INFERNO
ON
FIFTH

INFERNO ON FIFTH

Marlie Parker Wasserman

First published by Level Best Books/Historia 2023

Copyright © 2023 by Marlie Parker Wasserman

All rights reserved. No part of this publication may be reproduced, stored or transmitted in any form or by any means, electronic, mechanical, photocopying, recording, scanning, or otherwise without written permission from the publisher. It is illegal to copy this book, post it to a website, or distribute it by any other means without permission.

Marlie Parker Wasserman asserts the moral right to be identified as the author of this work.

Inferno on Fifth is a work of fiction. Incidents, dialogue, and characters, with the exception of select historical figures, are products of the author's imagination and are not to be construed as real. Where real-life historical figures appear, the situations, incidents, and dialogue pertaining to those persons are entirely fictional, and are not meant to depict actual events or to alter the entirely fictional nature of the work. In all other respects, any resemblance to actual persons, living or dead, events, or locales is entirely coincidental.

Author Photo Credit: Gretchen Mathison

First edition

ISBN: 978-1-68512-432-8

Cover art by Level Best Designs

This book was professionally typeset on Reedsy.
Find out more at reedsy.com

To Mark, with love

Praise for Inferno on Fifth

"Wasserman moves with great assurance through the Gilded Age, creating a fascinating cast of characters in a tale that seamlessly merges fiction and history. The fast-moving mystery story will keep readers glued to the page, connecting with themes that resonate as deeply today as they did a century ago, as the book winds to an exciting finish."—R.J. Koreto, author of the Lady Frances Ffolkes, Alice Roosevelt, and Historic Homes mysteries

"Marlie Wasserman takes us on a hair-raising ride in her new historical novel, Inferno on Fifth, based on the infamous Saint Patrick's Day, New York City, Windsor Hotel fire in 1899, immersing the reader in a version of what might have happened. Through this fast-paced work, rich with historical detail and multiple upstairs/downstairs perspectives, we relive the horrific event and its aftermath. Her vivid characters, most rooted in actual history, transport us 120 years back when fire construction laws were archaic, palm greasing all too commonplace, and women sleuths underestimated."—Jane Loeb Rubin, author of *In the Hands of Women* and *Almost a Princess*

"What a great read! Wasserman keeps readers on the edge of their seats, delivering a hair-raising account of one of New York City's most horrible fires. *Inferno on Fifth* takes us back to 1899, lets us in on the fallen grandeur of the Windsor hotel, the secrets of its wealthy patrons, the impoverished staff, and the whodunit of it all. This story puts us inside the very flames and has us praying we'll make it out alive."—Chris Keefer, author of *No Comfort for the Undertaker,* a Carrie Lisbon Mystery

"Was it a freak accident, intentionally set, or the result of inadequate regulation? Marlie Wasserman's meticulously researched novel imaginatively reconstructs events leading up to the disastrous 1899 Windsor Hotel fire in New York. Through a diverse cast of characters—rich and poor alike—whose lives unwittingly intertwined on a fateful spring day, she explores the complex motivations behind acts of bravery and flights of conscience."—Kathleen B. Jones, author of *Cities of Women*

"In Inferno on Fifth, Marlie Parker Wasserman meticulously reconstructs the story of the luxurious Windsor Hotel fire, the deadliest fire in New York before the Triangle Shirtwaist Factory fire, which, twelve years later, led to dramatic and long-overdue fire safety legislation. In Wasserman's riveting account, the workers—whose lives did not interest contemporary reporters—join the wealthy protagonists of the late Gilded Age to play a critical role in a gripping historical narrative."—Edvige Giunta, coeditor of *Talking to the Girls: Intimate and Political Essays on the Triangle Shirtwaist Factory Fire*

"Author Marlie Wasserman has approached this story like a detective on the trail of a scent. Alternating POVs give a multi-faceted look at this overlooked historical tragedy. The narrative is passed along from character to character like a flame at a candle service. We know the fire is coming. But we don't know who will escape. Wasserman's narrative keeps us guessing and worrying that our favorite characters won't survive. *Inferno on Fifth* gives us a reason to hang on and follow the narrative to the very end."—Julia Park Tracey, author of *The Bereaved*

Hugh Bonner

He heard high-pitched screams, saw flames rising. More screams. Three blocks from New York's Windsor Hotel, at 3:16 in the afternoon on March 17, 1899, Fire Chief Hugh Bonner sat on the edge of the front seat of his fire wagon. A fireman on the back bench swung around to clang the brass bell mounted on the wagon's side. Not loud enough. Bonner twisted to ring it himself, then shouted above the rising noise, ordering the driver beside him to hurry. As Bonner turned, he saw three other fire wagons behind him, rushing too.

"Hold tight." The driver snarled as he prodded the horses around the St. Patrick's Day revelers on Fifth Avenue. But even at fifty-nine, Bonner didn't need to hold on. He had ridden these wagons since he turned seventeen. He'd also marched with the revelers every year. Today, he cursed them for blocking his driver's path.

From three short blocks away, Bonner's eyes fixed on the upper floors. He saw women dangling from ropes, spinning, their full skirts billowing. Four struggled down a few feet, and then must have let go, plummeting. Two more didn't try the rope. They jumped from the fifth and sixth floors. More women sat on windowsills, bracing to jump. A man plunged down.

From a block away, Bonner could hear only the sound of ringing alarm bells and the yells of the crowd, but he had seen enough fires up close to imagine sickening thumps as he saw women fall and jump to the unforgiving sidewalk on Fifth Avenue. One struck an iron-spiked fence. Impaled.

The driver struggled to keep his horses from rearing and managed to maneuver the fire wagon into a narrow space at the curb. Bonner and his men leapt down. The Chief saw twisted bodies, maybe dead, maybe injured, lying amid police vans and ambulances. Mostly women's bodies, some in silk dresses, some in cotton maids' uniforms. Two men's bodies, both in fine suits.

Bonner pushed through the mass of yelling bystanders, necks bent back, chins up, coughing, scanning the windows. Following their gaze, he saw dozens of his firemen—the men who arrived first, from closer stations—climbing on ladders linked together, straining to pass women, some limp, some flailing, from one man to another. Good men, trained men. His firefighters would do their best. He estimated that with the men in the wagons beside him, fifty would soon be on the scene.

Bonner spotted Ninth Battalion Chief John Binns, until now the top man at the site, giving orders. "How the hell did it spread so fast?" Bonner asked. "Alarm called in at 3:12, from the red boxes." He checked his pocket watch. "3:19 now."

Binns shrugged. "The hell I know."

Two hours later, Fire Chief Bonner paced the site's perimeter, a square block in midtown Manhattan. The magnificent Windsor Hotel no longer existed. Bonner saw collapsed walls, leaning chimneys, piles of rubble. A burial ground. Handlers had moved the bodies on the sidewalk to the hospitals or the morgue, but Bonner guessed that under the rubble, diggers would find body parts, charred flesh, blackened bones. The smell of burning wood hid the smell of smoldering flesh. He suspected no one would have an accurate count of the dead and injured.

As Bonner looked over the ruins, staring in disbelief, he couldn't assess the cause of the inferno. In his three decades with the New York City Fire Department, he had never known a fire to spread so fast, to cause such destruction. Already he was hearing rumors—a careless cigar smoker, or maybe a thief setting a fire to drive hotel guests away from their valuables. Bonner trusted his sharp-eyed firemen and the police chief's detectives to investigate.

Hugh Bonner could not know then that one woman caught up in the fire would question the choices of the survivors and the victims. She would question, as well, the cause of such devastation.

Marguerite Wells

In January 1898, fourteen months before Hugh Bonner sped to the Windsor fire, Marguerite Wells eagerly awaited the ritual she had enjoyed yearly since graduating from Smith College in Massachusetts. She asked the principal of the New Jersey elementary school where she taught if she could leave in March for a European tour with her parents. Marguerite loved her students, but she loved her parents more. The snobby school principal always approved a three-month leave of absence, believing six months of Miss Wells's superb instruction towered over nine months of instruction by teachers trained at the New Jersey State Normal School. Marguerite then took the short train ride from New Jersey, and her parents took the long train ride from North Dakota—where Marguerite was raised. The family met in New York City, usually staying at the Windsor Hotel on Fifth Avenue for a week until their steamship departed for Europe. Each spring, Marguerite met with friends while her mama shopped, and her papa met with business associates.

In the year before the fire, Marguerite's circle of acquaintances centered around Smith College graduates who had settled in New York. Under normal circumstances, she would never have met Angelica Gerry. Marguerite's father was a prosperous banker from the West, while Angelica's father was one of the richest men in the East. The paths of the two unmarried women crossed for the first time when their families happened to sail to Europe on the same day in 1898 aboard the same steamship, the RMS *Campania*. The Wellses had sailed on the *Campania* before, but not until this trip did a steward slip a card under their cabin door inviting them to dine at the captain's table. Marguerite suspected someone at the Cunard Line had discovered the extent of her papa's wealth.

For years, Marguerite vividly recalled dining at the captain's table—the meal and the company. Her father had offered one arm to her and another to his wife Nellie as the family walked into the first-class saloon. He handed the maître d' the coveted invitation.

Extending his white-gloved hand, the maître d' took the invitation and inspected it. "Table one, sir. With the family of Mr. Elbridge Gerry. Follow me, please."

Marguerite heard the maître d's emphasis on the name Elbridge Gerry. Where had she heard that name before? As she and her parents approached table one, Marguerite saw a man in his sixties, with exceptionally heavy, white whiskers partially masking weak jowls, a woman about the same age, beautifully dressed, and a plain-looking younger woman, dressed in an even more beautiful gown, delphinium blue. The Gerrys' finery overshadowed the Wellses' evening wear. Mr. Gerry stood for introductions.

Marguerite's father squared his shoulders and began the formalities. "Mr. Gerry, may I introduce myself and my family. I am Edward Wells of Jamestown, North Dakota, and this is my wife Nellie and my daughter Marguerite."

Having spent time in the east, Marguerite expected snide reactions to the mention of North Dakota. Mr. Gerry and the younger woman at his side showed no reaction to North Dakota, while the older woman tightened her lips.

Mr. Gerry offered a firm hand. The men shook. "Pleased to meet you, Mr. Wells. I am Elbridge Gerry of New York, and here is my wife Louisa and my daughter Angelica." At that moment, the ship's Captain arrived, smiling at Mr. Gerry. Marguerite could see from their ease with each other that they had met before. More introductions, this time between the Captain and the Wellses.

In the dinner that followed, Marguerite learned why the Gerry name seemed familiar. Mrs. Louisa Gerry managed to work into the conversation the tidbits that her husband's grandfather had signed the Declaration of

Independence and that her grandfather had been governor of New York. The Captain added more details. Elbridge, a prominent lawyer, had served as Commodore of the celebrated New York Yacht Club, a position now filled by J.P. Morgan. Elbridge also owned substantial real estate in the city, though neither the Captain nor the Gerrys mentioned specific sites.

Throughout dinner, Mr. Gerry maintained a modest demeanor—no boasts—and Marguerite's papa maintained an even temper—no talk of politics. The wives failed to achieve such control. Mrs. Gerry held to her condescension, and Marguerite's mama turned competitive. "Yes, we live in North Dakota," she said, "but my husband has business concerns throughout the country. He served in the Dakota Territory Legislative Assembly and now he is a bank president. With holdings in real estate, insurance, milling, steel, and, oh, several railroads."

Louisa Gerry perked up.

One topic of conversation that stayed with Marguerite centered around the Gerrys' daughter, Angelica. She turned to Marguerite. "Miss Wells, you said you were in college in Massachusetts. Radcliffe, or I suppose you called it the Harvard Annex then? My brothers went to Harvard."

"No, not Radcliffe. I went to Smith College in Northampton. I graduated in '95. Now I teach school in New Jersey, but in the summers I tour Europe with my parents. And do some volunteer work." Marguerite did not specify the nature of the volunteer work.

"So we are both unmarried." As Angelica made that observation, her mother glanced at her. Then the eyes of the two mothers met, sharing concern for their spinster daughters. Marguerite looked at Angelica, saw her stiffen. Angelica moved the conversation to another topic. "I never went to college, not for me. I garden and tend my delphiniums. When we are at the country house, that is."

"Delphiniums? Does that keep you busy? Even in winter?" Marguerite heard her own tone. Too dismissive. "Tell us about those plants."

"Oh, my, yes, they are not easy to grow. They don't like hot summers, and they need staking. I divide them in spring. I watch which varieties attract bees and segregate those. I keep records of which kind of bees are attracted by each variety. And in June, I pull off early blooms to give us more flowers in the summer. The gardeners help, but I love to do the work myself. And I ride too. I even drive carriages and coaches. And breed horses."

Mrs. Gerry frowned at her daughter. Marguerite guessed Louisa Gerry wished for more talk of soirees, less talk of leisure pursuits related to flora and fauna.

Angelica's list of activities surprised Marguerite. In other settings, gathering with her friends, Marguerite talked about politics, the fight for suffrage, and sometimes such everyday matters as the weather, but never horticulture. Perhaps her friends would see Angelica Gerry as an aging debutante—later that year, Marguerite read in the society pages about parties and balls the Gerrys attended—but the young woman was not a ninny. Angelica studied what interested her.

Never during dinner did the Gerrys ask where the Wellses stayed when they visited New York. No one had a reason, at the time, to raise the topic of lodgings.

The Gerrys and the Wellses did not dine again at the captain's table on that crossing. But onboard the RMS *Campania*, the two daughters—both twenty-six that year—often spotted each other on the deck. The first time they met this way, Marguerite felt unprepared. She had been strolling along, alone, thinking about her work with the New Jersey Woman Suffrage Association. Their efforts to give women the vote had been ineffective, with no hope in sight. Ahead, Angelica stood at the railing, dressed beautifully again, watching the parade of passengers taking the air.

"Hello Miss Wells, good to see you again."

Marguerite stopped beside Angelica and tried to imagine a safe topic of conversation. She assumed Angelica had little interest in the musings of a suffragist. Maybe frocks?

"Yes, Miss Gerry. We both enjoy the open air. Your gown today is lovely, just like the other night."

"Last night. Let me think. Last night I wore Worth, House of Worth. Today, Jacques Doucet. Blue usually." She grinned. "But, really," she said, looking favorably at Marguerite's plainer shirtwaist, "I don't need many dresses for the crossing. Mother always pushes for more. A reporter once wrote that we traveled to Europe each year with fifty trunks." She rested her chin on her palm. "I am sorry to say he reported correctly."

"Fifty, my." Marguerite, still standing with Angelica, shifted her gaze to the sea. "That's ten times what we take, and we are more fortunate than most."

"Ah, yes. Every time I feel embarrassed about our good fortune, I remind myself that Father oversees good works, many good works. He's President of the Society for the Prevention of Cruelty to Children. His Society promotes the cause of neglected children. He doesn't get credit in the press, but I know how much he does for those boys and girls."

"That's admirable," Marguerite said. She had read a bit about the Society, though she had never had reason to note the name of its president. "Is the Society's focus on the poor children or their cruel parents?"

"Well, Father certainly cares for the children. He provides healthy meals and clean clothing. But he's particularly interested in bringing the parents to justice—prosecuting them in the court system for their neglect." Marguerite nodded in appreciation, though she had heard that such prosecutions often singled out the Irish and new immigrants.

"My papa too, though not at the level of your father, is civic minded. He helped fund Jamestown College, near our Dakota home. But he is a snob about education. I had to come East."

They laughed together. Later, in the weeks after the fire, Marguerite recalled her impression as she and Angelica talked. The women shared a love for their fathers, admiration, too. Neither felt anxious then.

Elbridge Gerry

Two years before the Wellses sat at the captain's table with the Gerrys, Elbridge Gerry sought a new manager for his hotel, the Windsor. "I cannot think of a better man to run my hotel, Mr. Leland," Elbridge said to the portly gentleman sitting on the other side of the desk. "You have my full confidence. We will make good partners. I own the hotel and the land, but as manager, you'll rent the building from me and retain a portion of the revenue."

Elbridge's guest sat up straight and sucked in his stomach.

Warren Leland smiled when Elbridge said partner. Elbridge had chosen that label carefully, knowing that his new manager would not take the word literally. Both men understood that Warren Leland would never serve as a true partner to Elbridge Gerry. Warren's grandfather, Simeon Leland Sr., opened the Chester Tavern in Vermont in 1818, forty-two years after Elbridge's grandfather, the first Elbridge Gerry, signed the Declaration of Independence. Warren's wife had been the daughter of a successful shipbuilder, while Elbridge's wife had brought such wealth to their marriage that it defied calculation. The Lelands, though prosperous, never made the society pages that brimmed with the Gerrys' comings and goings.

"Mr. Gerry, we're both businessmen, different sorts of businessmen. You own the land and the structure. I will manage the hotel. But we'll work well together, and I'll never let you down. Oh, and please call me Warren. I expect to hire some Leland cousins to help staff the hotel, so the name Leland will become too common to be useful."

Elbridge chuckled. "Good, and please, Warren, call me Elbridge. That's much clearer. Too many assume Gerry is my first name, not my last." Whether Elbridge used his first name or his last, he knew it was yet another name—his mother's maiden name, Goelet—at the heart of much of his wealth, including real estate. He had owned the land and the hotel at 575 Fifth Avenue in Manhattan for two decades, thanks in large part to Goelet money. In 1896, he needed a new operator to manage the Windsor. Easily, he identified Warren Leland as the top prospect. Warren had grown up in a family of successful hotel managers and moved from hotel to hotel, always toward bigger and more prosperous establishments.

A week earlier, Warren Leland had asked to inspect the hotel before agreeing to take over its management. Happy to show off his property, Elbridge accompanied Warren to the site—a square block, between 46th and 47th Streets, and between Fifth and Madison Avenues.

"Who designed it? And when?" Warren asked, staring in admiration at the brick exterior with brownstone trim and a grand entrance on Fifth, highlighted by steel lamp posts guarding the door. Elbridge paused. He saw Warren look up to take in the impressive roof, crowned with two small turrets, one on each front corner, and a big turret in the center.

"Sorry to say, I'm not certain of the architect's name. My friends in real estate tell me it may have been John Sexton, a master of the Italianate style, but I can't confirm that. Hotel opened in '73. Let's walk around the hotel before we enter. You'll see the U-shaped plan. In the middle, you'll see a central courtyard that lets light into each suite."

"And what is the origin of the name Windsor?" Warren asked.

"Sorry again. I'm not certain of that either. But I doubt anyone could come up with a more exalted name for a hotel."

After viewing the rear of the hotel, as well as the sides on 46th and 47th Streets, the two men entered the main door and walked down to the basement and then through each of the seven stories, climbing up the elegant central staircase from one floor to another. Elbridge saw Warren nod his head approvingly at the 600 poshly decorated guest rooms, clustered into suites, each with a fireplace, each with a bathroom. As Warren scrutinized the security features, Elbridge kept up a running commentary.

"Extensive piping. Estimated at seven miles." Elbridge chuckled. "To be honest, I didn't count. Four water valves on each floor. I'm told they connect to a telegraph alarm in case of emergencies. Though I admit, that seems improbable. Ten fire escapes on the rear and sides. Added only a few years after they were required. A coil of fire safety rope in each room. Everything complies with the 1882 fire code, but changes may be on the horizon now that electricity has come to the city."

Three years later, observers would note additional features that took on tragic meaning—wooden stairs, paneling and furnishing made of rare woods imported from seven countries, and long and wide halls unobstructed by fire doors. But in 1896, Elbridge and Warren felt confident that the hotel complied with safety regulations. "Looks as you described it," Warren said. "Maybe even better."

Elbridge set the annual rent at $83,000. Warren agreed without negotiating. The sum seemed in keeping with the high value of the property.

Now, a week after walking through the hotel, the men put their cigars in their left hands to shake with their right, Elbridge's slender fingers meeting Warren's pudgy ones. With a flourish, Warren signed the legal papers.

"Can you keep all the rooms occupied?" Elbridge asked as an afterthought once Warren finished signing.

"That's what I've been doing my whole life. We Lelands—as I said, two of my cousins are likely to join me—we register guests and keep them happy. And we'll pamper the guests who live at the Windsor year-round, those wealthy widows and invalids who like the services." Warren smiled as he stressed the word wealthy. "We're going to build on that. We'll add telephones, a hairdresser, a manicurist."

Elbridge nodded approval. "Take the Windsor back to its heyday, Warren. Those were the days when William—William Henry Vanderbilt that is— and Jay—Jay Gould—held court in the lobby and the bar. They favored the Windsor because it was close to their mansions, even though it was far from lower Manhattan. You know, far from the center of financial activity."

Elbridge squinted, realizing he'd erred by suggesting Warren did not mingle with the city's financial elite. But maybe Warren was accustomed to worse condescension. Warren bobbed his chin slightly, so Elbridge continued.

"My crowd liked to call the Windsor the Wall Street Club and The Night Stock Exchange. But Wall Street hit hard times for a while. And I don't mind telling you, the Windsor lost some of its luster by comparison with the new hotels. Now, you have an opportunity. Under your management, the Windsor can rise to the top again. Guests who want to live well without ostentatious display will flock here once more."

"I'm going to take advantage of that opportunity, Elbridge. With the Grand Central Depot on 42nd, more and more travelers and businessmen come to midtown. And I hear talk of tearing down the Depot to build a bigger station. The area has turned fashionable."

Elbridge smiled in agreement.

"One question I've been meaning to ask you," Warren said. "Jay Gould's mansion, the one he left to his daughter Helen, I know it's across the street from the Windsor. Is it true that Gould built a tunnel between the mansion and the hotel because he wanted to use the Windsor as a safe house, to hide there if his enemies came after him."

"Ha, I've heard that one too. A myth, Warren. I checked with Jay before he died. No tunnel, no escape route."

Marguerite Wells

Three months after meeting Angelica Gerry aboard the RMS *Campania*, Marguerite Wells returned to New York for a week with her parents and added another unexpected new friend—Theodate Pope—to her growing circle. Edward and Nellie Wells attended a dinner hosted by a Manhattan-based railroad concern, leaving Marguerite to dine alone at the hotel her father had selected, the Windsor.

"Mrs. and Mr. Wells are away this evening, Miss Wells?" Marguerite knew the maître d' meant this as a question, but it sounded more like a statement. "Would you care for me to seat you with Miss Theodate Pope? Her parents are also out so she is dining alone."

"If you think she welcomes company."

"Oh, yes, she has told me so. The family often stays here, and Miss Pope's parents have many social obligations." The maître d' looked down. Did he worry he had revealed his curiosity about the guests and their activities? Marguerite followed him to a table where a woman with blond hair and a square jaw sat reading. He said, "Miss Pope, may I seat Miss Marguerite Wells with you tonight? I am certain you will find her good company."

Theodate set her book aside and smiled broadly. "Please do. Miss Wells, I enjoy conversation." Marguerite looked at Theodate's plate, filled with fish and fresh vegetables, an unfamiliar diet. Not a good start. But Marguerite would try. She took the seat the maître d' pulled out for her.

"I am here with my parents. We've returned from Europe, and they are resting in the city before they take the train back West. What brings you to the Windsor?"

"Ahhh, yes, I am here with my parents as well. They've just returned from their own trip to France and are headed back to Cleveland. Their stay in the city gives me a chance to see them for a few days because I live in Connecticut—by myself—and for me it's an easy train ride to the city."

"I live alone, too, in New Jersey, where I teach school when I am not traveling. My parents live in North Dakota. I suppose your family situation and mine are similar."

Seeing the waiter approach, Marguerite didn't hesitate. She ordered her usual roast and fried potatoes.

"I wish I could eat as you do, Miss Wells. My doctor has me on a healthy diet. He knows I get anxious when I am designing houses and thinks this might help."

"You design houses? Truly?"

"Yes, I'm an architect. Well, an architect in training. Age thirty-one and still in training." She shrugged.

Five years older than me, Marguerite thought.

"An art historian at Princeton took me under his wing and mentored me. I wasn't allowed in classrooms there, but I learned a bit. I've remodeled homes in Farmington—in Connecticut—and I'm designing a country estate there for my parents, even though my mother doesn't approve of my interests. The work's not easy for a woman, but I plough ahead."

"I'm not creative in that way," Marguerite said as she waited impatiently for her beef, "but I also have an interest that is not always popular. I work for the vote for women." She hesitated a second. "Of course, we haven't been successful, but I take pride in my organizing skills. And I raise money for the cause."

"Admirable. I wish I could join you, but my father is against women's suffrage. It's odd, because besides running a steel company in Cleveland, he loves the arts. I don't mean traditional arts, but the new European painters. Perhaps you've heard their names? Monet, Manet, Degas, Cassatt. My father saw their genius before others did. And he supports my interest in architecture. But the vote for women? That he cannot see." She chuckled. "Yet I love him. I'm proud of him."

Marguerite leaned forward, rested her hand under her chin. "My own papa supports my work on behalf of suffrage. But he, too, has his blind spots. Even so, I love him." She recalled her conversation with Angelica Gerry a few months earlier on the RMS *Campania*. Angelica loved her father, Elbridge Gerry. Now Marguerite heard how Theodate Pope loved her father, steel magnate Alfred Pope. These conversations about fathers would haunt Marguerite later.

Bridget Dunne

Above the Windsor's palm-lined lobby, above its elegant second-floor dining room, chambermaid Bridget Dunne and her flock of maids maintained the hotel's standards for cleanliness.

As Bridget let herself be sweet-talked into a scam, she still considered herself a maid, a managing maid, not a scammer, not a thief, and not the worse words some might use. She presided over four maids on the fifth floor, making her a queen, or perhaps more literally a corporal, in the Windsor's world of domestic servants. Her little army cleaned the seventy rooms that combined into thirty suites lining both sides of the long, wide fifth-floor hall. Each suite had a well-fitted bathroom, where the wash basin's drain collected the hair of the female guests and the whiskers of the male guests, one fireplace that collected soot, and rugs that collected Manhattan's dirt. The queen of the floor herself, or the servants she managed, dusted and cleaned each bedroom, changed linens on the seventy beds, made them up daily, polished grates, washed windows, scrubbed bathrooms. They did not wash sheets or towels. Another little army of laundresses handled that chore. Occasionally, a guest asked a chambermaid to do more than clean, perhaps iron a dress or purchase sundries at a nearby store. The guest tipped the maid for that extra duty. If guests tipped for any unspeakable tasks, that was their business.

The queen of the fifth floor, Bridget Dunne, saw the other maids smile as they said her full name. Bridget, sometimes shortened to Biddy, served as the universal name for an Irish-born maid in America. The other chambermaids, even her friends, used that name to tease her, to remind her that she might manage an entire floor, but she was still a biddy. Bridget thought they meant well, mostly, but she knew too that they envied her slightly higher wages, her thick wavy hair, her comely figure, the light splash of freckles across her cheeks. When they tired of teasing her, they switched from Biddy to Bridget or the shortened Bridge.

Bridget and the maids she worked with on the fifth floor and the maids she roomed with in the servants' quarters welcomed their work at the Windsor. Most of them came to the hotel after working in private homes, where they handled laundry and cooking along with cleaning. Work in the Windsor was easier, safer, more sociable. Decent pay. As the number of Irish immigrant women had decreased since the height of the famine, fewer numbers commanded higher wages. The Windsor maids knew this would not last because the Negro women moving up from the South would work for less. So far, this threat remained distant because the hotel housekeeper, Mrs. Wrigley, following manager Warren Leland's dictates, didn't hire Negro maids to clean on the guests' floors. Those servants at the Windsor worked hidden in the basement laundry or in the kitchen.

Bridget Dunne started in service at age thirteen, in 1890, working for a wealthy family. When her employer moved, the woman of the house wrote Bridget a recommendation that led to her employment at the Windsor in 1894. For three years, Bridget labored as a chambermaid, working under the carping queen of the fifth floor, Fiona Ryan. Bridget never missed a chance to bring her admirable labors to the attention of Fiona, or to ensure that Fiona pass along a good report to chief housekeeper Wrigley.

"Fiona, you're giving me a half hour to clean 517 before the Robinsons move in?"

"You've done it before. They're regulars. Do it again. And don't go light on me."

"I'll clean good, Fiona. And fast. But put in a good word to that cocky Wrigley. Never know when I'll need it."

Thanks to talk like this, Bridget Dunne made sure she was known and admired by Mrs. Wrigley. These efforts paid off in November of 1897.

"Bridget." Mrs. Wrigley tapped Bridget on her hip as she stood on a ladder, dusting the cornices in 511. "Step down. I need to talk to you. Be quick about it. Busy day for me. I have news. Fiona Ryan's been hired away. By the Hoffman House. She'll be chief hotel housekeeper, like me." Mrs. Wrigley smiled. "Maybe not quite as good as me."

Bridget smiled back. "Good for her." Bridget looked at the wall beyond Mrs. Wrigley. Didn't want the gleam in her eye to show.

"Bridget, I need a maid to take over as queen on five. I reckon you're ready, right? Three more dollars a week."

"Glory be." Bridget couldn't hide her glee any longer. "When do I start?"

"Right away. Bad time to be without a queen for five. The President arrives tomorrow, November 27th. He's celebrating his brother's fiftieth birthday and plans to stay here, near him. Mr. Leland wants his hotel spotless. Or, I should say, wants his hotel to stay spotless. Some of the President's entourage might need to stay on five." Mrs. Wrigley smirked as she said entourage—one of the few times Bridget heard the chief housekeeper imply her distaste for the privileged guests. Like everyone else, Bridget knew that Abner McKinley, the President's brother, frequented the Windsor. The maids who could read followed reports of Abner's underhanded dealings, and they listened attentively to Hortense Webb, the tattling first-floor maid who cleaned his suite. Hortense spread the word about Abner's valuables, his wife's jewels.

"You're a hard worker, Bridget. You earned this. And it doesn't hurt that the other maids like you, and, I've noticed, the male guests too. Mr. Leland wants his male servants handsome and his female servants lovely."

"Tomorrow it is, then, Mrs. Wrigley. Thank you."

The minute Bridget's workday ended, she scurried to the hotel bar. Mrs. Wrigley forbade the maids to use the elevator, so Bridget ran down five flights. One of the manager's dim-witted cousins bartended there. He sold her a bottle of whiskey for half price. Then she climbed to the seventh floor where she roomed with other servants. Her friends were already seated in the drab scullery, resting after scrubbing all day.

"Ladies," Bridget said, using the term they loved to throw at each other, almost as much as biddy, "ladies, I have news. Yuh know Fiona Ryan, the nitpicking queen of the maids on my floor? She's been hired away by the Hoffman House." Bridget paused for effect. "Mrs. Wrigley asked me to take her place."

In front of Bridget at the rickety table sat three of her friends, each wearing a long white apron over a plain black dress with a starched white muslin cap. Bridget knew how they would react before they opened their maws. They proved her right.

Tara Regan chimed in first, as usual. "Bridge, you deserve that job. Now, you'll need to keep Mrs. Wrigley happy. A fussy one she is, even more than Fiona. Nothing's ever clean enough for Wrigley. She'll expect you to crack the whip on the others." Tara rubbed her cheeks, fiddled with hair, trying to tame the frizzy tendrils.

Crabby May Gleason, who roomed with Tara, jumped in. "Shush, Tara. Nothing wrong with Mrs. Wrigley. She keeps up high standards, like Warren Leland wants. That's why she's housekeeper." May turned her thin neck to glare at Tara.

The third maid, Molly Dugan, offered the slightest of smiles. "Bridge, happy for you." Molly's black hair fell out of her cap, over her face, almost covering her wandering right eye.

With a flourish, Bridget swept her right arm out from behind her and plunked the hidden bottle onto the table. "Ladies, I'll be making a bit more money. To celebrate, I ran down to the bar and bought whiskey off Fred Leland. He's Warren Leland's kin. Works in the bar in the afternoons." She opened the bottle and set out four glasses.

"I know Fred. He's too old for yuh," Tara said. "And too peculiar."

"Stop snickering at me, Tara," Bridget said. "You know what I wanted from Fred. A deal on this bottle. You have your Sean and Molly, you have your Frank." Bridget didn't even glance at May, the maid too contrary for courting. "And someday, I'll have a sweetheart myself. Not one of those fellas I meet in the dance halls. They like to touch, but then they get too drunk to know what they're touchin'. I set my sights higher than those clods."

The men Bridget met had little to offer, that is, until apprentice carpenter

Clayton Byrne, a tall Irishman with copper hair and blue eyes, came to the Windsor to work with the hotel's chief carpenter in the fall of 1898. Clayton offered Bridget lust. He also offered her his cunning.

Clayton Byrne

"The shaky railing on those stairs needs alignment. That's a good task to start you off." The Windsor's chief carpenter, John Connolly, spoke to his new apprentice, Clayton Byrne. Connolly pointed to the Windsor's magnificent staircase that started in the lobby and ascended six floors, skipping only the seventh-floor servants' quarters.

"Mr. Connolly, please remember, sir, I'm an apprentice. I'm not good with this fine wood, this mahogany. Didn't you say the armoires in some of the guest rooms need to have their doors realigned? They're walnut, right? I've worked more with walnut in my training."

Connolly lifted his eyebrows. Clayton worried that he took a chance by asking for a different task, but he needed to check out the suites, not the lobby.

"So you like walnut, Clayton? No problem. You can start with the rooms on the south side of the fifth floor. Those armoire doors do squeak too much."

"Thanks," Clayton said, smiling. Then he told a funny story, how he had built a walnut dining table for an aunt who never entertained. He had a bundle of stories, aimed at distraction.

The next day, another job. "The dining room doors," Connolly said. "Use the saw and sander. Shave them down. The waiters, they push through the doors when they run from the kitchen to the tables. They hold heavy trays and need those doors to open easily."

"Mr. Connolly, you told me some of the doors in the guest rooms need shaving too, 'cause of the new thick carpets. Why don't you let me do that and you can do the dining room? You're dressed better than me. My rags don't go well with the elegant dining room furniture. All that curved and carved wood. Louis XV style, that's what they taught us in carpentry workshop."

Connolly looked up and down, checking Clayton's attire. "You're fine. I wouldn't call those rags. But all right, you take the guest room doors." Now Clayton had another story up his sleeve—how his flatmate had left at dawn for the job, donning the wrong clothes in the dark.

The third day, same thing. Clayton kept to his pattern. Connolly wanted his apprentice to adjust the flagpole in front of the hotel. Clayton angled his head for a second. "Mr. Connolly, you sure you don't want me to replace the woodwork around a few of the windows in the guest rooms on the west side, the Fifth Avenue side? The storms last month left rotting wood. I saw it when I walked to work this morning. Those posh guests forget to close their windows." More stories, this time about bluebloods forgetting their heads. Connolly added in stories of his own. "One more thing, Mr. Connolly. Please call me Clay. Keep it short and simple."

Clayton Byrne ran a risk with his special requests, maybe pushing too hard. He should have been thrilled to have this job, temporary as it was, and accepted any task. "You'll get to use your skills and rack up some new ones," last year's apprentice had told Clayton. "And if you run into problems, Mr. Connolly, he's a good boss. He'll help. He won't yell." Clayton had been thrilled when the United Brotherhood of Carpenters and Joiners Union recommended him for the four-month Windsor apprenticeship in October of 1898. He saw an opportunity—more than one.

Once Clay started at the Windsor, he made it his business to learn what he could about the hotel's chief carpenter. John Connolly had worked hard for years, building shelves, repairing furniture, fixing squeaky stairs, hanging drapery rods, sanding floors. He kept up with the workload from mid-January to mid-October. But every October, he explained to Clay, the workload picked up along with the city's social season. Routinely, Connolly asked hotel manager Leland for permission to employ an apprentice to help. When Mr. Leland approved, as he always did, Connolly asked the United

Brotherhood to send him an apprentice carpenter on temporary assignment. Each winter, when the assignment ended, the apprentice continued his training elsewhere as he worked toward journeyman carpenter status with the union.

By mid-November of Clay's apprenticeship, he continued to wangle for tasks in the guest rooms, especially advanced tasks. Even as the two men grew chummy, Connelly still looked baffled by the requests. He rarely commented, until a few days before Thanksgiving.

"Clay, you're always asking for the harder jobs. Trying to show off?"

"Me, show off? Just trying to help you out, old man." Now, a friendly grin.

"Well, I got no problems with your work. All good. And did anyone ever tell you that you have the gift of the gab? I like your stories—gets lonely working by myself most of the year."

Clay rested easier. Seemed that Connelly had begun to appreciate that, for a few months, he could foist off the harder jobs. Then, one day, Clay saw Connelly on a guest floor, watching. Clay had taken a minute to gab with Bridget Dunne, the comely and friendly chambermaid who ran the fifth floor. The one with the thick waves and a sprinkle of freckles. Connelly didn't wait long to pry.

"Clay, my lad, you met a pretty one, right?"

"Yes, sir. She is that, she is. We met the first day I came to work here when I fixed the armoire in 523, and she changed the linens. And she has no sweetheart. Imagine that. I'll be taking her to a dance hall tonight."

"Good. You mind your manners. Don't break her heart."

"No worries, Mr. Connolly. She can hold her own."

As Connelly watched Clay, Clay watched Connelly. The old man loved his wife and two children, but he also admired pretty women, kept his eyes on them, maids and guests too. The man might be jealous. But Clay thought it through. If Connelly kept watching, he would notice his apprentice and Bridget together, laughing and talking in the halls, in the supply areas in the basement, and on the street when their shifts ended. He would assume that the pair was chattering nonsense as lovers do. He would not know that they had banded together for more than coupling, that Clay's gift of the gab had swayed his sweetheart toward his scheme. The chief carpenter would not guess that the very building he had kept in good condition, with his sanding and his nailing and his repairing, was now in danger.

Marguerite Wells

Marguerite Wells encountered Angelica Gerry a few times on their spring 1898 voyage aboard the RMS *Campania*, then not again for a while. After summering in Europe, Marguerite returned to her schoolteacher post in New Jersey while Angelica returned to the Gerrys' New York mansion on Fifth Avenue. The young women exchanged cards over the holidays, but not until March of 1899 did they find an opportunity to visit. Marguerite and her parents would tarry in New York for a week to shop and see the sights while waiting for the SS *La Touraine* to leave for Le Havre on March 21 for another enthralling summer abroad.

From New Jersey, Marguerite rode the Pennsylvania Railroad to Jersey City, then took a ferry to Manhattan to meet her parents after their exhausting five-day trip from North Dakota. Edward Wells wanted to check into one of the newest hotels in Manhattan, but with the economy picking up, his first choices were full. Moving one or two names down his list, he chose the Windsor, a luxurious old hotel the family had selected many times before. Looming over a square block, the building resembled a city unto itself, a city for the privileged classes.

On the morning of March 14, 1899, immediately after arriving at the Windsor, Marguerite sent Angelica a note asking her to lunch. Marguerite stated her plans frankly because she had learned that Angelica had progressive ideas about more than delphiniums. The plucky, former debutant was known for driving a team of horses through New York's parks, while her society friends relied on their carriage drivers. Maybe Marguerite could persuade Angelica to join the suffrage movement, or, maybe, to contribute funds. "I invite you to join me and my parents for lunch in the dining room of the Windsor Hotel, where we are staying, at noon on March 20th. I have also invited Theodate Pope, who by coincidence is staying at the Windsor as well. You will enjoy her company. I am not teaching so I can travel with my parents to France. In the fall I will move to Minneapolis for a volunteer position with the Suffrage Association."

Angelica sent a note back immediately, on stationery engraved with the Gerry surname, confirming arrangements. "I will be delighted to lunch with you on the 20th and also to have Miss Theodate Pope join us. She is already an acquaintance, for although her family lives in Ohio, they are known by my parents. I will elaborate when I see you. And let us take full advantage of your stay in New York. Before our lunch next week, can you also join me for lunch on the 16th, the day after tomorrow? Our home is at 2 E. 61st Street."

Angelica added a postscript. "Your Papa has selected a fine hotel—one my father owns." Marguerite grinned at the postscript, mentioned it to her parents, and placed Angelica's note in the top drawer of her hotel bureau. She never saw the note again.

"Don't despair that the newer hotels had no rooms available, Papa," Marguerite said when Edward Wells complained about the uneven heat in the family's suite. "I'm happy to return to the Windsor. I like the guests, the permanent guests we see each year." She raised her hand dramatically and began to touch each finger in turn, ticking off five groups. "The unmarried women my age, the older widows, the invalids and their nurses, the Civil War veterans, the businessmen who peddle their influence."

Watching Marguerite, Nellie Wells tilted her head, a familiar gesture, her way to poke fun at her daughter's lists and categories. Edward Wells mirrored his wife's gesture and then spoke. "Businessmen who peddle their influence? You mean men like Abner McKinley? The most famous resident of the Windsor?"

"Yes, Papa. He pushes his weight around, lobbies for clients, promises access to his brother, the President. Do you really approve?"

Edward Wells set his jaw. "Don't all businessmen look after their interests and their clients? I certainly do. And that's what allows this family to live in high style. To have porters haul your trunks and your mother's."

"Self-interest is one thing. Hinting at access to the President, the President of the people, or maybe I should say the President elected by the men of America, well, that's another thing."

As she spoke, Marguerite saw her papa's scowl turn to a smile. They had had this conversation before. Edward Wells approved of decorum in business matters, but Marguerite knew he also approved of feisty women. Most importantly, he believed women should vote.

"And not only Abner McKinley," Marguerite added, "but that Colonel Ochiltree—you've seen him in the dining room and heard him too—that man with the Texas accent who hangs around Abner, trying to bask in his glory. Ochiltree wore a gray uniform. A lot of the other guests did too."

"You deserve your reputation, you know," Nellie Wells said.

Marguerite took a moment. "Oh, you mean nosy. Butting in where my nose doesn't belong." Her sisters and brother back in North Dakota taunted her, especially Stuart, four years younger and brash. An only son, popular with the girls, likely to provide Edward and Nellie grandchildren. "At least I'm paying attention. I'm inquisitive. I'm not running around the prairie like Stuart, wasting time." Why did she take the bait? She knew her retort was a lie—she sometimes did waste her time, wondering for hours about the people around her, snooping even. And she had no reason to mock Stuart. Her parents hid their favoritism as best they could.

"Back to single women," she said to her parents. "You notice I named that group with my first finger. Me, and Theodate Pope. I told you about her before, how she designs houses. She's here with her parents. Remember, we're lunching with her, and Angelica Gerry, on the 20th, Monday."

Edward Wells bobbed his head with unnecessary approval. Although he had few snobbish bones in his body, Marguerite expected her papa did not mind his daughter hobnobbing with the daughter of a Cleveland iron magnate.

Marguerite gave scant attention to the second and third groups of

Windsor guests she ticked off on her fingers. She could not have known then that most of the sweet old ladies and many of the younger invalids living at the Windsor would not survive. The fourth group she had named to her parents, Civil War veterans, was harder to ignore and piqued her curiosity. Soon after registering at the hotel, she stepped into the elevator with several guests in their sixties, one with an empty coat sleeve. She wondered if the long-time residents of the hotel, as they entered the elevator, realized how many of the men standing beside them might have been armed foes thirty-five years earlier. The chatter of maids in the hall increased her interest.

"Fancy medals. He has three."

"A wooden leg. The wife told me to dust it, do you believe?"

"Saw a photograph of the gent on the dresser. He stood in an army tent. Skinnier then."

Hearing such fragments, Marguerite suspected that the maids, mostly Irish or daughters of the Irish, remembered a war that killed many of their kin.

Marguerite didn't try to control her curiosity. Thinking of her Smith College days in the library and bored with shopping, she jotted down a list of names she knew or overheard. "Leaving to shop for gloves," she told her parents the day after arriving in New York. Gloves were such an easy excuse—abundant, required no fittings, always needed. Better for her parents not to know the full extent of her nosiness.

Marguerite walked two blocks south on Fifth, not looking at her reflection in the shop windows and not looking at the clothes on display. She had no reason to care about her appearance, except for her hair. She took pride in her abundant blond hair, a pride she never succeeded at tamping down. As the windows multiplied, she gave in to a flicker of temptation. Walking slowly past a leather goods store, she saw in the window's reflection a young woman, petite, with a round face and blond hair, pulled into a messy chignon. Good enough for what she needed to do that day.

As soon as Marguerite thought herself beyond the sight of any Windsor guests out for a stroll, she walked faster, dodging the newsboys and the street peddlers selling wooden toys, feeling the brisk wind on her right cheek as she walked south. She caught a streetcar to the beautiful, crowded Astor Library on Lafayette Street—the city's free public library.

"Civil war records?" she asked when she reached the front of the queue at the librarian's desk.

"Union," the librarian said, more as a flat statement than a question. A handsome man, looking tired, worn out by the long line of questioners.

"Both." He straightened up, looked at her oddly. "Sorry to put you through the bother."

"No, it's not a bother. We don't get many requests for both. Mostly, New Yorkers ask to see the records of their fathers and uncles."

Marguerite's own father had no record. At the time of Gettysburg, he was sixteen. During Marguerite's childhood, the War often came up at family gatherings. Her father folded his excuse into the conversation. "I didn't make the enlistment age, eighteen," he said, with a sad wince. Marguerite knew he had been tall for his age, knew younger neighbor boys had snuck into the ranks with a little lie.

"No," she said to the librarian. "Not my father. I need to research a group of men from across the country."

The librarian raised his eyebrows but didn't question her. He directed a young page to a back room. Marguerite soon had a stack of leatherbound books, organized by state, then, mysteriously, by units within states. She saw smudges on the pages, pencil marks in the margins. Many others had used these books. She dug in, puzzling out the system and checking the names on her list. She learned that three guests or their families had ties to the Union, including Dr. Morris Henry, the deceased husband of one of the hotel's widows. He served as a naval surgeon under Union Rear Admiral Farragut. At least six guests or their relatives served in the Confederacy, including Colonel Thomas Ochiltree, the profiteer and friend of Abner McKinley. Should she consider the Windsor's lobby a place for friction or reconciliation?

When she returned to the Windsor late that afternoon, Marguerite put aside her pointless research to focus on a more practical matter, organizing the laundry for the family. Her parents had traveled to New York with a maid—tall and bossy Belinda Mason. Belinda had tended to the family for a decade and always accompanied them to New York and then to Le Havre to manage the family chores. She ran errands, packed and unpacked, and ironed as needed. But Belinda never washed clothes, not even in the wilds of North Dakota, and certainly not in Manhattan. Back west, a local laundress handled the Wellses' wash every Monday. Even Belinda's clothes. The Windsor Hotel might have found a New York laundress to pick up wash and bring it back, but Marguerite, who had managed her life without servants in New Jersey and at college, worked out a different plan.

Leaving her family's sixth-floor suite for a walk before dinner, she took the nearby servants' stairs rather than walk half the hall length to the elegant central stairway or wait for the elevator. A uniformed, dark-skinned girl, maybe seventeen or eighteen, holding neatly piled laundry, passed by on her way up. Marguerite smelled starch. She turned around and caught the girl's attention. "Excuse me, miss. Are you a laundress?"

"No, ma'am. A lady's maid. I do for Miz Alice Price. She brings me with her for travel."

Marguerite glanced at the pile of laundry. "You wash for Mrs. Price too?"

"Yes, ma'am. I do her laundry."

"Would Mrs. Price allow you to do the washing for other guests? For wages, of course."

"You ask Miz Alice. If she says yes, then I can help."

"I will do that. And what's your name miss?"

"Tilly Brown."

"Pleased to meet you. And I am Marguerite Wells."

At dinner in the dining room that night, Marguerite asked the maître d' to point out Alice Price. He raised his arm discretely, indicating a beautiful woman in her early forties, dressed in black, probably a mourning dress. She sat at a table with other women, all older.

As Alice Price finished her meal and left the table, Marguerite walked up to her. "Mrs. Price, forgive my intrusion. My name is Marguerite Wells. I am here with my parents, sitting at the table to your right. I asked the maître d' to point you out to me. Earlier today, I met your maid, I believe Tilly Brown is her name, and asked her if she might consider handling the laundry for my family this week for extra pay. She agreed, if you approve."

Marguerite sensed Alice Price's eyes scanning her clothes, her face, her expression. The widow slowly offered a gracious smile. "Pleased to meet you, Miss Wells," she said, drawing out her words, revealing a heavy southern accent that Marguerite heard over the noise of clanging china and silver. "Yes, you may employ Tilly. She's not the best, I warn you, but good enough. Just don't overpay her. We wouldn't want her to get used to northern wages."

By the time of the fire, the Wellses had employed Tilly twice. Each time Marguerite asked a porter to leave a note for Tilly where the Negro servants slept. The first time, the porter stared at the note with a quizzical eye.

"Are you sure, ma'am?"

"Yes, Luke," Marguerite said, reading his nametag and guessing his meaning. "Let's assume Miss Brown can read." Like most posh hotels, the Windsor insisted Negro servants traveling with their employers bed down in the basement, even though white servants could stay in small rooms attached to suites or with the hotel's white servants in cell-like rooms on the stifling top floor. Marguerite knew better than to wander into the basement herself.

When Tilly Brown learned the Wellses had laundry, she climbed the servants' stairs from the basement to the sixth floor, knocked on their door, took the bags of clothing, did the wash that night in the basement, somehow dried the clothes, and returned them the following day, ironed and folded. She made herself as invisible as possible, never lingering in the hall. The first time, Marguerite thanked her and paid her a fair wage by the standards of any region. The second time, Marguerite asked Tilly a few questions. She was eighteen, had worked for the Price family in Macon, Georgia, for three years, and accompanied Alice Price on trips to Atlanta and Newport, Rhode Island. Later, Marguerite remembered that this conversation took place on the morning of March 17.

That afternoon, the day of the fire, Tilly Brown disappeared. For days after, Marguerite scanned every newspaper she could find to check on Tilly's whereabouts. Tilly became one of Marguerite's obsessions, first a mystery, then a tragedy, then, well, Marguerite didn't have the right word. Thinking about Tilly and the other missing servants, Marguerite chastised herself for counting on her fingers only five groups of guests at the Windsor. She needed a finger on her other hand for the sixth group—the maids, hairdressers, pastry chefs, furniture repairers, boilermen, washerwomen. Hundreds of workers, struggling to earn a living, had shared the hotel with people whose wealth must be unimaginable. Was the hotel a tinder box in more ways than one?

Elbridge Gerry

"Don't listen to those damn reporters." Louisa Gerry's fist struck the breakfast table as she spoke, her rings and bracelet making a clinking sound. Elbridge's refined and loyal wife never swore, except when she talked about his critics. He knew Louisa spoke of the slandering carpers who claimed he cooked the books, raising money for his Society for the Prevention of Cruelty to Children, then spending it on himself. The day before, March 15th, a libeler in the *New York Times* wrote that even someone generally honest "is absolutely certain, sooner or later, if uncontrolled, to make an ass of himself."

"You've done all you can Elbridge. You opened your account books to those naysayers. They will see how honest you are. That will be the end of it." Her hand struck the table again.

During their thirty-two years of marriage, Elbridge grew accustomed to his wife's prideful patter. She descended from a great American family, the Livingstons. But even the Livingstons couldn't compete with the Gerrys. Louisa would try to best him, halfheartedly, reminding Elbridge that Grandfather Gerry's surname, and so their family name, remained linked to a redistricting process mocked as gerrymandering. Then Elbridge would remind Louisa that she lived well off Gerry money, though it had come from his mother's side, the Goelet side. Mother had inherited mountains of Goelet money and property, passing it on to her son. Louisa did not argue with numbers. In private, she let Elbridge win the contest between families.

He knew that her pride in him, in his ethics, in his sense of civic duty, stood at the heart of her irritation with his critics.

Looking to each side, he saw that the cook and scullery maids were out of hearing range. Elbridge's lips slackened over his jaw. Tea trickled down his whiskers, onto the table, onto the newspapers. He didn't wipe away the drips, didn't notice as he explained. "Louisa, there's more. Carping about my account books was last week's news. This morning's news has pushed the Society and even those poor children it serves out of my mind. I can handle only so much slander at once. No, let's call it libel."

He looked at his wife, puckering his wet lips, waiting.

"What now?" she said, buttering her toast, covering every inch.

"One reporter, my, an enterprising fellow he is, tried to assemble all the trash he heard or thought he heard." Elbridge picked up the newspaper, ignoring the tea stains. He squinted, then began to read to Louisa. "'By July 1898, Theodore Roosevelt's Board of Auxiliary Vessels had added twenty-eight yachts to the Navy's Mosquito Fleet to battle the Spaniards in Cuba. Twenty-two of the yachts had been owned by members of the New York Yacht Club.'"

Elbridge raised his eyes to glance at Louisa. Back to the libel.

"'A few members donated their yachts. More sent their agents to negotiate fiercely. The agent for yeast manufacturer Charles Fleischman asked $175,000 for the *Hiawatha*, but the Board knew it cost $30,000 to build a few years previously. The agent for socialite Allison Armour asked $100,000 for the *Ituna*, but the Board knew it cost a small fraction of that to build. The Board paid $117,500 to industrialist Henry Flagler, $150,000 to financier Peter Widener.'"

He looked again across the table at Louisa. She busied herself re-buttering. "Do you wish me to read more? The list goes on."

She snorted.

"Eventually, the reporter gets to the *Mayflower*. He says the board paid $500,000 for Uncle Ogden's yacht. Go ahead, scoff, but this shines a bad light on our family."

Elbridge knew, as Louisa did, that $500,000 was an outrageous exaggeration for the price of his uncle's 273-foot *Mayflower* despite its library, murals, smoking room, and twelve staterooms. Uncle Ogden's estate, or more specifically the Goelet estate, from which the Gerrys benefited, received a mere $450,000 from the sale, technically less than the yacht cost Uncle Ogden to build. But in the public's eye, the Goelets, and by inference Elbridge himself, gouged the American people.

"Elbridge, enough. It was your uncle's yacht. You did not negotiate that price." Louisa started to butter a second piece of toast.

"No, I didn't. But I could have encouraged Theodore to offer less. For the good of the Navy, of the country. As the Club's leader, I could have encouraged the other yachtsmen to accept lower prices. But I was distracted. Too busy defending myself in this Society mess. Now, I am defamed. The Gerrys are defamed." Elbridge threw the paper down on the table.

"Elbridge, don't overdo it. Self-righteousness and self-pity are rarely becoming. Remember, you didn't try to sell your own yacht while the greedy men at the Club bargained hard for good prices. You could have gotten a fortune for the *Electra* if you wanted. And President McKinley's brother—Abner. Didn't he have some peculiar business about a boat? Even a McKinley. So, no need to sound doomed. Don't pay attention to foul talk. You are a man of wealth and standing."

As always, she buoyed him up. "Yes, Abner. You're right. He's coming to see me later today. Maybe together we can figure this out."

"Really, Elbridge, I'm not sure you need that Abner. Ohio. Those brothers were born in Niles, Ohio. Can you imagine?"

"I will see what he has to say."

Louisa stood up to leave the breakfast table. She stretched her head high to have the last word. "And don't for a minute think this will get in the way of my plans. Gladys is arranging the place settings, even now. The dinner tonight goes on. The Fishes and Vanderbilts will not care one whit about overpriced yachts." She pivoted on her silk shoes. As he heard the rustle of her dress fade away, he heard another rustle.

"Coffee, please." Angelica addressed the scullery maid. His daughter entered the dining room and took a seat, not sitting back, looking more somber than usual. Had she heard them talking? Wasn't she too busy with horses and delphiniums and dresses to read the papers? He studied her. She knew. When the maid brought the coffee, Angelica ignored it. She sat staring at the stained newspaper on the table.

"Father, no one will believe that you took money or helped friends get money. Improper money." She said the phrase with dismay, with bafflement. "Why in the world would you skim from the accounts?" Her words were like Louisa's but steeped in kindness. Reassuring.

Listening to Angelica on the morning of March 16th, Elbridge gave no thought to the Windsor, which Warren Leland was managing without a hitch.

Bridget Dunne

Four weeks after chambermaid Bridget Dunne, queen of the Windsor's fifth floor, met apprentice carpenter Clayton Byrne, the two outlined a plan and agreed on separate assignments. Bridget took the first steps. At the end of the workday, she climbed to the tiny servants' kitchen on the seventh floor, where she knew she'd find three maids, the usual gaggle, sipping tea. Sure enough, Tara, Molly, and May sat around the rough pine table, gabbing. She could count on them to share their stories and their loves with each other, arguing only over borrowed clothes and unrepaid loans.

"Here's tea for you, Bridge," Tara said, wrapping her worn shawl tighter around her starched uniform. "I'm so cold. Those damn boilers in the basement never get steam heat to the top floor." Tara angled her chin toward the maid on her right.

"Don't be looking at me, Tara," Molly said. "The cold's not Frank's fault." Molly's wandering eye roamed aimlessly. Bridget and Tara giggled, not at Molly's eye but at her denial.

"Come on, Molly," Tara said, chatty as usual. "Frank's your sweetheart. Can't he get more steam up here? For you, if not for the rest of us."

"Yeah," Bridget said. "He's Chief Engineer in the basement, right? He sure gets heat to the guests on six."

Bridget spoke the last three words dismissively. The Windsor's snooty architect had saved the top floor, seven, for white servants who boarded there, sharing cell-like rooms. But even the good views on seven could not outweigh the heat in the summer or the frost in the winter.

"While we're talking about sweethearts," Tara said, "Bridge, you sweet on that good-looking chap? Clayton, right? Great red hair, tall. Has a mouth on him, like me." Tara leaned back, waiting for Bridget to start bantering. Bridget happily took the bait, to keep the maids at ease.

"Don't be lookin' too hard. Clayton's mine." Bridget stuck out her chin, used her playful tone, meeting Tara's expectations. May stayed silent, scowling at the jests. She patted down her hair, already in place under her cap.

"How much longer will Clayton stay an apprentice?" Molly asked. "I hear journeymen carpenters earn nice wages."

Bridget chuckled. She roomed with Molly, knew her up and down. "Oh, you ladies are so predictable. Molly, you go for the money. Tara, you go for the lookers."

No one blamed Molly's obsession with money. The oldest of nine children crammed into a tenement with sickly parents, she sent her earnings home. Hard to know if worry caused her wandering eye and her moodiness.

May stood up, brought her cup to the sink, and washed and dried it carefully. "I need to get back to the room, wash my uniforms for the week."

"Goody two-shoes speaks," Tara said, staring straight at May. No sign that May minded the nickname.

Molly rose. "I suppose you can call me that too Tara. Have to go. I'm ironing shirts for a gent on my floor. Pays good."

Tara stood up next. Bridget had a chance, took it. "Tara, keep me company. No need to run." Tara loved to talk.

"All right, Bridge, for a little." As Tara settled back down, Bridget rambled on about the low sugar supply for tea and the limited hot water on seven. Then she heard Molly and May move down the hall, open doors.

"I'll tell you about Clay, Tara, but I want to hear about your Sean too. Tell me, spit it out, what's it like keeping company with your fellow, with that long dark hair and that cute cleft in his chin? Does he take you with him to Paterson?"

Tara adjusted her cap, stalled.

Bridget knew that a year before, Tara, as a spectator, had stood at the edge of a crowd gathered on Fifth Avenue for an Irish nationalist rally. One of the rabble-rousers spotted her, the prettiest woman in the crowd. The man caught Tara's attention before she walked away. He learned her name and called on her the next day. "Sean Mack," Tara told Bridget at the time, "he's the handsomest man I ever saw. And he knows it."

Most of the chambermaids thought little about international news. Just chatter in the background. But Tara Regan started to soak up Sean Mack's ideas, ideas that leaped from cause to cause. Sean had grown up on the same block as a girl named Sophie, whose Irish parents settled in New York. When Sophie turned seventeen, she took a job in New Jersey, where she met and married an Italian immigrant, Gaetano Bresci. He was a silk weaver and active in an anarchist cell in Paterson. Sophie introduced her friend Sean to her husband Gaetano. The men had weaving in common—Sean's parents had been Irish linen weavers before they crossed the ocean. Sean took a job where Gaetano Bresci worked, earning enough to rent a bleak room in New York. The room was close to the Hudson, halfway between the Windsor Hotel and the Paterson silk mills.

Bridget waited. She wanted Tara to answer questions about Sean now that May and Molly were out of earshot. "Sean's a darling. He's good to me. Maybe we're too close, if yuh know what I mean." She looked to the side. "But no, Sean doesn't take me to Paterson. Do you believe, Bridge, those Italians let him into their meetings? He's the only Irishman. But he doesn't want me to be seen around there."

"Tara, don't you worry about him?"

"All the time. Those men, they're anarchists. Dangerous. Well, dangerous if you're a king or queen. Sweet Jesus and Mary, every year, those anarchists kill another royal shit. The coppers questioned Sean last month. They had a lead on him, followed him to meetings in Paterson. They think he's helping Gaetano Bresci and the other anarchists. Not a good kind of help. Sean thinks the coppers are watching him, now that McKinley's ignoring Ireland and cozying up to England. And they're not watching Sean for his good looks." Tara winked. "Ya know, Bridge, for Sean—he's a good Irish fellow—England's the enemy. For his Italian friends, their king's the enemy. The coppers don't care if those enemies deserve to be enemies."

Bridget's eyes drifted. Hard to follow Tara's tale of politics, but no matter—the next step was clear. As Bridget finished the cold tea, she asked her next question. "Tara, do those Italians think Sean can get them bucks? More than they can get for themselves?"

Tara winked. "He's poor as they are, but it helps that he doesn't look like they do. They think he's a firebrand who can help. And he'd like to be a big shot."

A year after the fire, when Bridget read that Gaetano Bresci traveled from Paterson to Italy to assassinate King Umberto, she thought back to her conversation with Tara. But even now, in late November of 1898, Bridget had her ears on alert. She didn't know Bresci and didn't care about kings, but she could tell Clay that her friend's sweetheart might want a job, one that paid well. Meanwhile, best to keep Sean's interests in the shadows.

"Don't talk about Sean to May or Molly or to the other maids," Bridget said. "It's fine that you're sweet on Sean. You're good together. Think about the kissin', not the killin'."

At first, Tara heeded Bridget's warning to keep Sean's politics to herself. But more and more, Tara held forth as the maids collected laundry or congregated in the halls on slower days. Bridget, walking into the crowded servants' washroom, heard Molly mention one of the maids' least favorite guests, Abner McKinley. "Posh Abner, he checked in for the winter. Warren Leland's telling the supervisors to kowtow to that gent. My sweetheart Frank told me. His crew in the basement is happy to stay there, hidden behind the boilers."

The McKinley name opened the flow for Tara. "McKinley," she said, almost shouting. "Abner's bad. A nasty man. His brother's even worse. It's William I hate. President McKinley, he doesn't mind England ruling Ireland. England, that bloody empire builder." Tara had been listening to Sean, picking up his words.

In mid-December, the Windsor filled up with guests in New York for the festive Christmas season. After the workday, Bridget joined the other chambermaids in the seventh-floor kitchen, as usual. Tara still blabbed about her favorite topic. "Abner, all the McKinleys. Jaysus, they're despicable."

Bridget winced. "Tara, keep it down. Mind your harping and swearing. You'll get yourself in trouble if Warren Leland or Mrs. Wrigley hear yuh." Everyone knew the chief housekeeper followed the hotel manager's orders. She allowed no disrespectful talk about the Windsor's best-connected guest.

"Right Bridge. But I can't help myself, especially when I'm near that maid who does Abner's suite, Hortense. Bad name, since she looks like a horse. She struts around the Windsor and yaks about Abner's wife's rings."

Bridget felt relief. Tara was mouthing off about riches, not politics.

"And his daughter. What a spoiled brat."

"Tara, have a heart," May said. "The poor girl is crippled."

"Right. But even with one leg shorter than the other, she's engaged to marry a doctor. Dr. Baer. I have a silk weaver, and Bridge has a carpenter, and Molly has an engineer. And we're all pretty, with two working legs. How do you explain that?"

May jumped in, this time not to urge compassion. "Girls, enough talk about your fellas. You're forgettin' me, I need a sweetheart, too. And not one of Sean's friends. Those rabble-rousers aren't my kind." May glanced at Tara. "But Bridge, your Clay, he's more upstanding. Can't he talk me up to some of his friends?"

Upstanding, Bridget thought to herself. Clay pulled that off well.

"Dunno, May. No one's ever good enough for you." Bridget added slowly, "Or upstanding enough."

May adjusted the strap of her apron, nodding in agreement.

The girls smiled. They had been goading each other for years, with a teasing tone. But the chatter and May's nod confirmed what Bridget thought. Stay wary of that one.

Two days before Christmas, Bridget noticed that May had left for a few hours to visit her sister in Brooklyn. Bridget swiped biscuits from the hotel kitchen and asked Molly and Tara to join her for tea, this time in the cramped room she and Molly shared. "Much warmer here," she explained, "especially if I close the door."

"You didn't nick these biscuits from the kitchen, did you?" Molly asked, tilting her head and drumming her fingers on the table, overriding any rebuke.

"Course not. Devan set them aside for me. The pastry chef made so many treats for Christmas that Devan said no one would ever notice." Everyone knew Devan Farley, the assistant butcher in the kitchen who came from County Mayo and loved the maids, whatever their county of origin. The lad's missing front tooth took nothing away from his pleasing disposition. Bridget suspected neither Molly nor Tara would worry about three pilfered biscuits. She was right. Sitting on cots in the nearly bare room, the maids bit in.

Bridget paused, unsure. She took the risk.

"Ya know, there is more to pilfer in this hotel than biscuits."

Bridget watched Tara. First, Tara stiffened, her body and her jaw. Slowly, her face softened. A few seconds of silence as Tara decided what to say.

"Yeah, art, jewels, money. Ha."

So far, Bridget thought, just a list, stated firmly, nothing more, not a game plan. She looked at Molly, then saw Tara looking at Molly too.

"Rings, brooches, watches, pearls, diamonds," Molly said quietly.

Still just a list. Bridget paused, then stared straight at the others.

"So, let me tell yuh—I've been talking to Clayton, right? His work with John Connelly's almost done, but Clay has a plan. He'll do all the work. We'll be out of it, don't need to get our hands dirty." Bridget chuckled. "Well, not any dirtier than they already get from cleaning commodes."

She looked up to check—they still looked at her, eager for more. "It's December now, and Clay's plan is for March, March 17th. We know about the rooms where the guests are long-time residents. Clay's been in a lot of those rooms already, doin' repairs and such, but we don't know who will be in the other rooms in the middle of March." She checked their eyes again. Still eager. "On March 16th, midday, can you both have lists? Jewels, valuables, art. Only the best stuff because Clay won't have time for more. He needs to work fast. You can start now, for the long-time swells, but not for the rooms that change over."

Tara glanced down. "Tara, I know you can't write a list. But you can draw, right?"

Tara gave a slight nod.

"Clay can pay. Twenty to each of you for the lists. More if he scores."

Molly jumped in. "We can cover most of the floors. You're good for five, Bridget, and I'm good for four. And Tara for two. May works on four, with me. She can help. And what about three and six?"

"Don't worry about three and six. Clay'll have his hands full with the floors we can cover. And let's leave May out of this," Bridget said, looking into space, away from the other eyes. "We love 'er, but she's a prig. Don't tell her anything." Tara, May's roommate, bobbed her head in agreement. Molly scrunched her lips, nodded slightly.

"And let's not say anything to Frank," Molly said. "My sweetheart's, ah, virtuous. Well, not in all things."

Over the next few months, the maids checked in with each other. They started to keep lists, lists they changed as guests moved in and out. Tara kept pencil drawings. Molly kept neat notes, but each time she added a valuable, she had a pang of fear. When the roommates went to bed, Molly climbed onto her cot slowly and deliberately turned down the rough sheets—no smooth sheets in the seventh-floor rooms. Then the whining started.

"Bridge, what if Mr. Leland finds out who pointed to the best rooms? I'm sending my wages home, to my ma. She's still coughing, bad. Pa's sickly, too. I can never send enough. I want to add in the money Clay'll be payin' us. But I don't mind telling you—I'm scared. What if we get caught? What if I lose my job here, or worse, end up in jail?"

"Bollocks Molly. We worked it out, so don't squawk. Clay's paying each of us twenty to set him in the right direction. If he does well in the rooms we tell him about, he'll double that. But he won't do all the rooms, only the best, or the easiest. It will be St. Patrick's Day, and we'll all be out watching the parade, on the roof. We'll ask up there some of the servants, our friends, to keep us company, and they'll be able to vouch for our whereabouts. You can trust Clay. If he gets caught, he'll say that when he worked for John Connelly, he learned guests left valuables in their rooms. That they were too lazy to use the hotel safe. If he gets caught nicking, he'll take the blame himself."

Bridget didn't say more. Or add the names of Clay's gang. Felix Kain and Lon Langmore. They'd run in Clay's gang for two years. And, yes, now Sean Mack, Tara's hothead lover. At least Sean had a head on his shoulders. Bridget had suggested Clay enlist Sean to help, offering him part of the haul. He could strengthen his position in the anarchist cell, passing money along for the cause since the Italians, with their accents and looks, had few gainful opportunities. No need for Molly to know Sean would join the gang. She thought he was a reckless firebrand, as May did. Tara knew Clay had recruited her beau, but she would keep mum.

With three maids and four hustlers, the gang covered a lot of territory at the Windsor. Clay sorted through the lists, picking only the most promising rooms and dividing them up among the chaps. Bridget admired Clay, trusted him. Loved him. Clay had thought through the timing, the gang, and promised to share details the day before snatching any valuables. She had no idea he planned a distraction of flames.

Marguerite Wells

On March 15, when Marguerite Wells researched Civil War veterans at the Astor Library, she took a quick break from the leatherbound military records to find newspaper articles on the Gerrys—their mansion and Angelica's activities, as recorded in the gossipy social columns. She would be prepared for lunch at the Gerry home. She would know what to talk about, what to avoid.

The following day, Marguerite left the Windsor Hotel and walked sixteen short blocks north on Fifth, past St. Patrick's Cathedral, past banks and stately townhouses, past Vanderbilt Row with its mansions between 50th and 58th. She had walked south often, but rarely north. These blocks seemed quiet. Few hawkers, no commotion. Again, she checked her reflection in a shop window, to ensure that her chignon remained intact. As she did so, she noticed a tall, red-haired man who passed her on Fifth, walking rapidly in the other direction. She couldn't know the stranger expected to get several lists of booty from three maids.

Marguerite arrived at the Gerry mansion at noon. It looked as she had imagined, like a French Renaissance chateau, built of brick and limestone. She wondered what Angelica and her parents would make of the Wellses' ranch in Jamestown, North Dakota. Edward Wells owned the largest, best furnished home for hundreds of miles around, but in a different category from the Gerry mansion. Marguerite pushed the comparison out of her mind, confident that her family could hold their own in any circumstances. She skirted the covered carriageway and rapped on the gleaming brass knocker.

"Miss Angelica is waiting for you," a uniformed butler said. "Follow me, please." He led Marguerite up a grand and winding central staircase, past ornately carved windows, tapestries, antique French furniture, a picture gallery, drawing rooms, and what appeared to be a well-stocked library. She smelled lemony furniture polish, mixed with the scent of roses on side tables. Later, Marguerite learned of two items less visible to guests—workers had brushed fireproof paint on all the woodwork, and the Otis elevator toward the back rested in a fireproof shaft. No flames would wreak havoc on this mansion.

"Wonderful to see you after so many months." Angelica spoke first, running from the settee, her blue frock swishing across the red Persian rug. She embraced Marguerite.

"Yes, for me too. And we will have time to catch up before I leave for France." Did Angelica hold the embrace for longer than expected? Marguerite gently eased her aside and looked at her face. Gloomier than usual.

"Are you not well?"

"Oh, no, I'm fine." Then silence. Angelica stared at Marguerite. "But I do want to talk. Let's go down to the dining room. Gladys will serve us lunch."

As Gladys hovered with silver platters, the two friends talked of New York, of shops, of Europe. Marguerite glanced at the lobster salad and smelled the fresh rolls.

"Thank you, Gladys," Angelica said. "Lunch looks excellent. We will be fine for a while."

Must be a hint—the maid turned to leave. Marguerite paused her chit-chat, staring at Angelica. "Do tell me what's on your mind. Is it that cad, Wadsworth Ritchie?" Marguerite had read his name in the papers the day before. Angelica had been engaged for months, then she, or maybe Ritchie, or maybe Father Elbridge called it off.

"So you know about that."

Marguerite winced, embarrassed. "I'm sorry. I should not have brought up his name."

"No need to apologize. Wadsworth has married someone else, and I'm happy to be free. I know I'm a plain-looking woman. Not even my French frocks can hide that, and at my age, I'm unlikely to get more proposals. I will remain free, busy with my girlfriends."

A quick memory of Smith College flashed through Marguerite's mind. Yes, she had had a crush—that's what they called it—on other girls. She had barely thought of them in a while. But then she barely thought of men either.

"No, Wadsworth is not on my mind," Angelica said. "It's my father. The Commodore. You met him aboard the *Campania* last year."

"Yes, of course. Is he not well?"

Angelica fiddled with her crystal water glass. She looked down.

"I will keep your confidence."

More fiddling. After a moment, Angelica looked up. "I have no one to talk to. I can't speak to my friends, you know, my parents' set. The Belmonts, Whitneys, Astors, Morgans, the Roosevelts, Stokeses, Vanderbilts. You've heard the names. I can't speak to their daughters either. And I can't talk to Mother. She's angry at everyone. And stubborn in her ways."

"But I am a creature of the West. And more interested in suffrage than tattling. You need not say anything if you don't want to, but should you wish to, whatever you say is safe with me."

Angelica set her mouth, then opened it. She looked behind her at the door Gladys might use. "My father is going through a difficult time. I sat with him at breakfast this morning. I also heard some of his conversation with Mother. He looked sad. It's not his health. He worries about his reputation. And reputation is important to us Gerrys. We are proud." She smiled. "Proud with reason to be proud, I like to think."

Marguerite gave a nod of encouragement.

"I will keep my tale short. It has two parts. The first I mentioned to you when we sailed on the *Campania* last year. My father manages the Society for the Prevention of Cruelty to Children. The Society helps abused girls and boys. But Father has critics. Disagreeable men who think he's pocketing donated funds instead of passing them along to children. They asked the Attorney General of New York to inspect the Society's account books."

Marguerite looked at Angelica, aghast. "Not possible. Why would your father retain funds?" She waved her open palm toward the antique furnishings, the silver tea set. "Are you certain of the charges?"

"Don't doubt me, Marguerite. Oh, my, I'm sorry to snap, I'm all nerves. I know it's hard to believe. Father writes letters to the editors of the newspapers to defend himself. I'm not sure that's effective, but it makes him feel better." She paused. "And then there's the second part. Father is active with his yacht club, the New York Yacht Club. He knows the men who own large yachts. With the war in Cuba, Roosevelt—he's Assistant Secretary of the Navy now, and he's a friend of the family—is buying up yachts for the fleet. Outfitting them as battleships. Papa's friends want him to put in a good word to Theodore, to drive up the prices of their yachts. Father won't do that, but the reporters think he has. They say he's a profiteer."

As Angelica said "profiteer," quietly, she teared up.

"Outrageous." Marguerite was satisfied that her brain had supplied the appropriate word, with the right amount of outrage. "What can I do to help?"

"Just listening is a help. Now you understand why I can't talk to my friends about any of this. And why I wanted to see you before our lunch on the 20th, to talk privately, before lunch with Theodate Pope."

Marguerite raised her eyebrows. "Tell me how you know each other."

"You are from North Dakota. Then Massachusetts. You may not know what it's like here. Everyone is connected to everyone else. Theodate's father is Alfred Pope, a wealthy industrialist and art collector. I am about to spout many names. No need to remember them all—just absorb the sense, the links in the chain. Alfred Pope seeks advice on collecting from Louisine Havemeyer. She married Henry Osborne Havemeyer. The Havemeyer family owns the American Sugar Company. As you can imagine, they are wealthy. Mr. Havemeyer is a trustee of the Museum of Natural History, as is my father, as, by the way, was Theodore Roosevelt Sr, the father of the current Mr. Roosevelt. And Mr. Havemeyer had a yacht, as does my father. And his widow lives on Fifth and 66th, five blocks from here.

Though taken aback, Marguerite continued to eat the food Gladys served.

The lobster salad tasted amazingly rich. Angelica could choose for herself to stop eating, but Marguerite gestured politely for a second helping. Between chews, she demonstrated her concern, asking questions about Elbridge Gerry's critics, their false evidence, the extent of the slanderous reports. She felt almost certain Mr. Gerry wouldn't steal money from poor children. She felt fairly certain he wouldn't profit from a war. She felt absolutely certain Angelica wouldn't lose faith in her father. She felt certain at that moment. She also felt certain this was not the moment to talk to Angelica about women's suffrage.

Marguerite misjudged.

"Now let me change the subject, Marguerite. In your note, you reported you plan to take up a position with the Suffrage Association in Minneapolis. Tell me what they are up to."

Marguerite stared.

"Don't be surprised at my interest, dear. Here is your chance to take my mind off Father's Society and his friends' yachts. We Gerrys want women to get the vote. Do you know that Elizabeth Cady Stanton is a Livingston, like my mother? Well, the Livingstons are a huge family, but if I remember correctly, Mother's great-great-great-grandfather, James Livingston—again, no need to remember the details—was the younger brother of Elizabeth's great grandfather, John Livingston. Or something like that. And there's more. Elizabeth gave Father a signed copy of the proceedings of the 1867 meeting of the American Equal Rights Association. He keeps it in his library on the second floor. I will show you." She chuckled. "You look surprised, Marguerite. We don't march in the streets, but our hearts are in the right place."

"You make me smile. If you have an hour, I will tell you about Minnesota. And then you can show me your dear father's library."

Bridget Dunne

The chambermaids held up their end of the plan. Now, the day before St. Patrick's Day, they needed to turn over lists and suggestions to Clay. Since the housekeeper, Mrs. Wrigley, paid little attention to the seventh-floor servants' quarters, Clay faced no trouble when he joined the maids in the tiny garret room Bridget and Molly shared, timed with their lunch break. Bridget made sure Tara came too. Tara's roommate, the self-righteous May, was out on an errand. Bridget had arranged for her to pick up a supply of green ribbons from the milliner, offering her first pick of the bows for decoration the next day.

Lunch break lasted twenty minutes. Bridget wasted no time. "Show Clay," she said to Tara and Molly. Looking at Clay's eyes, Bridget saw he took in her proud smile. She managed the maids on the fifth floor, and she could excite Clay, but she could also scheme and hustle. "We have three floors covered—two, four, and five." Bridget handed Clay her list of valuables for five. Molly handed him the list for four, starting with the valuables in 410. Tara, waiting to the end and looking at the wall, past her friends, handed Clay a few sheets of paper. She had drawn the valuables on the second floor, including rough sketches of ten paintings in Alfred Pope's suite. She had circled two, probably the ones she liked best.

Clay looked over the sheets of paper while listening to Bridget. "That's what you'll find tomorrow. Mostly, the jewelry and art belong to resident guests. If we added things that belong to non-resident guests, we made sure they were not checking out before tomorrow. That was easy—each week, Mrs. Wrigley gives us a chart with dates that we use for the deep clean between guests." No one spoke as Clay studied his opportunities.

"My lovelies, good job. You came through. Me and the chaps will figure out how many floors we can handle."

Bridget caught Molly's stare. "Wait—chaps?" Molly asked. "Bridge, you never said nothing about chaps."

Clay looked at Bridget and Tara with a faint nod, then sat up straight. "My doin' Molly. Don't go blamin' Bridge. I can't do this alone. Can't even do one floor myself, let alone a few. Have to get in and out, quick. Let me give you your earnings first, then I'll explain."

Clay reached into his pocket, took out three crisp twenty-dollar notes, handing them around. Bridget, expecting to get more from Clay later, smiled, as did Tara. Molly took the bill, looked it over slowly, then tucked it up her sleeve.

While everyone's attention centered on the bills, Bridget thought about Clay's chaps, his gang. Sean, eager and smart, but the Windsor would be his first job. Felix—thickset, older, but undependable and an unsteady drunk. Lon—dumb but daring, with an untrimmed beard. A tippler, too. She'd met Felix and Lon when they joined her and Clay at dance halls. She relaxed her jaw. Didn't want the others to worry.

"There'll be more money to go around if this works out," Clay said. "Maybe even for those of you whose floors I might not get to. Here's the plan. Three of the chaps are helpin' me. You don't need to know their names. Just before 3:00, when we start to hear the parade music—that's the cue—we'll enter the hotel. Well, not all at once—over a stretch of about ten minutes. Two of us will go to four. Another fella will go to either five or two. I'm not sure yet. Another to one—we don't need a list for the first floor. Bridget will open the maids' closets for us," he caught her eye, "one on each floor we cover except the first, 'cause she tells me that one has no closet. We'll linger in the servants' stairs 'til we see her. She'll tell us if the hallways look clear, and she'll let us into the closets."

Bridget concentrated, followed Clay's words. Added a detail of her own. "Since two and four ain't my floors, if any maids from there see me going into their closets and squint at me, I'll tell them we're short linens on five.

You know, all the maids' room keys work for all the closets."

Tara and Molly nodded.

"On four, and maybe two and five, me and the chaps will drop some cigar embers on the closet floors—just enough to get little fires started. Guests will run out without lockin' up. But I don't want the attention to be on those floors. I'm sending another one of our gang—again, no need for you to know names, he's a bit older than the others—to the smoking alcove off the dining room. He'll wait 'til a waiter comes by, again just after the music starts, at least that's the aim, then he'll throw his cigar on the lace curtain. He'll be the decoy, the man who everyone thinks is the culprit, but he's not. Then he'll go down one flight to the first floor. He don't need Bridget's help for that. He can wait in a corner near the telegraph office. The operator's name is O'Casey. Chances are he'll be out at the parade."

Bridget's heart stopped as she listened. She couldn't look at Molly or Tara, but she guessed their eyes were popping out of their heads. Embers? Fires? Why hadn't Clay told her before? He kept talking.

"All this happens when the marchers come 'round. Most of the guests will be out of their rooms, watching the parade, too. And there'll be a lot of music and noise covering up whatever we do. You girls have fun. Go up on the roof to watch the parade. If Mrs. Wrigley sees you there and she's angry you're leaving your floors, that's not bad. She'll know you have nothing to do with what's going on down below. And Bridget's going to ask someone from the kitchen, what's 'is name?"

"Devan. Devan Farley. The lad who's missing a front tooth." Bridget attempted an even tone. "The girls all know him. Assistant butcher." She still couldn't look at Molly or Tara.

"She's going to ask Devan to come to the roof. He'll be a witness too. He can say you were all up there. Bridge tells me Mrs. Wrigley knows Devan a bit because her office is near the kitchen, but they're not good friends. That's perfect."

Bridget willed herself to look at the girls. Molly's eye wandered wildly, and Tara bit into her bottom lip.

"Ya sure the fires won't spread?" Bridget asked. She knew she should say something more. Clay had hemmed her in. Too late to back out.

"They won't. I just want the little fires to be scary enough for people to sound the alarms and for guests who are lazy enough to stay in their rooms during a parade to run out without locking their doors. A wee bit of commotion."

Wee, Bridget thought. Tara and Molly looked at each other, with blank stares. They were hemmed in too.

That night, Bridget watched as Molly smoothed the twenty-dollar bill Clay had given her, then slowly put it into an envelope she addressed to her ma. Tara, in the next room, was probably doing the same thing, but waiting until May went to the washroom, then addressing an envelope to Sean. Bridget, restless in bed, hung on to Clay's word, "wee."

Felix Kain

"Shit, you're telling me my job is to smoke? You joking me?" Felix Kain narrowed his eyes at his buddy, Clayton, ringleader of their little gang.

"Look, mate, I'm giving you the hardest job. Yeah, there's the smokin', but a little more that I haven't told you yet. I was waiting 'til now—the afternoon before St. Pat's," Clay said. "Last job you showed you can grab and run, but let's see if you can do more. I reckon you're ready. Lon's too young and short on sense. Sean, well, he's too new, untested."

Felix Kain smiled at Clay Byrne's words. Maybe Clay was telling the truth. Or maybe that son of a bitch wanted the oldest fella in the gang to be the decoy, the sitting duck.

"You need an old man for this job, right?" Felix said. "I turned thirty-five last week, so now I can play a feeble gent?"

"And you put on some extra pounds with each year. Even with that fat, mate, you can run fast. Well, fast enough." Clay cackled. "This time, I need your head and your feet both. You smoke, but then you run."

"And you, Mr. Clayton Byrne? You have arm muscles now that you're a fancy pants carpenter, but you can't outrun me with your puny legs. And stop joshin' your way out of the business end of this job. You're givin' me all the risk here while you sit on your rump and call yourself boss. Time to talk money."

"Slowin' up old man? Took you two minutes to get around to the big question." Clay smiled broadly. "Your share'll be the biggest. Seven percent of the haul, not five like Lon and Sean. After I pay off those maids—my girl and two other biddies—there's not much for me."

Felix grinned.

"Listen to the drill. Put on your fanciest clothes over your usual rags. Sprinkle white powder on that sparse hair of yours, and walk like a swell, like you own the place. When you leave the hotel, throw off the suit. Walk out in your rags. And here's a badge I made up for you, for the pocket of your old pants, just in case the plan goes south."

Felix looked at the badge, laughed, and pocketed it.

"Case the place tonight. Look for the smoking parlor on two, with a bay window, down the hall from the main dining room on the 46th Street side. Flowery lace curtain at the window. You got it?"

Felix rubbed his jaw, concentrated.

"Then check out McKinley's suite on one. Near the telegraph room. O'Casey's the operator. He'll be there tonight but might sneak out tomorrow for the parade."

Felix followed Clay's bidding. On the evening of March 16th, wearing his usual worn pants and jacket, he walked into the Windsor and began to climb the magnificent central staircase, which went to the top of the hotel. He stopped on the second floor to scout out the best place for mischief. That's how he thought of it—mischief, shenanigans, high jinks. Clay called it horseplay. To the left of the stairs, Felix spotted small dining rooms. He read the discrete signs next to each of the three doors. "Private parties." "Dining Room for Children Attended by White Servants." "Dining Room for Children Attended by Negro Servants." He had taken a wrong turn.

Felix moved to the right. He saw the main dining room, with guests standing in a circular reception area, waiting to be seated. Beyond the reception desk, Felix took in the elaborate oak floor and the frescoed ceiling. A small sign informed guests that the orchestra played from 6:00 to 8:00 each evening. A few musicians arrived, lugging instruments. Off the south end of the dining room, through a hall with floor-to-ceiling gilt-framed mirrors, Felix found the wood-paneled smoking parlor, as Clay described it. The parlor was in full view of the mirrored hallway that waiters used to get to the kitchen. A round walnut table stood in the alcove of the parlor in front of a bay window open an inch to air out smoke. In the window, Felix saw a lace curtain fluttering slightly. Again, as Clay had described it. Cream-colored lace, a rose pattern, repeated from rod to sill. Felix took out from his pocket one of the two Romeo y Julieta cigars Clay gave him, unwrapped it, and smoked for a minute.

Then down to the telegraph office. Man at the telegraph, probably O'Casey. He's sure to be off at the parade. Felix noted the suite off that hall. McKinley's. Piece of cake, Felix thought.

Alice Price

Three months before Clayton Byrne spread his twenty-dollar bills among the chambermaids, the Windsor's maître d' led pretty Alice Price to a round table at the edge of the dining room. Pulled out a chair for her.

"Welcome to the widow's table." Alice heard this peculiar but firm greeting from the oldest woman at the table. "Hope you don't mind my name for us. You see, no need to be coy about it, or, ha, to be coy about anything else, right?" The other widows at the table, slightly younger than their apparent leader, snickered in agreement.

"Oh, my, no. Y'all are gracious to include me."

"Yes, welcome," the old lady said. "I am Mrs. Henry, Mehitable Henry, the oldest widow here. My Old Testament name is a mouthful. You can stick with Mrs. Henry if that's easier. The name of my third deceased husband."

Alice pushed aside thoughts of the number three, falling back on her manners. "And I'm Alice Price, from Macon, Georgia. Here for a few months, to take in the sights."

The other widows, all with less formidable names than Mehitable, introduced themselves.

Alice wore a black crepe mourning dress, but flouncy, adorned with a diamond necklace and brooch. She saw the frumpy widows stare at her jewelry. At forty-four, Alice knew she looked lovely and radiated wealth. Despite grief and ailments, she took care with her appearance.

Raised to be sociable, Alice enjoyed her conversation with the widows. As the chatter allowed, Alice Price mentioned that her deceased husband

Willis had been a cotton merchant at the time of his death three years earlier. She didn't add that he left her a fortune, but when she lingered over the word cotton, she made her point. She didn't add that Willis had started out as a grocer. She blabbered more openly about her connections to Southern aristocracy. Willis's brother served as mayor of Macon, Georgia, the Prices' hometown. And, she added casually, her sister had married Allen Daniel Candler, Governor of Georgia. She saw the widows slow down their eating, look at her. They might guess the Governor fought for the South, but they'd still be impressed.

Alice didn't share the hardship that brought her to the city. She had one child, a daughter also named Alice. Thanks to the family's wealth and connections, the two Alices summered in Newport, where young Alice was a belle of the town. Young Alice also spent the winter's social season with her uncle at the governor's mansion in Atlanta. The Candler/Price family delighted in the Christmas season of 1898 when the mansion looked radiant with candles and musicians. A few days later, while the two Alices were still in the mansion, young Alice took sick. The Governor called upon the best doctors in Atlanta, to no avail. At age nineteen, Alice Price died on January 13, 1898. Typhoid fever.

Mother Alice had weathered her husband's death. She could not bear her daughter's death. The Governor urged Alice to seek a change of scenery and medical attention for her nerves. She traveled to New York, checking into the Windsor, where she had stayed with her husband before—a small suite on the fifth floor.

The outspoken widow, Mehitable Henry, lived in the hotel on a lower floor. The two women, one forty-four and lovely, one sixty-nine and beyond her prime in appearance but not in intellect, had little in common other than widowhood and wealth. After meeting at the widows' table, they kept their distance. Alice had learned from the prattling housekeeping staff that Mehitable's husband served as naval surgeon under Rear Admiral Farragut, the northern hero who blockaded ports and confiscated cotton. Alice's husband Willis was a young man then, not yet a wealthy cotton merchant, so Mehitable's husband didn't directly hurt Willis's income.

But southern whites never forgave harm to the cotton market. From a different prattling maid, Mehitable heard that Alice's brother-in-law, Georgia Governor Candler, fought under General Joseph Johnston and lost an eye in battle. Each widow stayed wary of the other, until by chance, they found themselves together one afternoon in the tearoom.

"I'm afraid Dr. Morris was not the first husband to die on me," Mehitable said. "As you may recall, he was the third. Yes, I am a widow three times over. I loved each of them."

Alice took a minute to let that sink in. She glanced at Mehitable. No bluster now. The widow's eyes, moist, looked down. Three deaths. Maybe this woman would understand.

"Let me, let me tell you about my loss," Alice said. "Not Willis, my husband, though that hit me bad enough. I have more to tell. My daughter."

So began their unlikely friendship, their trust. The women soon reached beyond the deaths to share stories of loneliness. They laughed over their initial impressions of each other, forged by memories of a war long over. Alice expected to return to Macon and Mehitable to her home in Boston. Alice had no reason to foresee otherwise. They would live far apart, would have nothing to fear from sharing their stories. Alice saw that Mehitable, unlike other women at the widow's table, grasped a lot about Manhattan, a lot about medicine, politics, the fighting in Cuba and the Philippines. To keep up, Alice started to read newspapers. The older woman talked too about the relatives who saw her as a source of money—the stepson who would inherit her fortune, the nephew who borrowed from her. When Alice couldn't keep up with the details of Mehitable's financial transactions, Mehitable didn't get sniffy. And when Mehitable acted bossy or overbearing, Alice, eager to take her mind off her own troubles, didn't complain.

Two days before the fire, the women sat in Alice's suite for tea, brought up by Alice's maid, Tilly Brown. Alice ignored the biscuits and slowly stirred honey into her cup. She saw Mehitable try to control her trembling right hand by bracing it with her left hand. Their conversation about other guests had started out with energy, then faded. Mehitable ran her tongue over her lips. A pause.

"Alice, that doctor you're seeing here—Sutton—is that his name? He doesn't know a thing about women. This elixir he gave you," she pointed to the top of the bureau. "Useless. Who recommended him?" Mehitable leaned forward and scolded the younger woman.

"The doctor in Atlanta, the one who came to the governor's mansion to see to young Alice. I asked him. He trained in Nashville with Dr. Sutton, who then moved to New York."

"So, is the elixir working?" Mehitable said, arching her brow. "No. You said it just makes you sleepy. I waited to see if, by some miracle, it helped, but now I'm not going to hold my tongue any longer. I know you think your problem is grief, and I understand grief, but you've also shared those other problems of yours. I want you to see Dr. McPhatter, Neil McPhatter. He was a good friend of my husband's, Dr. Henry, and the two men conferred a lot on certain cases when Dr. McPhatter practiced here, before he moved out West and then returned East. They had different specializations, but specializations that overlapped. I can tell you more about that later. Dr. McPhatter is a woman's doctor, a gynecologist. He might be able to treat both the problems in your body and in your nerves."

Alice winced, looked at the floor. "I don't know, Mehitable."

"Here's what we'll do. Dr. McPhatter is setting up his practice in New York, for the second time, moving everything from Denver to Madison Avenue. So far, he has a small number of patients. He has some time. Let me bring him to you. He'll examine you here, in the hotel, and I'll be nearby. Would that make you more comfortable?"

The women continued to talk about McPhatter. Then on to the news of American soldiers near Manila and the closer news of Mehitable's concerns about her trusts and estate. The next day, over tea again, Alice listened as Mehitable laid out arrangements. She planned to bring Dr. McPhatter to Alice's room at 3:00 on Friday, March 17, St. Patrick's Day. Alice nodded reluctantly. She understood the plan, worried about nothing beyond the doctor's examination.

Neither Alice nor Mehitable paid attention to Tilly, as the maid folded clothes and placed them in the wardrobe in the bedroom of the suite, fifteen feet away.

Harry Niehoff

Detective Harry Niehoff kept a trained eye on the Windsor Hotel six days a week. His watch began at 2:00 in the afternoon and ended at 11:00 at night. He worked hard, but not as hard as he had worked previous years as a copper on the New York City force. Now, in this hotel job, he scanned the lobby and the bar every hour. On a random schedule, he walked each of the hotel's six guests' floors, the white servants' quarters on the seventh floor, and the basement.

The job presented mostly nuisances. Some days he spotted vagrants drifting into the lobby to escape the cold, sotted hotel guests at the bar benefiting from an easy path upstairs to their rooms, forgetful guests dropping possessions in the halls, whores thinking they could score an easy five-spot or maybe even a sawbuck. The vagrants and the whores, he dragged them out. The dropped keys and coins, he gave to the hotel clerk for safekeeping. The drunk guests—well, the manager, business-minded Mr. Leland, urged only a gentle nudge to let them know they had reached their limit. At the end of each day, except Fridays, Niehoff wrote an incident report for Leland. Fridays were the detective's day off because on Fridays, generally, more people checked out than checked in.

On the evening of March 16, the detective's rounds took him to the basement, where he scanned the center and south end—the storeroom, linen room, boot room, baggage room, engine room, pantry, kitchen, laundry, ironing room. A dark maze. He spent more time at the north end—the rundown quarters of the Negro servants who accompanied hotel guests. For weeks he had noticed that the basement quarters were more crowded than usual, and rowdier. The recession of the '90s must be over. He stayed alert as he walked the narrow passageways that separated spaces built more like interior sheds than rooms. One of the halls ended at an area set aside for cooking and eating, with a worn table to the far left. As Niehoff walked, he smelled coffee and heard the chatter of servants at the table. He stopped to listen. They could not see him.

"Paintings, grand masters, that's what Mr. Pope calls 'em. He goes to France, takes me along, and then he comes back with a new haul each time." A male voice. Negro but easy to understand.

"What do they look like? Nice?" A woman's voice. Also easy to understand.

"Well, I don't got no schooling on art, but I'm growing to like 'em. The ones Mr. Pope teaches me about look like piles of hay. But maybe better than that 'cause the artist painted those piles at different times of day. His daughter, she loves those paintings too. Tilly, do your rich people in the South buy paintings?"

Now, another woman's voice, Negro, more southern, harder to understand. "Oh, you should see that govner's manse. But no hay. Just paintings of men, white men. All up and down the stairs. I went there to dress Miz Alice and Miss Alice, when there was a ball, cause the govner's their kin. Anyway, I never saw hay paintings on the wall."

The man's voice again. "Mr. Pope bought lots of paintings in France. He doesn't even know where to put 'em. He puts the new ones on the floor of his suite. Leans 'em against the wall. I keep 'em dusted."

Now, a woman's voice. Niehoff wasn't sure if he had heard her voice before. "Not the vault? Mrs. Kirk, she puts some of her jewels in the vault, but she keeps most in her dresser. I remind her to put 'em all in the vault, but she and her daughter want 'em nearby. For their parties."

"Can you imagine, if someone wanted to nick stuff, this is the place." The man's voice again, chuckling.

Niehoff sprung out from hiding.

"Stay there, all of you. Names. I need your names. I'm Niehoff, hotel detective." He saw a Negro man with a high forehead and a gold tooth, in his forties, in livery—Harry recognized him—and three Negro women, two dressed in nurses' uniforms and one in a maid's uniform. He must have seen all the women before, too, but he remembered best the maid, young, medium brown, fetching. All four turned silent, as he expected. The maid shrunk into herself.

"Names. Out with it."

"You know me, Mr. Niehoff. Leonard Stillman, Mr. Pope's man. His valet. Rooms 203 and 204. Last week I helped you find the owner of that lost ring in the hall in front of Mr. Pope's rooms. I wouldn't do nothing wrong. We just joshin'. And these here ladies—traveling servants too, good people."

Niehoff looked from Stillman to the women. "Names?"

"Sarah Parker, nurse to Mrs. Nancy Kirk. Fourth floor. She knows I'm honest."

"Sue Bland, nurse to Mrs. Margaretta Fuller. Fourth floor. You can talk to her."

Niehoff had never seen Negro nurses until he started work at the Windsor. He sensed only the usual fear in their voices.

"Tilly Brown, maid to Miz Alice Price. Fifth floor."

The pretty one spoke softly, shook. Like a mouse.

The detective pulled out of his jacket pocket a worn leather notebook he had used for years, along with a pencil. "I'm writing down all this talk and it will go in my report, tonight, to Mr. Warren Leland, the Windsor's manager. If anything goes missing from any rooms, you will all be in trouble. Take this as a warning."

He pivoted and strode away. Leonard Stillman? Niehoff suspected Stillman told the truth. After all, he worked for Alfred Pope, that rich one from Cleveland who owned half the iron in the United States. Pope wouldn't put up with nonsense from a valet. Stillman was just joshing, probably, but you could never be too sure.

Late that night, Detective Niehoff went to his hotel office to write his incident report for Warren Leland. Most days Niehoff wrote a few sentences, sometimes hinting at the likely intentions of one of the whores he had thrown out. He wanted to bring Warren Leland a chuckle. The hotel manager was a good man. And Niehoff knew that Leland valued all efforts that kept the Windsor safe. This time, Niehoff wrote a longer report, without any quips. At half past eleven, as he left the hotel, he handed his report to the night desk clerk, Frederick Leland, the dolt who also worked the afternoon bar shift. Frederick muttered a thanks, then pocketed the report. Manager Leland had hired his cousins, Frederick and Frederick's brother Simeon, to work as hotel clerks. Everyone on staff knew the brains in the Leland family settled on Warren, skipping over Frederick and Simeon.

Niehoff, exhausted, rode the streetcar home. He counted his blessings that he had the next day off, that he wouldn't have to keep the hotel orderly on St. Patrick's Day.

Tilly Brown

At 6:30 in the evening on March 16, after that mean detective left, Tilly Brown stared at her trembling hands. She shouldn't sit in the basement, talking to these folks from the north—Leonard from Cleveland, Sarah from Chicago, Sue from Pittsburgh. What did they know about life with Miz Alice? Sarah and Sue looked at each other. Tilly could tell they saw her shake.

"Tilly, don't pay that detective no mind," Sarah said. I know Mrs. Kirk will speak up for me. Leonard and Sue looked down. Tilly said nothing. She took her plate, still filled with food, to the trash, scraped it clean, rinsed it in the sink, placed it in the drying rack, and walked out.

"Need to check some clothes in the drying room," Tilly said from the hall, not turning around. "I do laundry for a family besides Miz Alice."

Again, Tilly thought, what did those servants know? They didn't live in Bibb County Georgia, where James Moore was lynched on August 12, 1886, Tilly's seventh birthday. That's the first she remembered. Willie Singleton, lynched in '90. Charles Gibson in '97. And those men didn't do anything, just looked the wrong way. The day Charlie swung from a tree, Tilly washed up for the cook during Miz Alice's sewing circle. The women knit tea cozies and blathered about how justice had been served. So, yeah, maybe in the north those folks around the table didn't have to worry. Maybe.

Remembering the detective's threats, Tilly felt sick to her stomach, and the fire wouldn't start for another twenty-one hours.

George McClusky

New York City's Chief of Detectives, George McClusky, didn't usually reach out to hotel detectives like Harry Niehoff. Though the two detectives shared their age—in the upper thirties—and their profession, McClusky operated on a different plane, an elevated plane. After rising to the rank of Chief, McClusky investigated front-page-worthy bloodletting crimes. He was in the good graces of powerful Police Chief Big Bill Devery and wanted to keep it that way.

Chief Devery's circle of associates also included Fire Commissioner John Scannell. In mid-March, Scannell found himself at the center of a scandal he wanted behind him. Chief Big Bill Devery asked his number one detective to take charge of the Scannell case to make his friend's embarrassment disappear.

Fire Commissioner Scannell's half-brother Edward worked as a clerk in the County Court Building. The Commissioner believed that a swindler posing as Edward sought out gullible men who passed the exam to become firefighters but were not at the top of the applicants' list. For a $250 bribe, the imposter pretending to be Edward offered to use his alleged influence with his brother, the Fire Commissioner, to secure a job. When a disillusioned jobseeker paid the bribe, but a job never came through, he complained to the police. John Scannell, furious that his name was being used, implored his friend Devery to come to the rescue—the Police Chief should help the Fire Commissioner. Devery asked McClusky to lead the investigation.

McClusky needed to talk to the Scannell brothers, the county clerk and fire commissioner, to gather details. He met with them on March 16, the day before their trip upstate to spend a long weekend in Lake Placid. Fire Commissioner John Scannell would have no idea that day how fortunate he was to leave the city. Preparing for the meeting, McClusky looked in the mirror, adjusted his well-tailored jacket, carefully combed his full mustache, and angled his bowler hat just so. He vowed to get to the bottom of the bribery case to keep Commissioner Scannell and Chief Big Bill Devery happy.

"See you at dinner," McClusky said over his shoulder to Ida, one of the two spinster sisters he lived with at 223 W. 70th Street.

"Pot roast tonight," Ida said. "Do I get some stories in return?"

"Hope to have a good one for you. Not murder this time, but a wild bribery scam."

"Then I'll get Margaret to add in her apple pie."

McClusky smiled to himself. His other sister excelled at baking. Margaret and Ida kept house and cleaned and pressed his suits while he provided stories for the dinner table and household expenses. With these sisters, he felt no need for a wife and certainly not for children. He took pride in his work, his income, his title, his growing fame, and his good relations with Chief Devery. It had taken him seventeen years to rise from lowly patrolman to Chief of Detectives, and he would do nothing to harm that status.

Abner McKinley

"Tom, I visit my brother in the White House, and I visit friends in Newport and Oyster Bay, but there's nothing like Elbridge Gerry's mansion. Take my word. You're going to love it." Abner McKinley raised his voice loud enough for Thomas Ochiltree to hear above the clanking of horses pulling their carriage along Fifth Avenue on the afternoon of March 16. The carriage passed the same cathedral and mansions that Marguerite had observed three hours earlier as she walked to lunch with Angelica Gerry, but neither McKinley nor Ochiltree paid much attention to anything other than their approaching meeting with Elbridge Gerry.

"Enough with the snob talk," Ochiltree said. You think I've been nowhere except the governor's mansion in Austin? You forget I'm Colonel Thomas Ochiltree, an American legend." He smirked, looking sideways at Abner. "I dined in Jeff Davis's mansion in Biloxi and Grant's little house in Galena, too." Ochiltree stretched out the word little, then chuckled.

"Tom, you always play both ends against the middle. Anything for a buck, right?"

Abner McKinley, at age fifty-two, earned a good living as a lawyer. During one of his negotiations, he met and befriended sixty-two-year-old Thomas Ochiltree. Few life histories could surpass Ochiltree's. He had been a Texas Ranger, fighting Apaches and Comanches, then a Confederate officer, then a lawyer, politician, and businessman. His exploits yielded stories enough, but Ochiltree famously embellished those stories. He claimed friendship with everyone, never letting politics get in the way of business.

Abner enjoyed doing business with Ochiltree. The man stood out in a crowd. His receding red hair had retained its wild curls, and easterners loved listening to his western twang, peppered with enough long words for people to understand that this Texan was well educated. Like Abner, Ochiltree excelled at wheeling and dealing. Working together, the friends connected wealthy men who presided over banks, cattle, mines, telegraphs, and railroads to powerful men who could grant favors. Abner stayed within the law, just, and rarely discussed his activities with his brother, the President. Reform-minded critics lambasted Abner for peddling influence, but they praised his attention to his family, including his love for brother William and his love for his own wife and daughter. The daughter, born with one leg shorter than the other, was perfect in Abner's eyes. The family stayed in a suite on the first floor of the Windsor, a floor noted for its conveniences—the hotel office with its new telephones, the telegraph room with the accommodating O'Casey as operator, and a well-stocked newsstand. Ochiltree lived one floor above the McKinleys.

The men had a minute left to get their story straight before their carriage entered the Gerrys' elaborate porte cochère. "The steamer, Tom, that's what Elbridge is going to ask me about. He thinks I opened a Pandora's box for the cads who are sniffing out everyone who profited by selling a vessel for the war effort. Elbridge wants to hear what I have to say."

"No problem. Just agree to whatever he says. Keep 'em all happy, that's my motto."

The two paunchy men lumbered down from their carriage. Elbridge's butler answered Abner's knock.

The butler, unphased by McKinley's name and frowning at Ochiltree, led the visitors to Elbridge's study, where the three waited for a "come in" before the butler opened the door. Abner took in the elaborate furnishings while Ochiltree thrust out his arm to offer his host a hearty handshake. "Elbridge," Abner said, "I want you to meet Colonel Thomas Ochiltree. He has accompanied me because I'm sure you wish to discuss business, and Tom and I often conclude deals together. Consider him my trusted colleague. I will not hide the fact that the Colonel designation is from the wrong side. But don't let that concern you. Tom here is a practical businessman."

Elbridge smiled weakly, gestured to chairs, and offered cigars.

"La Aroma de Cuba," Ochiltree said, nodding admiration at the offering. Elbridge helped the men light their cigars. Abner noted that their host lit the matches quickly, without the usual flourishes, maybe eager to get to the heart of the meeting.

"Tell me, Abner," Elbridge said. "The price reported in the papers for the steamer. Was it accurate?"

So I guessed right, Abner thought. Elbridge called the meeting because he read stories in the papers about profiteering, stories that covered Abner's negotiations on behalf of a client who owned a steamer, along with stories about the yacht owned by Elbridge's deceased Uncle Goelet and sold by the uncle's widow for a huge sum. Elbridge wanted to confirm that Abner's wealthy client purchased a tramp steamer for $60,000, which Abner, acting on the client's behalf, sold to the U.S. Navy for $500,000 for use in the war in Cuba, earning a hefty commission. Righteous Elbridge would consider those sales the very definition of profiteering, but he would look for a way to coordinate his responses with Abner's, to frame the purchases in a sensible light.

Before answering Elbridge's question, Abner looked at Ochiltree. A slight smile as their eyes met. Abner should answer as planned.

"Elbridge, that steamer, unfair to call it a tramp steamer. Yes, my client purchased it for $60,000, but he added value. You should have seen it. Paneled stateroom, gleaming galley, plush quarters. Should have been called a king's steamer."

Elbridge shrugged his shoulders, and Ochiltree smiled.

"Those doggone naysayers," Ochiltree said between puffs on his cigar. "Don't they follow the news? We'd never have won the sea battle at Santiago de Cuba if J.P. Morgan hadn't sold the Navy the *Gloucester* and his friends hadn't sold their yachts. Those giants of the sea—worth every penny Roosevelt's men paid their owners. Same with that tramp steamer."

"Well, worth every *dollar* Roosevelt paid," Abner said with a chortle.

He hoped by making a joke, he'd distract Elbridge from Ochiltree's faux pas. The garrulous Texan should not have mentioned Morgan's yacht. The financier had been Commodore of the New York Yacht Club before Elbridge earned that title, and the two were friends in the same elevated social circle.

"I see," Elbridge said, turning his head away from Ochiltree. "Well, none of us has done anything the least bit illegal. I can tell you that with certainty. I would never profit from such sales." Then Elbridge's voice dropped one degree in certainty. "And I'm sure you wouldn't either." He looked away, took a few puffs, then looked back at Abner. "But the public doesn't see it that way. I think our best position is to make our voices heard. Talk to those reporters. I'm writing letters to the editors. Silence will bring more attention to these deals."

Elbridge barely finished his sentence before Abner chimed in. "Agreed. I will speak up as needed. And that way, I can clarify that my brother and I do not discuss business matters."

"Yes, let's keep your brother out of this mess. He's your worry. For my part, I'm not worried that Roosevelt will frown on the cost of the vessels. Theodore knows he can trust me." Elbridge put down his cigar, signaling the end of the conversation.

Abner led the way out, wishing that he inspired trust, too. He left his half-smoked cigar behind while Ochiltree held onto his. On that day, March 16, beyond the mild embarrassment of his deal for the tramp steamer, Abner had no cares at all.

James Duane

When New York City Patrolman James Duane requested St. Patrick's Day parade duty, his sergeant, bless the man, had agreed, making up for the lousy assignments of previous weeks. Duane's parents had immigrated from Ireland, along with a quarter of the city's residents. Thousands of them planned to march in the parade up Fifth Avenue or gather there to see the sights. Duane would guard them—light duty—while he joined the fun. He smiled at his good fortune.

Patrolman Duane woke up to a perfect day—chilly and breezy but manageable, thanks to the bright sun. He arrived early at the staging ground, the Worth Monument at 24th and Broadway, where a granite obelisk honored a forgotten general. As Duane scanned the crowd, thousands of marchers, their clothes dappled with green ribbons blowing in the wind, cheerfully took their place in line. No need for Duane and his fellow patrolmen to do anything more than stand around, looking manful, steadfast. His wooden nightstick hung down from his belt, and he could feel the .32 caliber Colt revolver in his holster, all part of daily dress. But he wouldn't need weapons today. The marchers and bystanders looked peaceful. They would enjoy the company, the pageantry, and later, the drink and festivities. When the parade ended, they would dance and party.

Out of habit, Duane moved his head in all directions, taking in the crowd. He watched marchers hunt for their assigned places and listened as bands warmed up. The parade's grand marshal, decked out with a green sash and green badge, checked his notebook, shouted directions. Musicians of the First Regiment of Irish Volunteers took their place of honor at the front.

Next a platoon of mounted police steadied their horses. Then the lower order parade marshals, also mounted, found their places. Behind them, invited guests lined up their seventy-five carriages. After the carriages, the groups assigned to the middle fell into position. The Hibernian Rifles of Westchester and Queens Counties. The Men's Associations of County Cork, County Galway, County Leitrim. Regiments of Irish Volunteers. A float with four girls representing still more counties of Ireland. Thirty-five divisions of the Ancient Order of Hibernians, each with a band, each band with bagpipers. Behind this middle throng still more societies and clubs formed ranks at the back of the parade.

"I'm cold. Need to get moving," one of the shivering band leaders said. His bagpiper pulled out a pocket watch.

"2:30. Any minute now."

As though they heard the complaint, the marshals shouted "start." The order rolled down from group to group. Duane took his pre-arranged position near the middle. Moving north on Fifth, marchers covered two dozen blocks with an easy stride. Bystanders, roused by the bands' reels, jigged in place. The marchers passed office buildings, storefronts, newsboys sporting green fabric shamrocks on their caps, and food-cart peddlers. Duane scanned the crowd, seeing cheery faces. He saw the clock on the corner of 42nd and Fifth hit 3:00. Marchers were keeping their expected pace.

With his new blue uniform, adorned with two rows of brass buttons, and his new helmet with a high-rounded dome, Duane knew he looked good, maybe even handsome. He slowed his pace to walk alongside the pretty girl on the float who represented County Mayo. She had pinned a green ribbon to her hat, which she held onto with her left hand, and another ribbon on her coat.

"Are you cold, miss?" Silly. She had tilted her chin up, and he wanted to get her attention. Did she hear? She turned to look at him, but with a question, not the inviting look he sought.

"Up there, what's that?" the girl asked.

James Duane's glance followed her right arm, then her wool glove, which rose toward the building at the curb. Within a second or two, the girls on floats representing Counties Cork and Galway all pointed up and to the right. The image of girls' gloved hands rising would stick in his mind, years later.

The crowd slowed, then halted on Fifth near 46th. Still looking up, Patrolman Duane bumped into the patrolman ahead of him, who bumped into the patrolman ahead of him. The festive sounds Duane heard a minute earlier stopped, replaced by horses snorting, carriages screeching, marchers shouting, whistles blowing. Then worse noises—shrieks, yowls. His eyes smarted. The girls on the floats no longer pointed inexactly with flexed, gloved fingers, to flames and to smoke. They strained their arms, stretched their fingers toward women in high windows, women of all ages. Duane couldn't hear the shrieking women, only the bystanders.

"There, there. Near the corner."

"The older one on the sill. Fifth floor."

"The one in brown. Don't let her jump."

Duane could barely see the features on the faces of the women in the windows, but he could imagine their expressions of horror.

Later, Duane read that the musicians and marchers farther back sulked when the front and middle of the parade halted, for no apparent reason. The trailing contingent detoured east on 42nd Street, then north on Park, until meeting up with the delayed front of the parade at 126th Street for the promised dinner and dancing. Waiting for the festivities, the marchers from the back heard what they had missed from the eyewitnesses in the lead.

"And the women, you should have seen the wretched creatures. They were jumping to the pavement."

"The posh ones?"

"The posh in their silks and the servants too. They all died."

"Didn't know it was a hotel at first. Just thought it was an office building. But then I saw the women and heard it was the Windsor Hotel. Not fit for a king or queen no more."

Felix Kain

At 1:30 on St. Patrick's Day, Felix Kain dressed better than usual, donning the suit he wore to funerals over thin, shabby clothes. The pocket of his old pants still held the fake badge Clay had given him. Felix folded a burlap sack and stuffed it into another pocket. He dusted flour on his hair and then spent ten minutes brushing it off his shoulders. After admiring the disguise in his scratched mirror, he liquored up.

Confident about his preparations, Felix rode a streetcar to the Windsor, where bystanders had gathered an hour early to view the parade. He returned to the same walnut table he had seen the day before and checked his watch, filched during a previous job. 2:40. He stood, forcing himself into something resembling a relaxed pose. He looked out the window at the massing spectators. With a shaking hand, he lit the last of the Romeo y Julieta cigars from Clay. Puffed on it. Why didn't it smell as good as the cigar yesterday? Waiters sped by, though as the lunch service dwindled, they slowed down. Right before 3:00, Felix heard music roll up Fifth. The few guests in the hall would hear the music, too.

"Hurry, we're missing it," a woman snapped at her husband as the two walked toward the stairs.

"Going as fast as I can, Dora. You're not even Irish. What's the rush?"

A waiter walked behind the grumbling couple, carrying a tray. Perfect timing. At that instant, Felix coughed, while flicking the embers of his cigar onto the lace curtain. A firm flick. Just enough noise and motion. Not enough to be suspicious. Felix saw the waiter's eyes follow the embers and narrow in a squint. As soon as the waiter was out of sight, Felix scurried into the hall. Glancing back for a second, he wondered if the embers had been too big. Better check. He slowed down, then lurked in a corner where he could see the curtain while staying close to the central staircase. That damn waiter turned around. Son of a bitch. Must have thought to give the curtain a second look.

"What the hay?" Felix heard the waiter's question.

"Goddammit." The waiter again, louder now.

Ignoring the growing clamor, Felix scrambled down the stairs toward his second task—Abner McKinley's suite. No one manned the nearby telegraph office. O'Casey must have gone spectating. Felix entered the open suite door, removed the sack from his pocket, grabbed, grabbed again, and took time to ransack every drawer in every chiffonier. After a while, he struggled to breathe as smoke filled the suite. He stumbled around for a few more minutes, disoriented until he found the door to the hall, and then he stumbled again until he felt the handle of the side door on the 47th Street side. Opening it, he gasped for air, felt relief. Seeing the crowd, he remembered one of Clay's directives. Felix put his sack down, stripped off his funeral suit, and threw it aside, certain the crowd was looking up at the windows, not out at him. He never saw the face in a low window across the street. Never knew that a dark man, wearing a chef's hat, had returned to his employer's kitchen and was staring at the Windsor's side door.

May Gleason

"Great day for the parade," Tara Regan said to May Gleason as the maids woke up on St. Patrick's Day in their cold room. "Look for me on the roof this afternoon. We can sing along with the bands."

Even in her wake-up daze, May noted Tara's good cheer. That girl talked a lot as each day wore on, but not much at this early hour. Why sweetness and light this morning? Maybe she had plans tonight with her wild sweetheart, Sean.

"Right, Tara. See you on the roof." No point in questioning her.

The rest of the morning, into the afternoon, May worked fast to finish cleaning on four. She would usually hesitate to leave her floor during the workday, but the chief housekeeper, Mrs. Wrigley, told all the girls that she herself would head to the roof to watch the parade. "Just don't make it all day." The housekeeper winked as she warned.

To finish her tasks, May carried dirty linens in baskets down five flights to the basement, then handed them to the laundresses. As she entered the steam-filled room, she saw the ironing station off to the left and felt a wave of warmth. A cluster of prattling maids stood at wooden ironing boards, one ironing busily, the others looking impatient. May knew the maid who ironed. She was Hortense Webb, the gossipy chambermaid, the one with a long face who cleaned the McKinleys' suite. Holding the handle of a strange-looking iron, Hortense glided it over a peach-colored silk frock trimmed with lace.

"Mrs. McKinley pays me to do extra, pays well too. She's picky about her gowns.

May lingered near the ironing station where the maids had gathered, curious to see if Hortense gossiped more about the McKinleys.

One of the maids, must have been six feet tall, pushed her way toward Hortense. "Please," the tall one said, "can I use one of the new irons. In North Dakota, where I'm from, we don't have irons like this."

"Who do you do for?" Hortense asked.

"Mrs. Wells. I'm Belinda Mason, her maid. She and her husband and daughter stay on the sixth floor."

May recognized this tall Belinda. She had seen her in the quarters set aside for traveling servants and had heard her western twang. Hortense pointed to a board and an iron. Belinda offered a hearty thanks and began to press a purple-striped gown.

A pudgy maid with blond braids begged to go next. Hortense saw the woman and pointed to yet another board and iron. "Over there. And you are—"

"I'm Lotte Hansen, lady's maid to Mrs. Ada Pope, from Cleveland. My lady likes to dress early. I guess we're all here because of St. Patrick's Day. All those parties tonight. Society folks turn Irish for the day, even if they bash the Irish in private. Or maybe they use the day as an excuse for a dinner party."

As May turned toward the servants' stairway that would take her to the roof, she heard Hortense give instructions. "That shelf on the wall. When you're through girls, put the irons there."

May walked out, leaving the steam from the laundry and the sizzling of the irons. She ran up the servants' stairs. Reaching the fourth-floor landing, she noticed two young men, both good lookers, hovering, glancing down the hall. The man with curly dark hair wore an unremarkable gray cloth jacket. She'd never seen him before. The tall, red-headed one looked familiar. He wore a brown leather coat. Trying not to stare, she followed their eyes, glancing down the hall. She saw Bridget standing beside the maid's closet.

May passed the men, climbed up a flight, then stopped for a bit, wondering. What were they up to? She crept back down and peeked around the corner to the landing. The men no longer hovered there. She looked down the hall and saw Bridget come out of the maid's closet, not carrying towels or anything else she might have borrowed from a floor that was not her own. What could Bridget be doing in the closet with two men? Whatever it was, May guessed it wouldn't be right. Pondering if she should tattle to Mrs. Wrigley, May climbed to seven to collect her coat, then to the roof, expecting a jolly scene.

Marguerite Wells

"Should I wear green to go downtown? If you look out the window, Mama, you'll see nothing but green. The whole city's in green."

Nellie Wells leaned out the sixth-floor window of the family's suite. "You're right. Even from up high, I can see. You're excited about the parade. Me too." She turned around and cocked her head. "But green might be a bit much for us. No Irish blood here."

Marguerite Wells never gave a second thought to St. Patrick's Day until March 17, 1899. Every previous March 17, she had spent in North Dakota, at college in Massachusetts, or teaching school in New Jersey. The holiday meant little to her. Her mother was born a Johnson, and her mother's mother was born a Jewett—all from English stock and proud of it. Her father, Edward Wells—he was English, too. But staying in the center of New York, at a hotel on the path of the parade, Marguerite felt the excitement of the day.

"Maybe just this brooch, Mama. That's not pretending I'm something I'm not. Marguerite pinned a jade brooch to the bodice of her blouse.

With her mother, Marguerite left the Windsor at 10:00 to shop for the items they still needed for their trip to Europe. Edward Wells spent the morning sending telegrams from the first-floor office, settling business ventures—railroad and banking matters—in preparation for the trip. The three met up for a late lunch at the Windsor, dining lightly on soup since they had no conception of the energy they soon would need.

Usually a sedate place, the dining room that day bustled. Marguerite didn't recognize most of the diners. They were not regular hotel guests, but cheerful visitors who came to view the parade and decided to begin with a fine meal. She did recognize the uniformed men who waited on tables, but even they seemed different, more alert, moving fast. Maybe eager to finish the lunch service in order to catch a glimpse of the parade.

"What time will the parade pass the hotel?" Marguerite overheard one of the diners ask a waiter.

"They say 3:00. But don't worry. You'll hear the music coming up from the south. You won't miss it."

"Where's the best place to watch? Without getting trampled?"

"John, let the boy move on. He's carrying a tray, and he has guests to serve." The man's wife was unusually considerate, Marguerite thought.

"That's all right, ma'am. Everyone asks. I hear the best place is half a block west on 46th, looking toward the hotel. Or you can stand right at the hotel, but you'll be jostled."

"Many thanks, boy."

Marguerite turned to her parents and repeated the waiter's advice. "Thank goodness we can watch from our rooms."

After lunch, the Wellses returned to their suite on the sixth floor, facing Fifth Avenue, toward the south end of the hall. Seeking exercise, they avoided the crowded elevator and climbed four floors from the second-floor dining room, up the wooden central staircase, through the wood-paneled hall. They gathered in their suite's sitting room and pulled mahogany side chairs to the window overlooking Fifth, angling them to get a good view to the south. Despite the cold air, they opened the window to hear the marchers. After five or ten minutes, they caught sounds—wonderful lilting jigs that grew louder and louder, growing sounds of bagpipes. They saw mounted police, elegant carriages, marching bands.

From high above Fifth, Marguerite spotted her mama's tall maid, Belinda, with her mauve bonnet. She must have exited the servant's entrance and now she ambled to the edge of the crowd. Belinda's father immigrated to the Dakotas from County Mayo, so that morning she asked permission to watch the parade after she finished ironing. As the music soared, Marguerite heard the bands and the groups on the sidewalk, singing. A man sung Molly

Malone. Marguerite's Papa laughed as she started to sing along.

The music stopped. Instantly. Marguerite heard shouts. People below flailed their hands frantically, trying to warn others. Women ran out of the hotel without coats. Marguerite and her papa lurched from their chairs and looked down, then to the sides, then up. They saw flames shooting out of windows above and to the left and the right. Everywhere.

Mama stood, paralyzed. Marguerite opened the door. She and her papa looked down the smoky hall, dumbstruck at the flames popping out from the elevator.

"Nellie, there's smoke in the hall, and it's too late to use the elevator. We are caught like rats in a trap." Later, Marguerite remembered thinking she had never heard her Papa use that phrase. Never. He scrunched up his face, puzzling out what to do. Mama turned pale, looking at him, her chin sinking.

"Here, in the closet, the rope." Days later, Marguerite was certain she pointed. "It's called a life-saving rope." She smiled proudly, despite the fear—she knew what to do. Papa opened the closet door and dragged out the coiled hemp rope Marguerite had seen in the room on this trip and previous trips. A simple, thick, rough rope. No instructions on how to use it. Up to that minute, her memories followed Papa's, followed Mama's. Parallel tracks.

Then, the fog came along with the smoke.

Hours later, coming out of the blur, Marguerite found herself standing on the sidewalk with her parents, staring at the wasteland that had once been the Windsor. "Don't return those blankets to the firemen," her papa said. "You'll need them. Twelve blocks to the Hoffman House. Broadway and 25th. It's a Friday, a slow day for hotels. They'll take us in." Now he sounded like Papa, not the man who said "we're caught like rats in a trap" a few hours earlier.

The Wellses, along with maid Belinda, wrapped their blankets around themselves like shawls and kept their eyes on the ground. The smoldering hotel gave off warmth but not enough to notice, not enough to quell their shivers. Edward Wells led the way, wandering around clamoring fire wagons, police vans, lost stragglers from the parade, and bystanders still looking up. Marguerite couldn't hear her parents talk over the sounds of coughing and ambulance bells, but she didn't need to because they were nearly silent. Smoke followed the foursome. They straggled into the Hoffman House. Marguerite's papa took his place in line at the front desk, behind Windsor guests who had beaten the family to sanctuary.

"Mr. Wells, I can offer you the last two rooms," the clerk said. "Space for your lady's maid in the attic. The bellhop can help you with your bags."

Edward Wells looked at his family, winced. "We have nothing. Just the clothes on our backs." The bellhop looked at him with pity, then annoyance, realizing no bags might mean no tip. He shrugged and led them to the elevator while he gave Belinda the key to the servant's quarters and directed her to the side stairway.

As Marguerite looked over the other bedraggled guests huddled in the Hoffman House lobby, she heard her mama talking to Belinda. "Come to our rooms in ten minutes. No clothes for you to unpack this time. We will plan how to reach people in Jamestown to tell them we survived." Nellie Wells cocked her head. "Belinda, you haven't said a word." Marguerite stifled a laugh. Belinda's chattering was a family joke. "That's not like you. Did the smoke hurt your throat?"

"I'm all right, ma'am. I'll see you soon." She walked toward the stairs, chin down, blanket still wrapped around her despite the warmth of the Hoffman House lobby.

Marguerite and her mama spent the night telephoning and telegraphing family to assure them they had survived. Her papa busied himself calling business associates, asking for duplicates of the papers and licenses he had lost. He managed to contact the office of the Compagnie Générale Transatlantique to make sure they would honor the family's tickets to sail to France on the 21st since the tickets were ash. All this took time because other survivors at the Hoffman House also lined up to use the three house phones and to reach the desk of the telegraph operator. Marguerite managed to call her brother Stuart back in North Dakota—thank goodness her papa had installed a telephone there.

The hotel housekeeper brought a light dinner of soup up to the Welles' suite. She announced that reporters in the lobby wanted to interview refugees from the Windsor. Edward Wells went downstairs for a while and returned with stories. According to the prevailing view, a cigar smoker's carelessly flicked ember had caused a city block to burn to the ground. Or maybe a gang of thieves had set the fire to force guests out of the hotel.

By ten o'clock, all three Wellses were in bed, exhausted. Marguerite had no regrets, other than her papa's decision to stay at the Windsor in the first place. She saw no reason to fill in the gaps in her memory and no reason to question the cigar smoker theory, which sounded more likely than the preposterous robber theory.

David Dudley

David Dudley anticipated a peaceful day in the kitchen. He directed his sous chefs to focus on dinner preparations—preparing the turtle soup, seasoning the lamb, whipping the vanilla mousse. His employer, Miss Helen Gould, would be out for hours, calling on her broker, the same broker who worked with her father, Jay Gould, until his death. Using the calm afternoon to catch up on tasks, Dudley made sure the kitchen gleamed and went over provisions, placing orders as necessary for the weekend. He worked steadily and efficiently, so he could take a break to watch the St. Patrick's Day parade as it passed by the mansion on Fifth Avenue. Dudley was as far from Irish as you could get, but he loved the music. So did his friend, Ted Johnson. Ted knocked on the door of the basement kitchen at 2:45. Dudley checked his watch, chuckled. Ted was always a few minutes early, especially when fun lay ahead. Dudley opened the door and tilted his head approvingly.

"Hey, Ted, looking good." Ted had taken care with his dress today. Dudley never called his friend by his last name—too many Johnsons in the Negro neighborhood where they lived, but only one Ted. "I'll clean up too."

Dudley threw off his apron and donned the respectable clothes he needed for Fifth Avenue. The friends exited the servants' entrance of the elegant, mansard-roofed Gould mansion on the corner of Fifth and 47th. Once out in the cold, they walked fifty feet, joining the crowd gathered in front of the Windsor to watch the marchers and listen to the bands. Dudley's eyes, looking south, stopped at the flagpole in front of the Windsor.

"Smoke," he shouted to Ted, trying to raise his voice above the noise. The two men stared, expecting the smoke to fade. It grew. Their eyes met in horror. Dudley looked over the crowd. No one else noticed. But he had worked in kitchens—Mrs. Gould's, and less equipped kitchens too—long enough to understand smoke. He gave Ted's arm a nudge to follow. They ran into the Windsor. A liveried doorman sized them up, his eyes staying on their faces, not their neat clothes. He sneered but let them enter. They ran through the enormous, palm-lined lobby. Dudley dashed into the office, looking for anyone standing behind a desk. He saw a nameplate. Simeon Leland, day clerk. Pasty skin, wisps of colorless hair.

"Fire, sir, you have a fire in the hotel. Where's the alarm?"

Simeon Leland stared at the two men, then sneered, the width of his sneer exceeding the doorman's. "You're crazy." The sneer became a snicker.

Dudley's eyes met Ted's. No debate. They knew not to argue. They started to walk out, then Dudley noticed another, smaller desk in the office. Behind that desk stood a man about the same age as the chortling Simeon. Dudley gestured with his chin to Ted. The two walked toward the smaller desk and read the nameplate—Charles Squires, Cashier.

"Please, sir. You heard me talking to the clerk. The alarm. Warn the guests."

Charles Squires's eyes moved beyond Dudley. The cashier sought a sign from clerk Simeon Leland. No surprise. Squires gave the slightest shake of his head, then looked down.

Most days, Dudley and his friend Ted took the safe path. They stood in the hall for a minute, silent, eyeing each other. One sniffed, then the other. Burning wood.

"Dud, let's do it ourselves."

Ted, always brave, turned toward the central staircase to cry out an alarm. The two sprinted upstairs as a man dressed in a waiter's uniform came running down, almost crashing into them, yelling "Fire, fire." Behind the waiter, smoke billowed down the staircase. Behind the smoke, men and women, howling with fear, lurched down the stairs toward the lobby. Ted took a few more steps up, shoving past panicked guests.

Dudley staggered behind, then pulled Ted back. "Gotta get out." As

INFERNO ON FIFTH

the two turned to leave, they heard a roar, a crash. The elevator dropped through its shaft, with orange sparks entering the lobby, exploding into flames, lapping up the silk drapes. Shrieks came from the elevator, or maybe the guests in the lobby. Or maybe the guests rushing down the stairs. Dudley and Ted managed to stumble out of the hotel as guests laden with belongings and panting for air shoved them aside.

"Think those fools at the desk are burning up?" Ted asked.

"Don't goddamn care," Dudley answered. But he did care about his employer. Helen Gould had encouraged him over the years as she plucked him from dishwasher to butcher to sous chef and finally to head chef, to handle her meals and her dinner parties. That lady might be wealthier than the Vanderbilts and the Carnegies, but she had a heart. She took care of people. He stood with Ted, watching the chaos, but when he saw embers on the roof of the Gould mansion across the street, he knew he had to get back.

Ted wanted to stay with the crowd on Fifth, watching the hotel windows. The friends raised their hands in a goodbye gesture, each with a knowing grimace. Neither was surprised at their treatment by the Windsor doorman, clerk, and cashier.

As Dudley crossed 47th, he saw two firemen spraying a weak stream of water at the embers on the mansion. The firemen nodded at each other, signaling success. Dudley reentered the mansion and headed to the basement. He put his apron and chef's hat back on, but he didn't return to the ovens and sinks at the heart of the kitchen. Instead, he stationed himself at a window where he could see a bit of the sidewalk in front of the mansion, as well as 47th Street. He watched the fire trucks and the crowd.

Dudley saw a heavyset man stumble out the Windsor's side door, stop for a second to gulp air, then put down a sack. Oddly, the man stripped off his suit jacket and threw it aside. Shabby dresser. The man looked around, picked up the sack, and walked away. He didn't get far.

"Halt." Dudley thought he heard two coppers yell that word. He opened the window, despite the smoke, to hear more. "Don't move." One of the coppers grabbed the bum's sack.

Before Dudley could see more, he spotted to his right the Gould carriage pulling up in front. Helen Gould was returning from her monthly meeting with her family's broker. Dudley knew that since Jay Gould's death seven years earlier, daughter Helen had advised the broker on how to invest her father's fortune, not the other way around. The servants had their own gossip network with numerous sources. Miss Helen and the broker managed to add to her inheritance despite ups and many downs in stock prices. She could continue her charitable donations.

The Gould carriage's pair of horses, usually dependable, stopped suddenly, braying at the sight and heat of flames. The coachman skillfully calmed them, then rang his bell to summon the butler. Even over the cacophonous street noises—frightened horses, firewagon gongs, screaming victims—the Gould employees heard that bell. The butler ran to the carriage, stifling a cough. He didn't take his employer's hand, as usual, but put his arm on her elbow to steer her quickly into the foyer. Dudley abandoned the window and quietly walked up the stairs to the parlor floor, close enough to hear.

"Oh, Clarkson, the ride was terrible. Thank goodness we have such a fine coachman. He maneuvered us around hundreds of engines and vans. Smoke everywhere. Such crowds."

"Right, ma'am. I've never seen such a commotion here on Fifth."

"And I saw stretchers with people with broken bones, burns. I heard crying, screaming. On the last block, I saw bodies on the street, covered with bed sheets. All that misery, twenty feet from my home."

"Your house is all right, ma'am." The reliable Clarkson tried to put Miss Gould at ease. "The fire crossed over 47th and lapped at the roof, but the firemen put their hoses on it, fast. Only a little damage. Let's get you inside, away from the mob."

"No, we should help the hotel guests and the brave workers out there. For heaven's sake—all these suffering people."

"The police called more ambulances."

Helen Gould set her eyes squarely on Clarkson's eyes. "What's the Christian way?" she asked. Dudley, eavesdropping, was accustomed to his employer's piety. She paused another second. "Find a police captain.

Tell him we're opening the house to the injured. I'll get the parlors ready."

Dudley returned to the kitchen as everyone around him awaited orders. From the window he saw a footman wave into the mansion a fireman who was about to collapse, and three bystanders gasping for air. Dudley went up and down with water and coffee for the wretched guests. Over the course of the next hour, the police captain, enlisted by the butler, guided stretcher carriers to bring the wounded off the sidewalks, into Helen Gould's parlors while she instructed her maids to bring down mattresses and blankets. Soon, the front parlor, the back parlor, and the dining room filled up with the wounded, as well as doctors, nurses, frantic relatives.

Dudley finished brewing a new caldron of coffee, then huddled with the kitchen help, all anxious for news from their chef. White capped heads bobbed up and down as they stood in a circle around him.

"Ignored yuh, eh? They deserve to burn."

"Not all of 'em. Not those that work down in the Windsor basement, polishing silver and washing sheets."

"And now Miss Helen wants us to feed all these swells and coppers."

They heard Helen Gould on the steps, then heard her enter the kitchen. Dudley used his eyes to warn his kitchen help. He stopped talking. The others scattered, sheepish looks on their faces.

"What's this about? Is there a problem?" Dudley knew Miss Helen needed the kitchen workers to feed the hordes swarming in her front door. Not a good time for her to chastise the help.

"Sorry, ma'am," Dudley said. "We're just upset about the fire. It took the hotel a long time to call it in." He looked at her. "And the flames reached your roof. Could o' been disaster for you too."

Miss Helen raised her eyes. Maybe she didn't know much.

"Have you heard how it started, Dudley?"

He told his version. Standing on the sidewalk. Taking a break, a short break. Being the first to see smoke. Running into the hotel to warn the staff. He sped through his story, then slowed down.

"Ma'am. You treat me good. Made me your chef. Responsible for the kitchen and these good folks here." He gestured to the workers. They were quiet, trying to listen while looking busy. "But some people, they don't wanna listen to a colored man."

She looked up at him, wanting more. He told her about the doorman's sneer, the clerk's rebuff, the cashier's denial.

"Dudley, I am sorry that happened to you. Give me a little time to think about all this—how far the story should go. Now, let's talk about what food we can offer the people upstairs."

After he went over supplies with her, she returned to her parlors. A few minutes later, Dudley went up, carrying his fourth tray of coffee. Women in agony lay on blankets, on rugs, on cushions on the parquet. He saw Miss Helen in the front parlor, looking at one of the victims, about her age, early thirties. Blistered face, singed hair, red and black arms limp at her side. Miss Helen straightened up, looked around, determined. She spotted three men moving tentatively around the bodies of the victims, with notebooks in hand.

"Gentlemen, you are covering the fire for your papers, right?"

"*The Sun*," one answered. "*The Journal*," from another, moving in front of the first. "*The Times*," from a third, resigned to his place behind the others.

She pointed at Dudley.

"Over here then. We have a story for you."

Alice Price

As the time arrived for her appointment with Dr. McPhatter, Alice Price grew anxious, and her cramps worsened. A strange doctor, examining her? Back in Georgia, no one had touched her, looked at her there. Aside from Willis, and he'd been dead for years. The men she knew were content just seeing, admiring her face and form. Well, most of the men. Now she dressed for the occasion, even though she laughed at herself, knew she was silly to dress for an examination. Of course, she certainly wouldn't wear green, even if it was St. Patrick's Day. No need to associate with the Irish.

As usual, Alice wore diamond rings on her fingers, a diamond-studded brooch worth $3,000 on her bodice, and money tucked into her corset—eight hundred-dollar bills and five fifty-dollar bills. By habit, she carried money on her person, rather than leaving it around to tempt servants or chambermaids or hiding it away in a hotel safe she didn't trust.

Once dressed, Alice found a reason to send Tilly off on errands, far from the upcoming examination. "Tilly, I'm going with Mrs. Henry to shop in a few minutes. While we're out, go fetch the hat I ordered, down on Broadway. Here's money for the payment. Might take you a while to get there because of the parade. Don't worry. No need to hurry."

Less than a minute after Tilly left, Alice peeked out the door of her suite's parlor, glancing down the hall to see if Mehitable Henry and Dr. McPhatter were on their way. No one. Quiet. Back to the mirror to check on her powder, her coiled topknot. She walked into the empty hall to pace and to watch.

In an instant, calm became chaos.

Feet pounding. Then yelling. "Fire. Fire. Get out. Leave the hotel." Two hotel maids bolted down the hall, screaming, caps flying off their heads.

"No. I don't see fire." The minute Alice uttered those words to the fleeing maids, smoke poured down the hall, and Mehitable and a tall man with a full shock of light hair appeared—Dr. Neil McPhatter. Men and women emerged from their rooms, wide-eyed, some empty-handed, some carrying coats and valuables. All looked petrified. Except for Dr. McPhatter. He spotted Alice—raised his arm. Stay calm. He turned toward the stairs, saw the same heavy smoke that Alice and Mehitable saw. The guests who tried for the stairs turned around, ran.

"The windows. Let's try the windows," the doctor said, glancing up and down the hall. Alice realized he didn't know what room she had come out of. She turned to point, but in the smoke, nothing looked familiar. He wasn't going to wait for her to decide. He barged into a room that guests had fled from, guiding Mehitable and Alice beside him and then slamming the suite door closed. The three ran to the window, and the doctor shoved it open. Alice saw the tops of heads leaning out of the windows below and arms letting out ropes across sills. Even with the suite door closed, smoke crept in from the crack under the door. Alice started to cough, Mehitable to wheeze, but the doctor paid little attention. He busied himself hunting through the unfamiliar room until he found a safety rope.

"Mrs. Price, you first." Alice, trembling, didn't fight him. She felt his fingers tie the rope around her waist, twist to make a firm knot. Then, his hands on her shoulders, guiding her to the ledge. She looked at Mehitable, who wheezed too hard to meet her eyes. "Now," the doctor said. "Hold tight and kick off." Before Alice could get out words of protest, he pushed hard. She swung out. Rope fibers ripped into her palms. She shot down three floors, still hanging on as she bounced off the burning building twice, and then let go, falling the final part of the way.

Fifteen minutes later, in the ambulance, Alice Price regained consciousness. The ride to Bellevue Hospital seemed endless. She could not move her right leg. She screamed from the pain in her hip and lacerated palms.

Looking at those palms, she winced, and then her eyes rested on her glittering rings. She took them off her fingers and handed them to the ambulance attendant for safekeeping. This man would be more trustworthy than the hospital workers.

At last, the orderlies lifted her from the ambulance and carried her to a bed. For painkillers, she had to wait an hour until the harried doctors could reach her. She listened to them carefully. She would recover, they said. The paralysis in her leg was temporary. By evening, Alice rallied to the point where she could talk to Deputy Coroner O'Hanlon, who was making the rounds of the wards. Looking for the dead, she thought. Alice complained to him that she had not recovered her rings, though she had arrived at the hospital with her brooch and cash. She sang the praises of Dr. McPhatter, crediting him with saving her life. The doctor, O'Hanlon told her, was in a ward on the floor below, recovering from a broken ankle.

Later that evening, after the deputy coroner moved on to other wards, Alice asked if anyone knew what happened to her after she blacked out after she tried to slide down the damn rope. An orderly who had tended to Dr. McPhatter put two and two together and wheeled the doctor to Alice's bed.

"I will tell you what I know, Mrs. Price. What I remember." McPhatter, looking pale in the wheelchair, spoke in a kindly tone. "I saw men on the ground at the hotel who tried to break your fall. They couldn't. Not that you weigh much, but they didn't judge right. You struck the pavement, right side down. A doctor in the crowd saw. He pushed his way to you. When he discovered your injuries, he motioned for an ambulance attendant to carry you away. To Bellevue, but I didn't know it at the time. The minute that doctor on the street unfastened the rope from your waist, I yanked it back and tied it around Mrs. Henry, knotting it again. I pushed her out, like I did with you. But it didn't work." The doctor winced. "She thumped against one of the decorative ledges and let go. The same doctor below who tended to you, he tended to her. He called for a second ambulance carrier. I saw the sign on the carrier's van—Roosevelt Hospital. Then me. I yanked the rope up and adjusted it around my own waist. I secured it to a bracket and slid down. You see my ankle and my burnt hands."

"Terrible," Alice said. "Can I ask? Have you spoken to my doctor? Do you agree my paralysis is temporary?"

Alice saw McPhatter look at her quizzically, then look down. After a second, he offered a reassuring answer, then tried to wheel himself away. She didn't know what she had done wrong.

Clayton Byrne

Surrounded by the suffocating smell of bleach and scented soap in the fourth-floor maid's closet, Clay Byrne huddled with Sean Mack, his untested accomplice. Sean seemed fine, so far. Clay scattered scraps of paper on the closet floor, then removed a cigar from his pocket and lit it. He shook the cigar with a few strong, intentional flicks, watching as the embers caught fire on the papers.

Clay fingered the burlap sack in his pocket. Big enough to hold gems but small enough not to raise questions. Then he fingered the pistol on his side, secured by his belt, hidden by his leather jacket. Filched at an earlier job and pocketed today out of habit. He wouldn't need it. He saw Sean look down, place his hand under his jacket. Sean must be fingering an identical sack in his own pocket, where it sat next to his lucky Liberty Head nickel. Sean had shown Clay the nickel days before when they talked about the Windsor job. "It's already gotten me through some rough scrapes," Sean told Clay. "My lucky charm. Keeps the coppers from haulin' me or my Italian buddies off to jail."

Remembering those words, Clay cut through the tension with a joke. "Feeling that nickel today, before we go nickin'? You're the last chum I'd guess to be the superstitious sort." Clay smirked as he spoke. Then he turned away from Sean to open the door a crack. Flickers of fire jumped out to the hall. He closed the door and waited until he heard commotion. "More smoke than I expected. Faster, too." Clay spoke quietly as he crept out of the closet, Sean following. Panicking guests leaving their rooms for a smoke-filled hall would pay no attention to two strangers.

Clay and Sean ran down the hall. Squinting in the smoke, Clay saw a woman in her forties, half holding, half dragging an older woman toward the central stairs. Good. He pictured Molly Dugan's list of valuables, with gems in suite 410 at the top. The two women must be Mrs. Kirk and her daughter, Mrs. Haskin. He guessed they had not taken time to lock their suite door, which he knew from the list was halfway down the hall. In seconds, still more smoke. How had his few embers caused such havoc so quickly? Sounds of choking. Coughing. Yelling.

Sensing Sean stumble, Clay grabbed for the younger man's arm and guided him toward the suite the women had abandoned. Now confusion—Clay wasn't sure. Couldn't see room numbers. He pointed to the door at his right and pushed Sean toward it, while pointing ahead to another door, then his own chest, letting Sean know they should split up. Surely, one of the suites belonged to the rich ladies, Kirk and Haskin. Barely able to see or hear, Clay assumed Sean entered the room to the right through an open door. Bending low, staggering down the hall to the next room, Clay felt for the door handle. Unlocked.

This room, the sitting room, seemed empty. Through the smoke, Clay made out that the suite followed the pattern he had studied when he apprenticed to the carpenter the previous fall—sofa on the back wall, armoire on the right, and desk on the left. He opened the armoire. One woolen coat and two bonnets. Opened the desk drawer. Stationery. Not the right room. To the side, he saw the door to the bedroom, open, the smoke a little lighter there. A four-poster bed with an old woman lying in it, wearing a lilac-colored nightgown, gasping. Her eyes opened. Widened. She screamed. Did the noise in the hall cover her sound? Clay struggled to breathe, struggled to see. Struggled to think.

He reached into his leather coat, took out his pistol, aimed. He didn't hear the gunshot, The woman slumped, scarlet seeping into lilac. He replaced the pistol, dropped to the floor, and crawled.

At the stairs, Clay bumped into a body slumped on the carpet. Several men stumbled past the body, ignoring whatever they tripped over. Clay put his palms under the thin fabric that partially covered the body. He felt smooth, naked legs under his hands. He lifted. A woman? Clay would barely remember this flight, would not know what motivated him to help, the heedless passing men or remorse.

At the sidewalk, gulping for air and still carrying a body, he entered chaos. He laid the body on the sidewalk. Yes, a woman, in a yellow-flowered chemise that exposed her flesh. He considered checking for a breath, but he needed to leave, fast, in case the coppers were looking for him. As he pushed his way through the crowd held back by police, he heard a crash, maybe a wall or a chimney, from the spot where he had laid down the woman. He did not look back.

Clay walked south, wobbling around vans, horses, carts, screaming bystanders. Panting, wheezing. He supposed he didn't stand out—others escaping from the fire walked alongside him—but they had not just shot a woman. Maybe they hadn't saved a woman either. Twenty blocks, and Clay still struggled to breathe. He studied his reflection in a shop window. Leather coat, undamaged. Bulge in a pocket. Not much to draw suspicion. Maybe he smelled of smoke, but so did everyone who had been in that fire. He walked another half hour, cursing at his luck.

Clay spotted a few flophouses. He chose one, said little to the clerk, paid in advance for a cot—little more than a pallet—for a week. That night, after checking to make sure the flophouse's ne'er-do-wells were not wandering about, he walked into the alley with his revolver, threw it into the trash. He reached into the disgusting bin to cover the gun with dinner leftovers. The stench struck him. He held his breath, pushing the gun in deeply. Creeping back to his cot, he lay down on the horse blanket, trying to ignore his parched throat and the odors from unwashed bodies on cots near his. He stared at the peeling ceiling, wondering where he could run.

Sean Mack

The fleeing women had not stopped to lock their door. Sean brushed off his fear for a minute—he had hit the jackpot. The bedroom in suite 410—Sean knew from Molly's list that he stood in the right room—brimmed over with riches. Through smarting eyes, he gawked at rings and brooches in an open case on a bureau to the left, where Molly predicted. Even through the rising smoke, the jewels sparkled, at least in Sean's imagination.

In an instant, smoke swelled in.

Sean swiped the jewels into his burlap bag. Gasped for air. Dropped the bag. Couldn't see. Opened drawers. Scooped a gem into a pocket. Would Clay expect more to justify the five percent cut? Sean gasped again. A few more for the pocket. Then he tripped over an open drawer.

Tilly Brown

Alice Price had never, not once, told Tilly Brown to take her time running an errand. Strange, since this would be an easy errand—fetching a hat on Broadway. And what was Miz Alice up to with that old lady, name of Mehitable Henry, and a doctor? Tilly grabbed her light coat, more suitable for March in Georgia. Leaving the fifth-floor suite, she lingered on the first step of the servant's staircase to catch a glimpse of the hallway. 3:00. The old lady and the doctor would be coming for a visit.

Quiet. Then, in a sequence Tilly would forget, or maybe all at once—

Miz Alice walked the hall, pacing.

Two white maids rushed down the hall, screaming. Did they yell fire?

That old lady shuffled toward Miz Alice. A tall blond man barged ahead.

Doors banged open along the hall. People streamed out toward the elevator. An ear-shattering, crashing sound from that direction.

Still on the servants' stairs, Tilly ran down five flights, with white servants storming in on every floor, pushing behind her. On the street, more screaming, jumping, frantic waving. Should she go back to help Miz Alice? Tilly found a spot on the sidewalk to stop. Shopkeepers from across the street handed out blankets to some of the guests and white servants. Shivering, looking up, she tried to sort out her choices. Then, two voices to her left.

"Think a gang set this? To cover their robbin'?"

"With the parade and the fire, they'd find good pickings."

The words of two coppers talking to each other hit Tilly. Didn't matter. She had done nothing. That detective, Niehoff, he'd find her. Or he'd give her name to the coppers. She knew she should try to save Miz Alice. Or should she save herself?

Frederick Leland

Six hours after pocketing Detective Niehoff's incident report, at around dawn on March 17, Windsor night clerk Frederick Leland took the elevator to the fifth-floor hotel room where he lived. He emptied his jacket pockets as usual and added the March 16 report to the pile of others from the week on his bureau. Frederick noticed that the newest report ran longer than the others, but he didn't bother to read it this time. Niehoff—that bootlicking toady—always tried to impress Warren with tedious reports. A lost theater ticket, a drunken diner. Frederick had long ago given up trying to impress his formidable cousin Warren, who thought being hotel manager gave him the keys to the kingdom. Bad luck, too, that Frederick's supercilious brother Simeon thought being a day clerk gave him privileges over the night clerk.

Frederick went to sleep, waking at 1:30 in the afternoon just in time for his second job at the Windsor, helping in the wine room. He dressed, gathered the reports, and put them in his pocket. He was running late. He would bring the week's reports to Warren Leland's office later, at 6:00, when he left the wine room for his night job at the front desk.

Frederick knew a lot of the night clerks at other hotels. Young men, men who expected better shifts one day. At age forty-six, Frederick no longer hoped for daytime hours. Cousin Warren had assigned Frederick the lightest duty—keeping his eyes out for the occasional after-hours vagrant or opening the safe for a bejeweled woman returning from the opera. Even Frederick realized such an assignment made sense. Unmarried, he had no wife to go home to, no bed to share. And while he took pride in his work in the wine room, he took little interest in the details of the front desk. He tolerated his lowly nighttime position because he loved his afternoon job—storing bottles, serving glasses, filching sips.

On this particular day, Frederick observed that the wine stewards needed help, even in the middle of the afternoon. The bar filled with smiling tourists and guests, finishing their last drinks before stumbling out to enjoy the parade. Frederick replaced cases and made sure the whites sat on ice. He noticed two nearly empty bottles. Easier to finish them off than to add them to the ice. As he stood behind the storage shelves and drained a sauvignon blanc, he heard raised voices. He continued his emptying responsibilities for half a minute. Then he saw one of the stewards stand still and slowly open his mouth to yell.

"Fire. Fire."

Instantly, the room filled with sparks and smoke. Coughing, Frederick threw ice on the sparks. Useless. He tried to remember the best way out. The smoke blinded him.

Frederick did not remember that his jacket pocket held a week's worth of Detective Niehoff's daily incident reports. Neither Frederick nor the four servants listed in the report, at least one of whom feared for her job, could know that within an hour, those reports would turn to ash.

Elbridge Gerry

E lbridge Gerry sat in his study, scratching his full whiskers, then rubbing his temple. With luck, the noise from the afternoon parade would not get on his raw nerves. He checked his watch—3:05—then continued to review the records for his Society for the Prevention of Cruelty to Children. Yes, his accountant had recorded all gifts and expenses accurately, to the penny. The gall of those so-called reformers to suggest he kept for himself donations intended for waifs. He had to worry about that on top of his greedy fellow yachtsmen and his deceased uncle's widow, who embarrassed him with their price gouging, their profiteering. And Abner McKinley, whose shenanigans cast a bad light on all the yacht sales.

Still, thank goodness, no annoying music from the Irish bands. He thought he would have heard those bands by now.

The only noise, a half hour later, was the loud door knocker. Elbridge did not think twice when he heard it. The butler would answer. And if the butler lingered in his own office with the domestic account books, the parlor maid would answer. And if the parlor maid dusted out of hearing of the knock, the cook would answer. After a minute, Elbridge realized that all three must have answered, perhaps the butler first and then the others. He heard the commotion at the front entrance.

"Sir, Patrolman James Duane is here for you. I'm afraid there has been a fire. Don't worry—Mrs. Gerry and the children are safe. The fire is at the Windsor, sir, the Windsor Hotel."

Bounding out of his chair, Elbridge pushed past the butler and ran down the grand staircase to the hall where Patrolman Duane stood frozen in place, eyeing the lavish furnishings. He looked like a lad who had dressed up in a costume covered in brass buttons. Two idle house servants lingered in the hall, eyes wide.

"What happened?" Elbridge, usually polite, skipped the usual niceties. The patrolman stopped staring and slowly offered his report, addressing the floor.

"Sir, Mr. Gerry, I'm, uh, I'm James Duane from the East 51st Street Station. I was patrolling the St. Patrick's Day parade. When we approached the Windsor Hotel, we saw it in flames. I ran in, fast as I could, got as far as the lobby. I led three women out, screaming they were. Chief Devery, he saw me and told me to run here and tell you about the fire. He said you own the hotel."

"Devery, yes," Elbridge said. Big Bill Devery had had a checkered career, charged with bribery and extortion, but then winning appeals and, by some sleight of hand, promotions. Elbridge kept his eyes on the patrolman, wanting more.

"The Chief called in reinforcements right away. He's back there directing the men now."

"All right, Duane, is it? Patrolman Duane. Let's see what is happening. Did you get here on foot?"

"Yes, sir. I ran, like I said. All thirteen blocks."

"I'm going to change clothes, " Elbridge said. He turned to the butler. "Tell Tommy to get the carriage ready. The smallest brougham." Elbridge dashed upstairs and returned in a few minutes, dressed less poshly, with a hat pulled down over his head.

A minute later, Elbridge Gerry sat next to James Duane in the enclosed brougham, with Tommy Blount on the driver's seat, heading south on Fifth. Elbridge rubbed his whiskers, his eyes, the nape of his neck, while the patrolman rubbed his palm on the soft leather upholstery. The horses slowed, then lurched. Tommy drove with skill, but even he had trouble maneuvering between the police wagons and fire trucks racing to the scene. By the time they reached 48th Street, Elbridge saw flames, and his eyes burned from the smoke. "Enough, Tommy, he yelled out the window. Let Patrolman Duane off here." Elbridge turned to the young man. "Take care out there." The patrolman might be Devery's man, but seemed like a good fellow.

"Tommy, you can turn around and head home. Best to stay out of the fray."

Once back home, Elbridge climbed to his study and sulked. To keep himself occupied while he waited for the bad news, he checked his well-ordered files to confirm he had paid his huge insurance bill on the Windsor Hotel. Yes, he had, on December 29, for the following year. A large bill, even for a large hotel. He remembered that when he prepared to pay the bill, he called his insurance agent to question the accuracy of the amount.

"Yes," the agent had said. "Mr. Gerry, sir, you must realize that although your hotel conforms to the fire code, the code is outdated. The insuring companies need to protect their resources."

Remembering the agent's word, "conform," Elbridge relaxed a bit. He wondered if he should go downstairs to use his telephone, to call Warren Leland, the Windsor's manager. Or maybe he could call John Scannell, the Fire Commissioner. No, best to wait it out, see the damage in the morning.

Angelica knocked, then entered, her arms crossed over her chest. She had heard. She'd worry.

"Father, the Wellses. Remember the family from North Dakota? You met them last year aboard ship, at the captain's table." Elbridge scratched his beard, saw his daughter's impatience. "He's president of the James River Valley National Bank."

"Ah, yes, fine chap."

"I'm friends with his daughter Marguerite. She and her parents are in town, staying at the Windsor." She tightened her mouth. "I've phoned the Manhattan Hotel, the Holland House, and the Waldorf Astoria. They're not there. I can't get through to the Hotel Netherland or the Hoffman House. What if they didn't get out?"

"Angelica, I'm certain they're fine. Mr. Wells seemed fit and more than competent to help them escape. If I learn any details, I will let you know.

I'm going to skip dinner and wait for news." She nodded her head but didn't ease her mouth as she left his office.

Elbridge spent the next hour looking over his insurance paperwork again. As he put the documents aside, the second-floor maid knocked.

"Mr. Gerry, a call for you on the telephone downstairs. Mr. Warren Leland." Her voice sounded different, guarded. Elbridge felt faint. The lack of dinner, or a premonition? He stood up slowly, adjusting his suit jacket, his tie.

"Yes, thank you, Rose." He heard each step of his leather shoes as he descended the curving staircase. Downstairs, he looked around, making sure no servants stood in hearing range.

"Hello, Leland," he said. Elbridge heard sobs. He waited, trying to control his breathing, unsure what to say.

"Elbridge, my wife and my daughter. They are gone." The sobs continued.

"Oh, my, Warren." Elbridge knew how foolish he sounded. The man had lost his wife and daughter. But Elbridge needed to know more. As he formulated the rudest question of his life, Warren helped him out.

"Gone, the hotel is gone. Along with guests. Servants too. Maybe fifty. Maybe a hundred. We don't know."

Elbridge did not pause—the shock of those numbers reset his thoughts. Now he remembered what to say and managed just enough.

"Warren, don't worry about the hotel. Please take care of yourself. Where are you?"

"The Grenoble."

"You get some sleep, Warren. We'll talk tomorrow. God bless you."

Elbridge Gerry understood the role of the patrician in New York society. Any other time, he would have taken the lead, walked around the rubble, expressed sorrow for the loss of property and loss of life. But in March of 1899, he felt overwhelmed with crises—the Society, that business with the yachts, and now the Windsor Hotel. He returned to his study, closed the door, poured a whiskey, and chose silence.

J. H. Sullivan

Every year, for the decade since he started work at the Windsor, Chief Electrician J. H. Sullivan, known as Sully, took a break to watch the St. Patrick's Day parade on Fifth Avenue. Along with Chief Engineer Frank Corbett, Sully presided over a crew of hotel maintenance men—engineers, electricians, boilermen, steam fitters, and coalmen. Most of them, like Sully, had Irish roots. He allowed them to break for the parade, too. "Come along," he said the minute he heard the first note of a fiddle. "Bring your smokes." Three men in the basement crew eagerly grabbed their jackets and cigars and followed Chiefs Sully and Corbett, joining the crowd on the corner of Fifth and 46th a few minutes before 3:00.

Damn. Sully glanced at the hotel's first-floor office window. He caught a glimpse of that pasty-looking Simeon Leland, the day clerk, staring through the window. Sully's eyes met Simeon's for a split second. At six foot two, Sully was easy to spot. Simeon flinched first.

Did that smug, suck-up clerk begrudge the men a few minutes at the parade? Sure, Simeon was Warren Leland's cousin, but Sully knew that Mr. Leland thought even a clerk's job stretched Simeon's talents. Leland, not a stupid boss, promoted Sully from electrician to Chief Electrician while keeping Simeon a clerk forever. Same with Simeon's brother, Frederick, who never even made it from night clerk to day clerk.

Out on the curb, Sully willed himself to ignore Simeon and to look left toward the avenue, not right toward the office window. He heard the Irish bands' sweet and familiar sounds of Dirty Old Town, Whiskey in the Jar, and

Molly Malone, first faint, then louder and louder as the marchers moved north. Chief Engineer Frank Corbett, five years junior to Sully and much shorter, sang along. Half Irish, Corbett knew the words to Molly Malone. He sang, "In Dublin's fair city, where the girls are so pretty, I first set my eyes on sweet Molly Malone." The men huddling together knew Corbett took a fancy to Molly Dugan, fourth-floor chambermaid at the Windsor who always looked for a steady meal ticket. Black-haired beauty, despite her wandering eye.

Staring down at Corbett, Sully stretched his lips into a mock frown. "Corbett, you sure you wanna sing along? Molly in the song dies of a fever."

Corbett chuckled. "Yeah, but she...."

Later, the crew would not agree on whether they saw the flames first, smelled the smoke, or heard the shrieks. Unaware they might be asked to recall those details, they focused instead on remembering their drills. Just the week before, they had extinguished a fire in the hotel kitchen. Now, instinctively, they dropped their cigars and pivoted in unison back to the service door, Sully and Corbett in the lead.

When they reached the basement, the two chiefs ran the perimeter together for a fast, preliminary check. "No flames, no smoke," they shouted to the crew.

"We're going to divide up and check again," Sully said. He planted his feet on the floor and squared his tall frame. "But first, listen up, listen good. We peeked at the parade, one at a time, but we didn't abandon our posts. Got it?" No need to tell the men that Simeon had seen them. Sully could out-talk dumb Simeon any day.

"Got it," Corbett said, looking at the others, bobbing his head. He spoke for all of them.

The next few minutes proved the value of training and, Sully and Corbett boasted to themselves in the hours immediately after the fire, of their leadership. The chiefs flew into action in the basement. Sully and his electricians scurried to check the junction box breakers, the fuses, the conduits, and the wiring. They scrutinized the areas with the greatest electrical use—the boiler room toward the center of the basement and the kitchens—looking more quickly in the areas with little or no electrical use. They worked as thoroughly as they could, trying to see through the smoke. Meanwhile, Corbett and his crew were off inspecting the engine room.

"All good. No sparks, no smoke," Corbett said after running back to report. "I turned off all the engines except the one that exhausts steam. We filled the boilers with water to avoid an explosion. The men started the fire pumps. They worked. And thank God for the tanks."

Sully understood. The two tanks on the roof, each holding massive amounts of water, would feed the four standpipes—a system of vertical piping that connected to 3200 feet of hose. He and Corbett had asked Warren Leland to buy those standpipes and hoses the prior year.

For a few tense seconds, Sully couldn't recall if he or Corbett had ever tested the new equipment. But from what he could see, all the hoses worked, at least the hoses in the basement. In the days to come, Sully and Corbett would hear approving reports from others attesting to functioning hoses. Head porter John McGrath and photographer Chris Mullin, who stood on the street, together grabbed a hose and managed to turn on the water. They sprayed flames in the elevator shaft and first floor. Milkman Edward Killan, with patrolmen helping, used a hose on the main staircase until flames pushed them back.

Sully and Corbett would pay less attention to reports that painted a different picture. An elevator boy tried to use a hose but got no water. A guest found a hose on a shelf, intending to spray the elevator shaft, but also reported no water. Alderman John MacMahon, one of the first marchers to abandon the parade and enter the hotel to help, saw employees trying to use hoses with a trickle of water for their efforts. Many of these good Samaritans, who never saw the crew sweating in the basement, told others that they suspected hotel employees were watching the parade instead of manning their posts.

No one—not workers, not officials, not experts, not Chief Electrician J. H. Sullivan, not Chief Engineer Frank Corbett—anticipated the biggest problems. Not enough water and too much water. When firemen grabbed hoses from the hotel or connected their own hoses to pumps, they found they were pumping at half capacity because all the hoses, except those connected to roof tanks, drew from the same water source that supplied the hotel. And the enormous tanks on the roof, holding thousands of gallons of water, would collapse, turning a gruesome scene into an apocalypse.

Frank Corbett

Frank Corbett knew his business as Chief Engineer, knew how to care for his equipment and his crew, but he'd never fought more than a kitchen grease fire before. He felt relief that Sully, cocky but smart, took the lead. Corbett heard Sully send their best pipe fitter upstairs to check on the maids and waiters.

Corbett dropped the hose he was unwinding and ran to the man. "Hey, you know Molly Dugan? Maid, black hair. Check on her?"

"Yeah," the pipe fitter said, rushing to the stairs.

Sully kept yelling commands. "Corbett, send Walker to check the back courtyard." Corbett liked his assistant engineer, Robert Walker—a good man in a crunch. "The firemen won't know about that courtyard," Sully said. "No telling what's happening there."

Without hesitating, Corbett joined Walker. The men moved quickly toward the back door, expecting only smoke. As they opened the door to the courtyard, they saw two maids, one with a burned sleeve, both screaming and disoriented. Corbett hesitated for a second, only a second.

"Molly Dugan," he asked the women. "Fourth-floor maid. Is she OK?"

Walker grimaced at him as the maids gasped for air.

"Dunno," one mumbled. The other coughed.

As Corbett and Walker helped the maids out, dragging them the last bit to the street, the men heard screams behind them. They raced back to the courtyard. Corbett blinked from the smoke, or maybe because he couldn't believe his eyes. Two women on the fourth floor swung out on ropes. Howled. Released their hands. Plummeted. Their dresses billowed out, umbrella-like, but didn't slow the crashes. Amid the horror, Corbett and Walker saw manager Warren Leland flap his arms, shouting orders, asking if anyone had seen his wife or his invalid daughter, then shouting orders again. Leland collided with Mrs. Wrigley, the housekeeper, who ran blindly toward an exit. He grabbed her by the arm, yelling at her to save his family. As he begged, Mrs. Wrigley collapsed.

"Drag her out," Leland shouted to Corbett, before disappearing, maybe to check on another area of his ruined domain.

"Those women couldn't," Robert Walker said, then wheezed. "Couldn't hold on when the rope tore their palms." He winced at the women lying on the ground. Probably guests. Their palms were red, eyes closed. But they might still be alive. Corbett and Walker carried the limp bodies over their shoulders to the sidewalk, placing them down near an ambulance. Off to the side, they saw a fire wagon, grabbed the few remaining ladders tied to the side, then carried those ladders back to the courtyard to help more women.

How many women they saved, they would never know, but they would always remember a headline the next day. "Witnesses believe many of the hotel employees were watching the parade while the hotel burned."

W.E.D. Stokes

"Rita, I'm off to the baths. I may lounge there for a while. See you later." William Earl Dodge Stokes waited for his wife to acknowledge his statement.

"Good, take your time."

He heard Rita's grating voice from one of the rooms of their Windsor suite. She seemed happy to be rid of him for a few hours. His young wife brought to their marriage beauty and wealth, even more wealth than his own inherited wealth. He would put up with the bitch. Especially when Judith, almost as comely, lived on the fourth floor, one up from Stokes's third-floor suite where he had decamped for the year, along with Rita and their toddler son, while a construction crew worked on a new mansion for the family.

Stokes looked in the mirror as he pivoted to leave. Good enough? Eyes too close together, nose too long, start of an expanding waist. He should ask his tailor to let out the seams in his suit jacket. Or better yet, wire Gieves & Hawkes on Saville Row for another.

At 1:45 on St. Patrick's Day, Stokes walked out of the Windsor Hotel, around the corner of 46th, as though he were headed to the Turkish baths connected to the rear of the hotel. He chose this roundabout path in case Rita peered out the window of their suite to check his route. Once out of her sightline, he did not turn left into the baths, but walked beyond them toward Madison, then left on Madison, then another left on 47th, then entered the hotel again from the side door. He took a servants' staircase to the fourth floor. Before knocking lightly at suite 423, he reached into his briefcase, took out papers, and glanced at them as though preparing for a discussion of real estate with the occupant of the room. No one walked down the hall to witness his practiced feint. The door opened a crack. The heavy scent of perfume hit him as Judith let him in. She stood naked, except for the bracelet he had given her the week before, lined with pearls and glittering with diamonds.

A most expensive bracelet. He took out a loan for that purchase. Not because his money had been swallowed up by the rising stone walls of his new mansion. No. Because of the damned Ansonia, now a millstone around his neck. The magnificent structure he was building on the upper west side of Manhattan, a hotel that would outshine the Windsor, gobbled up his once abundant cash. In a year, the Ansonia would provide rents galore, but he had to build it first. No stranger to high finance, Stokes knew how to circumvent his cash shortage. His banker loaned him money with ease. After all, Stokes belonged to the family that owned Phelps Dodge, a fabulously successful mining company, and his wife Rita was the daughter of a steamship company executive.

Stokes had met Judith Jones months before at a private club. After a few engagements, he arranged for her to live at the Windsor, in a room close to the servants' staircase. She enjoyed life there, frolicking in merry Manhattan and frolicking twice weekly with him. After gazing at Judith's bracelet, Stokes's eyes moved to her long, lean legs, reminding him of his racehorses. Those vicious rumors about how he shagged with young girls at his Kentucky stud farm while watching a horse mount a mare were ludicrous. Just once. But he did like playing stud farm with Judith.

After their time together, around 2:30, Stokes knew he needed a bath, the bath he had announced to Rita. Judith donned a yellow-flowered, silk chemise and peeked out the door.

"Hall's empty," she said.

Stokes pecked her cheek and left to retrace his steps. Down the servants' stairs, a half block down 47th, and then to the men's floor of the Turkish baths. He'd begin in the steam room, as usual.

"Hello, Alfred." Through the steam, Stokes saw Alfred De Cordova perched in his usual spot on a bench. His dark hair curled in the humidity. De Cordova was a Jamaican-born Jew, the one Jew Stokes knew. The two men moved in the same social set. Family wealth outclassed religion. Not only were De Cordova and his wife Harriet living at the Windsor, like the Stokes, while their own mansion was being built, but De Cordova had an office in the hotel. What a great arrangement. Stokes's mistress lived on the fourth floor, always waiting in the nude, and his banker on the first floor, in an office filled with fine art and outstanding collectibles.

De Cordova, spotting Stokes, scooted over on the damp bench to make room. "Hope that bracelet provided what you needed," De Cordova said. Noting his banker's grin, Stokes replied with a grin of his own.

Ah, the consequences of having your banker half-naked with you in a steam room. Stokes knew he should not have mentioned last week why he needed that loan, but the atmosphere of the baths led to confidences.

An attendant carried in soft towels. If cigars and whiskey were allowed, the afternoon would be perfect.

Then another attendant, carrying nothing, arms whirling above his head. "Fire, sirs, fire. In the hotel. Get dressed and run."

"Guess this rest is over," De Cordova said calmly as he rose and walked to the dressing room. Stokes followed, trying to match De Cordova's leisurely gait.

In the few minutes the men needed to dress and grab their possessions, the baths filled with smoke. Even De Cordova began to move quickly. Neither man said goodbye to the other as they left the baths, shocked at the noise in the streets, noise that had been masked by the noise of steam. They separated, each headed to check on family and possessions.

In front of the hotel, Stokes, his hair still damp, spotted Rita holding the hand of their toddler. She had managed to grab her fur coat. At the same time, Stokes saw the customary wide-eyed stare of recognition on the face of a reporter standing a few feet away with notebook in hand. Stokes could almost see the reporter's brain working—the stunning woman must be Rita Hernandez de Alba Acosta Stokes, with her son Weedie. The reporter would push closer, especially when he saw the woman standing next to a familiar-looking patrician. William and Rita Stokes kept reporters busy covering the couple's social activities, horseracing interests, real estate ventures, and lately, their rumored plans for a nasty and expensive divorce.

"Sir, I," the young reporter started. By the third word, he raised his voice to be heard above the terrifying screams. "I write for the *New York Times*. Can we step back to talk for a minute?"

Stokes saw his wife hesitate, deciding whether to continue to watch frantic women on the upper floors of the hotel prepare to jump or to talk to the reporter. Rita did love to see her name in the papers.

"Yes, if you can find a place where we can hear each other," she said. The reporter pointed toward the west.

Picking up his son Weedie, Stokes and the little group headed away, darting between police wagons and fire trucks. Stokes walked behind the others. No one would see him look back over his shoulder at the women leaning far out beyond the fourth-floor windowsills. Judith was not among them.

The din remained loud, even a half block away. Stokes let his wife take the lead with the reporter. "I sat in my hotel room near the window, watching the parade, with Weedie on my lap. I heard screams. Then I leaned out and saw smoke and flames above us. I grabbed Weedie and our coats and hurried out." She opened her eyes a bit too wide—Stokes recognized that forced look of concern.

The reporter stared at Stokes, waiting for a different or a confirming account. He'd offer one. "I couldn't help them because I was in the baths, the Turkish baths at the back of the hotel. The steam there makes such a racket. We didn't even know about the fire until an attendant warned us. Thank goodness Rita and Weedie made it out by themselves." Stokes looked at the reporter, avoiding Rita's eyes.

The uproar from the hotel—screams, whistles, clanging—drowned out some of Stokes's words. The reporter struggled to hear. No wonder he would write that Mrs. Stokes had been in the baths, not Mr. Stokes. The reporter corrected his error in a later edition. Stokes hoped no readers would wonder about the different accounts.

As Stokes ruminated over the fire in the coming weeks, reading every detail he could find, he came to understand that, in most ways, he had been lucky. Most ways he would talk about. Only one friend—the banker, De Cordova—would guess what Stokes had lost. Stokes could count on De Cordova's discretion. And De Cordova, Stokes learned, lost nothing other than a leisurely bath. Neither man knew that thieves snatched Alfred Pope's art, keeping them too busy to get to De Cordova's collections.

John Connolly

For John Connolly, the workday never seemed to end. He remembered, longingly, how he had a helper during the social season. That luxury ended two months earlier, after the New Year's Day receptions and dinners. The yacking Irish fellow, Clayton Byrne, would have helped with this latest task. Odd lad, that Clay—he liked to fix furniture in the guest rooms.

Now Connolly had to fix everything himself, despite his exalted title of Hotel Carpenter. He'd rather slip out to Fifth today. His wife said she planned to take their sons and stand near the corner of Fifth and 47th about mid-afternoon to watch the parade. If he could take a break, he could meet up with them. But the hussy on the fourth floor was pestering him again.

"Fix my bed frame. Room 423. Between 2:45 and 3:45." The occupant of 423 had not signed the note she told the hotel porter to deliver. No matter. Connelly knew who stayed in 423. Almost everyone at the Windsor knew—probably even the hussy's lover's wife, that beautiful Mrs. Stokes, or, according to the newspapers, Rita Hernandez de Alba Acosta Stokes. Connelly had been to 423 many times, usually to repair a small problem other guests would have ignored. He suspected that the precise time written down by Judith Jones—that was her name according to loose-lipped desk clerk Simeon Leland—corresponded to breaks between customers. Judith transgressed twice over. First, she slept with Stokes, a married man, then she cheated on Stokes himself with other rakes. Almost everyone at the Windsor knew that, too.

Confirming on his gold pocket watch, his most valuable possession, that he had arrived at 423 at 2:55, Connelly knocked. "Ma'am, I'm here for the repairs," he said. He thought using the word repairs sounded better than bed. As usual, she wore only a silk dressing gown, smelled musky. Stale perfume and sex.

"That way. Frame's too loose." She pointed off to the bedroom, as though Connolly didn't know. He walked in, set his toolbox down, and spent a few minutes examining the connection where the headboard met the mattress frame. He heard the swoosh of Judith's robe in the sitting room, then her voice, thinner than before.

"What's that noise?

Connolly messed around in his toolbox, making sounds of his own. He couldn't handle another complaint.

"Come here." She sounded even more insistent than usual.

He walked to the sitting room, where she stood at the window. Did the slut expect him to fix the window frame too? Her head angled down, looking at the courtyard. She inched to the left, making room for him.

Now they were shoulder to shoulder, peering out. Stronger smell, like a whorehouse. He supposed he smelled sweaty to her. Or was he smelling smoke now? What the hell? He blinked, gawked. He unfroze first, opened the window a few inches. She stood still. Shrieks blasted in.

Connelly darted to the hall door. Slowly, he opened it an inch. Felt overpowering heat and heard screams. Slammed it closed. Behind him, Judith started to yell. No words, just wails.

"The rope. Where's the rope?" he asked. She looked at him, stunned. Her eyes, moving rapidly and settling nowhere, answered for her.

He ran to the closet in the bedroom. Lifting aside Judith's dresses, he found the coil. He unwound the rope, scraping his hands. He looked it over, thought of his wife, his sons. He wanted to see them again. He also wanted to tell them how their brave papa had rescued a pretty lady before thinking of himself. He pulled Judith toward him, started to wind the rope around her waist. Her eyes looked blank, but she spoke two words, coughing, while she pushed him away.

"Bollocks. No."

She opened the door and ran out, letting in suffocating smoke. He yelled after her, into the abyss. He knew better than to follow. He slammed the door closed. Then he opened the window further and looked down. Women lay on the ground below, some with ropes around their waists, some without. Not moving. Connelly spotted the top of Warren Leland's gray head. He was running in circles, grabbing one person, then another. As Connelly strained to make sense of what he saw, flames slithered along the carpet at his feet, coming at him from two directions.

Connelly wound the rope around his waist. Unable to see, he felt for the bed. He anchored the rope to a bedpost, perched on the sill, and dropped down, his gold watch in his pocket.

At that very moment, Eleanor Connelly and her sons stood one block away, shaking in horror, but with no view of the courtyard. She was among the more fortunate relatives because she would learn her husband's fate from a doctor at the third hospital she ran to, Flower Hospital. John Connelly had died upon arrival there, his gold watch still inside the pocket of his work pants.

Seventy-five feet from where John Connelly had fallen, a smoldering, collapsed wall would cover Judith Jones's broken body.

Bridget Dunne

After unlocking the maids' closets, Bridget bounded upstairs to her seventh-floor room. She grabbed a coat and climbed more stairs, seeing the fire escape as she reached the roof. She had never noticed it before. She doubted others had noticed it.

Bridget felt sweat on her neck, so the cold air felt good. Dozens of servants had gathered on the roof, huddled at the edge on the Fifth Avenue side. They craned their necks to the south to watch the parade. Mrs. Wrigley and assistant butcher Devan Farley—the gap-toothed lad who passed along pilfered biscuits—stood a few feet back from the huddle. Those two were Bridget's just-in-case alibi, though they didn't know it. Molly and Tara stood off to the side. May had found her way to the roof, too, claiming a spot away from the others.

Bridget pricked up her ears at the rising noise. Only music. She heard a third-floor maid admire the green bows atop the heads of the girls on the floats, bright enough to be seen from high up. Bridget sidled over to her friends. A tap on Molly's shoulder. An eye roll aimed at Tara. Bridget led them toward the back, avoiding the area where May stood. With luck, no one in the crowd, not even May, would notice the three maids walk away.

"Everything's fine," Bridget whispered, keeping her eyes on Molly's good eye. "Fine, really. Clay knows what he's doing." Tara looked puzzled, and Molly pointed to an ear. They couldn't hear above the music. As Bridget tried again, beginning to raise her voice, she caught a single word of warning from the street.

"Fire."

One terrifying word, half-muted by music. She stretched her palm in front of her and pursed her lips, signaling Tara and Molly to keep quiet. That word again. She heard right. She turned back to the crowd of servants to catch the attention of Mrs. Wrigley and Devan. That morning, she told them to look for her on the roof. She would have gossip for them—some silly story she would invent about the hotel's painter—so when they saw her motion, they walked toward her.

Bridget glanced at the huddled servants still at the roof's edge. Now they heard, too. They looked to each other with raised brows, open mouths, wondering where to go. No time to worry about them. For an instant Bridget questioned why she had been wary, why she had taken note of the fire escape a few minutes earlier. She pushed those thoughts aside. She steered her followers to the rickety stairs that jutted down. Seven stories to the back courtyard. They hesitated, until screams of fire made their choices plain. Bridget cursed with each halting step. The metal railings, hot on the top floors, blazed heat by the time they reached the middle floors. Bridget and Molly, Devan too, barely touched the railings. Tara and Mrs. Wrigley, less steady on their feet, grabbed the red-hot bars. None of them stopped. Shrieks from every direction drove them on. At the lowest part of the fire escape, hands reached up from the crowd to lower them into a crush of people.

Once down, Bridget lost track of Devan and saw Mrs. Wrigley, disoriented, stumble into the courtyard, hands whirling in the smoke. Tara sobbed. Molly stood still. Bridget grabbed Tara's elbow with one hand and guided Molly on the shoulder with the other hand. They pushed through the crowd until they saw an ambulance pull up on Fifth. Bridget yelled for the attendant, catching his attention before others could. As she waited, eyes smarting, he dressed Tara's burns. He worked quickly, glancing to the side at the serious cases bystanders dragged to him. As soon as he finished, Bridget looked around, searching for a gap in the crowd. She saw Molly shake her head.

"No. I'm not leaving." Molly said, turning to face the hotel. "Frank's in there. In the basement."

Tara, eyes wincing in pain, glanced at Bridget. Leave Molly to find her beau, by herself?

More high-pitched screams. The maids raised their heads, following the heads of the others around them. Five or six women and a man leaned out the upper floor windows, waving arms, begging for help. The heads of the crowd bent to the left. Screams and warnings changed to cheering. Dozens of firemen had arrived. They jumped off wagons, grabbed ladders. Rubber jackets, rubber boots, helmets. They ran through the crowd to the hotel, leaning ladders against the brick walls. Along with the other bystanders, Bridget couldn't take her eyes off the catastrophe around her. She stopped searching for a way out.

"Look." Molly pointed to a window on the fourth floor. "Mrs. Winter. From my floor." Molly recognized the young woman with a single black braid. Her arms were on the windowsill. "She's goin' to jump."

A man in the crowd yelled as if to answer Molly. "Better a broken neck than death by fire."

Mrs. Winter turned her head toward a fireman who scampered up. He used a funny-looking ladder with a pole in the middle and rungs on each side.

"Scaling ladder, that is." The man in the crowd kept up his babble. "Lets 'em move to the left or the right better. And it's light." The crowd turned to him. They wanted to know.

"Wait. Don't jump. Stay there." That's what Bridget guessed the fireman yelled, as she looked at the motions he made with his arms. No one could hear him. The crowd below, rooting for the woman, repeated what the fireman must have said. Maybe Mrs. Winter heard. She took her arms off the sill. As the fireman reached through the window to grab her, she leaned out and saw to her right a gray-haired woman two windows away, pressing her hands to her cheeks. The younger woman pointed to the older woman. Help her first.

Bridget saw Molly stare up, with no look of surprise. "Ya know," Molly said, as soon as noise from the crowd died down for a minute, "Bessie Winter puts her fancy clothes away herself. Opens her curtains in the morning too. A grand lady, even though she has more money than anyone needs."

The fireman hesitated a second, then reached over for the older woman. He dragged her out, bent her over his left arm, and carried her down to where other firemen waited to help. Then he rushed back up for Mrs. Winter. As he carried her to safety, flames shot out from her window.

Two seconds later, a woman sat on the windowsill of her sixth-floor room on the 46th Street side, holding her Boston Terrier. "Holy mother of God, it's Mrs. Winklemann," Tara said, speaking up against Bridget's ear, gabbing again despite her burns. "I can tell because of the dog. Yesterday, I was in front of the hotel, walking Mr. Bright's dog. He's on two, so I clean for him and do what he asks. That lady up there, Mrs. Winklemann, she saw me and asked me to walk her dog, too. For money." Bridget saw Tara turn to Molly, to repeat her story, but Molly did not look up. She looked to the right, to the left, to the right again. Her black hair flew out of her cap. Her right eye wandered.

"Stay here," Bridget yelled at Molly. "You can't get through the crowd, and you don't know where Frank is. He could be running down the halls, checking pumps and boilers."

Molly stopped bobbing her head up and back.

"And the coppers are holding everyone back," Bridget said. "If he's in the basement, he'll get out, no trouble."

Molly grimaced, pushed her hair back into her cap. She frowned and nodded at Bridget.

Bridget turned her eyes back to Mrs. Winklemann and her terrier.

"Don't jump. They're coming for you," people in the crowd yelled. The words did not rise above the din to reach Mrs. Winklemann.

The fireman who saved Bessie Winter had disappeared, but off to the left, another fireman, young and strikingly handsome, climbed a ladder while holding an odd, smaller ladder that Bridget and the other gawkers now knew to call a scaling ladder. He reached the fifth floor, Bridget's floor. She knew it even from the outside. The fireman leaned his scaling ladder against the wall, trying to get to the sixth floor. Glass from the fifth-floor window broke. Bridget couldn't see it but heard it. Ignoring the shards, the fireman kept scrambling up. He hoisted Mrs. Winklemann out of her window, bent her over his arm, and carried her—and the terrier—down the scaling ladder, one precarious step after another. Bridget held her breath, then joined the others clapping as he carried Emma Winklemann and her dog to safety.

A man in the crowd shouted. "Bravo McDermott."

The next day, the papers would confirm the handsome rescuer's identity—Fireman First Grade Bartholomew McDermott. He would be in demand, working tirelessly for two more hours.

Before the bystanders could rest their necks, another woman's face appeared in the same sixth-floor window. Bridget couldn't be certain, but she thought this new woman wore a uniform and cap—Mrs. Winklemann's forgotten maid. Bile rose in Bridget's throat. She forced it down. She forced down too the sick feeling that she had caused the chaos around her. Flames from inside must be burning the maid's back. She had one knee on the sill, readying herself to jump. Standing on a nearby ladder, yet another fireman, this one wearing a yellow jacket, motioned to her to stay.

"Don't jump." Bridget joined the crowd yelling this refrain, even though they knew the maid couldn't hear. The yellow-clad fireman grabbed the woman and carried her down.

Bridget's eyes returned to the handsome fireman. When he reached the ground, he dabbed blood from his face. The shards had wounded him. Tara watched the man, smoothing her frizzy hair. As though he'd notice her. Tara liked the good lookers, even bleeding ones. Instead of admiring Tara or seeking a bandage, the fireman looked up and around to see who needed help next. An elegantly dressed man with a square jaw and a shock of white hair grabbed the fireman's elbow and rapped him on the shoulder. Before Bridget could guess what the toff wanted, she turned at the sound of screams in another direction.

Later, Bridget would read in the paper that the toff was H. W. Pope, wanting help to rescue his paintings. But Bridget knew that the Mr. Pope who stayed in the hotel was Alfred Pope. Tara cleaned his suite, and she gabbed to the girls about the art he kept there—fuzzy paintings of farms and women. The papers would report the value of the paintings at $35,000.

On the sidewalk, listening to the piercing screams, Bridget forgot about the elegantly dressed man and steered Molly and Tara toward the sound, near the corner where Fifth crossed 47th. Tara kept jabbering, though no one could hear her, while Molly stayed silent, looking left and right, searching for Frank but not running off. Her short beau would be hard to see in the crowd.

Bridget and Tara looked up. They recognized the sickly face in the window—Isabella Leland, wife of hotel manager Warren Leland. Bridget remembered that Molly, who cleaned the Lelands' rooms, had grumbled about Isabella for years. She never tidied anything herself, but who could blame her. The woman was an invalid, often confined to bed. At least she tipped well. $5 at Christmas for Molly. Mr. Leland looked after Isabella and his epileptic daughter. Where had that one gone?

A fireman darted up a fire escape on 47th, joined by a policeman. They pulled out Isabella, no longer moving on her own, and carried her to an ambulance. The next week, in gratitude for carrying his wife out of the building, Warren Leland sent the policeman a check for $100. Fire department rules, stricter than police rules, forbid Leland from doing the same for the fireman. He received an inscribed gold watch. Leland made these arrangements the next day as he mourned doubly, because while the rescuers carried burned Isabella, soon to die, down to an ambulance, their daughter, separated from her mother in the smoke, fell to her death from a nearby window, in view of Bridget and the other maids. The young woman plummeted headfirst, her dress billowing down, revealing thin legs, brown boots. If the arms of bystanders tried to break her fall, they failed. She thudded amidst the crowd's screams.

Bridget, watching, felt the muscles in her neck pulse and her stomach roll again. She swallowed vomit for the second time. Gulping for a breath, she turned toward another cry—an old woman on four, leaning out her window, yelling for help, with a frightened Negro woman at her side.

"Margaretta Fuller," Molly said. "She's on my floor. And her maid, Sue.

Or she might be a nurse. Sue Bland."

A fireman climbing to the rescue spotted them, but then his head turned to an even older-looking lady off to the side, howling. He motioned for Margaretta and her nurse to wait. When they didn't budge, he pushed them inside. He grabbed the ancient-looking lady, then motioned to two other firemen to rescue the women he saw first. Wealthy Margaretta Fuller would live, along with Nurse Bland. But Margaretta's daughter and sister, staying on a different floor, perished.

Bridget saw reporters around her scribbling frantically in their notebooks and heard them yell to the crowd, asking for the names of the women and the names of their rescuers. She wondered how the reporters could keep the chaos straight in their minds or on their pads.

Bridget's stomach churned again. Mrs. Schuchardt, a gray-haired widow, leaned out of her fifth-floor window. The woman always hungered for conversation. When Bridget came to change the linens, she allowed fifteen minutes for chatter. A fireman lifted Mrs. Schuchardt out the window, unwinding from her waist the rope she had tried to tie, then, in an act the bystanders would praise for the rest of their lives, swung her across the brick wall to another fireman atop a ladder.

The papers would mix up stories. Was it Mrs. Schuchardt or Mrs. Southard? On the fifth floor? Or the sixth? Was William Green of Engine Company 20 the hero who saved Mrs. Winter or was that Edward Ford of Hook and Ladder Company 20? Did wealthy Alfred Fuller, unable to get higher than the third floor to reach his wife Margaretta, offer a bystander $1000 to rescue her? Would any bystanders accurately recall what they saw?

Bridget stood on the street shivering, surrounded by gawkers, penned in by screams. She grasped Molly's ice-cold hand and Tara's trembling hand, standing between them.

A different sound, full of dread—a roar, high up.

The roof.

The roof caved into the chaos of the inferno. Bridget and the others jumped back in terror as brick and stone smashed the sidewalk. Ears nearly burst. Dust and ash floated in waves, entered eyes. Silence for a minute. Only later did the onlookers learn to blame the collapse on the weight of the water tanks on the weakening roof.

No one left on the roof could survive. Bridget glanced at Tara's tears, knew she fussed about May Gleason, her roommate on seven. They had left May on the roof. And what about their loves?

As though on cue, Molly whimpered. "Frank, where is he? Buried in the basement?" She pressed her fingers into her right eyelid, to keep her eye in place.

"And everything we own, gone. Bullocks. Our clothes…." Tara focused on their clothes. But Bridget knew that Tara was really thinking about Sean, while trying to hide his role from Molly. The last of the bricks to fall drowned out Tara. The maids looked up. Their rooms on the seventh floor had disappeared. Friends had disappeared.

The heads of the people in the crowd no longer jerked up and down, left and right. No one remained hanging out of windows. No windows remained, just jagged, partial walls.

The crowd stopped yelling, started chattering. "The Hoffman House? Or maybe The Murray Hill?" Windsor guests, those who survived, headed off to other hotels. The clerks would know those well-dressed survivors were good for the rates, even if they had no cash in hand. That wouldn't work for Bridget, in her maid's uniform and worn coat. Molly's family lived nearby but had not a half inch to spare. Tara's family remained in Ireland.

"Bridge," Molly said, with blame in her voice. "How could this happen?"

"God damn," Tara said, her eyes piercing Bridget's.

Bridget twitched every plane of her face. "No point standing here, trying to figure this out. Frank'll be okay." As she spoke Bridget looked first at Molly, then at Tara, trying to convey that Sean would be okay too. "Let's find a place to stay. Claire. She's close."

Bridget's younger sister Claire lived five blocks away in a seedy boarding house in the Hell's Kitchen neighborhood. The sisters, separated by a year, saw their ma die from tuberculosis, their pa from an accident when a horse trampled him. Then and now, Bridget admired Claire. She studied hard in school and then enrolled in the Normal College across town. She cleaned offices at night and studied to be a teacher during the day. But Bridget remembered Claire's jibes.

Three months earlier, when the sisters shared a meal at Christmas, Claire put her hand on her hip and stuck her chin out. "Bridge, I'm cleaning to afford schooling to be a teacher. What about you? Sure, the Irish had to go into service after the Famine, but now Bridge, fifty years later? Still cleaning? Time for more." That cocked head, puffed up voice. Claire sounded like their ma, always nipping at pa.

"Damn, Claire. I manage four maids on five. The housekeeper says I'm her best. Why do yuh keep raggin' me?"

Bridget remembered seeing Claire's eyes look at her, then look up and sideways. Saw her reposition her hand on her hip and heard her lash out.

"You might be giving a few orders, but you're still cleaning. I clean at night myself, but it's to get money for school, 'til I get a teaching job. You're smart, Bridge. You could do something else."

Now, in front of the smoldering hotel, Molly looked dazed, and Tara rolled a frizzy tendril around her finger. The girls hadn't met Claire, but they remembered the stories.

"My sister will turn up her nose at us, and not a pretty nose it is, yuh know. But I don't have a better idea."

Bridget started to walk west, with Molly and Tara trailing behind. They couldn't see her tears. Clay, had he started all this? Not possible.

Five blocks later, Bridget recognized Claire's boardinghouse, a frame building with weather-beaten shingles and a rickety front porch. She knocked. A gaunt woman in a faded apron opened the door, eyeing the visitors with suspicion.

"Claire Dunne, please," Bridget said. "I'm her sister."

The gaunt woman yelled upstairs. Claire bounded down. Molly and Tara stared, as Bridget knew they would. Claire looked like Bridget, just thinner and plainer. Claire stretched out her arms and wrapped Bridget in an embrace.

"I've been worried sick. You got out." She had lost any trace of an Irish brogue.

Bridget reached her arms halfway around Claire. Two likely boarders, a scruffy-looking man and a woman with a cane, both staring, came to the entry hall where they joined the gaunt woman who introduced herself as Mrs. Brownhill, the landlady.

"Your hand?" the woman with the cane asked, pointing to Tara's bandage.

"Burns," Tara said, "Not as bad as others. There's some didn't make it."

The scruffy boarder chimed in. "We heard fire alarms for hours. We didn't know what to make of the noise. I walked to Ninth and saw three ambulances, drivers whipping their horses. What happened?" He wanted news, wanted to pass along stories. "Claire here, she told us her sister worked at that hotel." He looked at Claire.

"I knew I'd have trouble going crosstown from school," Claire said. "That parade. So I walked, a long way around. I heard about a fire, but I didn't know it was the Windsor 'til I got here, and Mrs. Brownhill told me."

"I heard it from the fruit peddler," Mrs. Brownhill said. "He does the hotels on Fifth. He made a delivery there just this morning."

Bridget looked squarely at the landlady and her boarders. Better to include them, keep them friendly. "Yes, we made it. These are my friends, Tara and Molly. They work with me at the Windsor. We'll tell you our story." Bridget turned to Claire. "But let's get to your room first."

The maids followed Claire upstairs, to her chilly attic flat. Bridget and Claire sat on the bed, one step better than a pallet, while Tara and Molly sank to the floor. Talking slower than usual, Bridget offered Claire a version of their afternoon of terror. Nothing about the lists, or about Clay, or Sean, or being first to leave the roof. Tara and Molly stayed quiet, listening.

Bridget caught Claire narrowing her eyes the way she did, like she knew the story wasn't right. Best to keep talking—about anything—and not to take the bait.

"Claire, no food here?"

"Sorry Bridge. Mrs. Brownhill served already. Let me see if I can get you girls something to drink."

Claire left for the first floor, then came back after a while with beer offered by the landlady and whiskey offered by the unkempt boarder. While Claire was gone, Bridget wrote a short telegram for Tara to send to her family in Ireland. "Escaped hotel fire. Staying with friend. Will get in touch when settled." Bridget made certain Molly prepared a similar note for her ma, without information about Claire or her address.

"Mrs. Brownhill?" Bridget looked for the landlady on the first floor, finding her in the kitchen. "I expect we'll sleep late tomorrow. Could you help us get these notes to our loved ones? This one goes near the wharves, so you can just find a messenger. The other is a telegram for Ireland."

"Happy to help. No need to pay me 'til I know the cost. Follow me to the pantry. I want to give that girl with the burns some linseed oil to rub on."

"You're so kind."

The landlady found the bottle of oil, turned it up and back in her hands, made sure the lid was tight. "Yes," she said, eyes on the bottle, "you girls have been through hell." A pause, eyes still on the bottle. "By the way, do you know how long you plan to stay here with Claire?"

Bridget knew she'd get this question eventually, but she had no ready answer. She frowned, shook her head. The maids had nowhere to go, but worse—they needed to hide. Bridget took the offered oil, mouthed thanks, and walked upstairs without looking at the landlady's expression.

Bridget and Molly helped themselves to Claire's stash of biscuits. Tara hurt too much to eat, but she joined in drinking the donated spirits. Then they tried to sleep, Claire on her narrow bed and Bridget and the others on blankets on the floor, crowded together. Bridget sensed Tara moving her burned hand up and back, hoping to curb the pain, and heard Molly breathing too heavily to be asleep. As dawn came, Bridget listened to Mrs. Brownhill puttering around in the kitchen. How many guests did she plan to serve?

Theodate Pope

Theodate Pope and her mother Ada left their suite at the Windsor at 2:35, ahead of the St. Patrick's Day parade. Their hansom cab driver would have no trouble getting them twenty blocks north on Fifth to Louisine Havemeyer's mansion by 3:00. Louisine, the art collector and friend of the Pope family, had invited Theodate and Ada to tea.

Theodate relished this invitation. She would learn more about the Cassatts and Manets her father collected. Maybe Monet's magnificent Haystack series, too. After that, she planned to bring up the stalled progress of the suffragists, another of Louisine's interests. Then Theodate could report what she had learned to her new friend Marguerite Wells when they lunched together. Alfred Pope did not support the suffragists as his daughter did—his only failing, she thought—so when the Havemeyers gathered with the Popes for dinner parties, that topic was off the table. But this afternoon, among women, Theodate would speak freely.

Opening the ornate door, the Havemeyers' butler smiled, then frowned, then apologized, explaining that Mrs. Havemeyer had left unexpectedly to attend to a friend who had taken sick. Theodate didn't bother to cover up her disappointment. Ada Pope asked the butler to pass their regards to Mrs. Havemeyer, then told the carriage driver that instead of waiting for them, he could drive them back to the Windsor. To avoid parade traffic, he turned across town, then south on Madison. As the carriage reached 49th, Theodate felt the horses slow, heard them snort. She smelled smoke. After a few more carriage lengths, she and her mother heard screams and clanging bells. They locked eyes, puzzled. Theodate leaned out the window.

"Driver, what's happening?"

"Fire, miss, a big one. Could be the hotel where I picked you up. I'm turning around."

Theodate and Ada looked at each other again. "Pray your father has lingered at his lunch downtown," Ada said. Alfred Pope, President of the Cleveland Malleable Iron Company, always had business in New York—both the business of iron and the business of art collecting. With luck, he wouldn't be inside the Windsor.

"Just Lotte we need to find," Ada said. She would never forget her dear maid.

"Driver, let us out here," Theodate shouted out the window. She opened the carriage door, jumped down, and lent Ada a hand. "Mother, walk east on 48th, then north a block on Park. You'll see Aunt Eunice's house. Wait there, and I'll come for you. First, I'll check on Lotte and look for Father." Ada shook her head. She would not leave. When she started to cough, Theodate hugged her and gave the wheezing woman a gentle shove toward the east.

The maid was one of Theodate's worries. She also needed to search for her friend Marguerite, who might be in the hotel, and do what she could to save her father's art collection, temporarily stored in their suite. She could see those paintings, so dear, in her mind. She had a third worry, one that would grow over time. As a fledgling architect, learning what she could from Princeton professors, she wondered if she had neglected to see the hotel's weaknesses.

Assured that her mother walked toward Aunt Eunice's, Theodate pushed her way through the smoke to 46th Street, trying to get to the windows of her family's suite. She skirted a line of police brandishing their batons to keep bystanders at arms' length. When the crowd pushed her to a standstill, she stood as tall as possible, bemoaning her short stature. Packed together, onlookers pressed against her, oblivious to all but the scenes in front of them. They watched the maelstrom, unable to do more than gape.

Theodate heard shrieks of terror, high-pitched, coming from above, joining sounds of screeching wagons and braying horses. She saw the faces of women in the windows, some submitting to their end, some defying their end. Her eyes watered from smoke. Blinking out the tears, then squinting, she recognized a woman in a sixth-floor window—Marguerite's pretty, round face, blond waves. A gray-haired man hovered beside her. Her father? Theodate had never met the man. Each of the windows on the 46th side told a story of terror, but Theodate fixated on Marguerite.

At the same time, a firefighter—Theodate noted that the man was nice-looking and fit—climbed a scaling ladder to reach a woman flailing her arms out another sixth-floor window. Theodate recognized Emma Winklemann—the woman who kept her Boston Terrier at the Windsor. Theodate bobbed her head between Marguerite and Mrs. Winklemann, while most of the other bystanders, attracted by the dog, focused on Mrs. Winklemann. At the sound of cheering, Theodate turned to the Winklemann window. The fireman ignored broken glass around him and pulled the woman and her pet through the window. He folded her over his left arm, descended the wobbly ladder, and smiled as others came to hold the ladder steady.

Theodate felt a man's hand on her shoulder. She pivoted.

"I thought you were at Louisine's," her father said, hunching his shoulders with worry. "I walked back from lunch and heard the commotion blocks away."

"Oh, Father! Louisine was called away, so we returned here. But we are safe. Mother is walking to Aunt Eunice's."

Alfred Pope settled his shoulders for two seconds, then tensed them again.

"The paintings, Theo. I must save the Monets and the others." He turned his head and scanned the crowd. He grabbed a nearby fireman, tapped him on the shoulder. The same man who had just saved Emma Winklemann.

"I'm going to look for Lotte." Theodate couldn't be certain her father heard her, but she needed to search. Her mother's maid had a room on the fourth floor. When the Popes checked in, the only suite available couldn't accommodate Lotte, but the smarmy clerk found a spare room. Alfred Pope's tip helped.

Walking around the hotel as close as the police allowed, darting around mobs of bystanders, Theodate spotted a rotund young woman on the ground near 47th Street. Her blond braids, wrapped around her head, had unraveled. Lotte. An ambulance doctor tended to her.

"Ah, Lotte, thank God. I promised Mother I would find you."

"I slid down a rope, I did. Not bad, not for a heavy one like me. But my hands are ruined." Theodate patted Lotte's shoulder as the doctor applied ointment and bandages.

"Stay here, rest. I'll fetch you in a few minutes. I need to check on Father."

Theodate walked back to the spot where Alfred Pope had enlisted help. The harried fireman, now with his arms stretched to carry canvases, each about two feet by three, hurried to turn them over to their owner.

"Did the best I could, sir. Had to break a window. Grabbed what I could. Hope I got 'em all."

"Not sure. Great you saved these. Can you check for more?"

"Not right," Theodate heard a loud bystander say. "That fireman saved that woman on the sixth floor, and he should be saving people, not damned paintings."

Theodate froze. She moved closer to her father, instinctively. She shared her father's love for those paintings. Not only their value, but their beauty.

Losing sight of the fireman, Alfred Pope pushed his way to the outer circle of the crowd to check the condition of the paintings he struggled to hold close to his chest. Theodate followed, until she saw her father's valet, Leonard Stillman, rush to help with the paintings. Leonard was a good man. No need to worry about her father.

"Lotte, Theodate said, "she's all right, but I need to rescue her from the crowd. Back in a minute." She wasn't certain her father heard her, but Leonard nodded with approval. He and Lotte had worked in the Pope household for years. Although the maid, whose parents came from Norway, and the valet, whose parents had been enslaved, were not friends, Pope servants looked out for each other.

As Theodate jostled her way toward 47th Street, she turned her head to the booming sound of a man's voice.

"Halt. Don't move."

Thirty feet away, she saw two police officers in threatening stances, standing before a man, thickset, with partly gray hair. Hard to determine his age. Shabby clothes. The man bent under the weight of the awkward bundle he carried. Theodate edged closer.

The older officer took charge. "Empty your pockets."

"No, sir, I'm a reporter from the *Chicago Times*." He pulled a badge out from his jacket pocket. The two officers studied it.

The older officer twisted his face into a smirk. "*Chicago Times*, huh. Paper went out of business years ago. You dolt—I used to live in Chicago."

"But wait, you see, I was walkin', and I saw the fire. Ran in. A woman on the second floor needed help. I carried her down. She told me to go back and save her ma. I climbed back. Saw an open door. Thought I could save the lady's property for her. I grabbed things then went to look for a policeman to hand...."

While the man jabbered, Theodate saw the younger officer grab the sack Kain clutched and start to pour over the contents. The officer fingered items—jewelry, shirts, jackets, and tossed them on the pavement, until he got to a silver card case, which he held up to his partner, reading the embossed name, "Abner McKinley." Then a leather portfolio with a name, "A. McKinley." The officers hauled Kain away. The next day, newspapers estimated the value of Kain's haul at $8000.

Theodate walked toward Lotte, forgetting her father and the paintings for the time being. She scanned the Windsor's façade with an architect's eye, curious about the source of the fire. Flames leapt from all floors. What had she missed?

Ellen Kirk Haskin

Smelling smoke, Ellen Kirk Haskin didn't waste a minute. Twenty-eight years earlier, when she was seventeen, the Chicago fire had left its impression. Her father's profitable soap factory in that city burned to the ground. The Kirk family didn't know then that James Kirk would rebuild, preventing a decline in the immense family fortune. No, Ellen would not risk tarrying when she sensed smoke in suite 410, rooms she shared with her ailing mother, now a widow in control of the Kirk family wealth. Opening the door a crack to check, Ellen witnessed chaos—maids screaming, men and women running this way and that. She grabbed her mother. "Out, don't take anything."

Matriarch Nancy Kirk, at age seventy-five, had retained her wits but not her health. Ellen met her mother's tearing eyes as their arms interlocked. Out in the smoldering hall, Ellen pushed ahead, but her mother fell behind, choking out three wasted words.

"Leave me. Run."

Ellen half carried, half dragged the older woman through the spreading smoke, down four flights. Midway, a flaming piece of wood broke away from the molding and hit Ellen's right arm, burning through her sleeve. On the stairs, she looked for someone to help. Later, she would remember the men who ignored her, running down on their own, bumping into her. She would remember too the man who carried down a woman in a flowered chemise. He gave Ellen a look filled with shared pity. But at that moment, Ellen felt only her own arm burning and the weight of her mother. Pushing aside the pain, Ellen did not stop until she reached the street. Her mother's body slumped, but she was breathing.

As ambulance attendants lifted unconscious Nancy Kirk into their van, Ellen felt a pat on her back. Sarah Parker, her mother's Negro nurse. They had brought Sarah along to New York and allowed her to take a break to watch the parade. Ellen would not know until that evening that while Sarah watched the hotel burn, she worried too about Detective Niehoff's warning the day before, as he insulted her and her friends.

"Mrs. Haskin, you go get that arm treated. I'll ride along with your mother." Sarah turned to the driver. "She's my mistress, my patient. A good lady, let me go with her." Sarah jumped into the ambulance headed to Bellevue Hospital.

"I'll be there soon," Ellen shouted. Need to check on something first." She turned around, facing the inferno. She felt pain from the burn on her arm, not relieved by the frigid air. Hiding her singed pink silk sleeve behind her back, she walked toward the Windsor's front door, ready to use her shoulders to push her way into the hotel. The police, two rows thick, stopped her as well as dozens of other pleading men and women. Ellen felt no shame about wanting the valuables she left behind in 410—they were part of her father's legacy to her and her mother. Nothing to be done, at least for now. Turning back toward the street, Ellen begged for a ride from the driver of the next ambulance she saw and rode to Bellevue ten minutes behind her mother's van.

Pushing through the crowd gathering in the hospital entrance, Ellen raced from one packed ward to another, croaking in her hoarse voice, crying out every name her mother ever used. "Mrs. Nancy Kirk, Mrs. James Kirk, Nancy Ann Kirk." At last, in the third ward, Ellen saw a beckoning, swaying arm. Sarah, her mother's nurse, the one Negro nurse in the crowd.

"Still unconscious," Sarah said. "But the doctor didn't find any burns, thank the Lord."

Helen sat with her mother and held her hand, with Sarah nearby checking on her patient's pulse, applying compresses to her forehead. Ellen tried to ignore her own burns, but she winced when the pain increased. "Oh, Mrs. Haskin, let me see your arm." Sarah rolled up Ellen's silk sleeve to check.

Both women saw blistered skin. "I'll need instruments."

Sarah asked the other nurses for supplies. They ignored her, first maybe because they were busy with more serious injuries. As Ellen's pain increased, Sarah tried again. Still no help.

"Mrs. Haskin, they don't believe I'm a nurse. They don't think a Negro woman could be a nurse. I reckon they never heard of Provident Hospital and Training School in Chicago." Sarah waited a minute, keeping her eyes on the nurses and doctors, then crept to a cart to grab tweezers, salve, and bandages. Ellen smiled, her first smile in hours.

Shortly after ten o'clock, Ellen's mother's face went slack. Sarah turned to Ellen with a kind look and told her to motion for a doctor. The exhausted man who came to the bedside checked for a breath, going through the motions. He blamed the woman's heart condition, spurred on by flames.

After spending the last hour preparing herself, Ellen knew she had done everything possible to save her mother. Ellen's regrets were small—she had insisted they have lunch that day at a restaurant her mother disliked, she had grilled her mother that morning on the unsavory details of one of Ellen's six brothers' business deals. Ellen's faults haunted her, out of proportion to the miniscule evil of each deed. But as she grieved, she also felt pride that she had dragged her mother out of the inferno. The Kirk family would have a body to bury.

She sent a messenger to telegraph her brothers. What could she write? Would they wonder why their sister lived but their mother died? No, they knew their sister, their only surviving sister, knew she would do everything she could. Ellen kept her messages short but assured her brothers that she would handle arrangements to transport their mother's body by train back to Chicago for burial. Sarah helped with the forms. Tears covered the nurse's face, but Ellen noticed more—Sarah didn't look at her, looked beyond her.

"Ma'am, I know this is a terrible time, but I need to ask you something. A couple days back, I visited with other servants, another nurse too, all Negroes, in the basement. One of them joked about all the jewels guests brought to the hotel. Art too. A detective was walking around. He checks the place, checks where the Negroes stay. He heard us joking, and he gave a warning. Then, an hour ago, I heard one of the men carrying stretchers say that a gang of robbers set the fire. Miz Ellen, I'm scared. They won't come looking for me, will they? You know I didn't do anything wrong. The only thing I ever filched is bandages for your burns. I was outside watching the parade when the fire started."

Ellen tried to focus, tried to look away from her mother's body to her mother's nurse, to listen.

"Sorry. I know I shouldn't be botherin' you with this now. You can tell I'm jumpy."

"Sarah, Mother admired you. She would want me to vouch for you." Ellen looked at Sarah. Why did those words provide only some relief? "Oh, and Sarah, I will write a strong reference. You will find another patient." More tears from Sarah, along with a nod of thanks.

The clock in the ward reached 11:00. Ellen saw no need to keep vigil over her mother's body all night. On her way out of Bellevue, she saw a mirror in the entrance hall. She checked her appearance, as she had every day for decades, even amid tragedies. She saw singed hair and bandaged arms, the silk bodice of her pink frock covered in soot. All signs of honor. She felt but couldn't see her strained neck, blistered skin, aching back. Sore from half carrying Mother out of the flames. Pausing at the mirror, Ellen saw, absurdly, the sapphire choker on her neck, in perfect condition.

She had nowhere to go, no hotel, no clothes, no possessions. But that sapphire choker gave her a purpose. Her father died a decade ago, but his surviving business—the world's largest soap company—supported eleven children, seven still surviving, and a swarm of grandchildren and allowed Ellen to be the most bejeweled woman in the Chicago area. She owed it to her father to search. She hailed a hansom cab, despite the darkness, despite being alone. She told the driver to take her to the East 51st Street police station. Nurse Sarah Parker was not the only hospital visitor attentive to chatter in the ward that night. Ellen had heard two nurses talk about valuables. One told the other that the police at the East 51st Street Station vowed to collect, catalog, guard, and store all found jewelry.

Hugh Bonner

As Fire Chief Hugh Bonner's wagon pulled up to the Windsor, he saw police running around carriages, barking at drivers to stay back. Two coppers, recognizing him and spotting the chief's insignia on his wagon, cleared a tight space for his driver between a pumper and an engine. He leapt down, sensing eyes on him.

Damn, flames on every floor. As he feared, hotel staff and spectators must have been slow to sound the first alarm. He calmed down when he saw Ninth Battalion Chief John Binns, until now top man on site, giving orders. A good chap, low-key and well-liked, with the usual gray mustache. Bonner had heard his men joke that the muckety mucks in the fire department all had gray mustaches. But Binns would always have a distinctive look. He had lost an eyebrow years ago when sparks fell on him, and he had a bowlegged walk.

Firefighters from dozens of companies surrounded Binns, waiting for orders. The men had not tarried. Despite the chaos, Bonner took a minute to count—six ladder companies, eight engine companies, three ambulances, and one horse-drawn water tank, crowded together on Fifth Avenue. Within an hour, he would count even more.

Bonner pressed through the smoke to check in with Binns. The battalion chief looked relieved, happy to transfer leadership.

"Every floor, Hugh, and front to back. Never seen such a rapid spread." Bonner took in Binns's report, though he could see the disaster for himself.

"John, stay here and help me with the orders. Too big a site for one man. You've done a good job. Keep at it with me now."

Together, they repositioned the hose lines and gave them a try. "Weak pressure or limited supply?" Binns asked. He screwed up his one eyebrow, looking to Bonner.

"John, there's not enough water in the East River to put out this fire."

As more firemen arrived, they looked to Bonner and Binns for instructions. The two deployed the firemen as best they could, but they didn't have enough men for a square block of fire. On the Fifth Avenue side alone, Bonner saw six women in hotel windows, flailing their arms. Binns, after scanning the side streets, told Bonner that another five women on the 46th Street side and yet more on the 47th Street side were screaming for help.

"Highest floors first, Bonner yelled." Binns raised his hand in agreement.

"The women in windows. Hope those already on ropes make it on their own, right?" Binns raised his hand again.

"Ladders?" Bonner asked, looking at Binns. Every firefighter knew Binns's skill with scaling ladders, the light ones with a single beam down the middle and rungs on either side. Binns had used them himself, either despite or because of his bowed legs, gathering awards for bravery.

"Thank God we bought more last year, scaling and regular. Should be enough." Binns yelled above the newest roar from the crowd.

"Wait, help's comin'. Help's comin'." Bonner welcomed the refrain from bystanders. They stood shoulder to shoulder, jockeying for sightlines, waving wildly and shouting assurances to the women—men too, young and old—straddling sills. But Bonner knew that when hotel guests felt flames searing their backs, nothing would matter. Along with the crowd, he saw jumpers swinging out on ropes, bouncing off sills and railings, spinning around, dresses inflating, letting go, screaming.

Bonner's eyes met Binns's. "What idiot thought up those ropes?" Binns said. Before he finished the question, Bonner replied. "A monster."

Bonner let himself look for only seconds. He shouted orders to Binns and to other men who gave more orders. Firemen from engine companies yelled their intentions to each other, dragging and hoisting hoses. Firemen from ladder companies—Bonner knew those were the heroes everyone would remember—grabbed their ladders.

Hours later, after the roof collapsed, after the walls collapsed, after seeing too many scorched corpses to count, Bonner paused to drink lukewarm tea handed around by clerks from the Caswell & Massey drugstore across the street. He saw Binns at the corner, supervising tired men loading hoses back on the engine. Bonner gestured to Binns to join him for a sip.

"That bloody fire code," Bonner said. "Out of date the minute it became law."

"We tried," Binns said. He didn't need to explain more, didn't need to shout over the din. City officials, supported by Bonner and Binns, had recommended more stringent fire codes. No one listened. The officials didn't have enough connections, couldn't find the right people to threaten.

"You know we're gonna see a witch hunt," Bonner said. "The reporters, the public, they'll blame everyone they can find. Us too. Bonner's eyes locked onto Binns's. The men touched each other's shoulders lightly.

Thomas Brady

Decades ago, Buildings Commissioner Thomas Brady worked as an assistant bricklayer, then a bricklayer. Before long, he mastered other trades. With the help of influential connections, by 1899, he was a wealthy builder. He learned to dress well and to hobnob. As a side enterprise, he moved from one appointed office to another. Now Brady headed the Buildings Department of the City of New York. He knew how to run his department, but the Windsor site would be his biggest responsibility so far.

Arriving on the scene as the sun set over the smoldering ruins, Brady nodded a greeting to Fire Chief Bonner, who stood near a pumper and sipped tea, looking exhausted. Brady knew Bonner—they had met at sites before. Brady didn't need Bonner now. He looked instead for two other men. With no trouble, he spotted William "Big Bill" Devery leaning against a pile of blackened bricks. Devery's unruly mustache, double chins, and protruding belly made him easy to find, even as dark came on, with ash clouding visibility. Although the taint of bribery and extortion hung over Devery, he weathered legal challenges and remained the city's powerful Police Chief. The other man Brady wanted stood beside Devery, seemingly glued to his every word. George McClusky, Devery's chief detective, looked taller and thinner than his boss. Brady knew that the two men differed by more than dimensions. Devery wore his impressive uniform, resplendent with brass buttons and gold stars, while McClusky, known for another kind of flair, wore a well-tailored black coat and a black bowler. Odd duck lived with his spinster sisters.

Brady looked around in dismay, shaking his head as he greeted Chief Devery and Detective McClusky. The site resembled a burned and sacked city—fallen walls, precariously leaning chimneys, piles of scorched wreckage, rivulets of water, ash everywhere. Devery straightened up, extending his hand. McClusky smoothed his hair, extending his hand too.

"Damned debris," Brady said. "I'll put in a call to Joseph Cody to haul away the bricks and rubbish. In January, we gave him a license for the year. Good timing. He has a big hauling operation. But Bill, you're not off the hook yet on this one. I can tell from that drooping gob of yours that you know that. My department will take charge of demolition, but I need police cooperation."

"You'll get it, Tom," Devery said. "When you clear the site, I should say when Cody clears the site, the priority is bodies." Brady twisted his lips—of course. "Next, valuables, jewels. Those toffs who stayed at the Windsor are already yapping at our heels, looking for their glitter. They're swarming the East 51st Street police station. We have two mobs out there. One wants to see if we brought their scorched moms and pops to the back room where we're laying out bodies, and the other wants to find their diamonds." Brady saw Detective McClusky squirm at the mention of diamonds.

"Chief, Commissioner, about the diamonds, can we look ahead a minute?" McClusky asked. "How many men will Cody hire to clear the wreckage?"

"I'll authorize 250. For a start."

"Those men will be laborers, day workers from off the street?"

"Detective, you're probably right." Brady smiled, pleased that McClusky anticipated the danger.

"Word is already out that riches are buried in this rubble." While talking, Detective McClusky swung his arm around to take in the whole square block. "Who's going to watch the laborers who keep their eyes out for jewels? If some Italian laborer fresh off the boat pockets a necklace, the rich guests will blame us."

Brady saw McClusky glance at Devery, looking for approval from the police chief.

Didn't need to wait long. Devery patted his chief detective on the back. "Good man to have on our force, right Tom? He knows what bullshit's coming and how to cover my ass."

McClusky seemed to enjoy the praise. He kept talking. "I'll station my detectives around the ruins to look over the laborers. And we need a system for checking them. No one will pocket anything on my watch. Not even a shoelace."

"Sounds good," Brady said. "Let's talk to Cody and work out a plan to keep the guineas in check." Like Devery, Brady worried about the politicians and their wealthy friends, the people who would keep him in office. Brady worried too about keeping those building contracts coming to his company. At least Devery and McClusky would do their part. The chief detective might be a toady, but he seemed sharp. They were all in the limelight together.

"By the way," Brady said, "where's John Scannell? Our Fire Commissioner can't even show up?"

"Ah, Scannell. That sly man had the sense to visit relatives in Lake Placid for St. Pat's Day," Devery said. "Probably wanted to run away from the gossip that he accepted bribes from job applicants."

Brady nodded.

"But our man McClusky here," Devery said, patting the Chief Detective on the shoulder again. "He'll get to the bottom of that mess and put the guilty ones in the Tombs, right?"

"I'm working on it, Chief." Brady caught McClusky's deferential tone. Brady also saw Devery scan the wreckage and stare at McClusky, who got the message. "And, yes, I'll find the cause of this inferno."

"A city block, enormous hotel, burned to the ground in an hour. How's that possible?" Brady said.

"That's what everyone's asking," Devery said. "And McClusky here's going to tell us."

Ellen Kirk Haskin

The clock on the wall of the East 51st Street police station showed ten minutes after midnight. The worst day of Ellen Kirk Haskin's life had ended, but the new day started badly. She had already stood in line for thirty minutes, trying to ignore the lingering pain of burns on her arm and the anguished looks of people crammed around her. They hunted for lost relatives, lost valuables. Finally, only six people stood between her and the front of the line. On the desk ahead, she could see a nameplate—Acting Captain John Lantry. The frazzled man struggled to tamp down the chaos. With her good arm, Ellen caressed the sapphire choker on her neck to calm herself and to remind her of her father, his legacy, the Kirk family legacy. The choker reminded her too of the jewels she left in the suite and took her mind off her mother's body, still at Bellevue Hospital.

"Me mum." A disheveled boy of about twelve pushed his way forward, cutting into the line. "You have to find me mum." Elbows shoved the boy. His lament fueled grousing from others standing behind Ellen.

"Boy, move aside. I got here first. Officer, she's twenty. My daughter. Pretty peach-colored dress." More elbows.

"Four thousand dollars. My wife lost her wedding jewels and her heirlooms. Where do I look?"

"My bank books. I need those books."

"With child. My wife's with child. Is she on your list?" Ellen saw the frantic man raise his fists, preparing to use them.

Captain Lantry tried to keep order at the front desk. "Listen up," he yelled over the crowd. He put his hands on his hips and glared. "My officers are doing their best. They're trained to handle gang wars, knifings, brutality you wouldn't believe. This is new for them. Patrolman Doyle at the table there," he pointed, "has a list of injured guests, servants too. Most of them are in hospitals or homes nearby. We get updates to the list every half hour or so. You might want to hang around. If you do, sit on the side. But if your people escaped the fire without injury, they won't be on any list. Look for yourselves at friends' homes, other hotels."

More questions, shouted from the crowd. Lantry kept talking, raising his voice. He turned to the loudest shouters, holding his hands up. They didn't recognize this as a call for quiet. They kept up their pleas. Lantry kept up his instructions, ignoring the din that threatened to drown him out. He rushed to finish. "Sorry to say this, but some of the guests, servants too, who didn't make it out, you know, if the firemen or police found them, they brought them here, in the back room. Police Chief Devery designated that space as a morgue. Two senior officers are in charge there. You can check, but one at a time, and be respectful. And those of you who came here for belongings, be patient. Carts are still bringing loads of jewelry. Clothing and papers too. Officer Pressley records the location where each item was found, if he knows it, and the date. He's attaching tags. You can go talk to him."

Lantry pointed to a table off to the side. Ellen hadn't noticed it before because of the crowd.

"Give the officer a list of what you've lost. But if you get in the way of them lookin' for loved ones, my men will knock you down."

Ellen slipped out of line, moving faster than the man behind her hunting for four thousand dollars in jewels. She walked ten feet to the table where Officer Pressley presided. "Sir, my name is Mrs. Ellen Haskin. My mother is Mrs. Nancy Kirk. We had rooms at the Windsor. My mother passed away an hour ago at Bellevue." Presley interrupted mechanically.

"Sorry for your loss, ma'am."

"Yes, well, I am not here for that, not exactly, I came because my mother and I lost jewelry in the fire." She looked around, bent forward, lowered her voice. "$80,000 in jewelry." She realized that a few people crowding in at her back could hear her.

Pressley stared. "Ma'am, did you not use the hotel safe?" Too loud. This man should not judge her. Not now.

"My mother and I enjoyed wearing the jewels. They were gifts from my deceased father. We didn't want to bother to get them from the clerk responsible for the safe and bring them back each day. We made a mistake. And now Mother's dead."

Pressley must have seen her eyes tear. He softened his tone. "Go over to that chair there and write me a list."

As Ellen thanked him and walked to the side, the wide-open eyes of the people waiting in the room followed her.

Bridget Dunne

"How did you know?" Molly whispered to Bridget as the sun peeked into the tiny attic window the morning after the fire. The two shared a rough blanket on the cold floor.

"How did I know what?"

"On the roof to keep us near the fire escape?"

"Didn't hurt to be careful. Clay said the fire would be just enough to scare the gents out of their rooms. Clay's smart. I trusted him. But yuh know, plans can go sideways. So I took care, just in case." Bridget guarded her words. She didn't want to admit remorse and didn't want Molly and Tara to blame her for pulling them into a deadly scheme. And she didn't want to admit her fear that Clay had not escaped. She raised herself on her elbow and looked at Tara who was awakening on the next blanket. "Tara, I didn't know the metal on that fire escape was hot. Sorry. Any better this morning?"

Tara stared at her bandaged hands. She sat up.

"Lucky we're alive, Bridge. If you hadn't herded us to that escape, we'd be missin' or dead, like all those other girls." Tara looked away from her hands and into space for a second, probably thinking about Sean. And maybe thinking about May, the maid she shared a room with, the dead maid. "You got Mrs. Wrigley and Devan out too."

Tara, the injured one, had a right to be angry. But she was kind this morning. Molly would be the one to squirm, to make connections. Bridget didn't have to wait long.

"So many dead. I feel sick. Bridge, are we in trouble because of those lists? Good thing I didn't tell Frank about them. He would've killed me."

"Molly, settle down. Remember, Mrs. Wrigley and Devan know we were on the roof when the fire started. They'll back us up. No worries."

"And what about our money?" Molly said. "I promised my ma. She needs help for all the brats. I'm the one that gave Clay the fourth-floor list. That's the list he smiled at the most. He's going to give me another double sawbuck, right?" Bridget concentrated on relaxing her face. No need to point out Molly's rapid switch from guilt to greed.

Molly looked at Bridget, waiting for an answer. Tara joined in the stare.

"Clay's good for his word. But first, he'll have to find us. Maybe he'll remember I have a sister in the city."

Bridget saw Tara's eyes widen. She must wonder how Sean, too, would find them. But Tara wouldn't say anything about her sweetheart in front of Molly. For Molly, Sean was a hothead, not to be trusted.

That first morning at Claire's, Mrs. Brownhill welcomed the chambermaids to the breakfast table. The boarders never stopped with questions.

"Any burns besides the ones on Miss Tara's hands?"

"Any friends jump? Any posh ones jump?"

"How many bodies? Broken or burned?"

"Do you think it was that cigar smoker? One cigar for the whole hotel? Really?"

Tara talked with the boarders, cursing the flames and pitying the jumpers. She jabbered when she worried. Bridget hoped Tara stuck with the drama from the sidewalk, not the action on the halls. Unfortunately, Mrs. Brownhill had no young male boarders to distract Tara from her focus on the fire.

The boarders listened to Tara, ignoring Molly, who sat quietly. She would be worrying about whether Frank got out of the basement alive. All three beaus, in jeopardy.

Marguerite Wells

The morning after the fire, the Wells family plodded down to breakfast, wearing the same bedraggled clothes as the day before. Marguerite removed the jade brooch from her dress—she didn't want a reminder of the color green. She tried to ignore the lingering smell of smoke with each step she took.

Breakfast was a disorderly affair, as the Hoffman House staff tried to feed unexpected guests. Undercooked eggs, weak coffee. Marguerite had no inclination to rehash details of the previous day, and her parents seemed eager to move on as well. The three focused instead on their trip to Europe in a few days. How would they replace their clothes before sailing? They needed frocks, shoes, coats. Papa needed suits. How would they learn the whereabouts of acquaintances from the Windsor? They made plans to keep busy and to regain their lives.

"Waiter," Papa said, "I know you are busy. I am sorry to ask, but can you bring us stronger coffee?" As Marguerite looked at the harried waiter to nod with empathy, she saw that he had been clearing a nearby table where departing guests left newspapers.

Soon, she would curse those guests, curse the papers, curse the reporters.

Marguerite leaned left, reaching for the newspapers. She held onto the *New York Times* and passed the others—the *Sun*, the *Evening Post*, *New York Journal and Advertiser*—to her parents. First, she read the *Times*'s reports of the fire, then the incomplete lists of the dead and the missing and the injured, wincing every time she saw a name she recognized. Next, she read the list of survivors and the hotels that had taken them in. Her family's surname was not on that list. They must have arrived too late for the reporters to spot Wells on the hotel register. As Marguerite scanned the remaining stories to make sure she had not missed anything, she spotted her father's name in a column on page two. She read it, then reread it. In the coming days, as she brooded over this story, she would give it her own headline—"The West on Display."

The *Times* reporter wrote with verve. "One of the most remarkable incidents in this hour of thrilling experiences was the cool courage displayed by Edward P. Wells, who, with his wife and daughter, was a guest in the hotel. Mr. Wells is past middle age, and is a resident of Jamestown, N.D. His experiences in that country taught him the value of clear-headedness in trying moments, and it is to this quality that he owes not only his life, but the life and well-being of his family, all of whom escaped without a scratch."

Yes, Papa was a man of the frontier, of the West, she thought as she read, but hardly a trapper or an Indian fighter. His clear-headedness focused on banking, not escaping calamities. The Wellses lived in the largest house in Jamestown, not even a ranch.

"In this emergency," the *Times* reporter continued, "Mr. Wells besought his family to remain calm, and he then proceeded with great deliberation to measure the chances of escape. He first played out the fire escape rope in the room until he saw that it would reach the ground, and hauling it back, he quickly but securely fastened it about his daughter's waist."

No mention that she was the one to find the rope. Also, how did the reporter know what Papa did in the privacy of the Windsor suite? When he went down to the lobby, he must have shared his story with reporters, his point of view. Marguerite kept reading.

"He then lifted the form of the girl to the window ledge and slowly allowed it to descend. He wound the rope tightly about his hands and braced his feet against the wall of the room, meanwhile slowly playing out the rope at the end of which dangled the almost inanimate body of his daughter. Smoke and flame shot out at intervals from the windows below, but the passage of the girl was not retarded, and in a few seconds, she had reached the ground."

Inspired by the reporter's account, Marguerite could almost hear her papa pant at the start of her drop while she felt certain he would hold onto the rope. She counted her blessings that she weighed little more than a hundred pounds. Did she have the sense to cross her legs as she came down? Then, her questions moved in a different direction. Was she passive? Inanimate?

The reporter pressed on. "The rope was quickly hauled back by Mr. Wells and exactly the same performance was gone through in the case of his wife, who had meanwhile stood at his side at the window."

Mama had stayed slender, even after bearing four children, but she weighed thirty pounds more than her daughter. Did she do nothing as the flames lapped her family? The mother who made a gracious home in a bleak wilderness long before wealth flowed in?

The reporter's admiration grew with each inch of the column. "For the third time, Mr. Wells pulled the rope back, after he had seen his family in safety, and he then made his preparations for his own descent…. He carefully tied his hands in towels. He then clambered out on the windowsill and swung clear. He shot down like lightning, but there were ready hands below to break the fall, and when the bandages had been removed from the man's hands, it was found that he had not even a blister on them… The firemen agreed that there might have been a number of persons saved had they exercised the same courage and forethought as did Mr. Wells."

When Marguerite finished the *Times*, she saw that her parents barely touched the disappointing breakfast or the foul coffee. They had their heads in the other newspapers. Noise from surrounding tables kept going—clinking glasses, conversations, scraping chair legs—but no one spoke at the Wellses' table.

Marguerite passed the *Times* to her papa. He handed her the *Sun*. Here she found an account of her family nearly identical to the *Times* coverage, with the headline, "Saved His Womenkind First." When Marguerite read those two accounts that morning, she didn't know that twelve days later, a sensational drawing of Papa's feat would appear on the cover of *Leslie's*

Weekly—Papa lowering her from a window while Mama awaited her turn. Brother Stuart would frame that cover to display in his home. And Marguerite didn't know yet about another remarkable story that would run in the *Wichita Daily Eagle*, a paper influential in her hometown.

The residents of Jamestown respected Edward Wells. They had elected him to represent them in the Territorial Legislative Assembly and named him Territorial Chair of the Republican Party in Dakota. The son of a clergyman, he started out as a teacher and now, thanks to ambition and intelligence, presided over railroads, insurance companies, real estate firms, banks. Marguerite worshipped him. But she had never seen him save anyone from death. Had he stepped up as depicted? She felt ashamed that she descended to safety first, leaving Mama behind. But also proud that she bravely opted to test the rope first. And growing irritation that she, a Smith College graduate and a suffragist, should be painted as a delicate flower of a woman.

Marguerite looked to her mama, who folded up the *Evening Post*, saying nothing. The women traded newspapers. Marguerite quickly found the *Post*'s version of the Wellses' adventure. She came to call this one, to herself, "Firemen Save Helpless Family."

"Firemen Brennan, Sweeney, Linck, and Tessler took scaling ladders, and, while flames were shooting out of all the windows, rescued Edward P. Wells of Jamestown, N.D., and his daughter. The firemen saw these two in a six-story window. The ladders only reached to the third floor, and, catching up a scaling ladder, Brennan ran to the top of the main ladder, followed by the other three. Brennan gave way to Tessler at the top of the ladder, and the fireman gained the sixth floor by means of the scaling ladder. There, he seated himself in the window and offered to hand the younger woman down. She refused to be saved first and insisted that her mother, who had not been seen, should be the first handed down. The fireman, seizing her father, passed him down to Brennan, who passed him to Linck, and then to Sweeney, who assisted him to the street. The mother followed, then the daughter, and the fireman said: 'She was the coolest girl I ever saw in a warm place.'"

After reading the *Post*'s story twice, Marguerite looked left and saw that her papa was ready to give her the fourth paper, the *New York Journal and Advertiser*. Marguerite did not need to invent a telling headline. The reporter had provided a memorable one—"Made Them Save Her Parents First," followed by a smaller headline, "Miss Wells, of North Dakota, Regardless of Her Own Danger." The daughter is the heroine determining the order of rescue, while the cowardly father lets himself be saved first.

Marguerite stared at her cold toast and played with the jam as her parents finished their papers, with impenetrable expressions. Never did the three discuss the accounts. No grousing. No preening. Whatever they took away from the papers, they took away separately and quietly.

But the different versions drove Marguerite's obsessions. She considered herself exceptional. Smarter than others. More perceptive. She had faced challenges and acquitted herself well. She excelled in her local school, was admitted to Smith College, made friends with snobby easterners, became a fine schoolteacher. Until the fire, most days Marguerite succeeded in tamping down the other Marguerite, the failure, the one who had no beau, no children. The one who worked for a cause, suffrage for women, that seemed elusive.

Until that morning, Marguerite would have had no doubt that in an emergency, with split seconds to make decisions and others at risk, she would have stuck out her jaw, narrowed her eyes, and acted. Now, she felt a crack in that confidence. Was her sense of moral superiority, of honor, earned or imagined?

What could she remember? Marguerite seethed at reporters who repeated accounts without confirmation, filled in gaps with their imaginations and invented drama. But she shared their confusion. Did she offer to go first to assess the danger? Or last in order to save her parents? Once saved, did she try to save other guests? Did her papa show the courage of an enterprising frontiersman? Was he afraid? If her family's experience, for the three Wellses, needed four accounts for the telling, and the Windsor housed 300 people, how many accounts could there be?

"Miss, excuse me, are you Miss Marguerite Wells?" Marguerite must have been staring into space because the bellhop repeated himself. She raised her chin. He searched through the slips he carried and handed her one, then ran off to deliver others.

The short message came from Angelica Gerry. "Are you safe?"

"Mama," Marguerite said, "I forgot that we planned to have dinner with Angelica on Monday." Nellie Wells glanced up from her uneaten breakfast. "The dear girl must have been calling all the hotels, hoping to find me. She did not know we checked into the Hoffman House."

Marguerite walked through the lobby toward the house phone to call Angelica. Guests had queued up ahead of her. While waiting, she glimpsed clusters of people she recognized as guests of the Windsor. Each cluster included a man in a badly tailored suit who asked questions and scribbled notes. Later, she would learn that plainclothes police went to the Hoffman House and the other hotels sheltering Windsor refugees to ask what they had witnessed, to investigate allegations of incendiary activities. Several of the women would swear that as they ran for their lives, they spotted thieves—unfamiliar men who looked strangely relaxed, given the smoke and chaos.

At last, Marguerite connected with the Gerry telephone. "I'm fine, Angelica. And Mama and Papa are fine. And our maid. I'm so sorry I didn't call earlier." Angelica sobbed with relief and explained she'd been worrying all night. She agreed to join Marguerite and her parents for lunch in a few days, now at the Hoffman House.

"Marguerite, will Theodate Pope still join us, as you planned? I believe she stayed at the Windsor, too, but I've heard that she and her parents escaped. Have you heard from her?" Angelica's voice sounded more hesitant than anxious.

"Ah, no. I will try to reach her."

When Marguerite put down the phone's mouthpiece, her mind, moving on from Angelica, lurched in circles.

David Dudley

When dawn came on March 18, David Dudley was still at work in Helen Gould's kitchen, across 47th Street from the remains of the Windsor. He supervised his staff and helped them prepare food for the police and the doctors caring for the injured in the mansion's parlors. But he was not too tired to grab the morning papers. His anger over his treatment at the Windsor simmered as he read challenges to his claim as the first to notice the fire, the first to act.

One of the morning papers reported that head waiter John Foy screamed a warning when he saw a cigar smoker ignite a lace curtain. Yes, but Dudley saw smoke and ran into the hotel minutes before he and his friend Ted, trying to climb the central stairs, heard Foy's cry. Reading on, Dudley saw that even white-skinned Foy met obstacles. According to the papers, he ran to a red call box on Fifth. A policeman, controlling the crowd, stopped him. Foy yelled "let me through," but the distracted policeman heard only the loud Irish music of his homeland. Foy kept running, looking for a different red box. By the time he found one, he saw another man on it, calling in an alarm. Perhaps that man was Richard Merritt, who also claimed first place, turning in an alarm at 3:07 when flames already enveloped the hotel. Fire department officials insisted the first box squawked at 3:12. Reports did not distinguish between boxes designed for a single alarm and those designed for multiple alarms, or between boxes that worked and those that failed. But Dudley knew that Foy hunted for a call box several minutes after the jackasses—clerk Simeon Leland and cashier Charles Squires—learned of the fire and could have sounded an alarm that reached the upper floors and called the fire department on the house phone.

Christopher Mullins, a photographer capturing scenes of the parade, also claimed to be the first to sound an alarm. Looking through his lens with a sharp eye, he saw smoke wafting from the hotel. He ran into the office to tell cashier Squires. Mullins reported that the cashier, Charles Squires, listened attentively. Dudley spat on the newspaper.

Even the milkman got into the act. Edward Killan, who delivered his milk earlier and decided to watch the parade, saw a curtain on fire, ran into the hotel, and tried one of the few alarm boxes in the hotel. When he couldn't get it to work, he ran into the street yelling, ran back to the hotel, and with two soldiers from the parade, did what he could to help.

David Dudley yelled an alarm to the office staff first. He knew that distinction, whatever the papers reported. And he knew that if the idiots had not distrusted his skin color, he might have saved lives.

George McClusky

"George, Devery here."

"Good morning, sir." Chief Detective George McClusky sighed to himself. He'd recognize the husky voice of Big Bill Devery anywhere, even coming through Manhattan's imperfect telephone wires. McClusky had reluctantly installed a telephone in his flat—the first telephone on W. 70th Street.

"George, the President's private secretary, Cortelyou, called last night after I got home. Two years ago, he told us to keep our eyes on the Paterson, New Jersey cell, you know, the anarchist cell. Now he thinks the Italians there might target the President, might try to get to him through his brother, Abner. Threaten him. Maybe kidnap him. So talk to Abner, right away. Cortelyou says Abner's at the Hotel Manhattan."

"He was on my list, sir. I'll report back." McClusky had already planned to talk to Abner McKinley. He didn't need his boss, Big Bill, to tell him what to do. This morning after the fire would be a busy day. McClusky also needed to get to the Windsor site as soon as possible, to put systems in place for protecting valuables.

"Oh, and Gunter too." Big Bill kept up his orders. "That's another one you'll have to talk to. Some fella named Archibald Clavering Gunter—says he's a novelist—saw an old man with gray hair puff on a cigar in a bay window on the second floor. The ceiling filled with flames. Then the man with the cigar ran away. Check this Gunter out. He's at the Plaza. Oh, and George, don't forget Scannell and that bribe."

"I'm working hard on the Scannell case, sir. And I'll talk to McKinley, then this Gunter, then I'll get to the site to add security."

Big Bill grunted approval, then hung up without a goodbye.

McClusky raced down Broadway, moving with his distinctive swagger. Twenty minutes later, he reached the Hotel Manhattan at 42nd and Madison. He flashed his badge in front of the desk clerk. "I'm here for Abner McKinley. Urgent business. Send a bellhop up. Tell Mr. McKinley that Chief Detective George McClusky needs to speak with him."

The clerk wasted no time. Neither did the bellhop. McClusky waited, allowing him to observe the crowd in the lobby. Two of his junior detectives were already there, interviewing refugees from the Windsor. Journalists hovered nearby, trying to listen in. McClusky watched as harried men and women rushed in to ask the desk clerk if their missing relatives had registered.

After a few minutes, Abner McKinley emerged from the elevator. All eyes turned to gawk. McClusky and the others recognized the president's brother from newspaper photographs. Stretching his waistcoat to button it, McKinley looked around, probably hunting for a man in uniform, or if not a uniform, a shabby suit. Clearly, McClusky thought with pride as he adjusted his tie, McKinley did not expect to see a well-dressed detective.

Don't freeze up, McClusky thought to himself. This swell is just another blueblood in a city full of them. The two men introduced themselves while the staff—honored that McKinley sought refuge in their hotel—stared, awestruck. The guests and junior detectives stared, too.

"Let's find a quiet corner where we can talk in private," McClusky said. A clerk and a bellhop heard the hint. They cleared a corner of the lobby, waving their arms to invite the two men to a pair of wingchairs.

"First, let me say I was pleased to learn your wife and daughter escaped the fire."

"Most frightening day of my life. My daughter, she does not walk easily. Needs crutches. And my wife lost track of her in the chaos. But we are the lucky ones."

"Yes," McClusky said. And I realize you are a busy gentleman. I will get to the point. I understand the President's Secretary worries about anarchists and believes they may have been involved in the fire at the Windsor, to get to the President through you. Is that likely?"

As McClusky spoke, an older gentleman approached the corner of the lobby. He patted McKinley's back, familiarly.

"Detective McClusky, meet Colonel Thomas Ochiltree. A great friend. Tom and I have business ventures together. Like the rest of us, Tom escaped from the Windsor, but he couldn't get into this hotel. Staying at the Waldorf-Astoria, eh?" Ochiltree grinned assent, still with his hand on McKinley's back. "Tom's valet—a young man—helped him get out a window. By the way, when the valet came back to Tom's room to save collectibles, some of your men, patrolmen, thought the lad looked suspicious."

"Right, they clubbed him," Ochiltree said. "You see, he carried out a lot of my valuables. I might have clubbed him too if I'd been in their position, but then I'm always accused of being, hmmm, let's call it overzealous."

McClusky sat silently for a minute, annoyed that Ochiltree had intruded.

"Sorry about your valet, Colonel Ochiltree." As McClusky offered his weak apology, he looked at McKinley, darting his eyes for a second at the other man. McKinley picked up on the question.

"You look worried about continuing our conversation, detective. No fear. Tom is a loyal friend. You can say whatever you like."

Knowing that speed took priority, McClusky relaxed his eyes to hide his annoyance. "As I started to say, do you have any reason to believe anarchists were connected to the fire?"

Ochiltree answered before McKinley could. "The boiler ran dry and exploded, and those useless hotel workers, engineers, and boilermen down in the basement, I saw them outside, from my window, watching the parade with the rest of 'em. I'm sure those flames came up to my suite from the boiler below. The hotel crew paid no mind."

McKinley and McClusky stared at Ochiltree. "Are you sure?" McClusky asked.

"For years, I lobbied in Washington," Ochiltree said while giving McKinley a knowing look. "For a deep-water port for Galveston. Texas. I spent a lot of time on ships to understand what they needed. I know boilers. And I know they explode."

Abner McKinley smiled. "My friend here is known for tall tales. He fought the Apaches and Comanches when he served with the Texas Rangers. Then he served with the likes of John Bell Hood and James Longstreet, and he'll tell you about those adventures, sometimes, shall we say, with embellishments. But he does know boilers. Now, though, I need to disagree with my friend Tom. I'm sure it's those anarchists. They've been chomping at the bit to get to my brother, and it's likely they're trying to get to him through me. I think the anarchists set up a scheme to rob the place, as a distraction, and to kidnap me to get to William. They know I'm not guarded, while William has at least a guard or two at the White House. It's a miracle we escaped, though my daughter and wife, they're still in shock. The anarchists must have hidden out near the telegraph room. Check into that. Or maybe it's only one anarchist, that Kain fellow you coppers nabbed yesterday. He stole my wife's jewelry and my business papers. A lot of wealthy families with jewelry stay at the Windsor. Most of them lost jewels, but why did I lose more than anyone else? Kain bagged an armload of my family's property."

"Maybe, Abner," Ochiltree said. "But the anarchists could have gotten to the boilers too. Would be easier to blow up the whole hotel than to pick off valuables, one suite at a time."

"Tom, that Kain chum didn't seem bright, from what the police told me. For men like him, it's easier to set a fire than to damage a boiler."

McClusky looked from one man to another, realizing they were little help. Each sounded certain. Could they both be right? He listened to more of McKinley's charges against anarchists, wondering to himself why fingers always pointed to whatever groups had crossed the Atlantic last. He then thanked the two friends and left, walking out with his usual confident stride. Once clear of the hotel, he checked his watch and sped up Madison to 59th, then west a block to the Plaza Hotel on Fifth. He needed to finish this next interview and get to the site of the fire. Preoccupied, McClusky tripped over a newsstand and righted himself in time to avoid dirtying his well-pressed suit. Too much to sort out.

At the Plaza, McClusky found novelist Archibald Clavering Gunter in the lobby. Gunter repeated the story he told a reporter, the story that Big Bill Devery relayed an hour earlier. A strange man flicking a cigar too close to a lace curtain. Unlike Devery, Gunter told the story with a novelist's pacing and images. McClusky could see the spark alighting the lace. Another witness, certain of the cause. Three so far: cigar, anarchists, boilers.

Elbridge Gerry

Thirty thousand dollars. The day after the fire, Joseph Cody, the contractor hired by the city, sent a letter by messenger informing Elbridge Gerry that as the owner of the Windsor and the land on which it once stood, he should expect a thirty-thousand dollar bill for removing debris. The amount concerned Elbridge less than the day's pronouncements by city officials, self-righteous in their patter. They speechified, offering ideas on what might have prevented the fire, giving short shrift to hotel manager Warren Leland's compliance with the fire code. Warren had done nothing wrong. Certainly, Elbridge himself had done nothing wrong.

That infernal knock again, with the servants scurrying to answer. He could escape to the New York Yacht Club on the corner of 26th and Madison. He could hide out in the billiards room or the model room. No, the paintings and models of yachts there would remind him of allegations that he had profited unethically from the sale of those yachts. Better to lie low in his summer estate in Newport or his wife's house upstate. Would reporters find him there, too?

"Mr. Donald Easton, sir," the butler said, standing in the doorway, looking nervous, afraid to step beyond the threshold. The butler held out his hand. "With his calling card, sir. Again. He came this morning. We sent him away, as you asked. Do you want us to send him away again?"

"Come in, come in," Elbridge said. The butler, glancing down, had registered his employer's irritation. Elbridge studied the card for the second time that day. President of the New York Board of Fire Underwriters.

Maybe worse to continue to avoid the man. "Bring him up." Elbridge paced for a minute, unsure what to expect.

Donald Easton, wearing a decent suit, looked about fifty. Tall, clean-shaven. He seemed respectful, but not obsequious. Elbridge suspected Easton had begun his career as a firefighter.

Mr. Gerry, I am sorry to meet you under these tragic circumstances."

"Have you come from the site?"

"Yes, I walked around the block yesterday evening, a few hours after the start of the fire. And an hour today. It started to rain as I was there, but not enough to stop the smoldering. As you can see from my card, I serve as President of the Board of Fire Underwriters. Before that, I served as head of the Fire Patrol Committee of the Underwriters. I work to minimize fire damage and losses to insured properties. We strive to decrease insurance claims."

Elbridge knew to sit tight, not to take the bait. The man continued in a kindly tone, a formal tone. He glanced quickly at the books and artwork around him, then pulled his eyes back to the task at hand.

"Before I came here," Easton said, "I talked to the inspectors—several have already looked over the site. This fire did not give anyone an opportunity to minimize losses. The hotel is a total ruin. And we must not forget the loss of life, which I cannot fathom."

Elbridge picked up on the cue.

"How many men are gone?"

"Oh, sir, more women than men. Maybe twenty. Thirty. Fifty. We don't know yet. The firefighters and the police continue to look for bodies."

"Tragic."

"Yes." Easton paused, lowered his eyes, then raised them to look directly at Elbridge. "I am here as a courtesy, to tell you what I have told the reporters, which will appear in the papers tomorrow. You are a businessman, so I will cut to the chase. I estimate the loss at one million dollars. That's the loss likely to be covered by insurers. According to the records on file—I checked last night—you insured the building itself for $600,000 and the contents at $275,000. You insured the rents for $75,000, to cover the first year of reduced income. I'm estimating that the guests lost valuables worth about $200,000, perhaps more. Some of them carried their own insurance policies. Some didn't, but that's not your problem and Mr. Leland did provide a hotel safe if they had chosen to use it. By the way, between us and not for sharing, Mr. Leland has a life insurance policy of $10,168. He somehow made it out."

Elbridge chose to ignore Easton's "somehow."

"I would expect such a policy, given the needs of his family," Elbridge said.

"Now, Mr. Gerry, back to the Windsor. A number of companies—twenty-six—distributed the insurance among themselves, but the largest of the insurers is Liverpool and London. That company can withstand the loss. As of today, though it is early in the investigation, I see no problem with your claims. Whether the fire was caused by a careless smoker or a band of robbers—I've heard both—I foresee no allegation that you committed any wrongdoing. Of course, if the investigators on the site discover Mr. Leland to be criminally negligent in complying with the fire code, that would reflect badly on you since he's your employee, but I know Warren, and I don't expect negligence to be the case. Perhaps some of his employees were less than vigilant, but not legally negligent. In short, I think you have no cause to worry. The fire inspectors will continue their investigation, but they have little to investigate because the hotel is ash. They doubt they will find the origin of the fire or proof of arson."

As Easton spoke, Elbridge maintained his impassive look. But now it was his turn. "Mr. Easton, I thank you for this update. I am certain Warren Leland and his employees took all reasonable preventive measures. I have no doubt that my insurers will honor my claims. But since you have been forthcoming, I will be forthcoming as well. A man in my position depends on reputation as well as fortune. I do not enjoy being associated with gossip on negligence."

Easton narrowed his eyes and dropped his chin.

"And, of course, I do not enjoy being associated with death. Terrible, such loss of life. I will be grateful for anything you can do to ensure that the newspapers report the accident fairly. My family, and my relations, the Goelets, we do not need bad—and unfair—publicity."

Easton offered a quick nod. Then he looked beyond Elbridge at the far wall, opened his mouth to speak, waited a second, then started.

"One more item, Mr. Gerry, before I leave. As I am sure you know from the newspapers, the very newspapers you and I often question, here in New York, in a few instances, men of means who face charges of negligence in accidents have been known to make certain offerings to inspectors or agents, offerings that could sway their reports. You would never stoop to such practices, and you have no need to. But since you bring up appearances, I thought it prudent to remind you that reporters, knowing your ability to influence others and knowing that you support Tammany Hall, might suspect you are using that influence. I urge you to keep a low profile until this fire leaves the front pages. I hope you don't mind my speaking freely."

"Tammany Hall. Those connections with the Democratic political organization simply help with my legal and charitable work. That's all. I understand the problem with perceptions and shall continue to be careful. You and I think alike, Mr. Easton."

Joseph Cody

A few months before the fire, when contractor Joseph Cody landed a contract offered by the Buildings Department to handle demolition for the city, that feat cost him just a lunch or two, not much in the way of bribes. After growing his business for years, Cody had risen to the top with his most lucrative contract to date. He celebrated with family, and with the twenty workers he kept on the payroll, mostly Irish, all good men.

On the morning of March 18, Joe Cody stood in the rubble with Buildings Commissioner Thomas Brady, the boss on this job. "Two hundred and fifty men, you think?" Cody asked, tipping his head to the side. "I have twenty."

"Not enough. Last night, I asked Tammany Hall to put a call out. To send word to barkeeps. Maybe they can find you more micks. The Tammany bosses keep watch on the greenhorns, the ones who become Americans and can vote. Mostly that's the Irish. But now Tammany's cozying up to Italians, too. If the bosses and the barkeeps run out of Irish, they'll send over those new foreigners, fresh off the boats. We might get bohunks, dagos, polacks—who knows what. With me being Brady and you being Cody, I wish we could hire our kind."

Cody tightened his lips. Fixing his eyes beyond Brady for a second, he switched the talk from country of birth to drinking habits. Safer territory. "And if Tammany rounds up men from the Bowery flophouses, we'll get drunks. Not what either of us signed on for, right?"

Brady, shrugging, sat down on a wide pile of rubble. Cody hesitated for an imperceptible second, then sat down, too. He pulled a notebook and pencil from his pocket. The men began to tally the equipment they needed to find in a hurry. Eighty wheelbarrows, a hundred and twenty-five shovels, six wagons. For a start. Explosives too.

Cody didn't recognize the well-dressed man swaggering toward him at a fast clip. The stranger tipped his bowler in recognition to Brady and extended his gloved hand to Cody.

Brady did the honors as he and Cody stood. "George, meet Joe Cody, a good man, head of the workers that'll clean up this place. Joe, meet George McClusky, Chief of the Police Detective Bureau. He's already seen this rubble—he was here with me and Big Bill last night. Don't let Detective McClusky's fancy clothes fool you." Brady grinned and touched McClusky's soft wool coat. "He's a good man, gets the job done."

"Gentlemen, sorry to join you so late this morning. I had to interview two men first—Big Bill's request. I came as fast as I could. Mr. Cody, good to meet you."

Cody looked down at his dirt-encrusted boots. Both Brady and McClusky had called Police Chief Devery Big Bill—all buddies. Cody had entered the inner circle.

"To make up lost time, I'll get right to the point," McClusky continued. "I need to make sure nothing happens to any valuables your men find. How many do you expect to hire?"

"Two hundred fifty," Brady and Cody said in unison.

"See there," Cody said, pointing. "The line of men looking for work is growing."

"Some of them will be Italians," McClusky said. Cody noted that the detective didn't say dagos. "Let's get ahead of the trouble their mischief might bring down on my detectives. Some of the laborers will read those articles about lost jewels. Even if they're hired to find bodies and cart away bricks, they're going to hunt around for more." McClusky paused and looked Cody in the eye for a minute. Cody nodded, slightly. "We're going to work out a way to keep track of the rascals. Make sure they don't get away with anything."

"Ya know, some of the men are regular workers for me. I can vouch for them."

"I'm sure, Mr. Cody."

"No need for the Mr. Call me Joe."

"Good, Joe," McClusky said without reciprocating. "Here's what might make you feel better. Put your own blokes, I assume they're Irish, in charge of the new laborers—we'll split the new ones up into teams of ten or twelve. Your men can be the foremen and approve the timecards. I'll assign two detectives to each side of the rubble. They'll watch the laborers. The order is bodies first, then rubble, then property, but tell them to give all property to a detective immediately.

"A few other precautions," McClusky continued. "We're setting up a perimeter of ropes. The laborers need to stay within those ropes. If they find jewelry, they can't turn it over to a friend on the sidewalk. And I'll assign a few plainclothesmen to dress as laborers and mix with them. More sets of eyes. Also, when the workers sign on, we'll give them a brass tag to wear, with a number on it. One of my junior men is on his way with tags we keep in storage. No one can come here off the street and claim to be a worker. And we'll check their pockets when they leave."

"Good idea, Detective," Cody said. "My men are up to it. They can manage the drifters."

"How are you going to handle shifts and wages?" Brady asked.

"Three shifts, eight hours a shift," Cody said, looking for a reaction, at least from Brady. He was listening. "Twenty-five cents per hour for laborers, thirty cents per hour for hod carriers, let's say thirty-seven cents per hour for the foremen. More for Sundays and hazardous work. Well, it's all hazardous, but you know what I mean."

Cody looked to Brady for approval. The Building Commissioner obliged. "Sounds fair. No need for them to nick a gem to pay for dinner."

"Just tell me, Detective McClusky..." Joe said.

"Ah, call me George."

Cody smiled. The detective must be warming up.

"Good George. Tell me, is there a particular reason you're worried about filching?" Cody prized his Irish blood as much as the next guy, but his daughter married an Italian. No need to mention that. Two years ago, Cody stopped making dago jokes.

"We're going to have all types here, Joe, a lot of desperate men. Can't be too careful. The rich, sitting in their posh hotels and mansions, they'll watch every move 'til they get their jewels back."

Cody shifted his shoulders.

"One more thing I should tell you while we're all together," Commissioner Brady said. "Last night, I talked to Big Bill about building a shed, a shanty sort of, here on Fifth. Just a little room. Joe can use it as a payroll office for the workers and, if we need to, as a temporary holding spot for jewels and bodies."

As the men parted, McClusky thanked them. "Great, we're all in agreement on arrangements." Brady smiled broadly. Cody walked away with a grim face that no one could see. He would start with 250 laborers. By the end of the week the number would be up to 900, a number that would include many Italians. Whatever the number, Cody figured that ninety-eight percent of those men would be hard-working laborers trying to feed their families. McClusky's men would be watching all of them.

Clayton Byrne

The morning after the fire, Clayton Byrne trudged out of his squalid room in the flophouse to join the line at the outhouse in back. He tried to fix his mind on San Francisco—that city should be far enough away. Would Bridget go with him? Or was she angry, blaming him? Molly and Tara would blame him. And the three fellas he recruited? Oh, damn, his bowels—the line moved too slowly.

"Yeah, at that hotel. The one that burned."

Clay's mind shifted from his rattling innards to the chatter around him. Two down-and-out men ahead in line knew about the fire.

"Thirty cents an hour's what I heard in the saloon last night. Course, they want Tammany men, Irish if they can get 'em. But if they don't have enough micks they'll hire anyone who's willing to cart away bricks. And hunt for bodies." Some of the bum's words whistled through gaps in his teeth. "And maybe jewels."

"Not sure I can handle the smell. Those corpses gonna stink soon," a young man in rags said to the bum with missing teeth.

The fire must have been even worse than he feared. Clay stopped worrying about the slow-moving line and focused on the Windsor. He planned to go there anyway, to check on his men. He'd assigned Sean to the fourth floor, Lon to the second, and Felix to the smoking parlor and then the McKinley suite. After the heist, they would find each other at the corner of Madison and 47th, but they must have run off, as he did, trying to escape the commotion. Who knows where they were now? And he needed to learn what happened to the old woman in the lilac-colored nightgown. Clay never panicked, not until yesterday. Unnerved, he had shot her. He wished he could forget, but he remembered the blood. Had her body burned in the fire?

Maybe finding Bridget, then running West wasn't his only choice. If he hadn't left a trail—if his gang kept quiet and if the old lady burned—he could make something of the plan he had the day before, especially if he could work the site. The outhouse door opened, and the man behind him gave a push. Clay barely smelled the stench.

He saw a pail in the yard and washed up in dirty water. His throat hurt from the smoke, but his voice was no longer raspy. He looked down at his coat. Rough, not the finest of leathers. Still, Clay thought, it might not be what labor recruiters expected. He left his coat under his cot and walked a block to a rag dealer, where he purchased a stained cloth coat and brown wool workman's cap, big enough to pull down over his forehead. Tucking his red hair under the cap, he hurried north for the long walk to the Windsor, afraid he might be too late.

Approaching 37th Street, Clay smelled lingering smoke, heavier with each block. The noise of men and machinery grew. At the site, he saw a line of forty men, none well dressed. He joined them as more men ran up behind him. A few officials milled around the edge of the line. They talked a lot, shared papers, pointed here and there, arranging things. The line hardly moved. A bald man ahead of Clay stood reading a paper, then folded it and got ready to toss it onto a pile of debris.

"Hey, mind if I read that?"

"Be my guest. This place was hell yesterday. Still is."

Clay skimmed the three-page story of the fire, looking for warning signs, any mention of his name or appearance. Nothing. Then that notice. John Connolly, the fifty-year-old journeyman carpenter at the Windsor. Jumped to his death from the fourth floor, dying an hour later of burns, a compound fracture of the skull, internal injuries. Clay adjusted his cap, using his thumb to swipe his eye. He remembered the carpenter talking about his sons, teasing his apprentice about Bridget, giving him assignments in public rooms. The night before, staring at the ceiling, Clay's guilt had centered on the old woman in the lilac-colored nightgown, not on the others, not on anyone he knew. Shivering in line now, he willed himself to forget Connolly, to stay focused. At least Connolly would not be around to see the workers, to identify anyone, to remember that Clay wanted to work in the guests' rooms, to put two and two together.

After what seemed forever, the man waiting behind Clay gave him a nudge. "Move it. You're at the front." The bald man standing ahead of Clay, the one who had the newspaper, walked away with a smile and some things in his hand. He passed muster. Now Clay faced an agent shouldering a large canvas bag filled with papers and items that clanged, like metal or tin.

"Name and previous work experience?" The official with the paperwork ran his eyes over Clay, up and down.

"Clayton Byrne. I'm a carpenter. Out of work."

"Back problems? Diseases?"

"No sir, healthy. Willing to work hard. I need the wages."

"Any chit from Tammany?"

"No sir, but I can try for one if you want."

The agent looked Clay over again, maybe registering that whether he had a friend at Tammany Hall or not, he was probably Irish.

"Here's a brass tag, number 199. Pin it on. Here's your timecard. Get it signed, in and out. Two dollars per day. If you find property, don't hold it, even for a minute. Give it to a detective or an officer. Now, over there." He pointed. "Gillespie's team."

Finally, some luck. Gillespie's team worked near the corner of Fifth and 46th, close to the old woman's part of the hotel, close to where Sean went, close to the Kirk jewels.

Gillespie gathered the newcomers to his team. He stood on a pile of bricks, either to look important or to ensure the men could hear. "You use the tools over there." Shouting above the noise, Gillespie pointed to a crate of picks and shovels. "Dig through the rubble. Look first for bodies, then for property. If you find papers or jewels, tell me, right away. I'll find a copper to guard 'em. Anyone fools around, pockets anything, you're out of here." Clay kept his grin to himself—another warning, so the coppers knew there were jewels around.

That day, Clay worked alongside the others—Irishmen who seemed to know only the other Irish, Italians who seemed to know only the other Italians, Slavs who seemed to know only the other Slavs. Gillespie tried to mix it up. He partnered Clay with Luca, another out-of-work carpenter. Other than gestures to his partner, and exchanged curses as the rain started, Clay kept to himself. He talked little, while his eyes wandered.

Alice Price

Still in a hospital bed two days after the fire, Alice Price had a visitor—one of the long-term Windsor guests, a sharp-eyed older woman who often sat at the Windsor's widows' table for dinner and had the good sense to go shopping at the time of the fire. Alice should have been doped up, too sleepy to converse with her visitor, but hours had passed since she received morphine. The overwhelmed doctors had exhausted their supply and awaited a delivery. Even the pleas of the private duty nurse sitting in the ward, hired by Alice's brother-in-law, Governor Candler of Georgia, failed to speed up the delivery. Alice forced herself to ignore the pain in her right hip, to ignore the numbness in her right leg, and to turn the wait to her advantage. She would ply the visitor with questions about the hotel guests, those who were part of her world.

"How is Mrs. Henry Wharton? From the sixth floor," Alice asked, propping herself up on her elbows, careful of her bandaged hands. Mrs. Wharton's husband had been a chaplain for the Confederate Army.

"Just bruised," the visitor said.

"Glory be. And Colonel Cowardin, from the third floor?" Alice asked. The president of the *Richmond Dispatch*.

"Escaped."

Alice smiled. "Joseph Lamotte Morgan?" He had hosted Jeff Davis's widow, Varina, at a dinner party the previous year at the Windsor.

"Escaped."

Another smile. "General John Cox Underwood? From four." He was captured in '63 by the Union.

"Escaped."

"Colonel Thomas Ochiltree." He had been a Confederate officer. Odd that Abner McKinley befriended him.

"Escaped too."

"Margaret Auze? Across the hall from me on five." Her dead brother had been a Confederate brigadier general.

"Missing. Presumed dead."

Alice stared at the visitor, winced. The private nurse looked at both women, shook her head, then turned aside.

One more. "Dora Hoffman? The spinster's elderly brother had fought with Stonewall Jackson.

"Dead," the visitor said.

Another wince. Finally, Alice ran out of sympathetic guests connected with gray. She moved on to her Union-leaning friend. "Mehitable Henry?"

Alice said the strange name softly. The visitor put her hand to her ear in a come-again gesture.

"Mehitable Henry?" Just loud enough.

"Ahhh, Mehitable. The blunt widow from our table. She lingered in agony for a day at Roosevelt Hospital. Serious burns and internal injuries. She died three hours ago."

"Oh, my," Alice said to her visitor. "So much smoke. I lost sight of Mehitable. Dr. McPhatter—he tried to help us—he must have lost sight of her for a minute, too. That's why he sent me down first. Or maybe he sent me down first because I was the youngest. But it wouldn't have mattered, right? None of us knew how to use a rope."

The visitor stared at Alice, then spoke, looking down. "Understandable."

"I have a picture in my head. Mehitable in the smoke. Wheezing. I'll have to tell Dr. McPhatter that she didn't make it. You're sure I couldn't have done more?" Alice waited only a second for an answer, then asked about her belongings, talking over the visitor's murmured, mild assurances. Alice continued to chatter as the visitor and nurse locked eyes.

Alice asked a few more questions. Nothing about Tilly Brown. Alice had forgotten about her maid.

Marguerite Wells

The day after the fire Marguerite sought out Theodate Pope, to be certain she and her parents had survived the fire, as Angelica had reported, and to confirm arrangements for lunch on the 20th. It didn't take long. Marguerite started with the Hoffman House clerk. That hotel had more refugees than any other. Success. The clerk confirmed that the Popes had registered there, right before the Wellses. Marguerite wrote a note and received one back that evening. "So relieved you escaped. Am eager to see you, but lunch on the 20th will no longer be possible. I promised my father to help him relocate paintings he kept at the Windsor. We have an appointment at a warehouse I need to check for fireproofing. Let us find another time."

Marguerite recalled that Angelica had asked, in a strange tone, about Theodate, so she called the Gerry mansion and left a message with the butler. "Miss Pope will be unable to join us for lunch on the 20th." Angelica sent a note back. "Thank you, Marguerite." Odd that Angelica seemed relieved, not disappointed.

Before Marguerite could suggest another lunch date to Theodate, she saw her friend in the Hoffman House lobby on Sunday morning, March 19. Alongside Theodate walked a lovely woman, taller than average, and a well-dressed man with a full head of white hair and a square jaw—a more masculine version of Theodate's jaw. Must be her parents. Behind the three walked a stout woman, plainly dressed, her hair in pale braids around her head and her hands wrapped in gauze. The two friends embraced.

"Marguerite, meet my parents, Ada and Alfred Pope. I'm so relieved to see you, even though I knew you survived. I stood on 46th Street, so I saw you escape."

Marguerite startled at the word "saw," then fiddled with her face. Quickly, she asked the woman in the plain dress how badly her hands hurt.

"Thank you for asking, miss. They still hurt, but at least we're all alive."

"Marguerite, this is Lotte Hansen, our maid. She was ironing in the basement, and when she went upstairs with Mother's dress, she heard the cries." Marguerite, still trying to steady herself after hearing the word "saw," stared at Lotte, who bit her bottom lip.

"Couldn't save Miz Ada's dress."

"I did love that dress, Lotte." Theodate ignored her mother's remark and asked after Marguerite's parents. Alfred Pope seemed distracted and kept his eyes on the front door. Soon, he excused himself, saying he had urgent business, while the women lingered.

Mrs. Pope explained. "My husband retrieved his paintings from our suite at the Windsor and asked the drugstore owner across the street to store them for a night or two." As Theodate's Mother spoke, Marguerite saw Theodate look away, toward nothing in the distance. Her mother continued. "Now he's out reviewing warehouses, and Theodate has offered to check those that he likes, especially to check for security. We are wary after the fire. You know, Theo trained with Princeton architects. Don't ask me why. Apparently, she didn't learn about fire prevention materials." For an instant, Ada Pope frowned at her daughter. "Today my husband is visiting a warehouse a friend uses. Louisine Havemeyer. You might recognize the name from the newspapers. The woman is an art collector."

"Mother, I am certain that Marguerite recognizes Louisine's name."

"Yes, I do. I believe Mrs. Havemeyer works on behalf of the Suffragist Movement too—one of my interests."

A small smile from Mrs. Pope.

"Marguerite, my mother shares our interest in the Movement." Theodate seemed to have found one area where she could defend the snobbish woman. "I am afraid my father does not, though he tolerates my interest as long as I don't take it up." Emphasis on the "I." "I hope we can introduce Marguerite to Louisine one day, when we are all in the city and the fire is a faint memory. And Mother, I hope you don't mind, but Marguerite and I are trying to plan lunch together, the two of us, before her family sails to France. I'd like to hear about her teaching and her work for the movement." Mrs. Pope nodded. Marguerite felt relief that Theodate was not asking her mother to join.

Theodate suggested lunch at Dorlon's Oyster House, two blocks south of the Hoffman House, on Tuesday. Marguerite would have just enough time that day since she would be sailing to Le Havre that evening with her parents. Le Havre—far away from the Windsor.

Thomas Brady

Buildings Commissioner Thomas Brady heard his doorbell again. More reporters, even on a Sunday, in the early morning, two days after the fire. He'd talk to them on the front porch to provide shelter from the rain. If he invited them inside they'd linger.

"Welcome. Not enough coffee in the pot for all you thirsty reporters. All right, you first." He pointed to one of the younger men.

"Commissioner Brady, what do you think of the rumors that a gang of thieves started the fire, as a distraction?"

"Rubbish. Don't blame thieves. And don't blame a cigar smoker. Like Fire Chief Hugh Bonner said to you chaps yesterday. Bonner was there, in the middle of it all. He should know. Blame the hotel. A firetrap. And the Windsor's not the only firetrap in this city. Bonner told you he knows of six others. I'd say that's an undercount. You could ask Fire Commissioner John Scannell too. He agrees with Bonner." No need to add that Detective McClusky had just cleared Scannell's brother from the charge of accepting a bribe to ease an applicant into a fireman's job, or that Scannell, recovering from the bad publicity, was lying low and going along with whatever other officials said.

"Would you care to elaborate, Mr. Brady? Since you're Buildings Commissioner and know buildings better than anyone. Which hotels should our readers avoid?"

"Trying to make trouble, eh? No, Chief Bonner wouldn't name them for you, and I won't either. Yes, I blame the hotel. But the blame goes beyond that. The hotels—all the ones on Bonner's mind—they're up to code. The

1882 code." Brady said the year slowly. Let that sink in. "You want a culprit to blame. Look at the code, the code, men. When the Windsor opened, the manager—wasn't Warren Leland then—had no fire escapes. We told the manager to add four. He dragged his heels for a few years, but he added them. The hotel followed the law, the antiquated law." This time Brady dragged out the word antiquated. "Sure, the code was modified, improved a little in '92, but the changes only applied to new buildings. I can't condemn older buildings that live up to the '82 code. All I can say is that guests registering at the city's older hotels might want to investigate before they register." Brady moved his head and eyes to signal that the oldest reporter could take his turn.

"Let's talk about the code. What's wrong with it?"

"How much time do you have?" Brady let himself snicker. "I'll do the basics, and this applies to both the '82 code and somewhat to the '92 changes. You can't build a hotel with beautiful wood and have no fireproofing. Long halls need firewalls. That way, if the fire starts in one place, it won't spread to another place. The paths to the stairs and the fire escapes should be obvious. Guests need instructions on how to use fire ropes, though I'm not sure those are a good idea in any case. Women clambering down ropes, in skirts. Ha. And with all this new electricity, we need different kinds of codes to prevent fires caused by that equipment."

"So why don't you make those changes?" The short reporter took his turn.

"Wish that was my department, but it ain't. We have what some call jurisdictional disputes. Those state lawmakers in Albany, today they're debating three bills to improve the code. And at the same time, the Building Code Commission is in session, hard at work on their own changes. Who knows what they'll come up with? Or when? And the city's Municipal Assembly wants to get in the act, too. A kitchen with too many cooks."

Brady felt confidence in his abilities as a good builder. With the annex to Macy's that his company had built on 14th Street, he took every precaution—firewalls, steel staircases, fireproof insulation. He understood fire traps and how to avoid them. Could he have pushed for better codes, or codes that included older construction? He went back into his warm house, for the one cup of coffee remaining on the stove. He accepted no blame, not from the carpers, not from himself.

Bridget Dunne

Sunday, Bridget thought, two days after the fire, and still no sign of Clay. She had to start making plans. "Don't know how long we'll stay here," she told Molly and Tara, after Claire left for her cleaning job. No rest on Sundays. "Clay will send word. I'm sure he's not caught." She told herself he got out of the building, alive. "Even if the coppers nabbed him, he'll keep us out of it. The other chaps will stay quiet, too. They follow Clay." Bridget read in the papers that two coppers caught Felix Kain with Abner McKinley's possessions. But Tara couldn't read, and if Molly had read the stories about Felix in the boarders' newspapers, it wouldn't matter because she didn't know the names of Clay's gang.

"Food, food too, need to figure that out." The landlady had been kind the first day, offering meals around her boarding table. By the second day, she stopped her offers. "And we'll need dresses." The three had escaped with nothing besides their uniforms and their coats, all smelling of smoke.

When Claire returned after work, she opened the door to her room, shot her uninvited visitors a look. Bridget knew the meaning—you're still here?

"Claire, we'll find other lodgings within a week. I just told your landlady that too. Promise." Bridget kept her head high as she talked. She wouldn't beg. "We need a little while to figure things out, look for a flat, look for work. And we need to borrow some clothes, even if the fit isn't right. One more thing." Bridget took a deep breath. "I have a sweetheart now. Clay's his name. I didn't tell you because he's a tradesman, a carpenter, and I know you think I should aim higher." Bridget looked straight at Claire, avoided Molly and Tara. "Clay knows I have a sister, and he might remember where you live. He'll worry about me. He might come here."

"Can't you go to his place?" Claire arched an eyebrow, smugly.

Bridget knew where Clay lived. She couldn't go there. Might be coppers around.

"Claire, he used to work at the Windsor for a few months. He's a hothead. Made some enemies. He might think someone wants to frame him for the fire. I guess he's in hiding."

Bridget saw Molly and Tara lock eyes. Claire watched them, then stared at her sister. Bridget understood that stare. Claire thought she heard a lie. Another lie, she would think.

"One week, Bridge. That's all I can take of this crowding—four in a room hardly big enough for one."

Later that night, while Claire chatted with a boarder and Molly was in the washroom, Tara asked the question Bridget had been waiting for. "Bridge, if Clay thinks you might be here, with Claire, will he tell Sean? I'm worried sick that if they separated, Sean won't know where to find me."

"No worries, Tara. Clay takes care of his gang. That's why Lon and Felix keep working for him. Clay and Sean will turn up."

The next day, Monday, the maids kept to themselves. They didn't ask much of Mrs. Brownhill, just some tea and toast. They filched only a little from the pantry when she was in the yard hanging wash. They stayed quiet. Bridget and Molly took turns wearing one of Claire's dresses, going out for air, donning Claire's biggest bonnet. Buying a little food with the five spot Bridget always kept in her undergarments. Tara didn't join them. She fussed with her hair, pacing. In the early afternoon, Bridget watched Tara look out the attic window, then turn around.

"Bridge, I need to talk to Sean's parents. See if they heard from him. Maybe they can tell him where to find me." She paused, staring at Bridget. "I know. I'm scared the coppers will be watching their place."

"Tara," Bridget said, "they might be watching because of Sean's connection to those Paterson rabble-rousers, right?"

Slight nod. Tara understood to keep mum in front of Molly about Sean working for Clay, maybe being in trouble for more than hanging around with anarchists.

"You gotta go in disguise, Tara." Bridget patted down a pillow. "Stuff this pillow around your waist to change your shape and carry wash. Like you're bringing it back to the Macks, all folded nice—we'll nick some sheets from Mrs. Brownhill's chest—then you can crumple the sheets up and bring the basket back, like they gave you more dirty knickers."

"Ahhh, Bridge, as though Sean's parents could afford a girl to do laundry." Tara laughed, the first time in days. Ten minutes later a pudgy washerwoman descended the stairs of the boarding house.

The Macks didn't live far—a short streetcar ride. Tara was back in an hour. Her feet sounded heavy on the floor. Maybe because she carried a load of laundry. The minute Tara opened the door to the attic room, she dropped the basket and fell on the bed, sobbing.

"Nothing. They heard nothing. They sent one of the uncles to check on his room. He spotted coppers who must have been looking for Sean. The uncle knew to be careful. But he found Sean's landlady. Said Sean hadn't been at breakfast or dinner for a few days. Jesus, Mary, and Joseph, his ma's crying too."

"Those anarchists got him into hot water," Bridget said. She patted Tara's shoulder but didn't say much. All the girls' sweethearts were missing and in trouble. Better for them to worry about those sweethearts than about shared guilt.

Tara's fruitless excursion changed the air in the room from bad to worse. By dinner time, she shifted her chatter from her lover to money, joining Molly's worry about their missing bonus. They expected Clay to pay up, wherever he was. Bridget saw the two girls talking in the hall. Maybe they thought she had pocketed their share. Damn, she would think that if Tara's Sean and Molly's Frank had made all the plans and settled on the division of the haul themselves.

Still no word from Clay, three days after the fire. Did he forget about Claire, or forget where she lived? Or had his own blaze killed him?

Angelica Gerry

Walking downstairs for breakfast, Angelica spotted the butler reading the *New York Times* in a hushed voice to two maids crowding at his side. He closed the paper as he heard her footsteps. This would not do. She strode up to him.

"You know, it's our paper, Commodore Gerry's paper."

The butler looked at her in surprise. She never reprimanded the servants. Left that task to her mother.

"Of course, miss." He quickly handed her the newspaper and shooed away the maids. "I haven't heard the Commodore come downstairs yet. I didn't think he would mind a glance."

Angelica took in the butler's embarrassed expression.

"I see. But do tell me what you found so fascinating."

Another embarrassed expression. Then silence.

"You must. Point it out."

"Page eight." She could barely hear his whisper.

Angelica pulled the paper away from the butler, more rudely than she intended. Sheepishly, he also handed her the *Sun* and the *New York Journal and Advertiser*, which he had tucked under his arm. She carried the papers to the parlor. She started with the *Times*, going right to page eight. A hateful headline. "Labor Men Think Public Should Know the Unsafe Buildings. Attack on Elbridge T. Gerry."

Beneath the headline, the story did not improve. "Among the subjects discussed by the Central Federated Union yesterday was the Windsor Hotel Fire. Delegate W. A. Perrine of the Iron Molders said that the fire was a subject which the body could not possibly overlook. The fire involved a criminal carelessness and neglect of duty on the part of self-styled philanthropists and of city officials who had sworn to do their duty and were well paid for it." The reporter quoted Perrine. "'If Elbridge T. Gerry, who derived such an enormous income from the building, had taken…trouble to make the hotel safe…this terrible catastrophe would never have occurred. This would have been a more useful and a better way to act as a philanthropist.

"'President Brady of the Department of Buildings,'" Perrine went on, "'also was, according to his own admission, aware of the condition of the building, and said that he knew that hundreds of other buildings, which he would not specify, were also firetraps. I am also astonished at the assertation of Chief Bonner that he knew for a long time about the condition of the Windsor Hotel.'"

Angelica put down The *Times* and picked up The *Sun*. A similar story ran on page two with the headline "Labor Men Blame Gerry." Next, she opened The *New York Journal and Advertiser*, where she found more slime on page three.

"Commodore Elbridge Gerry is a rich man and a humane one. He is President of the Society for the Prevention of Cruelty to Children…. But as the owner of the Windsor Hotel, the Commodore thought it more important to save a little money for himself than to save dozens of children and women from a hideous death. Although he had repeatedly been warned that the hotel was a firetrap and had been able to measure the extent of its danger in the unimpeachable barometrical reading of increased insurance rates, he refused to make any changes in its construction of any but absolutely unavoidable repairs. He did not even obey the laws requiring the building to be equipped with proper fire escapes."

The *Journal* couldn't get enough of the story. They ran an editorial. "There is one man in New York who will not express his views. He is Elbridge T. Gerry, and his home is a fireproof palace on Fifth Avenue. He has another fireproof palace at Newport and enough millions that he can live in a fireproof palace in any part of the world he pleases. The public is deeply interested in Mr. Gerry's views in regard to the awful tragedy at that tinder box hotel, but he is not willing to let the public know what they are. 'No,' said the butler at Mr. Gerry's door last night, 'I am instructed to tell every newspaper man—and there have been many of them here—that Mr. Gerry absolutely refuses to see any of them.'"

That very butler coughed, then entered the parlor. His eyes moved to Angelica's clenched fists.

"Miss Gerry, may we bring you coffee here." He was a kind man and wanted to make sure she continued to breathe. She had treated him unfairly.

"We have no choice. I can't keep these from Father. And you can't throw them out. It's best that I bring them to him myself." The butler relaxed his shoulders, offered a slight nod in agreement and in sympathy.

Marguerite Wells

While Marguerite fretted about her behavior during her escape from the fire, the other survivors resting at the Hoffman House focused on causes and blame. Heading the list was waiter John Foy's statement that he had seen a man, probably not a guest, flick his cigar onto a lace curtain. Three other theories competed with the cigar. A gang planned the fire to cover up their thieving. Or fun-loving hotel workers failed to monitor circuits and boilers. Or Buildings Commissioner Thomas Brady too readily accepted the city's weak building code and didn't enforce even its inadequate precautions. Marguerite heard a fifth theory that hit the Wells family hard. Manager Warren Leland and owner Elbridge Gerry did not take proper precautions to ensure the safety of their guests.

Edward Wells bristled when faultfinders mentioned Elbridge Gerry. The Wellses had dined with that gentleman aboard the RMS *Campania* at Captain Hubbard's table a year earlier. So when Angelica Gerry came to meet the Wellses for lunch in the dining room of the Hoffman House on March 20, three days after the fire, Marguerite's papa felt anxious and protective. Two hours before their lunch, Angelica sent a message asking Mr. Wells to reserve a table toward the back and asking to meet the family on a side street. They could enter the restaurant through the back door, rather than through the lobby. Marguerite realized she should have suggested a more secluded restaurant, but her papa, busy replacing his suits and documents, chose to stay in the commercial part of the city.

The three Wellses donned winter coats to walk a half block to the side street. There, they spotted Angelica, her driver standing with her. She wore her hat bent oddly over her face. The minute she saw Marguerite, she ran up and embraced her, even though they had seen each other at the Gerry mansion a week earlier. "Thank God you are unhurt," she said, looking at Edward and Nellie Wells to include them in her relief. Angelica thanked her driver and asked him to return in an hour. The foursome walked through the Hoffman House's back door.

As the maître d' led the way to a rear table, Angelica kept her hat on and chose a chair that allowed her to sit with her back to the crowd. "I am sorry I had to ask for these special arrangements. You see, Father worries that he will be blamed for some vague act of negligence regarding the fire. He did nothing wrong. Mr. Leland did nothing wrong. And I doubt the Windsor's servants did anything wrong."

She stopped as she saw the waiter approach. No one had given any thought to the menu. Angelica looked at Marguerite, at the table, at the linens. Not at the menu. Marguerite's mama noticed.

"Dear, would you like Mr. Wells to order for all of us?" Angelica nodded agreement, with barely a smile. The waiter arrived, looking cheerier than any of his customers.

"A bottle of burgundy and sherry for the ladies. Oysters to start. For our entrée, lobster for the ladies, and roast pork for me. Brussels sprouts for all of us. Oh, and sherbet with raspberries for dessert." Never would awkward moments keep the Wellses from food.

"Absolutely nothing wrong," Papa said to Angelica, picking up the conversation again after the waiter walked away. We must try to ignore those stories in the papers. Rubbish, all of them. Your father and Mr. Leland followed the laws of the city. Perhaps those laws should have been updated, but that is for others to decide. Miss Gerry, you should have no worries."

"You are kind to use that welcome word, rubbish. But the stories sting. Mr. Leland is a good man, kind too. And the poor man's wife and daughter died in the fire." Angelica fiddled with her napkin. "Let me see if I can explain my position. I am no longer a debutante, but I attend social functions with my parents, and reporters cover those functions. They know my name, and they know my appearance. I fear that many of the people in this dining room have lost friends or relatives in the fire. You will understand—I have limited my social events this week. And to be honest," she looked at Marguerite, "I didn't wish to see Theodate, since the Popes are part of my parents' set, even though they are from Cleveland. But I badly wanted to see all of you."

"We understand, Miss Gerry." Papa looked Angelica in the eye as he spoke. "No need to make apologies. Tell us, how are your parents faring?"

"Not well." Her eyes watered over. "Father is in hiding. And Mother, well, she takes a different approach. She has not turned down a single invitation, and she dresses to the hilt."

Marguerite's papa eyed his wife. "It is always difficult to know when to keep a distance and when to try to get in front of such problems," he said. From his quiet tone, Marguerite guessed he would have chosen a middle ground, between hiding and flaunting. But which stance did he choose three days ago?

Angelica may have seen the look between Marguerite's parents. She glanced at her friend, with a tight smile, then moved the conversation away from the Gerry family distress to the Wells family distress. "Enough about my worries." She looked at the faces around the table. "Your injuries were minor, but how minor? And were you able to contact your relatives, to put them at ease?" Mama answered. Then the question Marguerite feared. "How did you feel about the newspaper coverage you received?"

Marguerite took a drink from her water glass. Her papa answered. "Yes, the coverage. We didn't like all that attention, but it can't hurt with my railroad business connections here in the city. No, it can't hurt for them to see me as, well, in action, relaying my ladies to safety." He said this quietly, with a gentle smile, but with his shoulders back and his chin tilted up.

Marguerite looked at her mother. No expression.

Angelica must have sensed an awkwardness. She changed the subject again. "Now the reporters seem fixated on burial arrangements. Mr. Leland must bury his wife and daughter, and he hasn't forgotten those victims no one has identified or, how do I say it, claimed. Mr. Leland says they won't be buried in Potter's Field. He has offers from owners of different cemeteries. Mr. Leland wanted the Sleepy Hollow Cemetery in Tarrytown. But John Keller, he's the Charities Commissioner, he wants to bury the dead in Kensico Cemetery in Valhalla, a little farther away. You see, Kensico's Board of Directors met each year at the Windsor. They felt connected to the hotel. When they volunteered a free plot and a free train car for mourners, the Commissioner took the offer. But he hasn't told Mr. Leland yet. Mr. Leland called Father to tell him about arrangements for Sleepy Hollow, and the Commissioner called Father to tell him about arrangements for Kensico. What a mess."

Marguerite could see her mama look at Angelica, then past her toward the crowded room. Perhaps Mama was surprised Angelica shared her worries. Marguerite understood. The poor girl couldn't talk to her society friends. Her father forbade such talk. But the Wellses were safe. Their social circles remained far out West.

"Did your father have a say in the selection of cemeteries?" asked Papa. Angelica waited to reply as the waiter arrived with drinks and oysters.

"No. He's using his time in different ways. He writes letters to the newspaper editors, defending himself on charges of ignoring the risk of fire, but aside from that, he wants to stay out of the fray. At least until the coroner's report."

Coroner's report? Marguerite's mouth dried. Her brain clouded. Then she realized the coroner would not be investigating the many versions of the Wellses' escape, which stuck like glue to her mind, but rather the many versions of blame for the actual fire. She felt foolish, self-centered, thankful that no one else saw her preoccupations.

George McClusky

By noon on Monday, March 20, as the Wellses lunched with Angelica Gerry, Chief of Detectives George McClusky itched to resume his investigation of the fire. On Saturday, he had managed to interview a few Windsor guests sheltering at the Hoffman House, but Sunday was a wasted day. According to custom, he couldn't interview witnesses on church day.

Monday morning would be wasted as well. Even though he had closed the bribery case—his detectives found the culprit offering payoffs for firemen's jobs and cleared Fire Commissioner Scannell and his brother—a sensational murder case interrupted McClusky's time. Dentist Samuel Kennedy supposedly bludgeoned to death lady of the night Emeline Reynolds in a shady hotel the previous August. Now, as the trial approached, Big Bill claimed he needed to watch over the case because people tended to trust their dentists, to assume they would use pliers and other tools only for good. Or maybe Big Bill watched over the case to get salacious details. McClusky led the investigation and would be called to testify at the approaching trial.

On Monday morning the district attorney met with McClusky to go over his testimony, with Big Bill sitting in, nodding his head in approval at the prosecution's case. McClusky knew what he was doing, what to say. He didn't need the Chief looking over his shoulder. But he did need Devery's support. The Chief of Detectives was a new position. Devery created it and he could uncreate it. The dentist case put McClusky in the headlines, which his sisters loved. The trial would put him in the headlines again. But the fire nagged at him. Many more deaths than one whore.

Freed from Big Bill's scrutiny, on Monday afternoon, McClusky walked to the Hotel Manhattan at 42nd and Madison, where he interviewed Abner McKinley a few days earlier. Now McClusky needed to see Alfred Fuller, a Windsor guest who escaped without injury, and his ill wife. The papers brimmed with stories about the Fullers—their wealth, their connections, Alfred's alleged offer to pay for his wife's rescue. Wouldn't do to skip the Fullers. A doctor opened the door for McClusky, who introduced himself as Chief of Detectives and suggested they talk in the hall, out of the Fullers' hearing range.

"Doctor, I'm investigating the Windsor fire. Can I question the Fullers about what they saw?"

"You can try. No new physical problems for Mrs. Fuller. She arrived here in a state of shock, along with ailments she has had for months. She is distraught—her daughter and sister, missing."

The doctor led McClusky into the hotel room. Alfred Fuller sat hunched over beside his wife's bed. Fuller had made millions with his stockyards and coal holdings. As though his millions weren't enough, the man claimed to be related to Andrew Carnegie. A stretch, McClusky thought. Alfred's wife Margaretta had two sisters. One, Nancy Bradley, stayed in the Windsor too. The third sister, Lucy, married Thomas Carnegie, the younger brother of Andrew. Alfred Fuller's connection to Andrew Carnegie may have been roundabout, but reporters loved that morsel.

McClusky glanced at Margaretta Fuller, lying in bed. Though not injured in the fire, she appeared to be in a sorry state. Her breathing seemed labored, and her color poor. Margaretta was only one of Alfred Fuller's worries. His daughter Florence shared a Windsor suite with his sister-in-law Nancy, and neither had been seen since the fire three days earlier.

McClusky considered staying away from Fuller, to give the man some peace. But each passing day dulled memories. Turning toward Fuller, McClusky introduced himself and motioned to the hall. Fuller, who had looked barely able to move, jumped up and followed McClusky out the double doors, almost tripping on the heels of the detective who worked at minimizing his usual swagger.

"Any news? About my daughter? My sister-in-law?"

"No, sir, no news. I wish I came with a report. If you are up to it—I apologize for the bad timing—I need to ask you some questions about the fire, about what you saw."

Fuller's look changed again, from eager to incensed.

"I wondered when you would come." His eyes shot darts at McClusky. "Those stories about a cigar smoker flicking an ember onto a lace curtain. Hogwash. One smoker, on one floor—impossible." Fuller clenched his fists. "The entire hotel, all seven floors, burned up in a few minutes, well, maybe a half hour. You fools think one lace curtain did that?"

McClusky ignored the insult. He stared at Fuller, inviting more. "My son was with me. We were with my wife in the parlor of our suite, on the fourth floor, but we went downstairs around 3:00 to buy a paper at the newsstand. That's when we heard screams and saw people storm down the staircase. My son and I were frantic. My wife—you see her over there—she's an invalid, here in the city for treatment. No way she could run to safety. My daughter Florence, she's sixteen, she stayed upstairs with my wife's sister, Nancy Bradley, on the sixth floor. Florence isn't well either, even though she's young." Fuller's eyes welled over.

"Do you want to stop for a minute, Mr. Fuller?"

"No." He paused, started again. "My son and I tried to rescue all of them. We stumbled up the stairs, trying to get to the fourth floor, but the crowd and the smoke, never seen anything like that, made it impossible. By the way, behind me on the stairs, I caught a glimpse of that fellow from across the way, the chef from Gould's house, who said no one paid attention to his warnings. Anyway, I got as far as the third floor. My son, he's younger and fitter, he left the hall and ran to the fire escape. He thought he'd run up it, but he couldn't get there. He turned around and grabbed me. Praise the Lord—when the flames forced us out, the firemen—real heroes—they carried Margaretta down from the fourth floor. Even her Negro nurse. But here's what I need to tell you. On that third floor, well, I think it was the third, but I may have lost count, we saw a man, young, scraggly beard, not running, not dressed like a guest, walking in and out of rooms. Suspicious.

And I smelled oil, or maybe gas. My son smelled it, too. And one more thing. I didn't see a single hotel employee on any floor. No one. Just me and my boy, and frantic guests, and a strange man. Maybe that man was Felix Kain, the thief your men picked up the day of the fire, the one who stole from Abner McKinley. And if I saw one thief, I'm sure there was a gang of 'em, robbers using the parade and the fire as, what do you call it, a diversion. They knew the guests would bolt from their rooms and leave valuables."

McClusky asked a series of questions, but Fuller held to his story. With an arm on the elderly man's shoulder, McClusky guided him back to his wife's bed. Mrs. Fuller looked at her husband, hoping for news of her daughter and sister. Instead, she saw her husband resume his stooping posture and take a seat beside her.

In front of the Hotel Manhattan, shivering in the cold, McClusky bought a *New York Times* from a newspaper boy. Damn. Another witness, jabbering. Why did David Cohen spout off to a reporter when he should have talked to the police? McClusky raced south to the Hoffman House at Broadway and 25th, where Warren Leland, in mourning for his wife and daughter, had set up shop temporarily. The Windsor's clerk, Simeon Leland who ignored the chef's warnings, sat at a makeshift desk in the lobby, looking not the least embarrassed by his reported negligence. Warren Leland had tasked Simeon with keeping track of guests, so relatives could find them. David Cohen, Simeon said, sheltered with relatives a few blocks away. McClusky hustled to the house and found Cohen in the kitchen, sitting beside a woman in her fifties, both drinking coffee.

"I will tell you what I told the reporter yesterday," Cohen said, his jaw leading the rest of his upturned face. "And I'll tell you right now that no one is handling this right, no one is listening. I live, well, lived in a suite with my mother." He looked at the woman beside him. McClusky noticed that Mrs. Cohen seemed to forget her coffee, not refilling her empty cup, or her son's, and not offering any. "We stayed on the second floor, toward the 47th Street side. I stood outside at 3:00, watching the parade. When I heard "Fire," I ran to our rooms. I had to use the servants' stairs because the central stairway filled up with smoke and panicky guests. It's a miracle I made it to my suite and somehow guided Mother down. The story that the fire started on the 46th Street side with a cigar is hogwash." McClusky noted that David Cohen used the same word Albert Fuller had used an hour earlier. "The 47th Street side," Cohen continued, "the side of my suite, along with the airshafts on my side, went up in flames within a minute of the cry of fire. The fire started in the basement.

"You should look at the good-for-nothing engineering crew that works down there, not at some cigar smoker. I lived in the hotel for two years. I know that below our rooms is the hotel office, and the boilers are in the basement, below that office. I also know that when I watched the parade, I saw, on the street, off to the side, men from the basement crew. Shirkers. And you, Chief Detective, are barking up the wrong tree if you're still hunting for robbers or a cigar smoker."

"The wrong tree, for certain," the mother added. "A dead tree."

Clayton Byrne

The loud sounds of carts and falling bricks rumbled through the site where the Windsor once stood. Only the laborers heard the quieter sounds of rumors spread in Clay Byrne's work team, in different languages but always understandable. Two stupid workers pocketed a scorched bracelet and a silver watch. They hocked their prizes at a pawnshop. Fifty cents for the bracelet, two dollars for the watch. George McClusky's detectives, in touch with all the city's pawnshop owners, arrested the idiots. Then, two more rumors. Detectives arrested an eighteen-year-old laborer for hiding a silver spoon and an older workman for grabbing a corkscrew worth twenty cents. All amateurs, Clay thought. Didn't even know the good dealers, the reliable fences.

Clay belonged in a different league than those amateurs, or at least a different league once he could concentrate only on booty. Now, he had to stay alert for bodies too. Saturday, the day after the fire, workers found few bodies, but by Monday, as they moved to a new section of rubble, it seemed like one body per hour. Clay listened. Looked. Even, despite the nausea, studied. A worker thirty feet away found a foot, but not right for the old lady in lilac, the one he shot, and not right for Sean, the one he worried about the most. His other mate, Lon, probably made it out, and Felix was in jail, too drunk or unsteady to filch Abner's stuff properly.

A second worker yelled. He found an arm. The worker turned over the limb, in a lacy black sleeve.

Clay heard a yell from a third worker digging ten feet away. "I found a body over here. No, half a body." The man ran from it.

Clay did not like the looks of the half. His partner Luca gagged. Shaking, barely breathing, Clay and Luca turned the half over. Then Clay used his left hand to cover his right as he reached into the pocket of the scorched jacket covering the hunk of burnt flesh. A Liberty Head nickel. Sean's. Clay forced rising vomit back down.

On the ground, under where Sean's torso landed, Clay glimpsed charred threads of a burlap bag wound around brooches. Clay kneeled on all fours, letting his open jacket hide his hands and legs. While Luca pulled back from the stench, Clay stuck the nickel in his boot. Besides the scraps of the burlap bag, he saw jewels on the ground. So much debris surrounded him—bricks, charred wood, fallen sinks—that it was easy to push one of the jewels and the scraps of burlap into a hidden crevice. Clay stood up, made a show of leaning over the torso, and reached into Sean's other pocket. As expected, he felt jewelry, lifted the items, and waved them up and back with fanfare at the detective who stood twenty feet away with a handkerchief over his nose. "Here 'ya go. This gent managed to save some of his wife's valuables."

The detective reached for the jewels. He held them gingerly, walking quickly toward the shanty that held valuables along with the payroll. He kept his hand away from his side, as though he thought the jewels reeked or were cursed. Clay expected the detective to write out a tag, as he was supposed to, noting the body and the location. He wrote nothing, maybe eager to rid himself of gems that had rested against charred flesh.

The rest of the afternoon, Clay found reasons to return to the spot where Sean had landed and to kick more half-buried jewels into the hiding spot. He also kept watch for the body of the old woman in the lilac-colored nightgown. In Sean's last minutes, he was one room away from her. Clay hoped that if a worker found her, neither he nor the morticians would spend enough time with the rank remains to find a bullet.

When his shift ended, Clay joined the queue of hundreds of shivering men, waiting their turn at the shanty's payroll window. The number of workers searching for bodies and hauling away debris had swelled from 250 to 600 as contractor Joseph Cody hired more laborers to dig and load.

Workers griped about waiting in line for hours to get their wages. By this night, the third night, the wait grew longer than ever, and irritations piled up when workers heard that officials suspected them of pocketing jewelry. Police Chief Big Bill Devery, or maybe it was Chief of Detectives McClusky, discovered the police had been shirking orders to pat down the laborers. Tonight, that would change. The police would look in every pocket. A slow, humiliating process. Then there was the timecard fracas. Some foremen failed to explain the system or punched cards incorrectly. More grousing. Clay didn't care about the wages—he set his mind on bigger booty—but if he didn't stand in line to collect wages with the others, Gillespie, his foreman, would wonder.

Once the frisking began and the laborers felt the pawing, groping hands of the coppers, their grumbling turned fierce. The Irish felt particularly abused. The Italians, well, Clay suspected they had seen worse. Word went out to the police that the laborers might rebel. For their part, the laborers, cold and exhausted, busied themselves cursing in five languages.

"Use clubs on those thugs. They're gonna riot." About half the day laborers in line, including Clay, heard Police Chief Devery's order. The other half knew of the order from what they saw, as fifty police surged toward the payroll line, wielding wooden truncheons. Despite the darkness, lanterns intended to light the salvage work cast a yellow glow on the scene. Clay saw the coppers' brutish faces as they surged forward.

"Behind me," Clay said to his work partner, Luca. With light skin and red hair, Clay knew he looked Irish. Luca's darker coloring would bring down a club.

"Hey, mate, we're just standin' here. Mike 'n me. No need to mess with us." Clay spoke with a brogue he rarely used. He stayed in front of Luca, almost hiding him, while coppers beat up Italians and Slavs and took dozens away in police wagons. Strange, Clay thought, since it was the Irish who bristled the most at the searches.

"Thanks," Luca said. "Don't tell my wife I'm a Mick." Clay smiled, confident now that the laborer working alongside him would have imperfect vision the next day.

The melee slowly wound down as the coppers realized they had inflicted enough damage to make their point. The laborers who escaped beatings or the patrol wagon stayed in line, needing their pay. Clay cleared the checkpoints and pocketed his wages, not bothering to check the amount as the others did.

Rather than drifting south to his flophouse, Clay walked west to Hell's Kitchen, working out the next day's details. He needed Bridget. He knew where her sister Claire lived, two blocks from where he had lived. With luck, Claire would lead him to Bridget.

An old hag opened the boarding house door. Must be the landlady.

"Need to see Claire Dunne, please, ma'am." The hag looked him over, scowled. His clothes needed cleaning and pressing, but so did hers.

"Claire, a visitor," the landlady yelled up the stairs. Sounded like Claire wasn't in the hag's good graces. A young woman, who looked like a washed-out Bridget, traipsed down the stairs.

"Claire Dunne, right?" Clay said to Claire, with the landlady staring. "Sorry, we've not met. I'm looking for your sister." He didn't offer his name.

"Upstairs." She led the way, face down.

"Don't be long," the landlady said. "We have rules here."

Clay spotted Bridget hiding in the hall, peeking down the stairs, comely as ever. He had almost forgotten. Tara stood behind Bridget, Molly behind Tara.

Clay swung up Bridget, folding her into his arms. She hugged back, let him put his cold lips on her cheek. She didn't kiss back.

"Clay, it's been three days. Where've you been?"

"Don't have much time," Clay said. "I need to leave before that bitch landlady starts fussing." As he launched into his new scheme, Tara and Molly cut him off, talking over each other.

"Not so fast, Clay."

"Where is Sean? Have you seen him? And what about…"

"I know," Clay said, looking at Molly, ignoring Tara. "You want the rest of the money coming to you. I don't have it yet. I will soon if you listen up."

Bridget put out her palm to shush Molly and pushed it out farther to shush Tara. Clay talked fast but softly, laying out the steps for the next day. Bridget listened, but her eyes wandered. The minute he finished, Tara spoke again, spitting out the question she held back.

"Clay, do you know you killed May Gleason? Killed my roommate? She was on the roof when it collapsed." Bridget and Molly stared at Tara, then at Clay.

He answered swiftly, without thinking. "Don't be looking at me, Tara. The basement crew, men like Molly's sweetheart Frank Corbett." He looked straight at Molly as he spoke. "They were outside partying at the parade when they should have been inside. Lost precious time. And May Gleason? I don't even know her."

Molly and Tara glared at him.

"I gotta go, or that landlady will whip my hide."

Tara followed him to the front stoop.

"I don't know where he is, Tara. I'm searching for him." He turned his eyes away quickly, and then he rushed off.

David Dudley

Four days after the fire, chef David Dudley's kitchen workers still hustled to prepare food for strangers streaming into Helen Gould's mansion, across the street from the rubble. None of the injured remained in the parlors, but Miss Helen insisted on feeding the hungry firemen who doused embers and even the unwashed laborers who removed debris.

"Dudley," Miss Helen said, "I want you to meet Miss Angelica Gerry. She has come to speak with you." He looked away from the stove toward a short woman, unremarkable in appearance except for her striking delphinium blue frock. He had never seen her before.

"Pleased to meet you." He adjusted his features to neutral, waiting. Miss Helen rarely introduced him to her guests.

"Miss Gerry has questions about the fire."

Miss Helen paused. Although the name Gerry sounded vaguely familiar, Dudley could not know that Helen Gould was deciding whether to mention that the blue lady's father owned the Windsor.

"She has friends who stayed at the Windsor, who barely escaped the fire. She came to ask me what I know of it and if I could introduce her to you. She read in the papers that you were among the first to sound an alarm. An unheeded alarm, I might add. You see, her parents are friends of mine. Her father and my father, when he was still on this earth, they often discussed business matters together. She hopes you can shed a light on the likely causes—the cigar smoker, or maybe the basement staff, or a gang of thieves."

Dudley lowered his shoulders, took a deep breath. He looked at his employer with raised eyebrows.

"You can trust Miss Gerry. Tell her what you already told those reporters and anything else you can remember. I will leave you two alone. I must keep watch on the parlor, make sure those workers don't eat their sandwiches on my mahogany tables. I would lead you both to a room upstairs to talk, but honestly, there's less hubbub here."

With an unsure hand, Dudley gestured to the chairs around the table that the kitchen staff used for their meals. Miss Angelica looked uncomfortable, too. A Negro man and a posh white lady talking. But Miss Helen had done the arranging. The visitor glanced at the chair, saw it was clean, and sat, adjusting the layers of her dress.

"Mr. Dudley, I thank you for taking the time to talk to me. I know you are busy with provisions. It's so very kind of Miss Gould, with your help, of course, to feed the workers. But while the fire is fresh in your mind, I hope you can share what you know."

"Are you certain, ma'am? None of it is nice."

"Please proceed."

Dudley relayed what he had told the reporters the day of the fire. Spotting it, telling the clerks, suffering their looks. The lady nodded as he spoke. She had read all this in the papers.

"And is there anything else you can add? Any thoughts on the likely causes?"

Dudley shook his leg under the table.

"One thing. Just one. The next day, I remembered that when I returned to the house and looked out the window, I saw a man, dressed all fancy in a suit, come out the side door on 47th. He was carrying a sack. He gulped for air and looked around. Then he put the sack down and did the strangest thing. He took off his suit." Dudley saw the lady's embarrassed look, and he raced on. "Underneath, he had on different clothes. Shabbier. He threw the good clothes on the street. Then he picked up the sack and started to walk. That's when the police found him and searched the sack. The papers said he stole Abner McKinley's belongings. But the coppers didn't know he took off those fancy clothes. Probably the fancy clothes got hidden and burned up when the hotel walls fell in."

"Mr. Dudley, why didn't you tell the police that story when you told them about the clerks?"

His hand shook, along with his foot.

"It's like this. I don't want to get people in trouble, people who are just getting through the day. Those clerks, they were rotten, they must have caused at least some of those deaths. I wanted to rat them out to the police. But the man, he wasn't hurting no one, not really. He only tried to take some valuables from a gentleman who probably had more than he needed."

Clayton Byrne

Monday, the day Clay saw Sean's torso, the workers learned that contractor Joseph Cody had selected a time. At 3:00 on Tuesday afternoon, he would pull the switch. He would use thirty pounds of dynamite to knock down the stubborn tall brick chimney on the 47th Street side, the one remaining structure. Tuesday morning, Clay could almost hear a buzzing sound—the sound of anticipation—wafting through the worksite.

As the time approached, all work clearing the site stopped as laborers and spectators gathered to watch the explosion. Policemen formed a ring around Cody, to hold the crowd back. With a dramatic motion of his arm and a proud smile, he leaned down toward the switch.

Ten minutes earlier, as the laborers gathered to witness Cody's explosion, Clay meandered toward the hiding place where, little by little, he had buried the Kirk jewels as he found them. He bent down, swung his arms as though he was lifting bricks, and with small motions in between the arm swings, filled his pockets. If Luca, his partner in Gillespie's team, noticed, Luca said nothing. Luca would remember how Clay covered for him when the coppers beat up the Italians. And Luca hoped to get a spot on a carpentry crew later if Clay put in a good word for him.

Clay spotted Bridget with Molly and Tara, where he told them to stand, up against the ropes keeping the workers away from the spectators. They wore borrowed clothes, scarves around their chins, hair tucked into large hats, and huddled, holding shawls in their hands and leaning forward to see the demolition. Cody started the countdown. Ten. Nine. Eight. Clay moved toward the maids. Seven. Six. Five. He looked around. All was as expected. Four. Three. Two. As the boom echoed across the site and bricks flew, Clay did the handoff, some to each. All eyes stared at the pile where the chimney once stood.

Clay did not look at Bridget or her friends, but the back of his neck tingled. He sensed that as Molly touched the silver, she struggled to mask her hatred. She would blame him for claiming that Frank abandoned his post. And as Tara touched the silver, she would blame Clay for losing sight of Sean, even if she did not realize her lover was a charred corpse in the morgue. She blamed Clay, too, for killing some maid named May. And Bridget? Her passion would win out over her anger.

Marguerite Wells

On Tuesday, five days after the fire, Marguerite brooded over how much to share with Theodate Pope as they met in the Hoffman House lobby and walked down Broadway to Dorlon's Oyster House for lunch. Marguerite saw the men sitting in the restaurant booths turn to look at two unaccompanied women out on the town.

After they were seated, Theodate's warm smile and calm bearing helped Marguerite decide. Theodate would understand. For once, Marguerite ignored the fresh rolls a waiter brought. She leaned forward.

"Theodate, this is awkward for me, uncomfortable, but you are the one person I can ask. You said the other day that you stood on 46th Street, watching, and knew I survived. My memories of that day are cloudy." She paused, then raced through the next sentence. "Tell me what you saw."

Theodate stared. She looked puzzled, not embarrassed.

"Let me see, it was a crazy time. I felt hemmed in, with shouting all around. Half the crowd looked at that fireman, McDermott. I'll get to him later." She glanced down for a second, but not at her roll, then looked back at Marguerite. "The other half—me too—looked at your window. I saw your father tie the rope around you. Then you went down. But you didn't slide down like those other women, the ones who hurt their hands, like our maid Lotte. Instead, Mr. Wells—I could see him straining, and your mother next to him looking like she was about to collapse. He must have braced himself against something because he lowered you—let out more and more rope—until you reached the ground. Once the men untied the rope from your waist, I saw your father pull it up."

Feeling faint, Marguerite placed her wrist against the cold water glass. She searched Theodate's face.

"What happened then?"

"You mean with your parents? I don't know. About then, my father tapped me on the shoulder, and I went to look for Lotte. But of course, we know your parents are all right."

The waiter interrupted, pointing out the specials for the day. The women glanced at the menu, then ordered quickly.

Theodate narrowed her eyebrows. "Why are you upset? You all survived. Do you have nightmares?"

"No. I'll tell you." Marguerite blew her nose in her handkerchief and tried not to shake. "I've read four different accounts of what happened to my family. The *Times* says Father used a rope to send me down, then he sent Mother down, then he wrapped a towel around his hands and went down himself. Did I really agree to escape first?" She stared at Theodate. "The account in the *Sun* is similar to the *Times*. She paused, then started again. "But the *Evening Post* reporter paints a different picture. He says three firemen guided my helpless parents down and never mentions me. "The *Journal* adds a fourth fireman to the story. The heroes led us down, but I insisted on going last, and somehow Papa went first. Theodate, would he agree to be saved first? Is he letting the story spread that he rescued us when he didn't?"

The questions, the doubts, had lived in Marguerite's head. Now, she spoke them aloud. Hearing herself, she could no longer stop the tears. She held up a napkin to shield her face from other diners. Theodate looked across the table, squarely, mouth open, unbitten roll in hand.

"No wonder you're upset. Well, I can report that you did go down first, but only with your father's help, and I do mean help because he let out the rope slowly and carefully. As for what happened after you reached the ground, I can't say." She paused, bit into her roll, chewed loudly, looked to the side.

"Let me tell you about the Popes' conduct," Theodate said, "and then let's look at our stories together. I must swear you to secrecy." Marguerite wiped away the last of her tears and tipped her head an inch, agreeing. "As I've mentioned, my father collects art. Not just any art. He has surrounded himself with a circle of connoisseurs, including Louisine Havemeyer. She introduced father to Mary Cassatt, to Edouard Manet, to Claude Monet. Father has bought almost a hundred paintings. He's a patron of Impressionism." She looked quizzically at Marguerite, who recovered enough from her tears to smile. Yes, she understood. "My father likes to look at his possessions, to admire them. He lined up his newest paintings—about ten that he bought in France last month—along the wall of our suite. His valet, Leonard, kept them dusted, kept them away from the fireplace.

"A minute ago, I said I didn't see your parents escaping because Father tapped me on the shoulder. He looked frantic, imagining his paintings turning to ash. Not just the money, but the beauty. You should have seen his face. Like his world was falling apart. I saw him, I heard him, grab a fireman. He begged the man to save his paintings, pointed to the window. Father was dressed in his fine suit and top hat, and he speaks authoritatively. I heard him beseech—well, maybe I should say order—the fireman. I didn't say anything." Theodate paused again. "I had promised Mother I would look for Lotte, so I went to find her. She had come down on a rope and nearly ruined her hands. When I saw Father again, he was hugging his paintings. But here's the sore—the raw—truth. When Father hugged those canvases, women were still screaming in windows, coming down on ropes. Do you see? Father pulled a fireman away from helping people, to save paintings. And I let him." Her eyes welled over. "Then Father told the fireman to go back and get more paintings. And he did." More tears. "The fireman was Bartholomew McDermott. Before Father corralled him, McDermott saved at least one woman, maybe more. He could have saved others, too. Only one reporter noticed Father enlist McDermott. He wrote about it as a minor detail—thank goodness."

Theodate stopped talking, deciding whether to go on. She took a big bite of the roll, chewed again, swallowed. "At first, in the chaos, Father thought McDermott saved all the paintings. Father's notes on his inventory and the receipts for his purchases all burned. And no one thought clearly that afternoon. Now he believes two of the paintings in Monet's series, it's called, Haystacks—they are truly wonderful—are missing. To be honest, only yesterday I realized I lost a leather trunk where I kept my heirloom jewelry. Do you remember everything you lost?"

Marguerite shook her head. "Papa can't remember how many account books he had with him, and Mama can't remember if she left her pearls in North Dakota."

"Yes, you see, it's not surprising that Father was slow to realize his loss. He won't tell the police about the missing paintings—they could be stolen or burned—because he's tormented by what he did. He is a kind man. But he was in shock, and his paintings were like his children. He sees his culpability. And I know I should have stood up to him. Told him to let the fireman save those women. Told him to forget the paintings."

Marguerite reached across the table, over her uneaten roll, and held Theodate's hands. Diners and waiters stared. Neither woman cared.

Marguerite would always remember Theodate's next words. "Our parents raised each of us to look after others, to act kindly, to seek grace. And most of the time we do, when we give thought to our actions. But sometimes tragedy strikes. We make choices in seconds. We stumble, lose our footing. Then, we spend the rest of our years questioning our worth, our decency. We made choices. You descended first. You know your father would have it no other way, and you know maybe you were the test case for him, to see if his method worked. I chose to look for Lotte, not to correct Father. Who's to say what the right choices were that day? We must live with the choices we made and move on."

Preachy? Uplifting? Marguerite might have thought the first, but she chose to think the second. Their hands stayed together for another minute, despite stares from the other booths, until the waiter approached with their lunches.

Marguerite picked at her food, while Theodate wolfed hers down. "Do you notice," Marguerite said, "I am leaving food on my plate, a first for me."

"And I am gorging myself, a first for me. Ah, the stress of telling secrets."

They talked about their plans for the spring and summer. Marguerite would sail to France, she thought then. Theodate would not return to Cleveland in a week with her parents. She would stay in Farmington, Connecticut, where the family was building a country estate. The celebrated firm of McKim, Mead & White were the official architects, but Theodate was determined to have a say on the site and the floorplan. Reminded of Theodate's expertise, Marguerite asked the question on the minds of the Windsor's survivors.

"Theodate, from what you understand about architecture, about building, have you figured out the cause of the fire? Do you think one reckless cigar smoker could cause such destruction?"

"A cigar smoker, maybe. But not that fast. All the floors, all the wings, gone, in an hour or so. No, it had to be more than a cigar."

After lunch, Marguerite intended to head back to the Hoffman House, finish packing, and accompany her parents and their maid Belinda to the SS *La Touraine*. They would leave that evening for Le Havre. Marguerite would linger for six weeks in Europe, then return to the East Coast to visit friends from Smith College. In June she would head to Minneapolis to take up a volunteer position with the Minnesota Woman Suffrage Association, which was struggling to influence the state legislature.

She had planned these next months carefully, but lunch with Theodate spun her around, and she could not stop spinning. Theodate's memorable words calmed her, but they did not settle her. "We made our choices," Theodate had said. "We must live with them." Could she? Marguerite had always handled stress—the little she faced until the fire—by digging in, by looking for detail, for answers. Instead, now she planned to run away, over 3000 miles. And there was more. While Marguerite dwelt on her father's actions during the inferno, Theodate was trying to come to terms with her father's obsession with his art. And Angelica Gerry was pondering her father's reputation. The three young women had in common more than spinsterhood.

If Marguerite had any remaining doubts about changing her plans, those doubts disappeared when the Hoffman House desk clerk flagged her down, holding out two envelopes addressed to Miss Marguerite Wells that happened to arrive on the same day, both bearing a Special Delivery seal. The first came from Marguerite's brother, Stuart. Folded inside, she found the *Wichita Daily Eagle*, one of the bigger newspapers in the Wellses' part of the country. Reading the account, Marguerite understood why Stuart addressed the envelope to her, not to Papa. The *Eagle* concocted a new variation of the family's escape, with Marguerite taking the spotlight. She came to call the *Eagle* version Marguerite the Magnificent. The paper lowered her age by six years and described her as petite and pretty. Petite she agreed to. The paper changed their hotel floor to five, not six.

According to the *Eagle's* reporter, the Wellses didn't need help in the beginning. At her father's insistence, and despite her arguments, Marguerite escaped first. She descended on a rope, braced by her father. As he lowered her and she passed the fourth floor, she saw a woman in a window struggling with her own safety rope. Apparently while swinging in midair, Marguerite the Magnificent instructed the woman on how to use the rope. Maybe Marguerite pointed to a bracket. Maybe she told the woman how to regulate the speed of her descent, miraculously deducing the formula. Marguerite assured the woman there was no danger.

Once on the ground, so the story went, Marguerite tried to get the attention of a fireman, but the crowd yelled so loudly that he failed to hear. She seized him by the arm, shook him, and asked him to get her parents down. Mr. Wells, by that time, had found a second rope which he wrapped around Mrs. Wells, preparing to lower her. That's when he spotted the fireman Marguerite had enlisted. That fireman saved Mrs. Wells, bringing her down on a ladder with the rope still wrapped around her waist. The fireman went back for Mr. Wells. The *Wichita Daily Eagle* highlighted Marguerite's magnificent western spirit at its best. A fifth account to add to the four earlier ones.

The second envelope came from a close Smith College friend, a woman Marguerite had roomed with for several years, who now lived in Atlanta. The day after the fire Marguerite had telegrammed her friend to say the Wellses had escaped and moved to the Hoffman House. Along with a note, the friend enclosed an article from a small Georgia newspaper, the *Jackson*

Economist. The paper ran a long story on Alice Price, a socialite from Macon, how she had escaped with injuries, descriptions of the rings she wore on her fingers. The article concluded with a short sentence. "Mrs. Price's maid died in the flames." The laundress. Tilly Brown. Dead.

Marguerite dreaded trying to explain her decision to her parents but braced herself. "Mama, Papa, I know this is sudden, but I won't join you in France. I want to stay here in New York while you are away." They stared, stunned. Waited for more. "You see, I'm still rattled from the fire. I want to spend time with Theodate—she is rattled too. She says she will introduce me to Louisine Havemeyer, who can tell me about plans for the suffragists here, plans that might be useful when I get to Minneapolis. And Angelica Gerry is struggling too. You saw when we had dinner together. Perhaps I can provide some comfort. Oh, and I want to follow the Coroner's activities. Maybe learn how this fire started."

That last sentence was the truest.

"Don't feel anxious about me here on my own. My friends use a hotel downtown that's an oasis, that's the word they use, for single women, with strict rules and security. I've lived away from you before. I'll be fine. And it's only for a few months."

She suffered through fussing, questions, and frowns, but her parents had always admired her independence, and in the end, they offered their blessing. She accompanied them and Belinda by carriage to Pier 42 at the foot of Morton Street, a bustling spot where the luxurious *La Touraine* docked. When the ocean liner pulled away from the pier, Marguerite turned around, with a look of determination she felt happy her parents couldn't see. She hailed a cab and returned to the Hoffman House, collected her small bag of new clothes, and headed off to the Martha Washington Hotel for Women on 29th Street, thanks, in large part, to the generous trust fund her father had bestowed on each of his children.

After registering at the front desk, she glanced at an ornate walnut table in the lobby. The evening papers were spread open, with headlines bearing the word "bodies." She felt an increasingly common sensation. She wanted to read. She knew she shouldn't read. The pull to the papers won.

Four bodies so far, most unrecognizable black lumps. The reporters seemed to revel in gruesome details. A worker using a shovel to sift through rubbish at the rear of the hotel, near the 46th Street side, smelled burnt flesh. Pushing aside debris, he saw the burned trunk of a headless body, with little flesh remaining. Contractor Joseph Cody redirected a more skilled searcher to use his fingers to sift through nearby rubble. That searcher found a severed foot, arms, and parts of legs. No one knew if the parts belonged to a man or a woman, but Cody, looking down his list of the missing and paying attention to location, guessed the parts could belong to Frederick Leland—the night clerk, wine room worker, and cousin of manager Warren Leland. Marguerite gagged at the report. She had known Frederick by sight. Sensibly, contractor Cody established a routine: workers placed the body parts on a board and brought the board to the shanty, mortuary workers placed the parts into a pine box, a supervisor marked the box with what passed for a name—unrecognizable Body 1 in this case, and a hearse driver took off for the morgue.

The reports continued to Body 2, the torso of a woman encased in a steel corset seared into what little remained of her flesh, resting on a bit of charred mattress. Workers looking nearby found a brown kid glove with pearl buttons, a small gold ring, and singed parts of a skirt and jacket. Contractor Cody, checking his list again, guessed this torso belonged to sixteen-year-old Florence Fuller. Marguerite had known Florence, a charming sixteen-year-old. Same name as Marguerite's youngest sister, back home in North Dakota. Now the routine again: board to shanty to coffin to morgue.

Next, fifteen feet below ground, on the 46th Street side, Body 3. A small torso, charred head attached, hair burned off, bits of silk clothing with a Parisian dressmaker's label, no arms or legs. Could this be Mrs. Auze, a well-known guest of the Windsor? Her nephew, hunting for her, said that years ago, she had lost the index finger on her right hand. But with no arms, that clue to the identity of the torso was useless. The charred head had two gold fillings and a prominent jaw. Maybe the torso did belong to Mrs. Auze. Or not. Same exit routine.

Then Body 4. An unrecognizable torso.

Marguerite wished that the Martha Washington had a bar where she could order a sherry. She would not sleep.

Clayton Byrne

Clay felt alone for the first time in years. He no longer led a ring of robbers, but he couldn't stop thinking about them, especially Sean. Clay had not lost a man before, despite a couple years of hustles. As for Felix, no surprise the coppers picked him up. That sloppy fool should have been more careful. But Felix, despite his faults, always stayed loyal. He wouldn't give up Clay or the girls. The third fella, Lon—where was he? Clay had entrusted Lon with the Popes' suite on the second floor.

When Tara drew the valuables in that suite, for each painting she tried to copy the artist's name. Those names—Cassatt, Manet, Monet, reproduced with a hand not used to writing letters—didn't mean much to Clay at the time, not until two days after the fire when he read about Windsor guest Alfred Pope, a titan of the iron industry. According to the *New York Journal and Advocate*, Pope kept paintings valued at $35,000 in his suite. A fireman had supposedly recovered those paintings, but Clay knew that would have been difficult. Tara had drawn ten paintings—probably too much for even a strong fireman to carry. Lon, for all his drunkenness and bluster, was fast on his feet and could have nicked a few before or after the fireman showed up. Lon wouldn't know how to find Clay, and he wouldn't know the value of what he had stolen or how to fence it. If he walked into a regular pawnshop carrying fine paintings, the clerk would offer crumbs or, worse, turn Lon in to the first copper who came around.

The night after reading about Pope's collection, Clay sought out some of his associates who ran gangs in upscale neighborhoods. He offered an idea for their next heist, in return for the names of fences who could be trusted with stolen art. Someday he hoped to need those names.

On Wednesday, Clay's fifth day shoveling rubble, he heard a faint whistle coming from the sidelines near the rope holding back spectators. He looked up, through the drizzle. He saw Lon, with that silly beard, staring at him. Clay looked back down. Luck had been on his side so far. No one had fingered or questioned him, and he wanted to keep it that way. He had worked at the Windsor for one season, five months before, wearing an apprentice carpenter's apron. Now he wore shabby clothing, made shabbier still by days of labor, and hid his red hair under an oversized cap. His guise had worked. If the coppers suspected Lon, they might follow him, looking for others. Or had Lon escaped notice too?

Noise of machinery and shouts from foremen to laborers rang out around the site, but Lon knew to take care. He mouthed one word.

"Sore."

"Sore," Clay mouthed back, after checking that no one besides Lon was looking.

Sore—the gang's nickname for McSorley's, East Seventh Street, one of their watering holes.

At nine that night, the usual time for gatherings, Clay entered McSorley's. Lon sat at a dirty table in back, an extra mug at the ready. Drops of beer shimmered on Lon's scraggly beard. He looked like he'd been drinking for hours. Both men avoided a noticeably grand reunion. Lon started with small talk, the wet and warmer weather, Tammany Hall politics. They nattered on until the din around them from other drinkers grew loud. Clay tipped his head. Lon should start talking.

"Lucky break I found you. I went to the site to see the men hauling bricks from all that rubble. Best show in town. Never thought I'd see you there, not 'til I watched a tall man swing a shovel and spotted a lock of red hair peeking out of his cap. Now, Mr. Smarty, tell me what to do with those blasted paintings. Two of 'em. Hay. Shit, just piles of orange hay. Big, maybe two feet by three feet each. The ones the maid who couldn't write drew for her list and circled. Heavy. I carried 'em out fast, before detectives started checking everyone. I dressed good, like you told me. If anyone saw, they thought I was a guest, saving my own stuff. But most of 'em on the street were looking at the jumping women. I was out of there before that guy they're calling a hero, McDermott, went in and saved the rest. Brought 'em to my pal a block away, then home after dark."

"The papers say Pope got his paintings out."

"Not all of 'em. Not sure if he's lying or if he doesn't know how many he had. Are you sure this haul is worth something? I been worrying I grabbed the wrong stuff."

Clay hoped no one was watching because he couldn't help himself. He moved his arm across the table, ignoring the wet rings and cigar ashes. He put his hand on Lon's shoulder, squeezed gently, and smiled. "Good work with those paintings. I needed good news."

"Right. Felix blew it, I heard. Got himself arrested. What about the new guy, the hothead?"

"Sean didn't make it out."

Lon crossed himself and took another swig.

Bridget Dunne

An hour after Joseph Cody detonated explosives, Bridget returned to the boarding house where she combined the stash of Kirk valuables that Clay handed her with those he handed to the other maids. Creeping down to the dank cellar, she found a hiding place beside cobwebs in a corner, far from the laundry basin. By the next morning, March 22, she considered grabbing the jewels and slipping away, leaving Molly and Tara behind. For days, the women had slept crowded together, sharing what food they could find, wearing Claire's worn-out dresses, hiding under big bonnets. Mrs. Brownhill looked daggers at her unwelcome guests. But the maids couldn't be certain the police weren't hunting them. They needed to lie low at Claire's or find another place.

Bridget had seen Clay twice since the fire, but if he had a plan to run off with her, he hadn't shared it. She followed the papers and knew talk of a robbery had quieted down while talk of the cigar smoker and the irresponsible basement crew continued.

In the meantime, Molly sulked, and Tara fussed. Worse, May Gleason's name appeared daily on the lists of the missing, the lists that Molly read out loud, the lists that unsettled Tara.

"When I followed you to the fire escape," Tara said, "I looked behind me. I saw May, saw her face. She didn't look like a know-it-all, there on the roof. She looked scared."

"Tara, enough. Your jawing won't bring her back."

"Don't shush me, biddy." Ahhh, the contempt. "I keep going over what we did. I walked behind you. I didn't stop. Didn't grab her. Why did she have to go to the roof? Holy mother of God, wish I'd never seen the insides of that damn hotel."

"Shut your gob. Give us some piece." Molly snapped, putting her hands over her ears.

Tara stopped for a breath, started up again. "Those coppers investigating the fire, they know McKinley stayed on the first floor. He'll blame anarchists. What if the coppers pick up Sean, if they think he's a rabble-rouser who hates that the President cozies up to the English? They'll think Sean plotted to kill Abner McKinley to get at his brother."

Bridget knew what Tara didn't say, especially when Molly was around. Maybe Sean, along with Clay, murdered May. Not actually tossing her off the roof but causing the fire. Tara and Bridget never said out loud that Sean was part of the job. No need for Molly to know.

A knock on the attic room door silenced Tara. At the second knock, Bridget opened the door. Mrs. Brownhill stood there with a strange man.

"This gent is hunting for Claire Dunne. When I told him she was out, he asked about Bridget Dunne. He said the sister would do."

"You Bridget Dunne, Claire's sister?" the man asked.

Bridget nodded yes, grabbed a sealed envelope, and said a quick goodbye before closing the door. Tearing the envelope open, she found one brief letter and a smaller envelope.

"Dear Miss Dunne," Bridget read aloud. "I have an acquaintance who knows you and your sister. She provided your address. I asked my cousin to deliver this note, in the hope you can lead me to your sister and that she can lead me to Molly Dugan, the woman I plan to marry. Inside this envelope, you will find a smaller envelope, intended for Miss Dugan. If you do not know the whereabouts of your sister, or if she does not know the whereabouts of Miss Dugan, then destroy the letter. Sincerely, Frank Corbett."

Bridget handed the small envelope to Molly, who was about to pounce on it. She read it to herself, read it again, then read it aloud. "Dear beloved, I must stay out of sight. Too many fingers point at me. That infernal clerk, smug Simeon Leland, he blames me and Sully."

Molly looked up for a minute to explain. "Sully's the Chief Electrician, Sullivan." Bridget raised one hand. She knew him. Molly read on. "Simeon claimed he saw Sully and our crew out watching the parade when the fire started. Darn Sully, why did he have to be tall? Molly, believe me, I was in the courtyard, saving women. Sully stepped up, too. Now we're in the crosshairs."

"See," Bridget said, "Clay's right. Everyone suspects the maintenance crew for abandoning their posts."

"Yeah," Molly said, "but Clay sounded like he believed that garbage. How could you trust that scumbag?"

"Molly, he may be a scumbag, but we want his payments, don't we?"

While Molly read, Tara stayed strangely quiet. She wound a strand of unruly hair around her finger. Then, another strand. Bridget tensed up for what was to come. "Molly," Tara said, "Frank's in trouble, but so is Sean. All our beaus. Bridget and I need to tell you something." As Tara spoke, she stared at Bridget. "We shoulda told you before. I'll get it out, straight. Clay's gang. He had three mates helping him. One was my love, Sean Mack."

Molly's right eye ranged wildly, and her jaw contorted. Her left eye glared at Tara.

"Sorry for keeping mum," Tara said. "We thought the fewer people who could name the gang, the better. But now I'm thinking you should know we're all in this together. Don't be mad."

"Ha. I'm mad at the whole lot of you," Molly said. "And at myself, too. The three of us are cursed, and our loves. My Frank, he's in trouble, even though he's the only one who did nothing wrong. I'd storm outa here, leave you far behind, but I've no place to go, no money." Molly placed a finger over her bad eye in a useless effort to still it. "Can we trust Sean? If coppers snag him, they might promise to forget about him in a trade for names. He must know Tara and the rest of us made those lists, and he can name the others in the gang."

"Cut it out, Molly. We're not blaming your Frank, so don't you go blaming my Sean. Bridget and I just helped him out so he could make money."

"Big mistake," Molly said. "And I made a mistake, too. I shoulda said no to you, Bridge. Shouldn't have made that fourth-floor list you wanted. And it was my list Clay liked the most. I saw that asshole's eyes—sparkled when he read about gems on my floor. He took that floor for himself. Did he take Sean along on four? What good is money if we land in the clinker? Saints preserve us."

Bridget spent the rest of the day scrounging food from the boarders and, despite the rain, taking quick walks to get away from the others, from the sniping. When she returned, Tara and Molly were sitting shoulder-to-shoulder on the floor of the cramped little room, barely touching bread and cold tea. Oddly, Tara said little, and Molly seemed even more aloof than usual. When Claire returned from classes and went down to take her place at the boarding house table, Molly and Tara locked eyes. Molly tilted her head. Proceed, she seemed to say.

"Bridge, even when we bicker, you know it's because we're all worried, all on edge. May is dead. And those others too—maybe thirty, maybe forty." Tara, trembling as she spoke, lifted one hand toward Molly, beseeching help. Five days after the fire, Bridget thought, and just now, Tara and Molly are thinking about all those dead women.

"So here's the thing," Molly said. "We, we caused it. Well, Clay caused it. Along with his buddies. Tara and I talked. We want to tell you first. We're going to the station to tell the coppers what Clay did. We'll turn in the Kirk jewels. I read in the papers that even some of the hotel guests are blaming the engineers and electricians, and that means Frank, for abandoning their posts to see the parade. I don't curse much, but that's crap. Frank saved women." Molly stretched out the word saved. "I can't let him take any blame. And we can't hide out here forever. We need work, we need to find new positions." Bridget saw Molly look back at Tara. Her turn.

"We'll get into trouble for helping Clay," Tara said. "But the coppers will know Clay's the troublemaker. We'll get off easy, especially if we give back the gems."

Anger rose in Bridget's throat, rising up her head. "You won't. You won't go to the police. Molly, Frank stood outside watching the parade. I saw him out the window right before I went to the closet. He stood next to

Sully, and Sully's tall as a tree. No missing him. And Tara, I know what Sean does, with that anarchist cell, or whatever it is, in New Jersey. Maybe he doesn't have his eye on some English ambassador or on the President, but I could say he does. You girls don't want me to talk. You really don't. Just to keep your conscience clear and your beaus safe."

The looks between Molly and Tara stopped.

Ten minutes later, Claire returned. She removed a note from her pocket. "Bridge, a strange boy, maybe a newsboy, hid in the bushes on the side of the porch during dinner. He saw me through the window and got my attention while everyone else shoveled food into their maws. I coughed, then said I needed to step out for some air. He threw the note on the porch then ran."

Bridget grabbed the note, the second of the day, while Claire whined. "We can't keep going like this, girls. You need to move on."

Bridget read the note to herself, then looked up at the three women waiting for word. "Clay hasn't been caught. And he hasn't forgotten me."

George McClusky

His list should have been shrinking five days after the disaster. Instead, it had grown. Chief Detective George McClusky took another look at his notebook, leather-covered, with his initials embossed on the front. For most cases, he never bothered with a written list, but with this case, his memory couldn't hold it all. Every time he read a newspaper, he saw another article about some witness's version of events. Every time he picked up the telephone, he heard his boss Big Bill Devery on the other end, relaying hearsay from even more witnesses.

"Got a call from a woman today who lives in Baltimore." Devery's voice came through all too clearly in the earpiece. "Claims her ma is missing. Old lady, sickly, stays at the Windsor. The woman thinks her brother might 'a killed the Ma to get his inheritance, fast. The brother has gambling debts. I wouldn't think twice about this except one of the patrolmen found a bullet next to some shreds of cloth, says they're lilac-colored, and a leg bone. Looks like it came from a .32 caliber revolver. The woman hasn't seen her ma for years and wouldn't be able to identify the threads of cloth. What do you think, George?"

"What was the condition of the bullet? Look like it had been fired?"

"Ah, George, I knew you were worth your salt. I forgot to ask. I'll have that patrolman send it over to you."

McClusky hung up and pulled out his list again. He had revised it several times, developing categories. Now, he'd have to add the bullet toward the bottom, as well as the indictment he'd read about in the papers, charging Leland Warren with burning inferior coal. But the reporters still favored the cigar theory. An unknown man, smoking a cigar in the parlor, flicking it onto a lace curtain.

Cigar adherents
  Waiter John Foy
  Hotel steward Allen Clark
  Guests at small dining room event—Mrs. George Cort and Miss Emma Brown
  Fire Chief Hugh Bonner

In the next category McClusky placed advocates of the robber theory. A single robber, or a gang of robbers, set one fire, or several fires, to drive guests out of their rooms and provide a distraction.

Robber theory
  Hotel guest Alfred Fuller (maybe on third floor)
  Albert Nimis (on way to visit hotel guest, saw robber)

In the third group McClusky placed advocates of electrical problems or some sort of basement mischief. Maybe wires were poorly insulated, or were too close to wood, or circuits were overloaded. McClusky wasn't sure any of the advocates of this theory truly understood electricity. Or maybe boilers were not serviced.

Electrical or boiler malfunction
  Engineering News editor (fire had to smolder for hours to do such damage quickly, cigar story was rubbish)
  Hotel guest Charles Cowardin (smelled charred wood, felt heat in wall of suite for three hours before fire)
  Hotel cashier Charles Squires (excess charge of electricity through poorly insulated copper wires)
  Hotel guest Thomas Ochiltree (boiler malfunction, unwatched by crew)

Battalion Chief John Binns (started in basement)
Hotel guest David Cohen (started in basement on 47th side)

In a fourth category McClusky listed naysayers, complainers of all stripes, and ideas that seemed loosely connected to existing theories.

Random
Abner McKinley suggests anarchists going through him to get to President
Officials Scannell and Bonner think robber story absurd
Hotel clerk Simeon Leland claims basement staff out watching parade
Letter to editor reports hotel employees on roof watching parade, open windows throughout hotel that let in music also encouraged drafts
Bullet found near leg bone, lilac threads, must examine bullet
Unknown complainant accused Warren Leland of burning soft coal, which emitted dangerous gasses
Wide halls fed fire

At the very bottom of the list, McClusky scribbled his own thoughts.

Mine
Robber story faulty—thieves would accidentally burn up some of valuables they wanted and they would be wary of police escorting the parade

McClusky took pride in his list. Thorough. Organized. So what? Where did it lead him? Big Bill had assigned three junior detectives to the case. They were wet behind the ears and only comfortable interviewing common criminals. McClusky looked out the window, barely noticing the heavy rain. He needed to stay in Big Bill's good graces. To do that, McClusky needed to reinvigorate the investigation. Think differently. Or find help.

Marguerite Wells

Five minutes, that's all the time Marguerite Wells spent second-guessing her decision to remain in New York. Breakfasting alone at the Martha Washington Hotel for Women the day after her parents sailed for Europe, she realized this would be the first of many lonely meals. No matter, she would ignore her loneliness as she sorted out that damn fire. What had her father done? And the other fathers, Mr. Pope and Mr. Gerry? Was a single cigar smoker the cause of such distress and death?

She would begin with the only methods she knew. Research, in a chair, at a table, in a library. Marguerite rode a streetcar downtown through the rain to the Astor Library on Lafayette Street—the same library she visited earlier that month to research Civil War officers. On this second visit, she did not hunt for military records, but for newspapers. She wanted to reread the accounts in the *Times*, the *Sun*, the *Evening Post*, and the *New York Journal and Advertiser*, and look at them alongside the Wichita paper's rendition of her exploits. The same harried librarian who helped her earlier sat behind a desk. Four men stood in line, waiting for his attention. Marguerite took her place at the back of the queue, thinking appreciative thoughts about the city's plan to build a new, larger public library at 42nd Street. When it was her turn, she explained what she needed. The librarian seemed to listen attentively. He smiled. He may have remembered her Civil War research a week earlier. He gave directions to a page, who returned in five minutes with a large pile of newspapers.

"Miss, here are papers from the five days since the fire. All from Manhattan." She thanked him and found a large table by a windowed wall. Rain coming from the east splattered against the window, the only sound in the quiet, gloomy reading room.

Marguerite reread the articles, confirming her original take on their contradictions. Flipping through the papers, she kept her eye on the lists of dead, and even on the lists of missing, looking for Tilly Brown's name. Alice Price's Negro maid was not on any list. Then Marguerite's eyes caught another article about the fire, this one on the front page of one of the papers spread on the library table. An article about the Stokes family. She remembered glancing at it when it first appeared. Reporters couldn't get enough of William Earl Dodge Stokes, rakish and forty-six, and wife Rita Hernandez de Alba Acosta Stokes, glamorous and twenty-four. A reporter for the *New York Journal and Advertiser* chose his words carefully, trying, Marguerite suspected, to create an erotic picture of a gorgeous woman jumping out of the bath. "Mrs. W.E.D. Stokes had notified the police that she had left jewels in the Turkish bath house immediately adjoining the hotel, from which she had hurriedly fled on the alarm of fire." He added enticing details about the item. "Seven pearls, twenty-one diamonds, with a topaz clasp."

Shuffling the papers again, looking for more on the Stokeses, Marguerite found that the *Sun* told a different story. "W.E.D. Stokes called at the East 51st Street station and demanded that the police turn over to him the rams head bracelets with ruby eyes that were found in the ruins. 'They are my personal property,' he declared. 'I was in the baths at the time of the fire, and in the confusion I lost the bracelets.' The police surrendered them to him. Mr. Stokes left the station refusing to discuss how it was that he lost the bracelets in the baths when they were recovered in the center of the ruins of the hotel, far away from the baths."

The odd stories leapt off the page. Mrs. Stokes claimed she lost her bracelet in the baths. Marguerite knew the baths provided a separate floor for women, but she thought it unlikely a woman of Mrs. Stokes's stature would use that facility. Mr. Stokes claimed he lost bracelets, more than one, while in the baths. That seemed more likely. Men of all social circles enjoyed the camaraderie of the baths. And what about the married couple's differing descriptions of the jewels? Diamonds or rubies? Then Marguerite puzzled over the apparent suspicions of the policeman on duty that day. Why did he question the exact location of the bracelet or bracelets, as though he doubted Mr. Stokes's story? Many articles reported on found jewels, but no one had ever questioned the location where they were found.

An image of Rita Stokes's bracelet, glittering with jewels of one sort or another, stuck in Marguerite's head. She realized her fixation lined up with the latest fixations of reporters and their readers. The first day or two after the fire, reporters highlighted the leaps—women, and occasionally men, jumping from the upper floors, dangling on ropes, or ripping their hands while sliding down. After reporters exhausted the topic of leaps, they moved to the other topic of interest to residents of the city. Missing jewelry. Perhaps the financial titans of the city no longer congregated in the bars and parlors of the Windsor, but bejeweled women had walked its halls. Manager Warren Leland provided a safe, but half the residents ignored the safe, preferring to keep their jewelry close at hand, to don as the whim arose. The papers included long and fascinating lists of what the laborers searching the ruins found: necklaces, brooches, bracelets, earrings, rings, watches, all set with diamonds, rubies, sapphires, pearls, engraved with loving words from sweethearts and admirers. Could Marguerite use missing jewelry as a wedge into the mystery of the fire? Time, she thought, to move beyond library tables.

She gathered up the newspapers and brought them back to the front desk. By this time in the afternoon, as the rain increased, the crowd lessened.

"Sir, thank you for sending the page for these newspapers. They were a good source of information. May I ask you a question about the city?" The librarian widened his eyes, inviting more. "Who is the police chief now?"

He stared, not expecting such a question.

"Oh, no, I am not in trouble with the law." She laughed as light-heartedly as she could manage, then pointed to the papers she had placed on his desk. "I've been reading about the Windsor fire. I have thoughts on it to share with whoever is in charge of the investigation."

"The librarian continued to stare. "Miss, the chief is William Devery." He glanced left, then right.

Margaret knew the name from the papers, but she hoped for more than a name from the librarian, who made it clear from his eyes and his gentle tone that he wanted to help a young, pretty woman. Would he add to the gossip she had heard in the lobby of the Hoffman House?

He did. "Some call him Big Bill Devery." More glances. "Chief Devery is rumored to be a scoundrel. You might consider, instead, seeking out Captain George McClusky. He's Chief of the Police Detective Bureau. He comes in here from time to time to do research of his own. He looks like a gentleman. Good dresser. Might be better for a young lady like yourself to avoid Devery and seek a meeting with McClusky."

Marguerite returned to her hotel and sent a note by messenger to George McClusky, Chief of the Police Detective Bureau. Jewelry provided the excuse for a meeting. "My mother, Mrs. Nellie Wells, lost all her jewelry in the Windsor Hotel fire, including a pearl necklace of great sentimental value. She embarked for France before she thought to check if it had been recovered. I would like to visit you in your office to inquire about the necklace. I realize you are a highly regarded and responsible police detective and might simply direct me to the East 51st Street station that has taken custody of lost valuables, but I wish to meet with you for another reason besides my mother's jewels. I have come upon information you may find useful as you continue your investigation of the fire." That sentence, Margaret knew, was a stretch.

George McClusky must have been eager for any nuggets. An hour after receiving Marguerite's message, his clerk called on the Martha Washington Hotel's one telephone to set up an appointment for 9:00 the next morning, Thursday, March 23.

Marguerite had seen George McClusky out of the corner of her eye on Saturday, when she stayed at the Hoffman House with her parents, and he interviewed hotel guests in the lobby immediately after the fire. She had overheard the guests' observations after McClusky left the hotel.

"Debonair for a former police captain. Spiffy suit."

"Respectful. No-nonsense."

"Walks with a swagger."

"Smarter than the Pinkertons."

Despite this praise, and even though she was the one who asked for a meeting, she stewed about it, trying to figure out how much to say, how not to look ridiculous. As she ate dinner alone in the hotel dining room, she considered canceling. With no companion to talk to, she stared straight ahead, through the dining room door and into the lobby. The evening's editions were again spread out on an ornate table.

As Marguerite left the dining room, she vowed to walk quickly past the newspapers. She didn't. More bodies. She rushed over the vague descriptions of Bodies 5 and 6, then stalled at Body 7. Workers found him near the remains of the elevator shaft. Just a large part of a trunk, a portion of skull, pieces of leg bones. Using a basket, the workers carried the remains to the shanty. Contractor Cody, consulting his list, guessed the pieces belonged to Warren Guion, the talkative elevator man at the Windsor. Marguerite and her parents knew him, knew his story. All the guests knew him. He supported his mother, two unmarried sisters, and a brother who had not been right since birth. Witnesses reported that Warren ran the elevator up and down to save guests, rather than running out to save himself. One of the Windsor's wealthy residents, John Doane, had lived at the Windsor the entire twenty years Guion had worked there. Mr. Doane started a fund for the Guion family, seeding it with $500.

Marguerite firmly folded the papers closed, a gesture of respect. She would meet with the Chief Detective. She would do her part to figure out what went wrong in so many ways.

The next morning, Marguerite took care with her dress, selecting a fashionable frock. Her new wardrobe now included two dresses a kindly dressmaker had finished in short order and three lovely dresses that Angelica had delivered to the Hoffman House, claiming that since she had worn each once to a reception, she couldn't wear them again. Two of the three were delphinium blue.

Detective McClusky worked in police headquarters at 300 Mulberry Street, between Bleecker and Houston, far south of the Martha Washington.

Seeing from her hotel window that the rain of the previous day continued and that branches twisted in the wind, Marguerite took a cab and arrived early. She didn't want to get wet before her appointment, so she hovered under the awning of a building across the street, watching an endless stream of officers and criminals enter the imposing Italianate, marble-clad building. No women entered. At 9:00 she adjusted her hat, dashed across Mulberry Street, and announced herself to the front desk clerk.

"Miss Marguerite Wells, here to see Chief Detective George McClusky."

The clerk looked her over, head to shoes. "He expecting you?"

"Yes, he requested my presence at 9:00 this morning."

Eyes up and down again. "Morton, take this lady to McClusky."

Marguerite thought she saw a flicker of humor as the two men's eyes met. The policeman named Morton led her up four flights. She vowed not to pant. At the top, off to the left, sat George McClusky behind an impressive desk, chatting with two young men—maybe junior detectives—who stood nearby, looking attentive.

Marguerite congratulated herself on dressing for the occasion, guessing, accurately in this case, that McClusky would wear his trademark posh clothing. She had not guessed that when she entered, he too would keep his eyes on her for a long second, before gesturing to a chair. She noted his thick black hair, well-groomed mustache, slender but muscular build. She sat down, clutching a piece of note paper.

"Detective McClusky, thank you for agreeing to see me. As I said in my message, I know you are a busy man. First, here is a description of my mother's necklace. It is valuable in terms of dollars and more in emotion. It was my great grandmother's."

"Yes, Miss Wells, my men will check for you." She expected him to look bored. He did not. He took the note paper, gave it to one of the young men, and used his hand to dismiss them both. While walking out, the man holding the note glanced back at Marguerite, then at his boss, with an uncommon expression. After hearing the door click shut, Detective McClusky stared at his visitor. Marguerite interpreted the stare as an invitation to keep talking.

"I am sure you are curious about what I can add to your investigation."

"Miss Wells, I continue to collect information. Details." He paused. "Especially from guests caught in the fire. I have learned to search for all clues I can find before reaching any conclusion." He dragged out the last sentence.

"Is it possible, Mr. McClusky, that you harbor the same doubts I do about the rumors circulating?" She could tell from the slight shift in his jaw that he didn't want to smile, but resistance was futile.

"Doubts?"

"Since I know you are short of time, I will launch right into my thoughts. But first, let me tell you why I have these thoughts. As you know, my father and mother and I were caught in the fire. We escaped, but our memories of the specifics are cloudy. To help my memory, I have read all the newspaper accounts I could find, right up to today, and I have noted inconsistencies. The first concerns the Stokeses, that is William Earl Dodge Stokes and Rita Stokes. As you—"

The detective cut her off with a grin under his mustache. "Yes, I am impressed you noticed. First, the Mrs. tried to claim the bracelet, then Stokes himself claimed it. During the fire, he was at one end of the building, actually, the baths, and Mrs. was at another location, and the bracelet, well, we found that in a third location. It is possible that it got kicked or dislodged when laborers cleared the site, but they were careful to keep things, as we say, *in situ*. And the husband and wife described the bracelet differently. Odd indeed. But we think it's not about arson, but about, hmmm, the nice word might be carryings-on. You see, we questioned some of the people who escaped from the fourth floor. We believe Mr. Stokes may have kept a lady of the night there. Apologies for my frankness, Miss Wells."

From the detective's expression, Marguerite guessed he expected her to be shocked. She offered only a simple frown.

"But I will tell you this, Miss Wells, even if your nugget of information does not offer anything new to the investigation, it does show me your powers of observation and reasoning. Have you discovered anything else that seems peculiar?"

Bridget Dunne

For a week, Bridget hid out with Molly and Tara in Claire's airless room. Looking at Claire, looking at the landlady, everyone knew it was a week too long. At least no coppers had knocked on the door. Not to haul away Bridget for helping Clay burn down the Windsor. Not to haul away Tara for her drawings or her link to an anarchist. Not to haul away Molly for her list or her link to an engineer who left his basement post. Had they escaped scrutiny? No way for Bridget to know. But she knew they needed jobs, needed a place to live.

"We could try to find a rooming house for all of us," Bridget said while Claire was out, "but that's not a good idea. If the coppers find one of us, we don't want them finding all three of us. We need to separate. Last night, I didn't say what was in the note from Clay that the newsboy handed Claire. I had to think about it overnight. You're not the only ones angry at Clay. I'm angry, too. The fool thought he'd set a few sparks and make out with riches. He shoulda known better." She paused. "But he's still my love. I'll live with his mistake." She heard herself say "his." She knew it was not so simple.

"I'm going to meet up with him. He wrote—well, sort of wrote, he used a lot of abbreviations and nicknames since he wasn't sure he could trust the newsboy or Claire—that he can't stay at the flophouse any longer. He can't stand the filth. Even the note smelled. In a few days, if no one arrests him, he'll go to the union—the Brotherhood of Carpenters. Maybe he can find day work. And he says he knows how to get money from the fourth-floor haul. I'm putting the sack out back tonight, near the trash, and he's going to pick it up around midnight and then pawn the jewels in Philadelphia. He didn't write Philadelphia. He wrote bellburg because he knows that I know that's what he calls Philadelphia. The cops aren't looking there. Then he and me, maybe we'll have enough to get to San Francisco. If not, we'll find a flat in Brooklyn. I'll see if I can work for a family, private home."

Molly and Tara screwed up their faces when Bridget talked about money from pawning. "Don't worry, girls. Clay will have more bucks for you, like he promised. Don't even think about turning him in. If you do that, you won't get another cent." Tara was first to settle her lips. Molly's bad eye roamed, then settled too.

"Bridge, I have another idea for Clay," Molly said. "You remember, I cleaned on four. One of the rooms, a woman named Judith lived there. Pretty woman. Shapely too. Lived alone. Her suite was small, but the one next to it was big. Took me a long time to clean the big one. Sometimes when I cleaned near the wall next to Judith's suite, I heard noises." Molly snickered. "The kind of noises you hear at night." Another snicker. "When I heard the door open and footsteps head to the servants' stairs, I peeked. I saw the back of a head. It was Mr. Stokes. I'm sure of it. Posh. But wrinkles around the waist of the back of his jacket because it stretches over his stomach. He must be too vain to admit he needs a new suit. Well, he's a builder. Building the Ansonia, that gaudy hotel up on Broadway. Maybe Clay could talk to him. Mention Judith." A third snicker. "Get on at the Ansonia."

Bridget stared at Molly, then at Tara, then back at Molly. All three started to laugh. Molly hadn't said that many words since the fire and hadn't offered helpful words, ever. It must be the promise of the bonus that loosened her tongue and changed her tune. "The Ansonia," Bridget said, "great idea. I'll put a note tonight in the sack out back."

"You didn't think I had it in me, did you? Well, I'm learning from the best. I need to, because I'm scared all the time—scared to be with Frank and scared for him. Bridge, you're not the only one who thought a lot last night. Me too. I'm done being mad. I need to look ahead. I'm going to get help from Devan."

"The assistant butcher? The cute lad missing a tooth?" Tara asked. "Why Devan?"

"Remember, Bridge, you made sure he was on the roof with us, that he saw us there. And he ran out with us, down the fire escape. He reads the papers. He knows the coppers suspect Frank of leaving his post. But Devan doesn't know about the lists. He saw us on the roof when the fire started, so he wouldn't blame us. Devan's a good lad, and he likes us. I saw him for a minute yesterday when I walked a few blocks for air after the rain stopped. We talked. He has enough money for another week in his boarding house—he gave me his address—then he's moving back to Hoboken to live with his family 'til he finds a job. Devan said I can stay with them in Hoboken. I can't go back to my ma. She has no room, and if the cops look for Frank, they might look for me too, to lead them to Frank. Devan said he'd help me find a position. Maybe a private family like you, Bridge. I'll get a note to Frank somehow and tell him he can find me through Devan."

"So that leaves me," Tara said. I don't know how to find Sean. He wouldn't go back to his flat. He's probably staying with silk workers in Paterson. Thanks to that damn Abner McKinley, Sean's looking at even more trouble than Frank or Clay. I need to get far away. Far from New York. Far from Paterson. While Molly had her ear against the wall on the fourth floor, I made friends on my floor, two. You remember Colonel Thomas Ochiltree, talks almost as much as me, the one who hangs around with Abner? Well, Ochiltree has a valet. Oscar Petersen. He's from Galveston, in Texas. Ochiltree spends time in New York, but he lives in Galveston. That's where he met Oscar and hired him. Ochiltree always brings Oscar on trips. I got friendly with him, yuh know, maid and valet on the same floor."

This time, Bridget snickered. "This Oscar, is he another good-lookin' fella, Tara?"

"No, it's not like that. But you guessed right. He is handsome. Sean's still the one, for now. But Oscar said, months ago, that if I ever want to leave New York, he can help me find work in Galveston." Bridget angled her head. "Get your head outta the gutter, Bridge. He meant honest work. Says Galveston's a booming port, with lots of jobs. For girls like me, too.

But even if he didn't mean honest work, I need to get outta here. I told Sean about Galveston, when the coppers questioned him months ago about those anarchists in New Jersey. He said he would find me there if things started to heat up here. Said it'd be a safe place to hide out because it's far. I'll hunt for Oscar. Maybe he's staying at one of the hotels with Ochiltree. And maybe he's ready to leave that awful man. Ochiltree treats Oscar like shit." Tara looked down for a second, then at Molly. "You'll help me, right? Each day, even now, the papers list the hotels where the guests who escaped registered."

"Tara, I'll read you the list, but here's an idea. If Oscar stops working for Ochiltree and if you two lovebirds take a five-day train ride to Galveston, ask Oscar to teach you to read along the way. Maybe it'll take his mind off your bosom." Bridget saw Tara jut out her jaw. Molly stuck her jaw out farther. This time, the jabs were in good humor.

Clayton Byrne

A week after the fire, almost at midnight on Friday, Clay grabbed the sack of Kirk jewels from behind Claire Dunne's boarding house. The day before, he had asked his foreman if he could swap his Saturday day shift at the Windsor site for a night shift. Now, he had time to take the train to Philly.

For months, Clay had anticipated that if valuables went missing from the Windsor, the coppers would watch the local New York pawnshops. He made three trips to Philly during the winter to find an accommodating pawnshop on the edge of a fashionable neighborhood and to befriend the young and chatty clerk there, offering him one small piece of jewelry at a time. The past November, Clay grabbed a few plain rings from the bottom of overcrowded jewelry boxes in the Windsor's guest rooms, nothing he thought their owners would miss, while he did carpentry work. As far as the Philly pawnshop clerk knew, these rings had belonged to impoverished tenants in the apartment building Clay owned. The tenants had paid their rent in jewels. Clay suspected the clerk undercut his offer, but the take was still good. Now, when Clay arrived at the pawnshop with a large haul, the clerk might not be wary. Might even be happy to see Clay. Even so, Clay took care not to make the haul too large. He brought most of what he had stolen but held some back for another time.

"How'd you collect all this loot?" the clerk asked. Clay stared straight at the young man. Didn't look away. He could tell the clerk was straining not to drool at the sparkling gems.

"My renter had a whole floor. Didn't pay for months, then died on me.

Her posh aunt wanted to cover the debt, and she heard from her niece's neighbors that I would take jewels. Nice to have an aunt loaded with diamonds, right?"

The clerk looked at the jewels, then back at Clay, then back at the jewels. He scratched numbers on his pad of paper. Clay smiled at the total.

"I can give you half now. Don't have enough cash on me for the rest. Come back in a week."

Clay considered arguing, but instead pocketed the money and nodded agreement. He needed to get back to New York quickly to fetch the Haystacks from Lon, place them in an old piece of luggage, and meet with the fence his chums had recommended. The fence would be waiting for him.

Marguerite Wells

Marguerite savored McClusky's question. "Have you discovered anything else that seems peculiar?" he said. She had no ready answer, but she summarized for him the various theories of the case and commented on which ones seemed more likely than others. He nodded as she spoke, and when he had to leave for another meeting, he said he might call on her some other time to discuss the case.

Marguerite had not attended a women's college for nothing. She understood the value of companionship and knew her two new friends were also obsessed with the fire. They might offer insights she could share with the Chief Detective. She telephoned Angelica Gerry and sent a telegram to Theodate Pope, asking them to gather in a private side parlor at the Martha Washington on Friday, the 24th.

Angelica arrived first and offered a hug. A minute later, Marguerite confronted the awkwardness head-on.

"Angelica, I remember you were wary of seeing Theodate. You feared she knew from the papers that your father owned the Windsor and that she might believe the absurd charge that he had not taken care with his property. Please do not worry. You'll see as soon as Theodate joins us."

Minutes later, Theodate, dressed sensibly for travel, offered warm hellos and sank down onto the sofa.

"Angelica, it is good to see you. It's been months. And I'm so sorry about those reporters who slander your father. My own father practically spits on the papers when he reads those stories. He may live in Cleveland, but he follows Mr. Gerry's good works and knows he is a good man."

Angelica beamed.

Now Marguerite sat up straight, to do her part, to add balance. "Theodate, I hope I can prevail on you to share with Angelica your own story about your father and the fire. You told it to me in confidence, but you see, we are all facing questions swirling around our fathers. Knowing we are in the same boat may help going forward."

Theodate winced and moved forward on the sofa. "I understand. But please, Angelica, what I say should not go beyond this room. I must insist."

"Certainly." Angelica nodded as she spoke, with a slight twist of her mouth. She seemed miffed by the idea that she might tattle. Marguerite knew that Angelica tattled only to those she considered safe.

Theodate settled back in her seat and offered a short version of Alfred Pope's efforts to save his paintings. Angelica raised her palm to signal she had heard enough. "Oh, my. I'll tell you, if my father's precious library went up in flames, he, too, would send men in to save those tomes. And Marguerite, no need to persuade me to look into the fire. I've already started!"

Theodate interrupted. "Me too!" She laughed. Marguerite joined in, and even Angelica laughed.

"Ladies, let me go first," Theodate said. "You saw that the *Times* and the *Sun* reported on a story in the *Engineering News*, written by an engineer, David Stauffer, right? I sent him a telegram, signed it T. Pope, explaining I was an architect and wanted to meet at his office in the city to get additional insights on the Windsor. I went yesterday. You should have seen his face when I said I was T. Pope."

Marguerite gave a knowing smile.

"I had to insist I was indeed an architect. I came prepared with drawings. Showed him the plans for the houses I renovated and for my father's new house in Connecticut. I'm not sure Mr. Stauffer believed me, even then, until I started to use terms like balustrades and pilasters." More laughter. "Anyway, the man didn't have a doubt about the fire, not a single doubt. He insisted that one cigar smoker could not have caused the fire. He thinks the combustion began in the concealed hollows in the walls on the lower floors. Ha, hollows doesn't sound like an architectural term to me but I have to admit it helps visualize the problem. Cheap fire stops could have contained the fire to those separate, hmmm, hollows. He thought the fire could have smoldered for hours before it raged."

"Does that make sense to you?" Marguerite asked.

"Absolutely. Because the fire started everywhere, not just near the lace curtain."

Angelica pouted. "But the man is an engineer, not an architect."

"Right," Theodate said. "But would New York City architects ever blame one of their own? We don't remember who designed the Windsor, but they probably do."

Angelica moved forward to the edge of her chair "My turn. Let me tell what I learned at the Gould mansion. I visited there on Tuesday." She related what chef David Dudley said about the strange man who emerged from the hotel's side door, stripped off his fine clothes, and then was apprehended with Abner McKinley's valuables.

The three women looked at each other. Marguerite jumped in first. "This proves that the robbery was, I think they call it premeditated. Not just a crime of opportunity, when lowlifes see open hotel doors and enter and grab. But a crime that took planning."

"Yes, but maybe this lowlife," Theodate said, "or his gang if there was more than one, simply picked the parade day as a busy day, suitable for their plans, and the robbery was unrelated to the fire?" Silence.

"Let's see if we can question that thief," Marguerite said, looking at the carpet. "I've become acquainted with the Chief of Detectives, George McClusky. I met him when I inquired about my mama's pearls. I will ask."

Angelica leaned forward. "There's more, she said. "Simeon Leland called on Father yesterday. I'm sorry to sound unkind, but that man looks like a ghost. You probably don't remember seeing him. No color, wispy beige hair. He worked as the Windsor's front desk clerk, the one who ignored David Dudley's warning and then blamed the basement staff—the engineers and boilermen—when he told the police they had been frolicking at the parade.

Simeon admitted to Father that the men returned to the hotel when they heard shouts of fire. You see, Simeon's cousin is Warren Leland, the hotel manager who lost his wife and his daughter in the fire. He is friendly with my father. Warren doesn't want blame for employing irresponsible men, and he doesn't want my father blamed either. Even in mourning, Warren told Simeon to apologize to Father for stirring up a hornet's nest. Father thinks the basement staff tried their best to put out the fire.

As Angelica spoke Marguerite looked at one friend, then the other. "Does this undermine the theory that we should blame the basement staff because if they stayed at their posts, the fire would not have spread?" Theodate shrugged her shoulders. Angelica bit her bottom lip, disappointed that her rendition of Simeon's story had not been more conclusive.

"I suppose we have more work to do," Marguerite said.

"One detail," Angelica said. "My parents mustn't know we are looking into the causes."

"Nor mine," said Theodate.

"Nor mine," said Marguerite. "A fine lot of cowardly women we are." She used a different adjective in her private thoughts—self-absorbed. She suspected she and her friends dwelled on the reputations of their families more than the horrors of the fire for its victims. She remembered Tilly Brown, dead. She thought briefly of the maids and servants she had seen, out of work and probably scrambling for their livelihoods.

George McClusky

"Chief, a lady here to see you. Says she knows you."

Was the young detective smirking? George McClusky smiled narrowly. Miss Marguerite Wells entered, dressed in a blue frock, different from the one she wore the previous day. She looked lovely, eager.

"A pleasure to see you, so soon after our last conversation," he said. He pointed to a chair.

"Detective McClusky, thank you for seeing me, with no notice, late on a Friday. An hour ago, I learned more than I had read in the papers about that thief your men picked up during the fire. Felix Kain. Is he in jail? May I see him?"

McClusky laughed. "No, my dear, you may not." The "my dear" leapt out before he could stuff it back. Her eyes didn't show dismay. "He is at the Tombs, on Centre Street. It's foul in there. No place for a lady. Tell me what you heard."

Marguerite Wells repeated the story told by one of her friends. A Miss Angelica Gerry had visited Helen Gould's mansion, where she talked to the chef who couldn't convince the Windsor's clerk to sound the alarm. "When the chef returned to the mansion," Miss Wells said, "he saw your criminal outside the kitchen window. He threw off his best bib and tucker." McClusky looked at her blankly. "Oh, my apologies. That's an expression from the West. I grew up in North Dakota. Felix Kain threw off his fine suit, which had been covering ragged clothes."

"My, North Dakota. I never would have guessed. Tell me again who told you this? Angelica someone?"

"Angelica Gerry. The daughter of Commodore Elbridge Gerry. Her family has been friendly with the Goulds."

He knew, from Miss Wells's worry the day before about her mama's lost pearls, that her family had money. But that much money? A family from North Dakota? She saw the surprise on his face.

"I know the Gerrys only because I met them on a transatlantic passage last year."

"The Helen Gould you mention—is that the Miss Gould who's feeding the coppers on duty?"

"Yes, and Angelica told me Miss Gould vouches for her chef."

"Hmmm. Good. I'll go to the Tombs myself. See what I can learn."

"One more tidbit, Mr. McClusky. Angelica told me that Simeon Leland—he's the Windsor clerk who told reporters that he blamed the basement crew for the fire—he visited Elbridge Gerry. He's Angelica's father."

"He's the Gerry who owned the Windsor?"

"Right. Simeon Leland recanted his story. He said the crew returned to their posts quickly. He thought they tried to fight the fire. I doubt we should blame them for starting it or for how fast it spread."

McClusky puffed on his cigar. "That's not a tidbit, Miss Wells. That information will help me focus my investigation." My, the girl was more than pretty.

"Please let me know what you discover at the Tombs. I am staying at the Martha Washington Hotel for Women. The manager runs a fine establishment, highly respectable, and the guests look after each other." Why did she tell him where to find her, and then why did she mention other guests? Did she want him to find her, or not?

Tara Regan

Saturday morning, March 25, Tara asked Molly to help her send a message to Oscar Petersen, the valet who worked for Colonel Thomas Ochiltree on the Windsor's second floor. The papers listed Ochiltree's hotel as the Waldorf-Astoria, so most likely his valet roomed there too. Tara dictated to Molly. "Ready for Galveston plan? Meet me behind your hotel, 2:00 today." Using Claire's paper and pen, Molly started to write, then stopped. She covered a word with ink. "Let's use G," she said to Tara. "The first letter of Galveston. In case anyone, what's the word, intercepts the note."

The night before, Tara had explained to Molly and Bridget why Oscar might be ready for a change. Thirty years before, his parents left Sweden and settled in Galveston, where Oscar grew up. Seeking adventure, at age twenty, he signed on as valet for Ochiltree, Galveston's prominent promoter. At first, Oscar and Ochiltree got on. Oscar liked traveling and learning about business. The Colonel—who knew if he was really a colonel—had a circle of followers, told good yarns, and spent much of his time in New York. As years went by, Oscar came to see Ochiltree's deals as shady, especially those with Abner McKinley. Maybe the deals didn't cross a legal line, but they came close. Even before the fire, Oscar considered returning to Galveston. His parents wrote with news about employment at the wharfs—not only stevedores but bookkeepers and shopkeepers too. Tara knew he'd help her find work. Sean could find work there, too.

She'd heard some of the boarders recount a story in the papers that coppers had beaten up a valet trying to save his employer's valuables. Those bruits thought the valet was a thief. Oscar was not the only valet at the Windsor, but if the story was about him, he might be ready to walk out on Ochiltree.

Tara loved Sean's spirit, even developed sympathy for the anarchists he befriended. But she saw danger coming. Six months earlier an anarchist killed another member of Europe's royalty when Luigi Lucheni stabbed Empress Elisabeth of Austria. Coppers were sniffing around the anarchist cells. Time for Sean to get away.

Tara didn't tell the girls everything Oscar said when he first mentioned Galveston months earlier. "Don't worry, I know you are sweet on that Sean. He can come to Galveston too." Oscar tilted his head, then added a sentence. "But I won't cry if he doesn't come." Looking at Oscar's eyes look at hers, she suspected he thought he could win her affections on the long train ride.

Now, as 2:00 neared and Tara approached the Waldorf-Astoria, she pulled her coat collar up and her hat down, fearful that coppers hunting for Sean would hunt for her. The day was cloudy, with brisk winds from the east—others were bundled up too. Looking a half-block ahead, she saw Oscar, and saw that he recognized her gait and her half-hidden face. They embraced like old friends, friends who had not seen each other since the tragedy that befell them, that killed May and so many others.

Pulling away from the embrace, Oscar studied Tara's face. "You ready now?" he asked. What about Sean?"

"He's in trouble, Oscar. I can't say how. I want to run off. To Galveston. Sean says he'll follow, or I should say, when we talked about Galveston a few months ago, he liked the idea. Since the fire, I can't find him. He must be…hiding."

Oscar's blond brows met. "Hiding?"

"Is it all right if we don't talk about it? I'm trying to find him, to get word to him. But even if I don't right away, he'll know where I've gone. And you, are you ready?"

"I can't keep working for Ochiltree. I suppose I can turn away from his hustles, but he was a bastard during the fire. I helped him escape. Then he ordered me to go back into the hotel, while it was in flames, to collect his valuables and clothing. A copper saw me carrying out Ochiltree's things. He thought I was a common thief and bludgeoned me. I still have the marks on my shoulders. My neck." Tara grimaced as Oscar pointed to a yellow blotch under his muffler. "Ochiltree scolded the copper a bit, then turned to his valuables. He counted them, complained about the smoke stains on his silk robe. Never asked if I was all right. I detest that man."

Tara looked up at Oscar as he complained. Tall, handsome, even if she preferred Sean's dark curls. "We're both ready to go west. Enough of this New York misery."

Oscar told Tara to meet him two days later, at the 5:00 ferry going to Jersey City's Pennsylvania Station, where they would board the Pennsylvania Limited to Chicago. Then another train to St. Louis. Then another to Fort Worth. Another to Galveston. A five-day trip. His smile widened. He would advance her money for the train ticket.

"I can pay you back," Tara said. "I'm expecting a bit of money from a friend. Should have it by Monday."

Tara returned to the boarding house and begged Claire to let her stay two more nights. Next Tara needed Molly to scribble a short note. "For S. On way to G. Meet JC 5 Monday." No names. She gave a street urchin a muffin she pilfered from the pantry, telling him to deliver the note to Sean's parents, wrapped in the day's newspaper. Even if a copper intercepted the note, he wouldn't know G meant Galveston and, with luck, wouldn't guess that JC meant Jersey City.

Marguerite Wells

Two days after Marguerite first met McClusky, and one day after she informed him of Angelica's chat with David Dudley, the Chief Detective called on the Martha Washington's phone. He invited Marguerite to meet him again, this time for coffee that afternoon. If he realized, as Marguerite did, that they would be meeting three days in a row, his voice revealed no embarrassment.

When she arrived at the café, she spotted him seated at a table, dressed in his customary well-tailored suit. He glanced up, flashed a welcoming smile. "Miss Wells, good to see you. I have a little news, nothing conclusive. Last night, I followed up your lead about Felix Kain. The thief who stole from McKinley and flung off a suit of fine clothes—I believe you called it best bib and tucker." Marguerite cringed at the sound of her words. The detective looked uncomfortable. He did not mean to make fun of her.

"I went to the Tombs to see Kain."

"So soon. I admire your efficiency." Marguerite poured coffee from the carafe as she spoke, careful not to shake.

"Devery, that's Police Chief Devery, he has me working on many cases at once, but your information seemed valuable, so I went to see the thug. The warden put Kain on the third tier, along with other burglars. Crowded in—three in a cell. Not too bad, I've seen worse. Kain insists he worked alone. I doubt it, since he knew the location of McKinley's suite, and he didn't seem smart enough to have figured out the clothing ruse on his own. I asked to see the ragged shirt and pants the jailor took off him when he got to the Tombs. I found a cigar wrapper in a pocket. That doesn't prove much since half the city smokes cigars. But here's the key. The wrapper was from a fancy brand, fancier than what you'd expect. Kain isn't talking, isn't giving up any others, but the wrapper keeps the cigar theory afloat. Thank Miss Gerry for pointing me to Kain."

McClusky ran his hand over the rim of his cup. In the silence, Marguerite heard his foot tapping. "Miss Wells, having coffee with you is a pleasure, but I confess I have an ulterior motive. In view of your interest in the Windsor fire, would you consider doing me a favor or two? I sense you can go places where my men and I would be conspicuous. You can talk to people without alerting them to trouble. You see, for most people, if a New York detective shows up at their door, they clam up."

His mouth twitched, slightly. He must be misinterpreting her eager look. "I am sorry to say the department has no budget for extra help. I cannot offer payment."

"Mr. McClusky, I want to be of service. Do not worry about payment. Perhaps I should not say this, but my papa is a man of means. He adds to my modest salary as a schoolteacher in New Jersey. I do teach most of the time, though not this year."

She had given him an opening.

"You are not married?"

She shook her head.

"Nor engaged?"

"I stay busy with my teaching and other activities. I do some volunteer work. And I often travel to Europe with my parents, though I decided not to go abroad with them this spring."

He must have seen her glancing at his naked ring finger. "I am busy as well, but not with family, well, not in the usual sense. I live with my sisters on West 70th."

He gnawed on his thumb. Looked uncomfortable again. "You are alone in the city," he said, "but you must have friends here?" He wasn't going to say more about why he lived with his sisters.

"Yes, I do have friends, and to be honest, I came to talk to you the other day in part because I want to help them. One also stayed at the Windsor, though she was out at the time of the fire. She has questions about family valuables."

Marguerite paused for a second, thinking about Theodate Pope. At yesterday's meeting with George McClusky, Marguerite had said nothing about Theodate's talk with an engineer who believed the fire started long before any robbery. She had feared that the surname Pope might spark the detective's memory. He might connect Theodate's name to the brief mention in the papers of Mr. Pope's ill-timed directive to fireman McDermott to save paintings. That was unlikely, but this detective seemed smart. Marguerite would not say anything that might bring Alfred Pope into the discussion. She would honor her promise to keep mum.

"And another friend," Marguerite continued, "Angelica Gerry—the one who met with the chef—she did not stay at the Windsor, but she has a family connection to the hotel and knows the manager. And as for me," she looked at the bare wall across the room, "I was in shock when I escaped. I would like to know how we, how my family, how we saved ourselves. So, you see, I have many reasons for my interest in the fire and its causes."

For the second time, the Chief Detective ran his hand over the rim of his cup. "One more thing, Miss Wells. We would not want to spread around word of your help. Can we agree on that?"

Marguerite formed a reply in her mind, then stopped. She would deal with that later. For now, she smiled, a sign of agreement.

"Give me a day or two to collect the information I need to direct you. Let's meet again on Monday. Say 10:00. I will walk you back to your hotel."

Once back in her room, Marguerite looked in the little mirror and smiled at the confident woman she saw there. She felt contentment. Chief Detective McClusky viewed her as curious and clever. She hadn't exactly formed a partnership with him—he wouldn't admit he was working with a woman. He'd have to once she solved the mystery.

The next day, Sunday, passed slowly. The Astor Library was closed, the daily papers were winding down their coverage of the fire, Theodate had returned to Connecticut, and Angelica seemed occupied with her family.

George—Marguerite decided to stop calling him Detective McClusky or

Mr. McClusky—opened his office door himself on Monday, March 27. No junior detectives hovered around the office this time. Marguerite guessed they were running about fulfilling assignments. She sat in the same chair as before, but this time the room felt different. More inviting. She was about to get her own assignment.

George explained that nine days earlier, the day after the fire, he talked to Abner McKinley. Seemed like the right thing to do, given the President's concern about his brother's welfare. Abner wanted George to follow a particular path.

"Marguerite, have you heard the name Luigi Lucheni?" Ahhh, he moved to first names, too.

She wanted to make a good impression, but the name Lucheni meant nothing. She shook her head.

"Well, even I had forgotten about Lucheni until Abner reminded me. Six months ago, this Lucheni killed Empress Elisabeth of Austria. Stabbed her with a four-inch tapered file. Called himself an anarchist. A lot of those Italian anarchists come here, trying to convert others and plotting who knows what. Abner reminded me that there's word of an anarchist cell in Paterson. In New Jersey."

Marguerite bobbed her head, understanding. She began to remember stories about the Empress Elisabeth.

"Lucheni is on Abner's mind because there have been threats on his brother, the President. Abner worries about assassins. The President's wife worries, too. I talked to one of my detectives, a man we assigned last year to investigate the cells. Now here's where we connect to the Windsor. One of the men on that detective's list of people to watch is an Irishman named Sean Mack. Odd, right?—Irish. Word is that he's the only non-Italian allowed into that Paterson cell. So after the Empress's assassination, the President's guards sent word to police departments in cities across the East. Watch the anarchists. One of my detectives kept track of the cell that took in Mack. My fellow thought it odd to see a red-headed Mick attend meetings. Followed him. Learned he has a sweetheart. Can you guess who she is?"

His eyes twinkled. Again, she had no choice but to give George a blank look.

"A chambermaid at the Windsor. Tara Regan."

The name meant nothing, but she tried to twinkle her own eyes back at him.

"Here's my thinking," George said. "Maybe Mack wanted to harm Abner, either in the fire or maybe use the fire as a diversion to kidnap Abner, to get to the President. Or maybe those anarchists are stupid, and they think Abner McKinley is William McKinley."

Marguerite stopped trying to twinkle her eyes. Yes, the anarchists had taken to violent tactics. But she understood, as did her suffragist friends, that anarchists hated their governments because authorities often did the bidding of the rich, or to put it another way, of men. At least George limited his criticism to the word stupid. Many had said worse.

"And maybe," George continued, "this Tara Regan helped. But since my detective already questioned Mack once, a few months ago, about his connection to the cell, the firebrand will be on the lookout for us and say nothing. I'm thinking that if you can find Tara Regan, she'll have more to say because she won't know you're helping me. Of course, the connection of the maid to the anarchist could be a coincidence, a false lead. It might have nothing to do with the fire."

Marguerite sat still, hoping George was done with anarchists for the time being.

"There's more. Another path, you might say. Warren Leland was manager of the Windsor. You said your friend Angelica knows him, right?" Marguerite nodded. "He employed a detective named Harry Niehoff. Since Niehoff took Fridays off, he didn't work during the fire. When I interviewed him, he said that a day before the fire, he ran into a pack of Negro servants in the basement. One man and three women. He thought he heard them talk about robbing guests. He says he warned them off. Niehoff was in a sorry state, flustered, felt badly that he was the hotel detective, and the hotel burned down. I could tell he didn't like talking to another detective who might think he failed at his job.

"Niehoff couldn't remember the names of the servants. He wrote them down in two places—his notebook and the report he wrote for Warren Leland. But he kept his notebook in his Windsor office, and he gave the report to the night clerk, Frederick Leland." George paused and glanced at Marguerite. "Frederick Leland. We think he was Body #1." She didn't flinch. "Anyway, all the papers turned to ash. I'm hoping you'll talk to Niehoff. He might feel less awkward talking to you than talking to a detective who might judge him."

"I can certainly try."

"If you talk to Niehoff, try to persuade him to think back and remember names." He passed her a slip of paper, bearing the man's address. "And if you learn the names of any of the women servants, maybe you can find them. Question them for me. By the way, Niehoff isn't the only person who suspects robbery. Alfred Fuller does, too. He's a millionaire whose daughter and sister-in-law died at the Windsor. Daughter might be Body 2. He thinks he and his son saw a robber on one of the floors, maybe the third. He's not sure. A lot of cloudy minds that day."

Marguerite smiled to herself, conscious of her own cloudy mind.

Just then, a knock on the door. "Yes," George said, looking annoyed as a patrolman entered.

"Sorry to interrupt, sir, but I have orders from Chief Devery to deliver this to you."

George grabbed a small packet, wrapped in brown paper.

"And to sign for it, sir. So sorry."

George signed, looked at Marguerite, and unwrapped the packet. She saw him hold up what appeared to be a bullet, examine it. He glanced down at a tiny fragment of lavender cloth that had been wrapped around the bullet, then glanced at her. Again, she didn't flinch.

"George?"

"Well, damn—pardon my copper's language—I believe this bullet was fired."

Tara Regan

On Monday morning, March 27, Tara watched Claire rise from bed. "You look happy, Claire. Glad to see the two of us leave today? I don't blame you. Not easy for any of us. Thanks for not kicking us out."

"You really think Galveston and Hoboken will take in the likes of you down-and-outs? Ha. And I'll still have my sister hanging around."

The day passed slowly. Tara shuffled up and back across the room, holding Claire's borrowed brush in her hand, trying to tame her unruly locks. "Sit down." Bridget swiped her hand, pointing to the lone chair. "I can't stand your pacing and your brushing. One minute on the ferry, and your hair will frizz up again. You aim to look nice for Oscar or for Sean?"

Tara sat down on the chair's edge, leaning forward with her head in her hands. "I don't know, Bridge. You think I've done nothing but chatter and fuss since the fire, but these days, away from scrubbing bathtubs, I've been thinking. Especially today, now that I'm leaving. See, I reckon I came under Sean's spell. He has a cause, and he pulls people like me into it. Not sure I realized the danger, for him, for everyone around him. If I go to Galveston with Oscar, and if Sean doesn't come today, or soon, am I abandoning him when he needs me? Or giving him a way to get out of the mess he's in?"

Molly sat on the floor listening, sullen as usual, until she heard the word mess. "Mess isn't a strong enough word." She cast Tara one of her looks.

Tara stared out the attic window. "Bridge, you'll keep to our deal? No mention of our lads."

"I promise, Tara. Just be on your way. Ask Oscar to write from Galveston to say how you're doing. I'll send his parents a letter with my address once I know it."

"Here's Devan's address in Hoboken." Molly, her scowl softening, handed Tara a scrap of paper. "You tell Oscar to write me there."

"We had grand times until the fire, right?" Tara said. "It's only the last ten days that have been bloody hell." She made no effort to wipe her eyes. "I may never see you girls again."

"Who knows," said Bridget, "if Clay disappears on me, I may follow you to Texas."

Tara looked away. She and Molly suspected Clay would be in the wind before long, off to another con job. Tara put her old coat over her maid's uniform and tied the strings of her bonnet—the clothing she had worn escaping the fire. In a sack she carried her one dress, a dress that Claire had told her to take. After final hugs, Tara turned to leave. Mrs. Brownhill, looking content, offered a sandwich for the trip. "Happy to see me leave, Mrs. Brownhill?"

"Worth the price of a sandwich."

Tara rode a trolley to the Cortlandt Street ferry terminal. Oscar waited there, carrying more sandwiches. They boarded the *New Brunswick*, a double-decker ferry headed to the Jersey City railroad terminal. Tara stood on the ferry's top deck, looking out at the shoreline, not ready to tell Oscar that this was her first boat ride, her first trip west of the Hudson River. She would have plenty of time to tell him later. Reaching into her pocket, she fingered the bonus Clay dropped off the day before, using the same hiding spot behind the boarding house where he picked up the sack of Kirk jewels. Clay kept to his word. Now she could pay for her ticket, if she wanted to, and not be beholden to Oscar.

As the ferry pulled into the Jersey City slip, Tara saw a man with a scarf wrapped around his chin and long, dark hair. She motioned to Oscar to give her a minute and tucked her frizzy locks into her bonnet as she rushed toward the man.

He glanced past her and walked away. Not Sean.

Twenty feet away, Oscar paced. Tara loosened her bonnet strings, letting the wind blow her hair about. She turned toward the train station and whatever was to follow.

Molly Dugan

An hour after Tara said her goodbyes, Molly did the same. She left the boarding house, blessed too with a sandwich. Her escape from that airless room couldn't have come soon enough. She headed to the Vesey Street ferry terminal, not the Cortlandt Street terminal where Tara had gone. Clutching a bit of Clay's bonus money—she had mailed the bulk of it to her ma—Molly checked out the three ticket windows until she found the right one for the ferry to Hoboken. Like most of the chambermaids, she had never been on a ferry, had never crossed the Hudson. She boarded the *Bremen* and followed the crowd, taking a seat facing west toward Devan's home.

The blowing wind rocked the ferry. Molly's stomach flipped. She had no interest in her sandwich. She had told the girls nothing, but in her note to Frank, explaining where to find her, she used a form of shorthand and held nothing back. "With gap-tooth, have enough funds for month with his parents, feeling full." He would understand. He would come for her.

Bridget Dunne

Bridget looked around Claire's room and listened. Quiet. The day before, Tara and Molly had left. No more chatter, no more sourness. Soon, Claire would see no traces of the chambermaids. Bridget wore a frayed dress of Claire's and, in a satchel, packed her maid's uniform, still smelling of smoke despite washing. With the bonus money from Clay, she could stay in a hotel for a short time until Clay called for her and they could get a flat together. That sack hidden behind the trash in the backyard had let them communicate. Late on Friday, when Clay picked up the sack, filled with Kirk jewels, he found Bridget's note reporting on Molly's idea to seek work at the Ansonia. Bridget had chanced writing more than she should. Clay could drop the detail that he knew about Judith, Stokes's whore.

When Clay brought the empty sack back to its hiding place late on Sunday, he added the promised bonuses, along with a note reporting he'd been hired at the Ansonia that very day. "On at A.," he wrote. "Owner S. in hurry to finish so kept office open Sunday. Talked my way into seeing him. Did need to mention J. Not enough yet for SF. Find place to stay for a while and send word to A on your whereabouts." Bridget understood. Clay did not have enough money for them to reach San Francisco, though he thought he would soon. At least he would have steady work for a while. He was safe. But less eager than she expected to get together. Did he think of her as part of a past con, nothing more?

Bridget began to check seedy hotels off Broadway. The clerks looked her over, admiringly and suspiciously, but she had no choice. Rounding the corner from 45th to Broadway, she saw a man wave at her. Unruly beard, too long to be fashionable, too long for his age. She tried to place him. One of Clay's buddies. Ah, Lon.

"Bridget Dunne. Clay told me you were all right. Wahoo." He looked around, lowered his voice to a whisper. "We all survived, well, all except Sean. Miracle, right?"

"Lon, what happened to Sean?"

"Clay didn't tell you? We're not sure, but he's missing. We have to, well, assume the worst."

Bridget fell silent. She'd met Sean a few times. Saw him for a second that awful day she unlocked the closet for him and Clay. She should feel sorry Sean didn't make it, should feel awful for Tara, but she felt sorry, most of all, that Clay had not told her.

"Don't look so mad. Clay did well. Those jewels. Worth a lot. And the paintings. Those are the big hit. I'm grinning because that was me that lifted 'em. Didn't even know they was that valuable. Clay'll make a fortune if he finds the right fence."

Bridget forced a smile, then forced the smile to stretch wide.

"Right, Lon. Good find. Valuable?"

"That's what Clay says. Artist's name is Monet." Bridget heard the name as Mo Net. "Ugly pictures. Stacks of grain. But Clay thinks we hit it big."

Muttering goodbye to Lon, Bridget strode off, now looking not for cheap hotels but for a building she remembered on the south end of Madison Square, a building that housed an art gallery. She would not take Lon's word at face value. What did he know about artists? She would check. That was first. Later, she would write Tara about Sean, thankful for the distance between New York and Galveston. Later, she would murder Clay.

Bridget spotted the American Art Galleries. She knew her dress would not fool the fashionably dressed man she saw through the glass window into thinking she was a prospective buyer.

"Hello, miss. Can I help you today?" The man glanced at her face, her breast. He ignored her worn shoes. Maybe she had kept her good looks, despite the hurdles of the last week.

"Sir, I am here for my employer." Bridget hid any trace of her slight Irish brogue. "She asked me to inquire if you are familiar with a certain painter. If so, she will make an appointment to meet with you."

He did not seem surprised by her mission. "The painter's name?"

"Mo Net." Bridget repeated the name as she had heard it from Lon ten minutes earlier.

"Mo Net. Hmmm. I know many Americans pronounce the name that way, but the art world prefers the French pronunciation, mownay."

The man smiled, but not unkindly.

"We do not have any Monets at the moment. I am afraid Durand-Ruel & Sons, twelve or thirteen blocks north on Fifth, is where your employer wants to go."

Bridget grabbed the edges of her skirt in a modified curtsy and thanked the man. She turned right on Fifth and sprinted to the Durand-Ruel Gallery. No need to enter. She could tell from the carving around the door, the design of the window display, and the finery of the customers who entered that Mo Net or Mownay was a painter to be valued.

Clay had conned her.

Marguerite Wells

Harry Niehoff had worked as a detective, albeit for a hotel, not for the police force. Marguerite assumed he would dress like George McClusky—nice suit, pressed. No. Mr. Niehoff wore a rumpled suit when she met him at the entrance to the Astor Library. She suggested that location when she sent a message to Niehoff at the address George had provided. Niehoff's office at the Windsor didn't exist anymore, and the library seemed a respectable spot. Marguerite selected a table toward the back, nodding hello as she passed the smiling librarian at the front desk.

"Nice building, Miss Wells. I've never been inside." The other patrons stared.

"Yes, it's lovely, and private. But we'll need to keep our voices down. Before we talk about St. Patrick's Day, Mr. Niehoff, tell me how you've been doing since that awful day."

"Not good. I'm still hunting for work. The Windsor's manager wrote me a kindly letter of introduction, a reference, even though that poor man just buried his wife and daughter. Good people. They didn't deserve this. Mr. Leland treated me good all these years. And me, I was on my day off. Not sure I could have stopped a fire, but who knows? I might have spotted some shenanigans before it started."

"Yes. Mr. Niehoff, it is exactly that—shenanigans—I want to talk about. Detective McClusky tells me you mentioned that you overheard servants in the basement talking about their employers' valuables. He didn't think this would lead to much, but he thought since most of those servants were women, perhaps if I pursued that line of inquiry, I would have a chance of learning something. Women might be more inclined to talk to a woman than to a detective. I realize today is eleven days after the fire, but I hope you remember some details and can share them with me."

"I wrote up a report, nice and clean, and gave it to Fred, Frederick Leland. The night clerk. He probably died in the fire. I could have asked Mr. Leland if he had that report in a safe or something, but to be honest, I knew I had to ask him for a reference, and I didn't want to ask any more than I had to. He was grieving. All I have is my notes, the notes I used when I wrote the report. I told Detective McClusky that I kept my notebook in my hotel office and that it must have burned. But I was flustered when we talked—that was right after the fire. I forgot I had my notebook with me when I went home late that Thursday night. Otherwise, it would have burned up along with everything else. I reckon I should have found Mr. McClusky and told him I have it, but I've been kinda down lately, down about the fire, down that I don't have work."

Marguerite tipped her head slightly, signaling she sympathized. She waited, trying to hide how eager she was for him to share his notes. After what must have been two seconds but felt longer, Niehoff reached into his coat pocket. He pulled out a little notebook, worn and scratched, then flipped through the pages.

"Four of 'em, all colored. Leonard Stillman, he's a valet, works for Mr. Pope. Sarah Parker, she's a nurse for Mrs. Nancy Kirk." He looked down. "Mrs. Kirk, she died. Sue Bland, she's a nurse for Mrs. Margaretta Fuller and her daughter Florence." He looked down again. "Daughter died. Tilly Brown, she's a maid for Mrs. Alice Price."

Marguerite winced when she heard the name Tilly Brown. Then she stopped herself. Tilly couldn't have been involved.

"What do you know about them?"

"Well, here's the thing. Tilly Brown, she's probably dead. Sarah Parker, she went back to Chicago with Ellen Haskin, that's Nancy Kirk's daughter, to bury Mrs. Kirk. Sue Bland, she went back to Pennsylvania with the Fullers to bury their daughter, Florence Fuller. Now Leonard Stillman, Mr. Pope's man, he's still here because I don't think the Popes went back to Cleveland yet. I saw Stillman at the 51st Street station yesterday. Good looking man, gold tooth. I went there looking for some of the things—a clock, a picture frame—I kept in my office at the Windsor, and I saw him there, hunting for Mr. Pope's valuables. When McClusky sent you to ask about all this, he probably thought you could talk to the women, but they're all scattered. I don't know where you could find Stillman even if you wanted to talk to a colored valet, and I'm sure you don't."

"Mr. Niehoff, we have a strange coincidence here. The Popes are staying at the same hotel I stayed at until six days ago. Stillman must be with them. I will make inquiries."

Marguerite led the detective out of the library, thanking him for his help and wishing him well. As she walked back to her hotel, she knew she had to find Leonard Stillman. Theodate had mentioned his name. She believed some of her father's Monets were missing, but she never blamed servants. As a matter of fact, she said Leonard took special care with the paintings. If he did not steal the Monets, did he know of another servant who did? But she felt certain that Tilly could not have stolen anything. In any case, the poor dead girl couldn't defend herself.

Belinda Mason

Accompanying Nellie Wells as lady's maid, Belinda Mason berthed in steerage on the SS *La Touraine*, crowded in with other servants and impoverished travelers. At nearly six feet, Belinda had to stoop in her quarters, but she didn't mind. She had sailed to Le Havre before with the Wellses. Responsible for little more than Miz Nellie's wardrobe and coiffure, Belinda had time to walk the deck. But this voyage gave her too much time, time to think back to St. Patrick's Day. On that morning, Belinda had asked for an hour off. "Mind if I watch the parade, ma'am? You remember my pa was from Ireland." Since Belinda practically ran the Wellses' household whether the family was in North Dakota or Manhattan, there could be little doubt about Miz Nellie's answer.

"Of course, Belinda. As long as you get my dress ready for the party tonight, you should go out and watch the parade. Take as much time as you like."

Belinda had hurried down to the ironing room in the basement, where she was annoyed to see a gaggle of maids waiting for one maid, who seemed to be in charge, to parcel out odd-looking irons. That maid called herself Hortense. Poor woman had a horse face. Belinda pushed to the front of the group, grabbing Hortense's attention. If Belinda could iron Miz Nellie's purple-stripped gown quickly, then she could watch the parade. Hortense pointed to a board and an iron, offering vague instructions. Happy to get started, Belinda pressed the dress carefully, swearing to herself at the countless pleats, using words Miz Nellie forbade. When Belinda finished, she carried the dress up to the sixth floor and hung it on the front of the armoire. Belinda thought she heard the faint sounds of a band, so she grabbed her coat and mauve-colored bonnet. She mumbled goodbye to the Wellses who sat in the parlor up against the window. Then she ran to the street to claim a good spot.

Later, aboard *La Touraine*, Belinda thought back to that ironing room whenever she heard Mr. Edward and Miz Nellie talk about the cigar smoker, the robbers, the irresponsible basement staff. Belinda had an uneasy feeling but couldn't make heads or tails of her distress.

When the Welles reached Paris, they checked into the Grand Hotel du Louvre, one of the two or three luxury hotels popular with wealthy Americans. The clerk found a tiny room for Belinda on the top floor. In that floor's scullery, Belinda sometimes recognized other maids from America she had seen on previous trips. She paid attention to voices, eager to single out maids who spoke her own language, though rarely with her western twang. One day during her third week at the Grand, Belinda spotted a maid who looked familiar—plump, with blond braids circling her head.

"Hello," Belinda said, hoping for an answer in English.

"Ahhh, hello, someone I can talk to. I'm Lotte. Lotte Hansen."

"Yes, I think I've seen you before. Maybe at the Windsor? I'm Belinda Mason. Oh, the bloody Windsor."

"Yes, I was there with my mistress, Miz Ada, Mrs. Ada Pope."

Belinda looked at Lotte. Lotte stared back, widening her eyes, taking in Belinda's height, remembering. "We met in the ironing room, right? Can we talk? Maybe later tonight after our ladies are in bed?"

Marguerite Wells

Marguerite needed to meet Leonard Stillman, Alfred Pope's valet. She didn't want to ask Theodate to arrange such a meeting because at lunch the week before, Theodate insisted on silence about the missing paintings. She would not want Marguerite to snoop. Besides, Marguerite could not expect Theodate to buy into the improbable notion that thieves, intending to grab art, started the fire as a diversion.

Marguerite rose early on Wednesday, March 29, and walked six blocks down Madison Avenue, then through Madison Square Park. At the Hoffman House, she approached the front desk clerk before the Popes, who had not returned to Cleveland yet, were likely to be out and about. The clerk nodded hello. He recognized Marguerite from her family's stay there.

"Roger, good to see you again. Here's a note for Leonard Stillman, Mr. Alfred Pope's valet. You've quartered him downstairs?" She handed Roger a sealed envelope.

"Yes, he has a space in the basement." Roger looked puzzled, while Marguerite hid her relief that she had located the valet.

She anticipated that Roger would take a dim view of her communication with a negro valet. She had a ready explanation. "I am seeking the haberdashery that Leonard Stillman's employer frequented. My father admired Mr. Pope's top hats when we were all at the Windsor. I want to surprise Papa with a silk opera hat from Mr. Pope's hatter, but I must first learn his name. I could ask Mr. Pope himself, but he and Papa conduct business together. There are no secrets between those two."

With luck, Roger would not try to open the sealed envelope to read the true request she had written. "Mr. Stillman, I am a friend of Theodate Pope and known to her parents. I must ask you a question, in confidence, pertaining to the family's experience at the Windsor. I hope to meet you under the arch at Washington Square Park at 3:00 today. If you are unable to break away from your duties, please suggest a different time, sending a message to me at the Martha Washington Hotel." She prayed Leonard Stillman could read.

At 3:00 in the chilly, damp air of Washington Square Park, a tall, dark-skinned man with a noticeably high forehead and a gold tooth, wearing an immaculate coat, approached Marguerite at exactly 3:00, under the marble arch. He looked familiar. She had seen him at the Windsor. He must have considered this meeting carefully because he carried an umbrella and raised it over her head, even though the air had more mist than rain. She understood—it wouldn't be right to be seen strolling, even in daylight, even in a public park. But she could be seen talking and walking with a servant who protected her from the elements. Especially if the servant was not quite beside her, but a few inches behind.

"I have seen you at the Windsor, but we've never been properly introduced. I am Miss Marguerite Wells. I am assisting Chief of Detectives George McClusky in investigating the fire. Hotel Detective Harry Niehoff, too."

When Marguerite said Niehoff, she sensed the umbrella tilt over her head, saw Mr. Stillman pull his head back.

"Miss Wells, that Mr. Niehoff, he heard us joshing one day in the basement. We didn't mean no harm. Just joshing."

"Mr. Stillman, I know the Pope family, especially Miss Theodate. I am certain that Mr. Pope trusts you, as his valet, and would never keep in his employ anyone who would cause trouble. But I must ask you a question, and beg you to keep our conversation confidential, even from Miss Theodate." Marguerite paused. "This is a lot to ask from you, but my question would unsettle Miss Theodate." Marguerite's gaze held the valet's. "I need to ask about Mr. Pope's paintings. Do you know how many he had in his suite, and how many he retrieved?" Stillman looked puzzled by her question. "I realize you may not be able to help, but I am trying to sort out various theories of the fire. I urge you to share whatever you remember." Marguerite had little hope of an answer, but the only entry point into Niehoff's overheard conversation was the man standing slightly behind her, holding an umbrella above her dry head.

As she spoke, Stillman righted the umbrella. He relaxed a bit, though looking up at his stiff shoulders, she could tell he wasn't sure about her.

"His paintings? You mean the Manets? Cassatts? Monets?" Stillman pronounced the artists' names properly.

"I see you are familiar with the collection."

The compliment helped. He relaxed a bit more.

"Miss Wells, the paintings are beautiful. And, yes, I am his valet, but I also accompany him to galleries and to artists' workshops, and I carry what he buys, and hold onto his receipts and other paperwork for him."

"Ah, valuable assistance." She paused for a minute. He smiled. Perhaps pride in his work would loosen his tongue.

"After a buying trip, I also ship most of his paintings to his home in Cleveland. I crate them up real careful. But we had just returned from one of his trips to France, so many paintings were still in his rooms. I arranged them for him and told the maid I would dust them—she didn't have to. Mr. Pope and I didn't want extra hands on them."

"Then let me ask you, did Mr. Pope retrieve all of them? Or did you? Or a fireman?"

"I couldn't get them out myself." He looked at the arch, not at Marguerite, but she sensed more embarrassment than guilt. "I was working in the basement when the fire started, cleaning Mr. Pope's evening shoes in the boot room. It took me a while to find the polish I needed. See, the Popes had a social event that evening. Of course, that dinner never happened. When I heard screams, I grabbed the shoes, tried to get upstairs. Got as far as the lobby. People were rushing down. I couldn't get up. I dropped the shoes, tried the servants' stairs. They filled with smoke, and more people rushed down. Even some guests took those back stairs. I knew Miz Ada and Miss Theodate were paying a social call, and Mr. Alfred went to a business lunch.

I wasn't worried about them, only worried about the paintings. Especially the Haystacks. He bought two others in '91, they're safe in Cleveland, and on his last trip, he bought two more from a French dealer. Mr. Alfred likes to collect things."

"Haystacks?" Marguerite tried for a casual tone. "Do you think those two were saved?"

Now, Mr. Stillman was the one to pause for a second. "Mr. Alfred tells me so, but I'm not sure. I helped him take his paintings, the ones Fireman McDermott rescued, across to the drugstore for safekeeping that day, and then a day or two later, I helped Mr. Alfred take them to a warehouse. He said he had all his art. But I don't think he had the Monets, the Haystacks. I carried eight paintings to the drugstore, but no Haystacks. I didn't want to disagree with Mr. Alfred. I don't do that." He looked at her, drew in a long breath. "You won't say anything?"

"We speak in confidence, Mr. Stillman. Do not worry."

"I should be believing Mr. Pope, right?" He smiled, swung the umbrella away from Marguerite's head, and walked away.

Leonard Stillman did not steal the Haystacks or anything else. Marguerite felt sure of that, even if Niehoff had heard him bantering about valuables. Stillman loved those paintings. But his last line—"I should be believing Mr. Pope, right?"—stuck in her head. Was the valet protecting his employer from embarrassment? Could a thief, unconnected to the valet or without his knowledge, have realized the value of Impressionist art and set a fire as a distraction? If so, what would a thief do with the paintings? George had sent nothing but long shots her way. No matter, she would follow those long shots. But she would not tell the detective about the paintings for as long as possible.

When Marguerite returned to the Martha Washington Hotel, she sent a telegram, the oddest she had ever sent, to her former art professor at Smith College. "Perhaps you remember me. Marguerite Wells, class of 1895. Need guidance. Seeking Monets to purchase. Louisine Havemayer not available. Can you suggest NYC dealer?" The next morning the desk clerk handed her a short telegram. "I remember you. Only student ever from N.D. Durand-Ruel & Sons Fifth and 36."

Marguerite would ask at the Durand-Ruel gallery—was the value of Monets generally understood? If she could find a gabby gallery assistant, she might even find a way to ask if Monet's paintings had been stolen in the past, or if fences were already in the business of dealing with Impressionist art.

She needed more information before she visited the gallery. Back to the Astor Library. She chatted with the friendly front desk librarian. Ten minutes later his page delivered a pile of newspapers to Marguerite's favorite library table. She skimmed the columns on the art world for names that might lead to men who fenced valuable art. Within minutes she learned enough to decide against a visit to Durand-Ruel & Sons. Their gallery was in a building owned by Louisine Havemayer's husband. The Popes knew the Havemayers—Theodate and her mother had called on Mrs. Havemayer, a well-respected collector, the day of the fire. Skimming more articles for the names of other collectors and galleries, Marguerite began to realize the small size of the city's art world, and that everyone in it knew the Havemayers. If word got back to Mrs. Havemayer that a nosy lady came searching for two missing Monets, Theodate's father Alfred, and Theodate herself, might hear of it. Theodate could trace the leak and blame Marguerite for blabbing. Once the art world knew that Alfred Pope had saved valuable art but lost two Monets in the fire, the story of his focus on paintings over women's lives might spread. To learn of lowlifes who fenced paintings, Marguerite would have to look elsewhere.

As she refolded one of the papers, a headline in a small column caught her eye. "Windsor Thieves Arrested." Two laborers at the Windsor site had grabbed a bracelet and a silver watch from the smoldering ruins. They turned over their booty to Norton's Pawnshop, in return for fifty cents for the bracelet and two dollars for the watch. One of George McClusky's detectives, in touch with pawnshop owners near the Windsor, arrested the idiots. Marguerite jotted down Norton's address. Perhaps the pawnshop owner would offer help. She returned the papers to the page, smiled at the friendly librarian, and planned her afternoon excursion.

To prove her authority, Marguerite had only a calling card George had given her. That would have to do. She donned a somber black dress, the most official garb she owned, thankful that a harried seamstress had finished it the week before in preparation for an ocean voyage. Marguerite strode to Norton's on Third Avenue near 45th. Opening the door, she saw shelves and shelves of sad looking items—silver serving pieces in need of polish, chipped china, scratched valises. The musty smell of unwanted bric-a-brac hit her.

"Sir, I hope you can help me. Chief of Detectives George McClusky directed me here." She flashed his calling card in front of the pawnshop's proprietor, a little man with a few strands of hair slicked back in greasy rows over a bald pate, wearing a soiled jacket. "Detective McClusky understands that several paintings I own were stolen from my townhouse. He told me that neither he nor his fellow detectives are knowledgeable about paintings. He suggested I come see you personally to ask if any paintings have been pawned here."

The uneasy owner looked at the card and stepped back a foot. He did not need more trouble. "Ma'am, the detectives know that I do not accept stolen goods. Every now and then I accidentally buy an item that could have been stolen, but if that happens, I cooperate with them. Always." Sweat collected on his forehead. "And you should know that we are not in what you might call the high rent district here. If you are looking for valuable art, try McAleenan's on Broadway and 35th." He wiped his brow with his fingers, then rubbed his damp fingers on his jacket.

Marguerite walked southeast to McAleenan's. Entering the shop, she saw cases of glittering jewels and fine leather goods, displayed attractively. She sniffed. No musty smell in this shop. A well-groomed clerk greeted her. She offered the same story she had used at Norton's and flashed the same card.

"Ma'am, can you tell me the kind of paintings you lost? The artists?"

"Two Monets. Paintings of haystacks."

"Ah. We would know those paintings and would suspect theft immediately. The thieves who, well, who know their business, if you want to call it business, they know to avoid pawnshops, especially reputable ones like ours. They use fences instead." He paused. "Fences. I doubt you have heard that word before. That's the vernacular term for irresponsible men who deal in stolen goods. Fences have begun to specialize. A few deal in stolen art. We know of them because sometimes the police, like Detective McClusky, check in with us to see if by chance we've been offered valuable art, and then we read about the resolution of those cases in the newspapers."

"Very helpful sir. Do you know the names of any of these, what did you call them, fences?"

"You might try a man named Seth Sennett. He lives two blocks away. He had been pawning his possessions here almost weekly—we are the nearest pawnshop to his flat—but then I saw his name in the papers, along with his address." He looked at Marguerite, raising his eyes. "I don't accept his goods anymore. You see, I have been following his story. Two years ago, the police suspected him of stealing a Mary Cassatt pastel. He invited the police to search his flat, to talk to his banker, to check with his neighbors. The police found nothing. That's probably why Detective McClusky never gave you Sennett's name. But I am not sure the man is innocent. A week after the theft, Mr. Sennett came to our shop to redeem a gold watch chain and cufflinks he had left here. He had come into money. Up until then, he always wanted to sell, never to redeem. Suspicious?"

"Would you be able to tell me what this Mr. Sennett looked like?"

"Shorter than average, nice looking, wavy brown hair, neat scar on his chin, spectacles."

"I can tell you are a keen observer."

He grinned. "A clerk in a fine shop must be."

"And can you tell me the location of Mr. Sennett's apartment?" He could.

"You have a fine memory for details," she said. He grinned again.

"But please, miss, don't search him out yourself, though he does not look like the dangerous type."

"Of course not. I will pass along your information to my butler who will inquire on my behalf. We will not mention you or the name of your shop." With a look of appreciation, Marguerite left and walked around the block, in a direction away from the address the clerk had offered in case he decided to watch her from his window. Once beyond the clerk's sight, Marguerite reversed directions on a parallel street.

Mr. Sennett lived in a respectable building, on a respectable block. She couldn't barge in without a plan.

W.E.D. Stokes

Two weeks had passed since the fire. William Earl Dodge Stokes no longer doubted that Judith Jones perished. His whore's name never turned up in any of the papers. Fifty dollars had prevented day clerk Simeon Leland from adding Judith's name to any registry before the fire, and fifty more kept him from adding it to the lists of the missing after the fire. Still apprehensive, Stokes read every paper, looking for news. On the morning of April 1, he spotted a story headlined *More Missing from Windsor Fire*. He grabbed a shot of whiskey, despite the hour, then read on. Women fussing about missing husbands, husbands fussing about missing wives, toffs fussing about missing servants. But, thank the lord, Stokes found nothing about Judith. Also reassuring—she had never sent word to him. Had never turned up, asking for money, for a suite in his new hotel.

He had Judith's bracelet, though that had caused him no end of troubles since the damn distrustful copper guarding the guests' gems knew it was found in a place that had no connection to the baths or to his own suite. And then that copper had to blab to a reporter. Now, the bigger problem was Rita. She knew about the bracelet—all of New York knew about the bracelet—and she suspected he kept a woman. She always suspected that. His wife was a lot of things, but she was not stupid.

What would Rita think if she knew that Judith burned to death? That he did nothing to save the whore? That he never told her next of kin? He didn't know much about Judith, just that she had a brother somewhere in the Yukon. Most likely, Jones was not her last name, or her brother's. He could inquire about her family at the private club where he met her, but

Madame McGuire was discrete. He suspected she rarely asked about the families of her girls, and if she did, she would not keep records. No, his best choice was to spend an hour mourning Judith, perhaps donate to the bulging fund for the family of elevator operator Warren Guion, as a form of penance, and then move on. And visit Madame McGuire to see if she had welcomed any new girls into her parlor.

Marguerite Wells

Marguerite spent hours imagining how she could check on Seth Sennett, the man who might be fencing stolen Monets. The city detectives who investigated him two years ago found nothing worrisome. She would try herself.

A cafe down the street from Sennett's apartment opened at 7:00 in the morning. She could watch his building from a seat near the window and either confront or follow him. She would come to think of cafes as the perfect woman's detective office.

Marguerite expected she would need to wait days to find Sennett. To her surprise, after going through only one cup of tea, she saw a man with wavy hair and spectacles leave his apartment building. She couldn't see if he had a neat scar on his chin, but she felt confident this man was Seth Sennett. Since she had paid for her tea in advance, she followed him with no delay. He walked to a corner, where he stood for a minute looking north. When a trolley heading south on Broadway arrived, Sennett hopped on. She did, too. He hopped off at Dey Street and walked to an impressive five-story building, the Mercantile National Bank. He entered with a key before the bank opened.

Knowing she could not enter the bank that early, Marguerite strolled around the city for hours. At 10:00, she entered and saw Sennett behind a teller's window. He was looking down, counting bills. The other tellers were busy too, and the only guard she saw was giving a customer directions to the loan department. She exited before anyone could notice her. On a corner of Broadway and Dey, out of sight of the bank windows, Marguerite waited for the trolley headed north. She returned to Sennett's apartment building, hoping to learn if he had a wife and children. She guessed that a trained detective like George would not pay attention to a criminal's family, but she wanted to know everything she could about her prey. A handwritten directory in the well-swept vestibule listed the names of residents in the order of their flat numbers. "302, S. Sennett." She walked around the block, trying to imagine a reason to knock on that door. She devised a simple plan, one unlikely to get her in trouble.

Marguerite entered the apartment's vestibule again and climbed to the third floor. After pausing to catch her breath, she knocked. Footsteps inside, moving closer.

"Yes?" A woman's voice came through the door.

"I am Miss Mary Wilson from the New York City Woman Suffrage League on East 14th Street. I would like an opportunity to tell you about our efforts to persuade legislators in Albany to support the suffrage amendment."

The door opened two inches. Marguerite saw a sliver of a woman's face, staring. Lovely. Looking down, Marguerite saw an equally narrow sliver of a small child.

"I don't mean to be rude, not to a lady, but I have no interest in the vote. I trust my husband to vote for our family."

"If at any point you reconsider, please visit the League at our 14th Street address. And thank you for your time."

Marguerite smiled to herself as she walked back down to the vestibule. The teller—or was he a fence—had a family. She had learned from McAleenan's clerk that Mr. Sennett visited that pawnshop regularly, but if he had a decent job as a teller at the well-known Mercantile Bank, why was he a habitual pawner? The man needed money. Had he tangled himself up in gambling or women, the two obvious sins?

The next day would be Saturday, March 31, then Sunday. On those days, Sennett would have no routine. Marguerite had to wait two days to further her inquiries. Inquiries. Maybe she should start to label her efforts an investigation, and to label her methods surveillance.

On Monday, in the late afternoon, Marguerite found a cafe across from the Mercantile Bank. Cafe number two, she would name it later. She wore one of the three new hats she had purchased.

"I am waiting for my friend, but she gave me conflicting information about what day she might arrive, and I can't reach her. Don't be surprised if you see me occupying one of your tables a few times this week." She ordered the most expensive stew and dessert, to keep the waiter happy and quiet. Every dinner hour for the next few days, she either sat in the cafe or on a bench in front of the Mercantile. When she spotted Sennett leaving the bank, she followed him on the trolley. Monday, he went back to his apartment. Same on Tuesday. And Wednesday. She wore a different hat each day, but even if he noticed a woman taking the same path he did, he had no reason to suspect her motive. On the fourth day, Thursday, Sennett stepped off the trolley early, on East 4th Street, and headed a block to the bowery. Surprised, Marguerite just managed to exit behind Sennett before the trolley driver started up again.

Marguerite knew she would be conspicuous, alone and dressed as a lady, in that rundown section, but what else could she do? She followed Sennett, walking briskly. He turned into a disreputable looking establishment near Cooper Square. She guessed from the hurrying men and indecently dressed women coming and going through the door of the establishment that it must be a brothel. If so, Sennett would not be there all night. She walked up and down the block, feeling uncomfortable, hoping the people on the street were too inebriated or too absorbed in their own worlds to notice. An hour after he entered, Sennett exited.

Pleased with her surveillance, Marguerite caught a hansom cab to the Martha Washington. Walking through the lobby, she saw the evening editions spread across the ornate table, as usual. This time, she didn't even try to walk past the newspapers. That afternoon, April 3, laborers discovered the last chunk they could call a body. A supervisor labeled it Body 35. As was the case with most of the other bodies, no one knew whether 35 was a man or a woman, young or old.

Frank Corbett

The Windsor's Chief Engineer, Frank Corbett, hid inside his flat, going out only for necessities and to meet with J. H. Sullivan, the Chief Electrician, to plan their next steps. On April 3, while Marguerite Wells staked out the Mercantile Bank, Frank and Sully huddled in a back pew of the Church of St. Paul the Apostle on the corner of Columbus and 60th. No fingers would point at them there. They avoided their neighborhood church and the churches closer to the site of the Windsor.

"Look." Frank shoved an official-looking document in front of Sully. "A summons to testify at the coroner's inquest."

"That damn Simeon Leland," Sully said.

"Pipe down. We're in a church."

Sully lowered his voice a tad. "No one's here. It's Monday morning. Even the priest is asleep." Sully read the summons, then reread it. "Simeon's behind this. That weaselly hotel clerk puffs himself up because he sat behind a desk and because he's Warren Leland's cousin. Why did he have to go and tell coppers and reporters he saw us outside watching the parade? Everyone's blaming us for the fire. Some guests saw us too. But guests never pay attention to engineers and boilermen, right? They might not know who's who. Simeon's the problem. The coppers know he worked at the hotel for years. He'd recognize us. Still think we should let things play out and hope for the best?"

Frank shrugged. "Got a better idea?"

"Yeah. I have a plan." Frank listened, then offered a slight bow in mock surrender.

"Hey, Frank, why did you get a summons and not me? Must be that the sound of you singing Molly Malone in your awful voice was more memorable than my tall body sticking up over the crowd." Sully snickered.

Later that day, Sully paid a messenger to deliver a sealed note to Simeon Leland. The Windsor's front desk clerk still sat at a table at the obliging Hoffman House, keeping track of Windsor guests' whereabouts. "Meet with me and F. Corbett," Sully had written. "Hear us out, for your own sake and your family's sake." Sully suggested the next night and a bar far from the rubble. Frank told Sully to add "family's sake" to the note, guessing that might keep Simeon from sharing the name of the bar with the police. Of all the suspected causes of the fire, Frank doubted the basement crew had risen to the top of the list, but he couldn't be certain.

At the appointed hour, Frank entered the bar, standing straight as usual to mask his short stature. No police were in view. Simeon Leland cowered in a chair off to the side. His pale wisps of hair clung to his damp forehead. His narrow lips had almost disappeared.

Frank grabbed three beers from the bar and brought them to Simeon's table. Sully entered the bar then—two minutes after Frank, as planned—slouching to mask his height. "Sorry about Warren Leland's daughter and wife," Sully said, taking a seat and sliding a mug toward Simeon. "Awful to lose two relatives like that." Frank nearly choked on his beer. Sully was a smooth talker, but who could be this smooth? Would it make any difference? Simeon stopped squirming, but he wouldn't meet Sully's eyes. Didn't reach for the mug.

"Frank and me," Sully said, "we each saved some money over the years. We won't starve, but we need to find work soon. You're out of work now too, right?"

Simeon warmed up a bit. Someone cared about his income. "I hoped Mr. Gerry would rebuild. A new hotel. That's not looking good. And my cousin, he wants me to stay at my station at the Hoffman House to keep track of Windsor guests for another week. Poor man, he's still mourning his wife and daughter, then he goes and has an appendix attack a few days ago, and surgery. But he still pays attention to everything. Always checking on me. So I can't go look for work yet." Simeon reached for the mug, took a swallow.

Frank saw Sully sit up straighter. The small talk was over. Sully moved right into the plan he'd laid out for Frank the day before.

"Me and Frank are going around to other hotels, new office buildings too, that might need experienced engineers, electricians. We're calling on the managers at the Waldorf-Astoria and the Murray Hill tomorrow. Fifth Avenue Hotel the next day. Want us to see if they need an experienced clerk? In case Mr. Gerry doesn't rebuild? Or takes his time?"

Sully swigged his beer. Frank followed suit.

Simeon squinted at his supposed drinking buddies, took another swig himself, then said, "Put in a word for me?"

"Sure. We're all in this together."

Now, it was Frank's turn. Months before the fire, Molly told him about W.E.D. Stokes's girlfriend, hidden on the fourth floor. Frank wasn't sure whether Simeon, stationed at the front desk all day, would have noticed.

"And there's one other place we're trying," Frank said, keeping his eyes on Simeon. "You know Stokes, W.E.D. Stokes? The society rake who lived in the Windsor with that pretty wife Rita and their little boy? He's building a new hotel, enormous one, uptown. Calls it the Ansonia. Might be positions open there. You know him?" Frank paused a minute and didn't take his eyes off Simeon, then spoke slowly. "Know him well?"

Simeon didn't change his expression much. Just the slightest movement of his jaw. Either he didn't know about the woman Stokes stashed away or was careful not to let on. Frank and Sully thought that if Simeon did know about the woman, maybe he'd enjoy being part of a minor extortion scheme. Mentioning the woman to Stokes as they asked for jobs hardly seemed like a crime. But it didn't matter whether Simeon knew about her or not. The Ansonia was a good lead, in any case, to keep Simeon on their side.

"One more thing, Simeon." Sully took up the conversation to close the deal. "You told reporters that we left our stations that day. Well, right, you did see us watching the parade. We were out there for one minute. One. We ran back as soon as we heard the cry. Meanwhile, you were talking to that chef from the Gould mansion. You ignored what he said to you. You wasted precious minutes."

Sully's eyes bored into Simeon's.

"Hey, I went to see Elbridge Gerry a few days after the newspaper stories. I told him you went back inside, fast. My cousin didn't want anyone to think Gerry hired slackers." As Simeon spoke, sweat beaded on his forehead.

Sully tipped his head, paused for a second. "That's a start, but you didn't go back to those reporters or to the police and say the same thing, did you?"

"No. But be honest. One minute—or maybe it was five—could have made a difference." Simeon scratched his damp cheek, getting ready for his next line. "Maybe we all, in your words, wasted precious minutes."

Sully jerked his head back, the slightest of jerks, but continued as planned. "The reporters have both those stories already, the story about the chef and the fake story about us, but they didn't make much of any of that after the first day or two. Their readers only wanted to hear about body counts. And maybe the cigar smoker. Don't you think we should keep it that way? You stop talking, and we'll stop talking. Wouldn't want your wife and the little ones to have to answer for those wasted minutes, right?" Sully took another swig of beer, put his elbows on the table, and moved his reddening face close to Simeon's ghostly face. Frank could smell the clerk's sweat.

The three men left the bar together, Simeon trailing the others. On the sidewalk, Sully reached down to pat Simeon on the back. "We'll let you know how the job search goes. Whether any of the managers need a clerk." Simeon offered a weak thanks and scampered away, not thanking Frank for the beer.

Sully's plan had worked. Simeon understood he should watch his mouth.

As Frank walked quickly back to his flat, he thought about Molly Dugan. He knew from her cryptic note of the previous week that she was with the assistant butcher at his parent's house in Hoboken and that she had enough money to pay her expenses. Frank didn't spend much time pondering how she had acquired that money. He focused instead on Molly's word "full," the word they had used that winter for another maid in the family way. His eyes filled every time he reread the note and imagined himself holding an infant. Frank would fend off blame, find work, and marry Molly Dugan. His Molly would not resemble Molly Malone, the lass he sang about as the flames rose on St. Patrick's Day.

Marguerite Wells

Marguerite thought of herself as a Smith College graduate, as a suffragist, as a teacher, as a traveler. Not once had she considered herself a blackmailer. After she readily agreed to help George with his inquiries, she wondered if she had stepped out of line, her own line. How could she have agreed to help if it meant becoming mixed up with criminals? She prayed her parents would never learn of her antics.

In the dining room and lobby of the Martha Washington Hotel for Women, Marguerite saw other women unchaperoned and on their own. She began to relax, to sense that her openness to adventure could outbalance her fears. Or was she fooling herself? Did she simply aim to help George, to earn his respect, to find ways to keep meeting him? Had she avoided telling him about the stolen Haystacks to honor Theodate's demand for secrecy? Maybe, but Marguerite knew she also wanted to prove her cleverness to herself and to George.

On April 7, the day after Marguerite followed Sennett to the brothel, she waited outside the Mercantile Bank for him to leave work and return home. He walked out with other employees, all chattering to each other. She lurked behind until Sennett's companions turned in another direction, and he stopped to wait for the trolley. She slinked up to his side.

"Mr. Sennett, I believe. My name is Mary Wilson. I need to discuss a painting with you."

If she had any doubt that she had followed the right path, his look ended that. He did indeed have a neat scar on his chin, and he looked petrified.

"There," she said, pointing to a cafe a block south, not the one where she had set up shop near his apartment and not the one where she had set up shop close to his bank. Cafe number three.

Sennett looked around, wondering if he should run, looking her over, probably guessing she wouldn't run to follow him.

"I must get home. No time."

"I don't think you want to go home to your lovely wife and little daughter in apartment 302. Not yet."

They had spoken only a few sentences to each other, but Sennett knew he was in trouble. He let her lead the way to a table at the back of the cafe. They sat silently, speaking just to order tea. Marguerite hid her shaking hands on her lap.

"The Cassatt pastel, Mr. Sennett. Tell me about it."

He looked at the damp table as he muttered. "I did not steal the Cassatt. The police found nothing."

Still hiding her shaking hands, Marguerite moved to the Monets. "And the Haystacks?"

"Haystacks? What are you talking about?"

"Mr. Sennett, I do not think of myself as a mean woman, but I believe you are lying, and to get to the point, if you continue to lie, I will send your wife a note about your visit yesterday to a certain establishment in the bowery."

The man was more scared than she was. He lost all color. He began to whimper. He faced the wall, away from the cafe's other patrons. Marguerite squirmed, then she reminded herself that this man had committed at least two crimes, probably more. She moved her fingers in her lap into closed fists.

"Tell me how you came to get the Monets and what you did with them."

His eyes roamed from the table to the floor. He must be calculating what to say and what to hide.

"Miss Wilson, if that's your name, I will tell you part of the story. And I will admit my role in all this. But if I tell you everything, my life will be at risk."

She did her own calculating. Did she care what happened to those

Monets? She appreciated the new art, so, yes, she cared, but after all, Alfred Pope still had eight of his ten paintings. She reminded herself that she cared most about the first part of the crime, the fire.

"Start with the very beginning."

"My name showed up in the papers when I was accused—falsely, I tell you—of stealing a Cassatt pastel." The man's eyes still roamed, but his voice grew stronger. "Thieves in the city had my name, and some suspected—again falsely—that I could find buyers for art, valuable art.

"A man approached me two weeks ago. Tall, red hair. Ladies might say attractive. Looked Irish. Maybe in his late twenties. Said he might be able to get two Monet Haystacks. I didn't think he knew a haystack from a pile of manure, excuse my language, but when he showed them to me, I knew they were the real thing. I am a bank teller. I examine bills throughout the day. I have an eye for detail. And I do know buyers, out of state gentry, though, as I said, I did not reach out to them for the Cassatt. I am a likeable fellow, my friends tell me, and people of all sorts warm up to me without hesitation." Marguerite recalled the man talking animatedly to his companions ten minutes earlier. She nodded, coaxing him to continue.

"I will not tell you the identities of the bluebloods. They are vengeful men. I took the Monets on, you might say, consignment. The potential buyer has hired a specialist to verify their provenance. Coming from Boston next week. The buyer could have trusted my eye. I'm never fooled."

Once the man starts talking, Marguerite thought, he doesn't know when to stop.

"His name?" she asked. "Not the bluebloods. The name of the man who stole the paintings. And where can I find him?"

"He didn't give me his name, just his address, so I could turn over his share to him once the buyer pays. The thief didn't want any money going through banks. A smart man, smarter than I thought. Knows the police can trace bank transfers."

He gave Marguerite the thief's address in the West Forties, a neighborhood known as Hell's Kitchen. Then more whimpering. "Please, miss, I have said all I can without endangering my life. I am done with this business now. And done with the, the business, in the bowery. Keep my wife out of this. Victoria doesn't need to know, right?"

Vile man. He stole valuable art. More seriously, for Marguerite if not for the police, he betrayed his wife and child. And married a woman too stupid to want the vote. Marguerite wondered—when he said "Victoria doesn't need to know," was he referring to the art or the whores or both? But she had what she came for—information on the Haystacks. Looking at weaselly Sennett, she knew that enforcing the law, or morality, was beyond her plan.

The information she gathered from Sennett could lead to a gang of robbers who might have started the fire to cover their thievery. She could get closer to understanding how the fire started, or to understanding the split-second decisions people made that day. Did she selfishly descend first? Did Alfred Pope care more about his paintings than burning women? Was Theodate Pope too preoccupied to dissuade her father from his misguided passion? Should Angelica Gerry's father have insisted the Windsor have the same protections as his mansion? Should Marguerite's papa deal squarely with conflicting reports of his actions? Were the flames spreading too fast for anyone to think clearly? Or was self-preservation stronger than all other characteristics?

"Mr. Sennett, if I find the thief, that's sufficient. If I cannot find him, I will return." Marguerite stood up and walked away, leaving him to pay for the untouched tea. She made a point of remembering his wife's name, Victoria.

Tara Regan

To Tara's surprise, Galveston sat on an island, like Manhattan. The Gulf of Mexico surrounded one side of the thriving city, and the Galveston Bay surrounded the other side. When Oscar led Tara out of the Union Depot on 25th Street, she could see ships anchored in the busy port, more ships than she ever saw on the Hudson. The weather felt warm, too warm for Claire's old dress. Tara looked up, following a flapping noise. Enormous birds flew along the shoreline. "Brown pelicans," Oscar said. "If I wasn't in a hurry to get home, you could stand on the shore and watch them scoop up fish in their pouches."

Ten minutes later, the Petersens welcomed Oscar home. They had received his telegram explaining he would arrive with a young woman who had lost her housing in the fire. He had added nothing about whether this woman was a friend or a lover. After embracing Oscar, the Petersens sized up Tara. She saw their eyes move from her frizzy hair, to her worn dress, to her flat stomach. Mrs. Petersen offered the spare bedroom and some used dresses from a neighbor lady about Tara's size.

On April 1, the day after Tara and Oscar arrived, Oscar walked to the port and immediately found a job clerking at a cotton warehouse. That same day, Mrs. Petersen took Tara in tow, walking her through the bustling Strand district. When they reached the corner of Tremont and 24th Street, Tara spotted the Tremont House, a magnificent five-story hotel with a mansard-roofed tower.

"Mrs. Petersen, let me make inquiries here. Would you mind waiting in the lobby for a minute?" As they entered, Tara could tell that Mrs. Petersen had never been inside.

At the front desk, Tara asked to see the hotel housekeeper.

"She is off today. Can I help you?"

"I worked as a chambermaid at the Windsor Hotel in Manhattan—"

"Oh, my." The clerk interrupted her. Even with just those two words, Tara heard a twang, the slower sounds of the region. "The big hotel that burned to the ground?"

"Yes, so I am out of work and wonder if the Tremont needs chambermaids."

The clerk eyed her. "How long did you work at that hotel?"

"Three years."

"Can you provide a reference?"

"The Chief Housekeeper would certainly provide one if I could find her. But, you see, she lost her job too and needed to move in with relatives. I don't know how to reach her." Tara couldn't have Mrs. Wrigley knowing about Galveston.

The clerk puckered his lips, unsure. "Miss...."

"Regan. Tara Regan."

"Well, Miss Regan, the housekeeper here is ill. She's been ill for a while. The manager needs to replace her. If you were at the Windsor for three years, you might qualify for the position. But without a reference from your past employer, I'm not sure."

Tara offered her most refined smile. "May I talk to your manager? I'd like him to hear me out."

The clerk looked her over. Tara guessed he thought she'd try flirting. He led her to an alcove and asked her to wait. A minute later, the good-looking hotel manager arrived. Tara weighed her options. She made a quick decision. She didn't pat down her hair. She did call forth Mrs. Wrigley's rules for cleaning.

After a short time, Tara left the manager's office with the agreement that he would try her for a month.

In short order, Tara Regan began work at the Tremont House. She supervised twelve maids, holding them to the high standard she promised the hotel manager. On Saturday, April 8, on her lunch break, she borrowed from the hotel lobby the papers from Galveston, San Antonio, Houston, and cities throughout the country. Tara read them herself, slowly. On the train from Manhattan to Galveston, Oscar had taught her. Never before in her life had she had five days of leisure and learning.

She looked for stories about the Windsor. They were few and far between. She did see other stories, worrisome stories. French authorities caught an anarchist before he could assassinate the Minister of Justice. Italian authorities caught a different anarchist before he could blow up the Chamber of Deputies. Holy mother of God. Tara missed her own anarchist, Sean Mack. Was he in trouble? Was he on his way to Texas to find her?

In the meantime, every day, Galveston offered comfort and opportunities. As did Oscar Petersen.

Marguerite Wells

Armed with the address Seth Sennett gave her, the next day, a Saturday, Marguerite walked to the neighborhood known as Hell's Kitchen. She found the thief's address—an ordinary three-story wooden apartment building, no better or worse than the other rundown buildings on the block. She couldn't hover. She walked to the nearest busy corner where she could keep her eyes on the building and give the appearance of waiting for a friend. She lingered for a half hour, until a woman walked out of the thief's building. From her age, Marguerite guessed she could not be the thief's wife or girlfriend.

"Excuse me, ma'am. I'm looking for a young man, tall, red hair. Maybe Irish." Marguerite smiled, proud that she recalled Sennett's description. "I believe he lives here. I have a message from his employer."

"Ah, yuh must mean Clay. He's the handsome fella in the building." She winked at Marguerite. "But he hasn't come back since the fire, the day of the fire at the Windsor. That'd be, um, three weeks ago." Marguerite worked hard to mask her shock when the woman said Windsor. "He used to work there. Maybe he lost friends and, who knows what else. Landlady tells me he left all his belongings in his flat. She doesn't know if she should clean it out and rent it to someone else or wait. You have a message from his employer, you say? Maybe you should tell that employer to tell his carpenter to go back to his flat."

"I will do that, ma'am. Thank you kindly. But I can't recall Clay's last name, and I should have it. Can you remind me?"

"Clayton Byrne. As Irish as they come."

The Windsor. Marguerite didn't know where to find the man but now she had discovered the connection. Clayton Byrne, where were you hiding?

The woman who came out of the apartment building mentioned that Clay worked as a carpenter. Maybe just someone who picked up a hammer and helped a relative. Or maybe a real carpenter. When Marguerite returned to the Martha Washington Hotel, she saw construction across the street—a major building site for another hotel. Two days later, on Monday morning, she stood in front of the site. She spotted a man in his fifties, wearing a belt with tools hanging from it. He shouted orders to others. He turned away from the site, probably to take a break. She caught his attention.

"Sir, do you have a minute?" He stared. Looked her up and down. She raised her voice so he could hear her over the din. "A few men are building my home on the Upper West Side, one of the new areas, but they don't meet my standards. I am a widow, or I would ask my husband to handle these problems." The man did not seem to question her colorful dress. As a matter of fact, he seemed to relish it. "I see the fine work you and your men are doing here. Is there a central clearinghouse for carpenters, somewhere I might go to enlist new men?"

"Sure. I'd offer my own workers, but we're busy now. Try the new United Brotherhood of Carpenters and Joiners. 240 East 80th Street. But better if you send a man there to inquire."

She smiled. The rude man with wandering eyes had offered valuable information. East 80th—that was Yorkville, a German enclave far north of the Martha Washington. Marguerite hailed a hansom cab. After a forty-minute drive, she arrived at the Brotherhood's headquarters. A brick building, with a wooden plaque above the door. On the plaque, she noticed a shield, decorated with a compass and a plane and the words *Labor Omnia Vincit*—Labor Conquers All Things. For a second, Marguerite wondered whether the carpenters entering the building could translate from the Latin. Then she told herself to squelch such thoughts. Opening the door, she glimpsed a dozen men slumped on benches, smoking and talking quietly. Her mind wandered back to the Latin, and again she checked herself. She ignored the men's stares and approached the clerk at the front desk.

"I hope you can assist me," she murmured, trying to avoid the ears of the men on the benches. She had her story down pat, this time with embellishments. "My husband hired workers to build our home on the Upper West Side, but he died in an accident last month." She looked down, again hoping her colorful dress would go unnoticed. "When he died, most of the men working on the house disappeared, except for one carpenter, who tells me he needs a second carpenter to finish up. He recommended a man named Clayton Byrne but didn't know how to reach him. The man still working for me—he's extremely busy—suggested I inquire here. He thought you might know who has hired Mr. Byrne recently or thought you might have a record of his current address."

The front desk clerk looked unphased by the request. He grabbed a binder on the shelf behind him and searched his records.

"Clayton Byrne, Clayton Byrne," he said, louder than Marguerite had. "If he's a licensed carpenter, he'll be listed here." The clerk moved his eyes up and down the pages but didn't seem to make any progress.

One of the men on the bench shuffled toward Marguerite. Dark haired, head down. The desk clerk glared at him. "Pay him no mind, ma'am. An immigrant, in here waiting to see if he can pick up some day labor. Sometimes, a foreman needs another man for a job. Don't care if it's a foreigner or not for day work. So the men wait."

Neither the desk clerk's glare nor his words stopped the laborer.

"You asking about Clay, Clay Byrne?" The laborer had an accent.

"Yes."

"I worked with Clay at the fire site. We cleared rubble. But they don't need us any longer. Good man."

Marguerite stared at the laborer.

"Got it," the desk clerk said, "Clayton Byrne. Apprenticed at the Windsor Hotel, October 1899. Licensed on February 1, 1899. Resides at 406 W. 47th."

"But he doesn't live there now," the laborer muttered. "He's at a flophouse—a hotel downtown, in the bowery. I visited him there once, but I don't remember the address." He described the neighborhood, the look of the run-down building. "If you find him, miss, tell him Luca said hi. Luca from the rubble. And if he finds work, and the foreman is willing to hire an Italian, remind him that he knows where to find me."

It had taken Marguerite a week, but now she had found Clay Byrne, the carpenter turned art thief, and knew he was licensed and skilled. She didn't know if he worked in a gang or alone. But she did know that a man had to have some sense to be a licensed carpenter, to know a Monet from, as Mr. Sennett said, a pile of manure, and to find a fence specializing in art. Clay Byrne was no petty thief. He had selected St. Patrick's Day, when routines would be upended. He had set a fire to drive out guests, who would leave without bothering to lock their doors, clearing the way for the takings.

But she did not want to confront a thief, any more than she wanted to tell Victoria Sennett about her husband's infidelity. She would turn all this over to George—should have done so sooner—to look for his gratitude or more. To continue to honor her promise to Theodate and protect Mr. Pope, Marguerite would need to find a way to tell George about Clayton Byrne without mentioning the Haystacks. While she thought that over, she would move on to the remaining loose thread. Where could she find Tara Regan, the chambermaid who could lead George to Sean Mack? And was Mack really an anarchist who wanted to get to the President by causing harm to his brother? Seemed more roundabout than an art heist.

Elbridge Gerry

"You can't hide behind your desk forever, Elbridge." Louisa stood tall in front of him, jaw out, voice quiet but firm. His wife had tried to coax him out for social calls ever since the fire, but he'd have none of it. Not until the hubbub blew over. "I know Angelica is saying no to events, but you should set an example for our daughter." Louisa wiggled the high collar of her silk dress. She craned her neck toward the maid dusting bookshelves on the far wall. "Mary, you should have opened the shutters, let some air in. The days are finally warming up." She turned back, lowered her voice. "We need to be out and about. That's the best way to quench rumors."

Rumors. All around him. In his head. In the papers. In the hushed voices of servants loitering in the corners of his mansion. When he thought straight, Elbridge knew he did not need to worry, but these days he struggled to think straight. First, that business about steam yachts. As though the grandson of a signer of the Declaration needed to profit from war. Then, the business about his Society for the Prevention of Cruelty to Children. As though he'd take food out of the mouths of orphans. And now allegations that he, or his hotel manager, had been negligent.

Louisa wasn't through. "And remember those stupid charges in February, before the fire? No problems there either."

"Yes, I remember," Elbridge said. "A complainant charged Warren with burning soft coal and so violating the Sanitary Code. Supposedly, it's a smoke nuisance. I followed that case. Rufus dismissed the indictment on Asa's recommendation." No need to give his wife the full names of officials

Judge Rufus Cowing or District Attorney Asa Gardiner. He and Louisa knew them from social gatherings. Asa was a Tammany man, as was, in a modest way, Elbridge himself. Only Rufus was a Republican, but one who moved in the right circles. "Thankfully," Elbridge said, "no blame stuck to Warren. Poor Warren."

For two seconds, Eldridge saw Louisa's jaw soften. The couple locked eyes and shared their sorrow. Warren Leland not only lost his wife and daughter in a fire at the hotel he managed, but he had suffered an appendix attack, and on April 4 he died. Did he die from his illness? From a broken heart? From guilt that others died while he survived, if only for eighteen days?

The moment of shared sorrow waned.

"Louisa, even though I'm a lawyer, I'm thinking about more than negligent employees or burning the wrong kind of coal. You think I'm sulking? You're right. I'm sulking about my reputation." Elbridge scratched both sides of his whiskers, digging into his cheeks. "Thomas Brady, that long-winded Building Commissioner. He had to talk to reporters. He said older hotels like the Windsor were unsafe."

"Yes, Elbridge, but Asa shrugged off Brady's damned accusations. Said he needed facts."

Elbridge barely winced at his highborn wife's foul language.

"I just thought of something," Louisa said. "Isn't the Chief Justice of the state Supreme Court—that carper who thought Tom Brady should have closed down unsafe hotels—a Tammany man?"

As she said the word Tammany, Eldridge's mind wandered back to the admonishment from Donald Easton, President of the Board of Fire Underwriters, the day after the fire. Avoid influencing any investigation, Easton had warned. Elbridge had no need to even contemplate applying pressure. Not necessary. His crowd stuck together. Or, Elbridge liked to think, they knew right from wrong.

Marguerite Wells

George McClusky had asked Marguerite to hunt for chambermaid Tara Regan, who might lead the police to anarchist Sean Mack. That was over two weeks ago. Marguerite had heard little from George since, aside from a quick note delivered to her hotel. "I hope to talk to you next week," he wrote. "Chief Devery keeps me busy with other cases." Marguerite followed the crime columns and so had a sense of this herself. George testified at the trial of the debauched dentist accused of killing his mistress. Marguerite tried to imagine George's reactions to the reported indecencies. Then, in April, George led the successful hunt for a kidnapped baby. That story, along with his name, ran on the front pages, pushing aside the Windsor fire.

On the morning of April 12, George left another note at the Martha Washington, asking Marguerite to dinner that night—he remembered a shred of information that might help her search. What would she wear? The dresses she had bought in a hurry for Europe and now wore in New York looked too stodgy for dinner. She tried one on, wondering as she fussed with her bodice if she foolishly imagined that the detective's interest went beyond investigations. Regardless, the dress wouldn't do. She rushed with it to a seamstress and asked her to quickly remodel the neckline and add a flounce, offering extra payment in return for speed. Marguerite saw the seamstress look up from the dress, stare.

"For the opera," Marguerite said.

Six hours later, after picking up the dress and admiring the improvement, and taking extra care with her chignon, she heard the bellhop knock. A gentleman caller awaited her in the lobby. She took the elevator down, still anxious. She had not sorted out whether to tell George what she learned from Mr. Pope's valet, what she learned from Seth Sennett, or what she learned from Luca about Clay Byrne. Would George grumble that she had not shared her discoveries with him immediately? If he had summoned her for a meeting earlier, would she have shared then? Was she piqued at his silence over the last two weeks, when she assumed his interests had moved on? Now, was he looking for information, or a chance to see her again?

Marguerite stepped out of the elevator. George's eyes went from her blond hair to her bodice. She took in his freshly shaved skin, trimmed mustache, and the scent of vanilla and clove. He led her out of the hotel, to a nearby steakhouse. She noticed he did not assume his customary swagger—she had read about that in the papers—but matched his stride to hers. She doubted that he dined at this steakhouse regularly, on his detective's salary, but she had also read in the papers that Chief Detective McClusky thought of himself as a bon vivant. Maybe he had inherited money. He ordered for them both—a boneless ribeye and a bottle of cabernet.

George paused until the waiter walked out of earshot. "I want to celebrate with you. You've read about the case of the dentist, Samuel Kennedy, the one who killed his, well, his girlfriend, Emeline Reynolds?" Marguerite looked down, thinking that's what he expected. "I testified at the trial. All very unpleasant. The jury found Kennedy guilty, and the judge sentenced him to die in the electric chair. Bad for him but good for me—Chief Devery seems pleased with the outcome. And then next we had to find the kidnapped baby. I'm sorry those cases took me away from talking to you more about the fire."

"Excellent work on those cases, George. Is it hard to keep Big Bill—I know that's his nickname—happy?"

"Yes." George fiddled with his mustache. "You see, jobs in the force are political. Even mine. Not always based on merit. I need to solve cases to stay on Big Bill's good side. That's how it is. I support my two sisters, both spinsters. Ida and Margaret, they teach singing lessons, but not often. I need to retain my position as Chief of Detectives."

Marguerite saw George look down. He thought he had said too much. Perhaps he had. Apparently, George McClusky did not buy his fine clothes and eat steak due to an inheritance.

"Oh, I see."

He paused, slowly looked up again. She could hear him tap his foot on the carpet beneath the table. She tried for a reassuring smile. It came easily. The tapping ended.

"Back to the Windsor. You remember that bullet? The one I examined when you came to my office? Big Bill got a call from a woman in Baltimore, saying her mother stayed at the Windsor a lot and she hadn't reached her. She was afraid her brother—the brother was desperate for money—shot the mother and then maybe started the fire. The woman hesitated to contact the police because she's close to her brother and didn't want to bring shame on the family. But when she grew desperate for news, she called Big Bill. The brother lives in New Jersey. I had detectives check him out. He's paid off his gambling debts, and on St. Patrick's Day, he marched in his own town's parade. So, that theory is gone. With no clues, the bullet is a dead end."

"Poor woman, the mother that is. I guess she'll be missing forever."

"Marguerite, let's move from the bullet to another lead. After the fire, I interviewed the hotel's housekeeper, Susanna Wrigley. She told me that the last time she saw Tara Regan was when the two of them, along with the assistant butcher and some other maids, ran from the roof down a fire escape. Mrs. Wrigley had no idea where Tara would be now. I forgot to tell you about that interview. It came back to me when I reviewed my notes yesterday. Would you consider interviewing Mrs. Wrigley yourself? Worth a second try?"

Marguerite heard the word forgot. This was her chance, if she wanted, to tell George about her discoveries, about the stolen paintings. If he had forgotten to tell her something, she could have forgotten to tell him something. As she imagined how to tell her stories without mentioning Theodate or Alfred Pope, George reached over the table to put his hand, a well-groomed hand, over hers, firmly. She felt his touch, felt more. This was no apology for his scant information or for asking her to do more.

Thirty minutes later, George walked Marguerite back to the Martha Washington, again matching his stride to hers. As they rounded the corner near the hotel, he put his hand on her shoulder and steered her gently into an alcove in a nearby building. He moved his hand to the back of her head and held her there as he kissed her. Startled, she began to pull away, and then instantly, almost before he realized, raised her own hand to his shoulder and kissed him back. As she felt the force of the kiss, she wanted it to last, but she pulled away and smiled. George walked her around the corner, into the lobby. They said a formal goodnight in front of the desk clerk. Marguerite entered the elevator.

She was not misinterpreting George's intentions. Business, yes, and more. Memories of her Smith College crushes on girls were forgotten.

Molly Dugan

"I'm done hiding." While Devan Farley was out looking for a butcher's job, Frank Corbett sat in the kitchen of the Farley family apartment in Hoboken, not touching the beer Molly put on the table. "Sully's done hiding too. And more. They're taking me on as an engineer at the Murray Hill. Not Chief Engineer this time, but the pay's decent. And Sully's got on at the Waldorf. We'll both take our chances with the coroner's report." His eyes moved to Molly's belly. He saw her follow his look and smile. "When."

"Middle of October, I think."

"No time to waste. Next Sunday. I already checked with Our Lady of Grace on Willow and 4th. Mostly German worshippers, but the priest says they welcome the Irish, too. He can marry us next Sunday. In four days."

Molly's eyes, both of them, stared straight at Frank. "I have a little money saved up for white satin. Devan's ma will help me sew a dress fast. But, Frank, before we marry, I need to see that priest."

"Confession...?"

"Yes." She would say no more.

Marguerite Wells

The day after the steak dinner with George, Marguerite found Susanna Wrigley at the address he provided—a small flat in Brooklyn. Marguerite took a chance, showing up unannounced. She thought she might gain an advantage by catching the housekeeper unawares. A trim woman in her forties answered the door, dressed neatly even though she wasn't expecting a visitor.

"Mrs. Wrigley, I am Marguerite Wells. My family and I were guests at the Windsor." The housekeeper's expression alternated strangely between annoyance and sympathy. "We all survived, and with no injuries. I was sent here by Chief Detective George McClusky, who asked me to call on you." At the mention of McClusky's name, the housekeeper opened the door wider, motioned for Marguerite to enter, and led her to the parlor. This woman was accustomed to making way for authority.

She had made the best of her modest dwelling. Marguerite glanced at the attractive furniture and well-displayed bric-a-brac. Off to the left, in the kitchen, a girl played at a table. Marguerite waved hello. Straight ahead, against the mantel, she spotted a photo of a young man, the frame draped with black ribbon.

"Mrs. Wrigley, I am sorry to intrude, especially since I know you already talked with the chief detective a few days after the fire. He's gathering evidence about the cause of the fire and asked me to assist him." The housekeeper gave Marguerite an odd look. "To be honest, many of the people affected by the fire are women, and the detective thought they might be more comfortable speaking to another woman." This explanation, technically correct, seemed to satisfy Susanna Wrigley. Her eyes moved halfway to a more regular position. "I'm here for a little more detail on the information you kindly provided him."

"Yes, that man asked hundreds of questions, fast like. And when my burns were still raw. They're almost healed now. Thank the Lord that Frank Corbett dragged me out."

Marguerite narrowed her eyes.

"Frank, the Chief Engineer. Good man. I ain't never seen any robbers. And Mr. Leland had a safe. All the guests should have put their valuables there. Not my fault if they didn't. Not my maids' fault either. I kept watch on my maids. Once or twice, they asked me if they should remind guests about the safe. I said don't. Keep to your place. You don't want them to think you spend time looking at their jewels." Mrs. Wrigley stuck out her chin, bobbed it up and down.

"The last thing I am here for is to affix blame. I know you lost friends and workers in the fire. And you lost your job and burned your hands. You are a victim, too."

The woman repositioned her eyes to a fully normal position. She stared at Marguerite with a sudden switch as a tear fell from her left eye and her shoulders sunk.

"We are trying to find Tara Regan. I understand you saw her last when you climbed down the fire escape before—before—the roof caved in."

A tear from the woman's right eye followed a parallel track down her face. She removed a handkerchief from her pocket and dabbed at her eyes while Marguerite waited.

"Yes, so sad." Marguerite tilted her head, signaling commiseration.

"Can you tell me a little more? Did you see a man waiting for Miss Regan at the bottom of the fire escape or anywhere near the hotel?"

"Oh, no. But it's hard to remember."

Marguerite smiled. Exactly.

"Here's the little bit I do remember," the housekeeper said slowly. "Bridget, Bridget Dunne, she's the head of the maids on the fifth floor, smart lass, pretty, with wavy hair and freckles, she must have paid more attention than the rest of us. I was watching the uniforms, listening to the bands. When Bridget heard screaming, she motioned for a few of us—let's see, Tara Regan—and Molly Dugan—and Devan Farley, too. You could say Bridget saved our lives."

More tears. Marguerite waited, gave her a chance to catch her breath.

"I'm sorry, Mrs. Wrigley, but I have more questions. Can you tell me about these people, Tara and Molly? And Devan, too?"

"Tara, she talks too much. But pretty, even with that frizzy hair. Now Molly, the one with the wandering eye, she's quieter, stone-faced. And Devan, he's the, was, the assistant butcher. All the girls like him."

"This Bridget you mentioned, or maybe Molly, would either of them know where to find Tara?"

"Hmmm. They might. All lived together on seven. Seventh floor that is. Don't know where they are now. All the servants' rooms—gone. But Bridget, maybe find her first. She has a sister, Claire's the name. I know because my daughter is a Claire." Susanna Wrigley moved her head in the direction of the girl Marguerite had seen at the table in the kitchen. "And this sister, she's an ambitious one. Going to school to be a teacher. That's what Bridget told me. To get money for her school fees, Claire works at night cleaning offices somewhere. She looks down on her sister. Not right. Bridget's queen of five. I mean, she manages the maids on the fifth floor. Nothing wrong with that. I started as queen of three, and now I'm—I was—chief housekeeper. Mr. Leland, God rest his soul, just a week since he passed, he knew I kept his hotel nice."

Marguerite nodded respect, glanced to the side. Hoped the nod would encourage the woman.

"Let me think. Oh, Claire cleans in the Tweed Courthouse. Night shift. You could go there to find her and then ask her where Bridget went."

"Thank you, Mrs. Wrigley. You've been helpful. I hope you find work soon. A position as good as the one you lost."

A few weeks later, Marguerite wondered if the housekeeper had more regrets than she let on.

Theodate Pope

Theodate Pope leaned over her drawings, suspecting the open spaces in her layout would fail to provide needed fire stops. For months, she had been working on sketches of Hill-Stead, the country home for her parents on 250 acres in rural Connecticut. She started with two goals—design a comfortable colonial revival style estate and allow spaces for her father's magnificent art collection. Now, she had a third goal. She needed to learn from the Windsor conflagration, to make certain that no fire could threaten Hill-Stead's inhabitants or its art.

Soon, she would send her sketches to the architectural firm her father had hired—McKim, Mead & White. She understood that the firm's associate architect, Egerton Swartout, would turn her sketches into official plans, with proper notations and elevations. Swartout! The man was three years younger than she was. No matter. The house was her design, her concept. No firm, no upstart associate architect, could take that away from her.

When the house was finished, would she admire her vision or would she look at the walls and be reminded daily of those missing Haystacks, of her father's misplaced priorities, of her own questionable priorities?

Marguerite Wells

Immediately after leaving Susanna Wrigley's apartment, Marguerite took the streetcar from Brooklyn to the Tweed Courthouse at 52 Chambers Street. She ignored the elaborate portico with its four Corinthian columns and instead walked around the building until she saw a narrow door used by messengers carrying portfolios and guarded by a man in uniform.

"Sir, I need to get a message to a maid on your night shift. I prefer to deliver the message myself rather than leave it. Can you tell me when the shift begins?"

With four hours to waste, Marguerite walked north to shop along Broadway, still trying to replace her incinerated clothing, and ate a simple dinner at a tea shop. At 8:00 that night, she walked back to the side door of the Tweed Courthouse, careful to stay under the gaslights. No guard stood at the door this time. Apparently, the courthouse hired a guard for day duty but not for night duty. Why bother protecting the cleaners? Somewhat reassured by the large number of pedestrians still walking through the area, Marguerite asked each woman who entered the side door if her name was Claire. The third woman to enter paused and glared.

"My name is Marguerite Wells. I lodged at the Windsor Hotel." She had prepared a long-winded explanation, an invented name. "I am trying to find Teresa Tuttle, the chambermaid who cleaned our suite. I owe her money for doing extra chores for my family. I feel terrible that I have not paid. Surely she can use the money, now that she lost her job. I asked Susanna Wrigley, the hotel housekeeper, if she knew where to find Teresa. Mrs. Wrigley had no idea. But she said that since Teresa worked on the fifth floor, and Bridget Dunne managed the maids on that floor, if I could find Bridget, then maybe I could find Teresa. Mrs. Wrigley thought I should begin by finding you and remembered that you work evenings at the courthouse." Claire looked doubtful. She must be thinking her questioner went to an awful lot of trouble to pay a maid some small fee. Marguerite stared intently at Claire for a few seconds. Claire stared back.

"So you're looking for Bridge? She wouldn't tell me where she was going. We don't get along. She doesn't tell me much. But you can look for her sweetheart, Clay." Claire said the name slowly, with a sneer, stretching out the "a" sound. "A couple weeks ago, I heard her tell one of the boarders that her Clay's working carpentry at the Ansonia, the big hotel going up on Broadway and 73rd. Byrne's his last name. If he wants to tell you where she is, that's his business."

Marguerite strained to keep her eyebrows down, her jaw relaxed. She thanked Claire and hailed a cab to return to the Martha Washington. The minute she sat down on the carriage seat, she grabbed the notebook from her handbag to check the scribbles she had made after her unpleasant talk with Mr. Sennett about the tall, good-looking Monet thief and then her friendlier talk six days ago with the woman who came out of the building where the Monet thief had lived. Yes. The same name. Clayton Byrne. The man who stole the Monets and tried to sell them to Seth Sennett was the same man courting maid Bridget Dunne.

Bridget Dunne

Two weeks had passed since Bridget moved to the cheap, airless room at the Stratford Hotel. She had enough money for one more week. Sitting on the Stratford's lumpy bed for hours, she seethed about Clay. He didn't cut her in on stolen art. Since the fire Bridget had spent half her time feeling remorse for conniving with Clay, contributing to the inferno, and half her time trying to survive. Since she learned about the stolen art, survival—without a lover—almost blocked memories of the dead.

Bridget could find Clay at the Ansonia, hammering away. She could send him a note, telling him she was at the Stratford. What then? Did she want to take up with a man who had betrayed her? He was her way out. A clever carpenter, who would have steady work, a decent salary. She could stop cleaning. Instead, he dragged her down. Molly Dugan had managed—she'd probably marry Frank. Tara Regan was off to Texas with that valet. Of the three maids, Bridget fussed to herself, how could it be that she, the prettiest, the cleverest, the most ambitious, was stuck in a dismal room, and without a man. She would wait until the coroner's verdict came out, see if the coroner fingered Clay, see if he fingered her, and then decide.

Marguerite Wells

Forty-four blocks north of the Martha Washington Hotel—a half hour up Broadway by carriage—Marguerite saw the Ansonia Hotel.

If Claire Dunne had provided accurate information, Marguerite would find Clayton Byrne at the construction site. She could probe. Did he set the fire to steal art, or was it a tragic coincidence that the fire and the theft happened together? She had to answer the question without endangering herself. Then she should let George handle the rest, taking care that he not blame her for withholding information and that he not harm Alfred Pope's reputation.

Marguerite guessed the odds were good that Clayton Byrne had never met the fence's wife, Victoria Sennett. On the morning of April 14, Marguerite dressed simply, pushed her politics to the side, and looked out the carriage window as her driver approached the Ansonia. The huge structure soared upward seventeen stories. Every part of the building looked ornate—mansard roof, round corners, turrets. Marguerite had visited London and Paris, but still she was impressed. She had never seen such a grand building in America. As she stepped out of the carriage, noise surrounded her. Hundreds of workers made a racket, hammering and drilling. She walked around the block until she saw someone who stood still while the others worked—a foreman.

"Excuse me, sir." She yelled to be heard. "I'm looking for one of your carpenters, Mr. Clayton Byrne."

The foreman looked her over.

"And what's your business?"

"My name is Mrs. Victoria Sennett. My husband owes Mr. Byrne money. But my husband has taken ill and sent me to give the money to Mr. Byrne. If you tell him Mrs. Victoria Sennett is here to pay him, he will want to see me." She smiled.

The foreman would not stand between his carpenter and payment. He raised a finger. She should wait a minute. He disappeared, then returned with a tall, red-haired, handsome fellow.

"Mr. Byrne?" He moved his forehead toward her in a yes. No sign he saw she was not the real Victoria Sennett. "I need just a minute," she said to the foreman, motioning to the carpenter to follow her to a quiet corner.

"I don't believe we've met," she said, looking at the carpenter for confirmation.

"No, but your husband's a good bloke. He has settled matters, I take it?" Clay looked at her eagerly, his gaze resting on her handbag, not her figure.

"Almost."

Clayton Byrne frowned, keeping his gaze on Marguerite as she spoke. "You see, the interested party is a bit worried. He knows the paintings belonged to Alfred Pope and that Mr. Pope escaped the fire. The interested party wonders if there is a connection between your—your possession of the paintings—and the fire. Doesn't mind if there is a connection, but wants to know about it, to be prepared, to understand the risk. And wonders if there is fire damage to the paintings." Marguerite threw in the last line on an impulse. She caught the carpenter off guard. He stayed silent for a few seconds, undoubtedly weighing confession against profit.

"Well, Mrs. Sennett, see, I set a tiny fire, a little distraction. To encourage guests to leave their rooms. Two things you need to tell Mr. Sennett to pass on to that interested party. I got the paintings out before the fire came to Pope's suite. No damage. You can see. Look for yourself. And there's more. That big fire, not my fault. My fires were little, I tell you, little. Most of that big fire started somewhere else. Maybe the basement, maybe the wires in the walls. I dunno. No one can lay the blame on me."

Marguerite willed herself to nod. Told him she would pass along the information and that he should expect payment in a few days.

She would have skipped back to her carriage if no one had been looking. She had learned that Clayton Byrne set the fires, many fires. Did he have help from the gent with the cigar or the laggard basement crew? The carpenter showed no remorse, no guilt. Either he didn't think he caused the conflagration, or he was a stone-cold killer. But back to the Haystacks. When Clayton said that Victoria Sennett could assess the lack of damage—"just look for yourself," he said—he let on that the paintings were in the Sennett apartment.

Marguerite left the Ansonia, returned to her hotel to look over her few belongings, and realized she needed to shop. Within an hour, she put together the costume of a widow in her fifties, including a gray wig, black veil, and black cloak, and filled her handbag with cheap instruments and a sheet of fine paper. Hungry as always, she gobbled braised beef with noodles in her hotel's dining room. She thought about lingering there, with the great smells and the company of law-abiding guests, but instead, she ordered a dessert for fortification and left for her room. She made a point of passing the front desk clerk and chatting with him about the books she planned to read in her armchair that afternoon. Then she dressed in her new costume, exited a side door out of sight of the clerk, and found a hansom cab to take her to the Sennetts' apartment. She asked the driver to wait while she went upstairs.

"Mrs. Sennett, I am Amanda Jensen, from the Adams Art Museum in Boston." Victoria Sennett, the real Victoria Sennett, opened the door the same two inches she had opened it on Marguerite's first visit. Through that space, halfway down, Marguerite spotted the little girl she had seen before. The woman looked anxious, not suspicious. She seemed prepared for the visit.

"I expected a gentleman."

"You are getting a gentlelady. Many museum curators these days are women." Marguerite touched the veil covering the top half of her face. "As a widow, I must earn my living."

Victoria Sennett sighed, then opened the door. She led Marguerite to a room off to the left, then pointed to a wardrobe at the far side.

There they were. Two glorious Haystacks, on the bottom of the wardrobe, leaning against the back. Marguerite's eyes and breath collided. Large piles of hay, at different times of day. Even in the dark closet, she sensed Monet's skill at capturing light. The simple haystacks looked more sublime than ordinary.

Marguerite bent down on her knees, complaining of stiffness. She took two kinds of magnifying glasses out of her handbag. Taking her time, she looked closely at the paintings, with one piece of equipment, then the other. Finally, she stood up, rubbed her knees through her dress.

"Mrs. Sennett, these paintings are legitimate, as your husband stipulated. He knows his business. My employer authorized me to accept the artwork on his behalf." She took out of her bag the sheet of paper and a pen. I am writing a receipt and will sign and leave it with you." She paused, looked down, and added, "Of course, the receipt does not include specific descriptions of the art, as, shall we say, a precaution." Victoria Sennett's expression showed no recognition of the sham. "You can trust my employer to transfer funds by tomorrow morning. Now, please help me wrap the paintings. They are large and heavy, but I have a carriage and driver waiting."

Marguerite would never know what Seth Sennett had told his wife. She either assumed he served as an intermediary between two respectable parties, or she colluded in the scheme but didn't realize that a trained curator would be unlikely to work for a buyer in the shadows. The little girl in the apartment was sure to hear screaming when her father returned home after work, to an empty closet.

Fifteen minutes later, Marguerite walked into the Martha Washington, flanked by the porter she enlisted to carry the paintings, wrapped in brown paper, from her hired carriage. The clerk didn't recognize her in the gray wig and veil. She asked him for Marguerite Wells's room number, explaining she needed to deliver portraits, and that Marguerite expected her. The clerk smiled, certain that Miss Wells was in her room. Accompanied by her porter, Marguerite unlocked her door, set down the paintings, paid and dismissed the porter, then ripped off her widow's clothes.

She brooded over the mess she'd created. What to do with the treasures resting on her bureau? If she delivered them to George, he would ask Alfred Pope why he had not reported them missing, and that would put his actions on the day of the fire under the spotlight. Theodate would blame Marguerite for the renewed attention. And then there was the matter of Bridget Dunne. Marguerite had sought out Clayton Byrne to get the full story of the Haystacks, and because he might have an address for his sweetheart, Bridget Dunne, who in turn might know the whereabouts of Tara Regan, who in turn might know the whereabouts of the elusive Sean Mack, wanted for anarchism. Marguerite cringed—so roundabout. After a lonely dinner of oysters at her hotel, she collapsed into bed, exhausted.

The next morning, Marguerite returned to the Astor Library, pleased to see it was open on Saturday and that the usual librarian sat at the desk.

"More about the Civil War? Or the Windsor fire?" The librarian recognized her immediately. Smiled. Too warmly.

"Kind of you to remember. No, today I am…." Marguerite quieted her voice. "I am looking for newspaper articles about Paterson, New Jersey. Specifically," still quieter, "anarchist cells."

The librarian stared. "Anarchist cells?"

"Yes."

"I'll gather the Paterson evening and daily papers." He dropped his voice, too, almost to a whisper. "Also, I think I can find some newspapers and weeklies written by anarchists stored in the back." He raised his index finger to signify a minute, then slanted the same finger to point to a nearby chair. She was to wait for him. This time, he did not send a page to fetch materials. The line at the desk had diminished, so the librarian went himself.

After a short while, Marguerite saw him approach, carrying a stack of papers. He gestured again, toward a table at a far corner of the reading room, and followed her there.

"Are you looking for evidence of criminality?" The librarian's odd question, stated solemnly, startled Marguerite.

"No. Not at all. I want to learn, to read what I can."

Unexpectedly, he sat down, looked around. He placed the papers on the table.

"These men, these immigrants. They don't believe in government because government has been bad for them, especially in Italy. Some want violence, but some only want a better life." He stood and walked away.

The librarian had known where to look. On the desk, Marguerite found anarchist newspapers from Paterson, including *La Questione Sociale*. She read columns by Enrico Malatesta, one of the anarchists' leaders, and a woman named Maria Roda. George had railed against anarchists, and over the years Marguerite had read of their violent tactics. But in suffragist circles, her friends talked about anarchists in more nuanced terms. She needed to come to her own judgment. As she suspected, in the smaller papers and weeklies the librarian had brought her, she never saw a call to arms, just articles about low wages for the working class, about ways for women to become more active in politics. Nothing about assassinations. Nothing about McKinley. Whatever George suggested, she would not hunt for Tara Regan, hoping the chambermaid would lead George to Sean Mack. She would not play a role in bringing the force of the law down on a political activist.

Marguerite returned the newspapers and weeklies to the desk, waiting until no one else stood nearby. She smiled at the librarian. "Thank you. I read these with interest. Your view is correct. Not all these men are criminals. If I can trouble you, I would like to read the March 18th papers once more, the major papers that reported on the Windsor Hotel fire."

She felt awkward asking for those newspapers again, but the articles on anarchists had unsettled her. George seemed to accept the view that anarchists were evil, or maybe he simply mirrored the thinking of Chief Devery. Reading the articles carefully, she reached a different interpretation. She recalled the lessons of her Smith professors—a single story could be read in multiple ways.

Back at the library table with a huge pile of newspapers, she reread the accounts written immediately after the fire, looking at them differently, almost gasping in recognition. Most of the guests whose stories appeared in the papers were single women, descending on ropes or jumping, but many guests trying to escape seemed to be part of a family or household group. Mrs. George Wheeler and her daughter Dorothy appeared in the windows together. Mrs. David Salomon and daughter Rosalie and friend Laura Bates climbed to the roof together to await rescue. And some guests, according to the papers, bravely tried to help others. Nellie Thomas, descending on a rope, took time to tell another struggling woman to wrap her feet around the rope. Bessie Winter, telling her rescuer to help someone else first, was described as "probably the coolest woman in the burning hotel," language strangely close to a fireman's description of Marguerite herself—"She was the coolest girl I ever saw in a warm place." Maybe the most noteworthy story, because it included a man, reported on Lieutenant J. H. Higby, who met up on the fourth-floor hall with two frightened women, and the three appeared in the window together.

Marguerite imagined what might have happened in the chaos and smoke of the fire. Reporters, looking from one horrific scene to another, scribbled notes, guessing at identities. They could innocently have confused stories. She sat up straight, looking out the window at the bright afternoon sunlight. Her reading during the last hour had not solved the mystery of the fire, but it did give her another way to look at her own personal mystery—the confounding accounts of the Welles' escape.

She took a deep breath, then another. Already that morning, she had rethought the common understanding of anarchists and had worked out that journalists reporting on her actions and her father's during the fire might have confused them with others trying to escape. Maybe now she could think afresh too about a practical problem. What to do with the stolen paintings? She could help Theodate by restoring the paintings to the Pope family, bringing them to an expeditor to crate up and send by rail to Cleveland. With that plan, she could explain how she retrieved the paintings, letting the family worry that the art had instigated a deadly fire, or she could refuse to provide a sender's address. Or she could deliver the paintings to George, explaining how a pawnshop clerk led her to Seth Sennet, who led her to Clay Byrne, but that plan would point a finger at Alfred Pope. George would know Pope had focused, to a fault, on saving his paintings. Marguerite doubted Theodate's father would suffer repercussions but passing on that information would undo a promise.

A better possibility crossed her mind—Louisine Havemeyer, friend of Alfred Pope's. She collected art, she lived in New York, she would know the value of the Haystacks, and she would know they belonged to Alfred Pope. If a destitute mother could leave a foundling at a church door in the middle of the night, couldn't a desperate suffragist leave a painting or two at a mansion's door in the middle of the night?

Hortense Webb

Hortense Webb had roomed by herself in an east side boarding house, not on the seventh floor of the Windsor like many of the other chambermaids. Now, without a job, she had no money for rent. A week after the fire, she sought refuge with a cousin in North Tarrytown, a village north of the city. "I won't be a burden to you," Hortense said to her cousin. "I'm sure I can get on as a housemaid in town. When they hear I cleaned for Abner McKinley and his family, they'll be happy to have me."

"Try Millionaire's Row," the cousin said. "One mansion after another."

John D. Rockefeller and other business titans lived in North Tarrytown. They served as a magnet, attracting wealthy friends to build nearby estates. The first morning of Hortense's search, she dressed plainly, respectably, pinning up her hair. Most days, she avoided the mirror, not wanting to be reminded that the Windsor maids called her Hortense the Horseface behind her back.

"Breakfast?" her cousin asked. "Don't you want to eat before you make the rounds?"

"Maybe later."

"I miss your stories. You always had stories about the other maids, about the guests."

"I don't feel chatty now." Hortense paused, not looking at her cousin. "Lost too many friends."

The first day, Hortense walked two miles, leaving her cousin's modest neighborhood. The residents of North Tarrytown—gentry and servants alike—were out starting their day in the chilly air, walking their dogs, shaking out rugs, grabbing milk from their stoops. They did not seem to carry burdens on their backs, their shoulders, their hearts.

At each mansion, Hortense knocked at the back entrance, offering Mrs. Wrigley's letter of recommendation. *"Miss Hortense Webb worked tirelessly at the Windsor Hotel for five years, cleaning and tidying as required. She was the maid I assigned to the suite of Abner McKinley, brother of President William McKinley. Mrs. Abner McKinley spoke highly of Hortense. I commend her to you without reservation. She would still be employed at the Windsor if not for the fire of March 17th. Yours respectfully, Susanna Wrigley, Chief Housekeeper, Windsor Hotel."* When Hortense first read the letter, she knew that Mrs. Wrigley must have been in a charitable mood while writing it. No mention of Hortense's endless chatter and occasional lapses. Mrs. Wrigley would be less charitable had she known of Hortense's greatest transgression.

Neither Hortense nor her cousin, a nurse at a local clinic, realized the seasonal pattern of employment in town. The housekeepers Hortense encountered at each estate began with compassion. "Oh, my dear, the Windsor. You must have been through a lot. Thank the Lord you escaped. Unfortunately, I don't have good news. We hardly ever hire in the spring. The housekeepers at the other estates down the road will tell you that too. The social season's long over, and my missus is already thinking about summer in Newport. Same for all the society folks here. Either Newport or Saratoga Springs. Before you leave, would you like a cup of coffee to help with the morning chill?"

"Kind of you, but I'll be on my way." Hortense refolded Mrs. Wrigley's letter, tucked it into her handbag.

A few more tries on the same road with the same results.

After each morning of fruitless inquiries, Hortense trod to the wooden pews of St. Theresa of Avila's. On her first visit there, March 24, Father Joseph Sheahan heard her confession. Later, when he saw her slouched on a hard pew every day, he respected her privacy, whispering hello when they passed in the aisle or patting her shoulder and wishing her a good day.

Father Joseph and Hortense Webb were the only people besides Susanna

Wrigley who knew that the chief housekeeper's deceased husband's brother, John Wrigley, had moved west. That John went to work for the Electric Appliance Company of Chicago. That he offered to help assess the Company's newest appliance, an electric iron, a good invention, but not perfected yet, not ready for household use. That he told his boss that his former sister-in-law was chief housekeeper at the Windsor, managing fifty maids and watching over twelve guests' maids. That those maids worked for wealthy men and women who were particular about their clothing. That Susanna Wrigley agreed to have a crack at those irons and report back, in return for a bonus, with five dollars of that bonus going to Hortense who would demonstrate for the other maids. That Mrs. Wrigley selected Hortense because she worked for Mrs. Annie McKinley, the President's sister-in-law, who would be happy to have her gown in perfect condition for the St. Patrick's Day balls. The rest of the confession even Mrs. Wrigley didn't know—that Hortense advised the maids to store the irons on a wooden shelf. That she forgot to tell them to disconnect the irons. That in her rush to finish ironing, to finish instructing, and to get outside to see the marchers, she may have ignored the smell of burning wood.

For the rest of her days, Hortense would believe she and Father Joseph were the only two who knew those tragic details.

Marguerite Wells

April 17, a month after the fire, Marguerite fretted that she had heard nothing from George McClusky in five days. He had sent her in two directions: find Tara Regan, who might point the way to Sean Mack, the anarchist, and talk to Harry Niehoff, to learn about the servants who might have had robbery on their minds. She wanted to share a bit of what she had learned, and peck away, carefully, at George's distaste for anarchists.

Perhaps Big Bill Devery kept George busy with other investigations. Should she wait for him to call a meeting? No, this was a professional matter, not a courtship. She could act first. She used the hotel phone to call his office to suggest a short meeting. One of his detectives called back ten minutes later. 4:00 would work for Chief Detective McClusky.

In her hotel room, Marguerite looked in the mirror to arrange her hair, and to practice what she would say about anarchists. Most of the young men were nonviolent, exasperated with unjust rulers. Even on her third try talking to her image, she couldn't manage to sound more informative than judgmental. She knew that with anyone other than George, she might be willing to sound judgmental. Maybe in person she could achieve the right tone, especially if George offered an encouraging smile.

Two hours later, Marguerite entered the Chief Detective's office. He looked at her quickly, with a standard greeting that he might give to any visitor.

"George," she said, "I expect I will disappoint you with my findings."

"Marguerite, no apologies needed. I am certain you did your best." Had he never expected much?

"I will start with the deadest end. I talked to Susanna Wrigley, the housekeeper in charge of the maids. I know you talked to her, but your instincts were correct that she would be more forthcoming with another woman. She suffered a great deal. Burned her hands, lost her job, lost many of her employees, her friends. She didn't know how to find Tara Regan." Marguerite saw George's stare skip over her, go to the wall behind her. "The housekeeper told me I could hunt for another maid who might know Tara's whereabouts. That nugget led nowhere. I'm afraid I have no path for you to find Tara's anarchist sweetheart." She would leave it at that. She would defend anarchists in another time, another place.

"I'll let McKinley's secretary—George Cortelyou—know we tried. The detectives I sent to stake out the Paterson cell haven't had luck either. No sign of Sean Mack. If Cortelyou still worries about an assassination attempt, and he should, he better find a way to safeguard the President." George frowned when he said "and he should." Yes, save the anarchist lesson for another time.

Marguerite shuffled in her chair, tried to will George to look at her. "There's more, I'm afraid. The hotel Detective, Mr. Niehoff. He directed me to a valet who was present in the basement discussion about valuables. The valet acknowledged that conversation. He insisted he and the other servants were joking around. I know the valet's employer, know he thinks well of his man, trusts him. I believe that's a dead end, too." Again, she would leave it at that. No need to mention the missing Monet Haystacks. Or Seth Sennett. Or Clayton Byrne.

George shrugged his shoulders. He didn't seem surprised at the lack of progress.

"George, what about the coroner's inquest? Didn't the jury gather last Thursday? Won't they have a verdict soon?"

Marguerite saw George purse his lips, look back at the wall behind her, decide how much to say.

"I wouldn't put too much stock in the inquest. Word leaks out, you see. The coroner, Ed Fitzpatrick, my men tell me he arrived forty minutes late for his own inquest. Claims he wasn't feeling well. Then one of the witnesses called in ill, and another went away on business. Fitzgerald adjourned the jury early. On the next day, last Friday, Fitzgerald addressed the jury and said they were unlikely to find the cause of the fire and that the people in charge of the building may have followed all the laws. He hinted that the water supply, or lack of water, might be to blame."

Marguerite heard taps. George was shaking his foot again, as he had at the steakhouse. The office was so quiet that the taps sounded loud. George glanced around—to make sure no junior detectives were close?

"The coroner shouldn't talk like that before the jury has heard witnesses. Well, now that it's Monday, the inquest is starting up again, but this time, Jacob Bausch is taking over from Fitzpatrick, who has the grip. Or so he says." More foot tapping. More looking around. "And Bausch, well, he's Tammany through and through. And one more thing on Fitzpatrick. When he was a state committeeman, he endorsed Mr. Gerry for mayor. Not that Gerry ever ran. But Fitzgerald admires Gerry. Hard to imagine that coroner presiding over an inquest that would charge Gerry with negligence. You could say none of that matters because Fitzgerald's in the sickbed, and Bausch is now the presiding coroner. But the same thing, at least in terms of likely results. Bausch started out as a woodcarver, and he's on record as standing up for labor whenever there's a dispute. Hard to imagine him presiding over an inquest that would charge the basement crew with negligence. I shouldn't be telling you any of this."

Marguerite ignored his self-reproach. "George, implications? Are both these coroners unprincipled?"

"Oh, I would never say that." Now his eyes shifted to the ceiling for a second, and his voice shifted to a whisper. "But I would say neither Fitzgerald nor Bausch would be likely to blame a friend."

As their conversation wound down, Marguerite got up to leave, thinking that George would set another time to see her, perhaps to go over the future verdict of the inquest, perhaps for a meal. He did not.

Marguerite left the police headquarters. Unthinkingly, simply following the route she had trod before, she walked south on Mulberry, then west on

Houston, then waited for a streetcar on Broadway. She paid no attention to the braying horses or the street peddlers soliciting her business. Her failures overwhelmed her. She had not defended anarchism, she had not been forthcoming about the theft or Seth Sennett or Clay Byrne, and George had lost interest in her.

Bridget Dunne

Bridget followed the stories in the papers. She knew Coroner Fitzpatrick fell sick, and Coroner Bausch took his place. Two witnesses never appeared. The sense of disruption grew when two jurors failed to appear. Bausch threatened to issue them contempt of court subpoenas. On April 24, the jury finally heard testimony. Patrolman James Duane testified he turned in an alarm at the nearest firebox. Battalion Chief John Binns testified he thought the fire started in the basement, although at first, he thought it started on the second floor. Chief Engineer Frank Corbett insisted the fire did not start in the basement, that the tanks had enough water to feed the standpipe system, that all the hoses worked, and that he had not deserted his post to see the parade. Mrs. Emma Winklemann said she saw smoke out the window, shouted fire, grabbed her dog, started to climb out her window, and was miraculously rescued by Fireman Bartholomew McDermott. Chef David Dudley complained that no one paid attention to his warnings of fire. Waiter John Foy insisted the fire started at the bay window, where he saw a gentleman smoking and a curtain catch fire. Desk clerk Simeon Leland claimed he rang the hotel fire signals.

As Bridget read the accounts, with each sentence she felt a swell of relief—no attention to the robber theory. At the same time, she had no idea what a jury would do with such wildly different stories. She didn't need to wait long—just one more day—April 25.

The jury took fifteen minutes to deliberate. How was that possible? The verdict: "We find that the origin of said conflagration was due to accidental causes and not in any way due to the lack of proper and usual facilities for extinguishing fires. We also find that within three minutes from the time the alarm of fire was received in this instance by the Fire Department, the first company was at the scene of the fire and had water upon the flames."

She was in the clear with the law. Clay was in the clear. She could go back to him with no fear. Back to the liar and the cheat?

After reading about the verdict, Bridget walked around the city for the first time since the fire with no hat pulled low over her face. She ran into a maid from the Windsor, who told her of openings at the Hoffman House. They needed chambermaids and a seamstress. Then, by happenstance, she walked past the American Art Galleries, where she had first inquired about Monets. She spotted, on the door, a discrete sign. "Seeking assistant for front desk." In the window, she saw the same fashionably dressed man who had taught her the correct pronunciation of Monet while eyeing her bosom. She caught his eye. Even though the sign did not say "No Irish need apply," she would leave behind the few Irish expressions she used. She would become Bonnie Donne.

Angelica Gerry

"Champagne, Angelica? Let the steward pour you a glass, to share with Mother and me. We are celebrating. I have early word from a man I sent down to the courthouse to monitor deliberations. 'Accidental cause,' the coroner's jury said. Elbridge Gerry stood tall and smiled, swallowing from a crystal flute he held in one hand and looking at a piece of paper he held in the other. "'The fire, the jury concluded,' I'm reading from my man's notes, 'was due to accidental causes and not in any way due to the lack of proper and usual facilities for extinguishing fires.' So Leland Warren—may he rest in peace—his reputation as the Windsor's manager is untarnished."

Angelica looked at her father while registering her mother's expression. Yes, both women knew. Elbridge Gerry, always kind and proper, would focus on the fate of his friend Warren. But her father would be pleased that his own reputation remained intact, at least regarding the matter of the Windsor. Maybe the fracas over the yachts would take care of itself. And likewise, regarding the Society for the Prevention of Cruelty to Children.

"Father, bravo for you, for Warren, and for the American jury system," Angelica said. "My friend Marguerite—you remember her—she's the daughter of the Dakota banker, Edward Wells—has been looking into the causes a bit, and she was always certain that Warren was in the clear. She put my mind at rest."

"Of course," Louisa Gerry said, flicking her flute, just short of a spill, toward her daughter's chin. "Never any doubt."

Angelica drank her champagne and asked the steward for a refill. Her father nodded, indicating his approval. He caught the steward's attention and pointed to his own glass and his wife's. "Yes, let's sit for a few seconds."

As Angelica and her parents took their seats in the dining room, she kept her eyes on the ornate federal bow and swag chair railing and the rose-colored silk drapes. She did not let her eyes look down the nearby service hallway where renowned architect Richard Morris Hunt had chosen to place the Gerrys' Otis elevator—the latest model, which she knew rested in a fireproof shaft. The Gerrys' elevator would never crash in a fire. Angelica would enjoy the festive moment, enjoy her dear father's reprieve.

Marguerite Wells

On May 1, Marguerite received a telegram from Theodate. "Must see you quickly. Have shocking information on Windsor. Lunch tomorrow noon Old Homestead. Confirm by telegram."

The Old Homestead, on Fourteenth and Ninth, was convenient neither to the Martha Washington Hotel nor to the station Theodate would arrive at when she rode the train from Connecticut. Theodate must want privacy. Marguerite immediately confirmed arrangements and spent the rest of the day in an anxious state, eager to hear the news. She arrived at the Old Homestead early. Theodate arrived a minute later, early as well, with her dress rustling and her hair flying out of her hat as though she had run to the restaurant. The day was unseasonably warm, so when the women embraced on the sidewalk, Marguerite could feel perspiration on Theodate's neck. Quickly, Theodate pulled away, then pivoted to enter the restaurant and follow the waiter to a table.

Theodate ordered her usual meal, heavy on vegetables. Marguerite, not intimidated, ordered the meat lunch special of the day. The minute the waiter moved out of hearing range, Theodate began her story, breathlessly.

"Lotte Hansen—you met her for a minute at the Hoffman House—she's Mother's maid. Lotte's been with our family for years. Loyal woman. Responsible. She tends to my parents on their European trips. Travels with them. You know that at the time of the fire, my father had returned from a buying trip to France, and after the fire he went back to Cleveland. He didn't stay there long. In early April, he and Mother took another trip to France. Maybe he wanted to, ah, to replace those two paintings I told you about."

Marguerite looked at her napkin and refolded it, straining to hide her expression. She hadn't expected Theodate to mention the Haystacks again.

"Or maybe Father wanted more art. I don't know. Anyway, Mother went with him and took along Lotte. Can you guess where they stayed?"

Marguerite could. One of two or three hotels frequented by Americans. "The Grand Hotel du Louvre?"

Theodate grinned. "Right. Lotte stayed in a servant's room in the attic."

Marguerite started to catch on. "She met Belinda there? My parents stayed at the Grand, too."

Theodate kept grinning. "What you might not know is that Lotte and Belinda had seen each other before. At the Windsor. On the day of the fire. Lotte needed to iron a dress for Mother."

Without skipping a beat, Marguerite finished Theodate's sentence. "At the same time that Belinda ironed a dress for Mama. It was the striped, purple silk she planned to wear to a party that night. She never saw it again."

Theodate bobbed her chin up and down, then chattered on. "The maids talked at the Grand. You see, both of them had been worrying. When they were in the ironing room, they wanted to use new electric irons that another maid offered them. This other maid was a big talker. She cleaned the McKinley's suite, so Belinda and Lotte thought she knew what she was doing. She told the maids to use the new irons. She said the hotel's chief housekeeper wanted all the maids to give the irons a try. Lotte and Belinda said that the maid, the talker, didn't really know how to turn the irons off or how to store them."

Marguerite stopped breathing, locked eyes with Theodate, and waited for her to continue.

"Lotte thinks the maids never unplugged the irons and stored them on a wooden shelf while they were hot, or that the electrical system couldn't handle lots of irons all at once. Lotte's not certain. She talked to other maids for a few minutes, and then she hurried up to bring Mother's dress to our suite. Once she got to the hall, a stampede of guests pushed her to the ground, almost crushed her. In view of the short time between when she left the basement and when she saw that stampede, she thinks the cigar started the fire, but she fears other causes added to the first fire and helped it spread. Lotte dropped Mother's dress and managed to stand. She saw an open door and grabbed a rope. She didn't have far to go—we were on two—but she still rubbed her hands raw when she dropped to the sidewalk. That's where I found her when I should have been with Father."

The waiter approached with the orders. The second he left, Theodate started up again.

"With the horror of the fire, Lotte forgot about the irons. But when her hands recovered, she began to piece together the events of that day. She wondered about those irons—the maids used at least four that afternoon. Then, in Paris, she and your Belinda spotted each other and shared their regrets that they hadn't spoken up.

"Both the maids can read," Theodate added, "but they saw few English newspapers at the Grand, and those they did see were dated. Remember, though, Lotte had been in America for two weeks after the fire. She knew about the investigations. She told Belinda the authorities were blaming the cigar smoker, and the basement engineers, and maybe robbers. The maids talked it over. They decided to tell their stories to Mother. She can be a stubborn woman, but she guided them well. She told them they did the right thing talking to her and that when she and Papa returned—they just returned two days ago—they would visit me, and the three of us would decide how to proceed.

"Honestly, I suspect Father was happy for the spotlight to shift away from thieves and stolen merchandise. In any case, when my parents visited, I told them that you had been talking to the chief detective." She stretched out the word talking, and grinned again, this time from ear to ear.

"Talking, Theodate." Marguerite paused. "For the most part."

"I told Mother you would know what to do."

"The detective, the irons, the next step. Where do I begin? First, Theodate, I haven't seen Chief Detective George McClusky since April 17th, two weeks ago. I haven't heard from him either. Chief Devery had George on other cases. You remember that dentist accused of murdering a young woman in a hotel, and also the baby kidnapped from Central Park? Those stories were all over the front pages. George is ambitious. He wants to stay in Devery's good graces, so he works on whatever case the Chief worries about the most. And I'm sure you heard about the coroner's inquest. When the jury said the fire was an accident, George had no reason to keep investigating. And what's more, he knew I wasn't helping. I found out a lot of things, but nothing that pointed to one cause. I liked him Theodate, I truly did, but he liked me only as a partner in an investigation, nothing more."

Theodate put her hand over Marguerite's, in comfort.

"And now, to the irons," Marguerite said.

Theodate interrupted. "Before we get to the irons, I need to tell you about the Haystacks. My Father and I thought they were lost forever. But ten days ago, while he was still in Paris, he received a telegram from Louisine Havemayer—our collector friend. You won't believe this. When her maid went to fetch milk from the back door, she found two paintings, wrapped in brown paper. The Haystacks!" Louisine asked a curator to verify that they were Monets, and then sent them to Cleveland." Theodate started to laugh, almost choking on her vegetables. "The thief had a change of heart. But, seriously Marguerite, Louisine has no reason to think the paintings, or their theft was connected to the Windsor fire. What a relief."

Thank goodness, Marguerite thought. Should she admit to her role? Then Theodate would know that Marguerite had been mucking around, possibly stirring up stories about Alfred Pope's actions during the fire. Better to let Theodate imagine a remorseful thief.

"So happy for your father. One day, if I come to visit your family in Cleveland or if they move to Farmington with their art, maybe I can see the Haystacks for myself.

"Now, back to those irons," Marguerite said. "My God, do excuse my language, I never, never guessed that one. Faulty electrical this or that. Well, in my judgment, Lotte and Belinda have no need to tell George or anyone else about the irons. Their story will not change the verdict of the coroner's jury." Marguerite paused, swallowed a mouthful of meat. "Is it possible that all these things happened at once? Frayed wires? Badly insulated wires? A smoker burning a lace curtain? Robbers causing the flame or using it as a diversion? Insufficient water? Failing hoses? Malfunctioning boilers? Too much wood? No fire doors? Inattentive crews? Bituminous coal? Others might add anarchists hunting for the President's brother. Or maybe some combination of these?" Marguerite took a deep breath, then looked at Theodate, almost in triumph.

Theodate took up the analysis. "I believe you are on the right track. I've been talking to architect friends and to the builders working on my parents' home. And I had another chat with the engineer I spoke with earlier. I've learned a lot. Sometimes detectives can guess a fire's speed by the amount of char on remaining materials. But nothing remains of the Windsor. Sometimes, lines of demarcation between damaged areas and undamaged areas offer a clue about the pattern of a fire. But no lines remain. We do know that when small fires merge, they may become more intense than the individual fires, and all fires rise."

"Here's another thought, Theodate. The timing—St. Patrick's Day—makes it less of a coincidence that multiple fires started at once. The parade provided a distraction if thieves wanted to get into rooms. And the maids needed to iron clothes for the festivities. And guests left their windows open to hear music. Maybe the boilers worked too hard to heat water for baths."

Theodate bobbed her head up and down. All this was possible. All this was unknown.

"My next step is to make a choice," Marguerite said, "the choice to live with uncertainty."

George McClusky

The demotion came as no surprise to George McClusky. Big Bill Devery always blew hot and cold. For months, he had asked George for favors, to stretch the rules on a case, to cozy up to an official, to look the other way at illegal gambling. George occasionally did fiddle with the facts of a case, but he tried to do so only in the cause of justice, not in the cause of Devery's well-being or pocketbook. When Devery asked one time too many, George ignored him.

Talking to reporters, Devery justified the demotion, claiming George was too secretive about his progress on key cases. Such rubbish. On the bright side, George's buddies in the force all stood up for him, speaking about his good character, his upstanding work.

George was no longer Chief Detective, just a captain at the Grand Central Station. Every day, he passed the barren site of the Windsor, a few blocks from that station. Every day he thought about Marguerite Wells. It was already mid-August. Had she left for her teaching job in New Jersey?

On Thursday, August 17, the five-month anniversary of the fire, he entered the Martha Washington. The desk clerk said Marguerite Wells was still there. George left a note.

The following day, he sat in the lobby of the Martha Washington at 5:50, unsure whether he would see her. A few minutes before 6:00, the elevator doors opened, and she stepped out—small, lovely, but not smiling.

"Good to see you again, Marguerite."

"Yes, George." Still no smile.

He looked around the crowded lobby. She followed his gaze. "We can talk at the steakhouse."

They said little on their way to the restaurant. Once seated, their conversation centered on the menu, the wine, the smells of beef from the kitchen.

"George, you are tapping your foot. You seem uncomfortable?"

"Yes." In the silence that followed his one word, he heard the talk at other tables, the clinking of glasses. "I am uncomfortable. I've been foolish. Chief Devery. He had me running around, solving cases. You must know that he demoted me."

"Are you still able to support your sisters?"

"Yes. My salary is lower. Not by much. But I am happier."

"George, I have not heard from you for five months. No notes, no calls. I realize you must be preoccupied with the changes in your circumstances, but don't you think you owe me an explanation?"

"Marguerite, I am a detective, a good one. A few days after our dinner here, our first dinner, I learned from my sources that you have been active in the suffrage movement. One of my sisters is too. The problem for me was that Devery hates the suffragists. He's always asking police to break up their rallies. I froze with fear that you would be at one of those rallies. That he would learn that I…that I kept company with a suffragist. And that I would need to bail you out." He couldn't look at her, but he knew she glared at him. "I didn't call you for weeks. And then weeks turned into months, and I didn't think I could undo the damage. I feel ashamed."

He squirmed in his seat. "That's not all. I know some suffragists think more kindly about anarchists than the police do. And more kindly about immigrants. Even though I'm not as, well, as intolerant as most on the force, and I'm willing to listen, I convinced myself that you wouldn't want to be with the likes of me.

"But hear me out." He raised his head. "In other matters, I've been upright. For the most part, when Devery crawled up my back about every case that made the news, I did what he asked. Then some cases came along where I saw an opportunity to clean up gambling, maybe illegal brokering. Devery wanted me to ignore those crimes. He must be taking bribes. I couldn't ignore what I saw. That's when he replaced me as chief. How foolish could I have been—worrying what a scoundrel would think of me?

"During all this," he said, "I learned something. I'm going to use flowery language for once." He leaned forward, willed himself to lock eyes with her. "Honor means a lot to me. I sensed the same thing for you, the second time we met. You said you wanted to know how your family saved yourselves. The way you said it—you wanted to be certain your actions that day were honorable."

"Yes, George, honor means a lot. But honor means different things to different people. I need to tell you what it means to me."

Marguerite Wells

Marguerite rode the train from the New Jersey town where she taught school to Jersey City, from where she caught the ferry to Manhattan. Then streetcars to 46th and Fifth, a pilgrimage of sorts, one year and a day after the inferno. A low wood fence walled off mounds of rubble. No plaque marked the burned-out site.

She hailed a cab, asking the driver to take her to Kensico Cemetery in Valhalla, New York—the cemetery the Charities Commissioner selected for the unidentified and unclaimed Windsor victims, ignoring Warren Leland's wishes to bury them in Tarrytown's Sleepy Hollow cemetery. A year ago, Angelica Gerry told the Wellses about the confusion over the burial site.

To Marguerite's eyes, Kensico was a beautiful cemetery, overlooking Mineola Lake. Again, she saw little to mark the specific site. She knew a monument committee planned to erect a stone to honor the dead, but that would take time. Now, about twenty people crowded around a grassy square that marked the graves of thirty-one—more or less—unidentified souls. According to the accounts she read, grave diggers buried seventeen caskets. Sixteen contained bodies or portions of bodies that appeared to be a single person. A seventeenth casket contained fragments of what could have been as many as fifteen victims. Marguerite heard rumors that one or two guests may have used the fire as a means of escape, to hide from their troubles or their lovers or their spouses. If they were counted among the dead, the precise number of victims would remain a mystery. Marguerite guessed at eighty-six fatalities, including the unidentified, the identified, and the unfound, and subtracting for two people who may have intentionally disappeared.

In the small gathering, Marguerite glanced around. She recognized only Fanny Leland, the manager's surviving daughter. Looking unwell and teary, she introduced herself to Marguerite and the others. She had come from Chicago for this anniversary of the death of her mother, Isabella, and younger sister. Marguerite remembered that Fanny's father, Leland, died a few weeks after the fire. The poor woman had lost three loved ones. The others must have remembered because the group moved aside to give Fanny a place next to the clergyman.

Marguerite glanced at her wristwatch. Almost 2:00.

She saw the man approach with a confident stride. He moderated his usual swagger to fit the occasion.

"I'm not late, am I?" Westchester County Sheriff William Molloy had sought George McClusky's help, outside his official duties in the city, on a double murder case. George had come from a meeting in the sheriff's office, two towns away. Happy to earn a fee to supplement his salary, George had suggested the day of the service—a Sunday when he was not on duty.

"Just on time," Marguerite said, sliding her arm into the crook of his arm.

"I'm afraid I need to go back to Molloy's office after the service. We didn't finish going over the investigation." Marguerite nodded. "I will see you later."

The crowd hushed as a clergyman walked to the front. Marguerite stood beside George. They listened to a psalm and blessings for the deceased, known and unknown. At last, she could focus on the dead, moving beyond her own family's strengths and weaknesses.

Afterward, Marguerite said a warm goodbye to George and a more formal goodbye to the others. She walked out to the driveway where her carriage driver waited. Off to the side, she saw a young Negro woman holding a cloak and umbrella as though she served one of the mourners. Marguerite looked twice, unsure. She climbed into the carriage slowly, letting all the mourners pass her so she could see if any approached the woman. None did. She asked the driver to wait a minute.

"Miss, you look familiar. Have I seen you before?"

"No, miss." The woman looked down.

"Are you waiting for one of the mourners? They have all left."

The woman's shoulders stooped as she tried to disappear into herself.

"You are Tilly, right? Tilly Brown?"

She clutched her props and started to dash away. Marguerite dashed after her.

"No, wait. Wait. I am not trouble for you. I am not. Can we talk?"

Marguerite knew Tilly felt cornered.

"Come, come to my carriage. I will take you wherever you are headed."

It took Marguerite halfway from Valhalla to Manhattan to gain Tilly's trust.

"That detective, Mr. Niehoff, he heard us joshing in the scullery, that one in the basement, about all the fancy things the guests owned. Pictures, jewelry, cash." Tilly sat forward on the carriage. "We weren't gonna do nothing about it. No way. But he scared us. Then, when that fire came on, I heard talk that robbers started it. That meant trouble. Coppers, and our masters and mistresses, well, our employers, they always blame us. And of all the Negros Niehoff heard talking, I was the youngest. And the one with a—an employer—who I knew would not stand up for me if she escaped that fire. So I ran. I had nothing but the clothes on my back and a little money Miz Price gave me to buy her a hat that day.

"I had an uncle in a boarding house near the wharf on the Hudson. He unloaded freight. He let me stay with him and found me a position in his foreman's house."

"Tell me, Tilly. One thing never made sense to me. The newspapers reported that Mrs. Alice Price and Mrs. Mehitable Henry, along with Dr. Neil McPhatter, had an appointment to go shopping that day. But that is strange. I can understand why two ladies might go shopping, but why would a forty-year-old doctor go with them?"

Tilly shifted in her seat in the carriage, finally leaning back. She twisted her lips into a strange smile. She waited.

"Why?" Marguerite said.

"I know that's what those papers reported. My cousin read it to me. Miz

Alice made that up." Tilly stopped talking and looked down again.

"You can trust me, Tilly. I want to understand, for myself."

"So you know I did your laundry a few times, but all the time, I did Miz Alice's laundry. I knew she had problems—lady problems. She was a nervous wreck after young Miss Alice died. That girl acted sweet, not like her mama. But the mama's nerves were not her only problem. I know she took some kind of drug—I dusted around it on her bedside—but it didn't help. That old lady Mrs. Henry wanted Miz Alice to try something else. Got her an appointment with the doctor. Dr. McPhatter. Miz Alice told everyone that they were going to shop, but the doctor was really coming to examine her when the fire started. I didn't know much about that doctor or about Mrs. Henry, and, I'm ashamed, but I can't read. I needed to find out more cause I'm curious, like you. In the house I work in, my uncle's foreman's house, the son, Ronald is his name, he's studying to be a doctor. And he is a good young man, kind. I talked to him, like I'm talking to you. And he checked all this out. Here's what he found. That old lady, Mrs. Henry, she was a widow. Her husband doctored people with skin problems. I forget the fancy word. And he did more than that. He also helped people with the clap—sorry, Miss Wells. Ronald calls it venereal disease. That Dr. Henry was famous for his help with the...venereal disease. And Dr. McPhatter, well, he was a lady's doctor. Can't remember that word either. But McPhatter, he did more than that. He did surgery, too, and he fixed women with all sorts of problems. The two doctors knew each other. Ronald thinks maybe they were working together on ladies venereal disease problems around the time that Dr. Henry died. So the old lady wanted Dr. McPhatter to treat Miz Alice. I don't know nothing more but think what you will. You can see why Miz Alice said they were all going shopping."

As Tilly talked, Marguerite stared at her, dismayed at what she heard. She wasn't the only survivor digging for the story of the Windsor.

"Ya know, Miss Wells, I always felt bad I ran away. Didn't try to save Miz Alice. Or any of the maids. Or the porter who took a liking to me and didn't make it out. I took care of myself. That's what my ma told me to do, but she was born a slave, had no choice. Maybe I did have a choice. I came here today to pay my respects and to stir myself to do better."

Marguerite put her arm around Tilly, the first time she had embraced a Negro person, and she knew, from Tilly's expression, the first time for her too. Along with so many others, she and Tilly would weigh their choices and try to ease their burdens.

A Note from the Author

The Windsor Hotel burned to the ground on March 17, 1899. Because the Windsor was in Manhattan and because well-known guests stayed there, many newspapers covered the fire at length, telling countless stories about guests who survived and those who died. In contrast, reporters gave scanty coverage to tales of Windsor maids and kitchen staff. Occasionally they were mentioned, but even when I had their names, I could rarely discover more about them. As a result, all the guests in my story—along with the hotel desk workers, Frank Corbett, J. H. Sullivan, Harry Niehoff, Warren Guion, and John Connolly—are historic characters, but I imagined the names and lives of the maids, and of Sean Mack and Clayton Byrne. All the city officials I name are historic figures, including John Binns, Hugh Bonner, Thomas Brady, Joseph Cody, John Scannell, William Devery, George McClusky, Rufus Cowing, Asa Gardiner, Edward Fitzpatrick, and Jacob Bausch. Other historic characters include Helen Gould, David Dudley, Ted Johnson, Neil McPhatter, and Felix Kain. The commercial establishments in the novel really existed, except for Norton's pawnshop.

Investigators in 1899 had few ways of determining the cause of a fire, especially one as destructive as the Windsor fire. Judging from newspaper accounts, the investigation was rudimentary, at best. All the possible causes I list were considered and dismissed. The coroner's inquest did indeed conclude that the fire was accidental. I truly believe there was more than one cause.

According to newspaper accounts, Alfred Pope did redirect a fireman to save paintings while the fire blazed and women jumped. I have not been able to determine which paintings were saved, but since Pope collected Impressionist art, it is conceivable that the rescued art included works by

A NOTE FROM THE AUTHOR

Monet. I have no reason to believe that anyone stole two Haystacks, but that ties in with the robber theory. The details I relate about the Popes' experiences during and immediately after the fire are largely accurate, but I did change small details to simplify the story. I must emphasize that by all accounts, Alfred Pope lived an honorable life.

The three wealthy women who investigated the fire are distinguished historic figures. Marguerite Wells became the third president of the National League of Women Voters. Theodate Pope became a licensed architect in New York. Angelica Gerry became a philanthropist and gardener in Delaware County, New York. Bridget Dunne, Tara Regan, and Molly Dugan—let us imagine that their lives took on meaning in other ways.

I have tried to stay true to the historical record, whenever that record is known. But I have taken some liberties. Many historic figures named Helen filled the accounts of the fire. Guessing that Helen Gould was the best known, I changed Helen Kirk Haskin to Ellen and simply referred to Warren Leland's daughter, Helen, as Warren's daughter. I apologize to the memory of the other Helens. To differentiate between Fred Leland and Fred Johnson, I renamed the latter Ted Johnson. Ada Pope's maid was Jane though I chose to name her Lotte. In some cases I took liberties with the chronology (the timing of McClusky's demotion, the resolution of the Scannell bribery case, Stokes's effort to find the missing bracelet, the opening of the Martha Washington Hotel), switching dates slightly to fit with the plot. Experts I consulted on the electric iron insisted the appliance was unavailable in 1899. I went against their good counsel and imagined what might be called an early focus group.

All newspaper quotations are exact, except for minor changes for clarity.

I have tried to be precise about the fire itself. As I indicated in the novel, many newspaper reports were not clear. For example, a guest might be said to be on one floor in one account and another floor in another account. Some of the confusion may result from the different ways of referring to stories in hotels, where some count the ground floor as the first and others do not start counting until the floor above the ground floor.

My sources included the major New York City newspapers of the era, as well as biographies too numerous to list. I will single out only three: Shelley L. Dowling's *Elbridge Thomas Gerry: An Exceptional Life in Gilded Gotham*, Sandra L. Katz's *Dearest of Geniuses: A Life of Theodate Pope Riddle*, Claude H. Hall's "The Fabulous Tom Ochiltree" in the *Southwestern Historical Quarterly*.

Acknowledgements

Readers of this novel may conclude I am never at a loss for words, but in thanking the friends and family who helped me, I struggle to find the right words to characterize the enormous value of their contributions. My husband, Mark Wasserman, listened patiently as I tested out the plot over breakfasts and he suggested one of the subplots. My children Aaron Wasserman and Danielle Blass—also listened, offering encouragement. My sister, Carol McConnell, helped time and time again with research and technology and caught many errors in my first draft. My brother, Robert D. Parker, read every word, caught errors in logic and syntax, and made insightful and invaluable suggestions. My publishers—Verena Rose, Shawn Reilly Simmons, and Harriette Sackler—have offered their support, encouragement, and talents. I could not have written this novel without such a phenomenal team.

I also want to acknowledge the lives and deaths of the many people who did not survive the Windsor fire. I hope this book adds to marking their memories.

About the Author

Marlie Parker Wasserman writes historical crime fiction. Her previous books are *The Murderess Must Die* and *Path of Peril*. When not writing, Marlie travels throughout the world and tries to remember how to sketch. She lives with her husband in Chapel Hill, North Carolina.

SOCIAL MEDIA HANDLES:
  Twitter: @MarlieWasserman
  Facebook: Marlie Wasserman
  Instagram: marliepwasserman

AUTHOR WEBSITE:
  marliewasserman.com

Also by Marlie Parker Wasserman

The Murderess Must Die

Path of Peril

Printed in the USA
CPSIA information can be obtained
at www.ICGtesting.com
LVHW090043130124
768887LV00057B/1179

9 781685 124328